The OPEN ARMS *of the* SEA

JASPER DORGAN

TRISKELE BOOKS

The Open Arms of the Sea

First published in Great Britain in 2012

Published by JAP Publishing jappublishing@hotmail.co.uk

First printing 2012

Cover design by J D Smith

Printed in the United Kingdom by Lightning Source UK

ISBN 978-0-9574031-0-9

For Freda

ONE

The landscape of broken-glass rocks and parched earth stretched to the distant horizons. The noon-day Yemeni sun hurled a light so harsh that it bleached everything it touched and crushed the world to grey ash. At the furthest reach of the desolate plain the shark-toothed highlands pierced a cloudless, white sky.

Lieutenant Leslie Deacon of the 1st Battalion Royal Sussex Regiment stood on a low rise of baked desert gazing through his binoculars at the wonder of the Tihammah plain. He felt small in its presence, a mere speck in the vastness of the desert bowl, as insignificant as a particle of dust. The Tihammah had that power. The power to make you invisible.

He let his binoculars drop to his chest and rubbed his eyes with dust-gloved fingers. Shaking his head alert, he took a mouthful of warm, brackish water from his canteen and rinsed his mouth. He swallowed the resulting sludge in a forced gulp.

He trained his binoculars once more on the far mountains to search for the Adoo rebels. To hunt again for a tell-tale flash of coloured cloth or the glint of sun on gun metal. Deacon and his troop had chased the Adoo half way across the baking plain and now that the rebels had found refuge in the mountains ahead, he was wary of pursuing them further. The rebels had stolen mortars with them and Deacon was not planning to get caught in open ground and in range.

He saw no colours or glints, only the ocean of rocks and the volcanic, black mountains at its shores. He was about to return to the truck when a small plume of desert dust and rocks erupted like a geyser from the desert floor about a mile in front of him. Deacon heard a soft boom echoing from the far mountains. Then another geyser erupted beside the first. The dusts fell slowly back to the plain.

Deacon stood still and retrained his glasses. He saw the faint trail of mortar smoke still drifting in the sky and tracked it back down to its mountain source. He marked its direction with his foot.

"Mark the grid and direction, corporal," he said.

"They are bombing us, sir."

Corporal Lockett stepped up beside him. He was a small man, barely coming up to Deacon's chin, but he occupied his space with a confidence and youthful brio that made him appear taller. Lockett had been with him for more than six months but Deacon had never really settled in his un-servile care. The corporal had a way of always having an answer, or a question, and of always being there, like an eager shadow.

"I am aware of that, corporal. Just mark it."

Deacon turned and checked on the troop. The men had been sleeping beside the truck under canopy shade, but the sound of the mortars roused them to a drowsy concern. Sergeant McNish rolled himself from his doze on the truck running board and blinked about him. His barrel frame strained at his jacket buttons and he farted loudly. Shaw and Ambrose were struggling into their shirts and Kenny crouched on one knee with the Sterling already primed and lapped.

"Pulling back, sir?" said Sergeant McNish.

"No." said Deacon. "Relax lads. We are out of their range. They're just firing their toys. They have 81mil mortars and the mountains are over four miles away. We're safe here."

The men groaned and slouched back to the canopy. They sank in its shades.

"Compass bearing eighteen degrees, sir," said Lockett.

"Radio it in, corporal. Contact and grid," said Deacon.

"It's getting late, sir. Still four hours back to Aden."

"Don't you ever obey an order, corporal?"

"Only inadvertently, sir."

"I think they can still shoot you for that."

"Army will shoot you for anything, sir."

"Radio it in corporal. Now."

"Yes, sir."

Deacon watched the distant mountains for a while but there were no further mortar launches. The Adoo would be packing up and heading further into the highlands. No British Army patrol could follow them there. The mountains belonged to the Adoo, and the piard wild dogs.

Deacon wandered out onto the desert plain to have another look at the circle of rocks that the Adoos had used for their last over-night camp. A bare, scratched hollow among small boulders blackened by the petrol-can fire and littered with cigarette ends, goat bones and human dung. Petrol coloured flies hovered above it in small clouds.

They had discovered the camp while tracking the fleeing Adoo. Deacon and his men had been chasing them for almost a day and a half across the wadis and wastes of the Tihammah. The sun had beaten hard most of the way and the discovery of the camp was an opportune excuse for a break for chow, vehicle checks and light dozing. It had been a long patrol and Deacon wanted the men rested and cooled before they made the long afternoon run back to Aden.

Deacon walked the circle of the Adoo camp site, but found nothing of interest. It was when he widened his search that he noticed a glint low in the rocks. He squatted down and saw a small metal disc lying in the dirt. It was no bigger than a half-crown. He blew the dirt from around it with soft kisses of breath; then he carefully probed under it with his knife. The disc lifted without wire or resistance. It wavered in his fingers. His limbs were beginning to shake with fatigue. In the heat of the Tihammah every move was an act of will. The disc was light in his palm. Deacon wrapped it in his neck cloth and put it in his belt pouch. He rose up unsteadily and walked the camp again but found nothing more to take the eye.

He headed back to the truck. The sound *Unchained Melody* on Private Shaw's transistor radio rippled in the heat towards him.

Lockett came out to meet him. "Message sent, sir. Receipt confirmed."

"Right, we'd better get the men do a line west to east. Twenty minutes out, then back. And you can tell Private Shaw that if I hear that damn song again I will confiscate his radio. He knows the patrol orders. And I am sick of that damn song."

Corporal Lockett grinned. "More a Rolling Stones man, me, sir. *Can't Get No Satisfaction*. Now that's a soldier's song for you. I expect you are more of a jazz man."

Deacon did not snaffle the hook. It was the corporal's game to probe beneath the officer's uniform. To unearth some fragment of his non-soldier self. It was Deacon's game to not oblige.

"No, Kipling's more my line, corporal. When wounded and left on Afghanistan's plains and all that. That's a song for the troops."

"*And the women come out and cut up the remains.*
Just roll to your rifle and blow out your brains.
And go to yaw Gawd like a soldier."

Lockett grinned puckishly and spread his hands to signal the end of his impromptu performance. Deacon tried to ignore him as he always did. Lockett was too independent of spirit and far too clever for a corporal. But for all his oddities he was a dutiful and efficient one.

"Where exactly did you go to school, corporal?"

"Anywhere there was trouble, sir. I sort of picked it up on the way." Lockett adjusted his Arab-style headscarf and crabbed his fingers through his hair. Then he dusted off his smart army jacket with a few deft slaps. Even on the fourth day of a patrol Lockett looked as tidy as if it were his second. "Learned there is always time for a smoke though, sir." He offered Deacon a flicked cigarette from his pack and a cupped palm for the light.

"Remind me why you joined the army, corporal."

"Couldn't disappoint the Queen, sir."

Lockett was twenty, just four years his junior, but he made Deacon feel old. Deacon sucked on the cigarette and let the smoke burn through him. He returned to the truck.

"Sergeant. Line west. Get the men moving. I want to be heading back to Aden in an hour."

Sergeant McNish gazed warily at the plain. "West, you say?"

Deacon hitched a thumb over his shoulder. "That way. Keep the twin peaks for bearing."

Sergeant McNish gazed after the thumb to the distant horizon. "Ah. The titties there. I see'em. Right. And what are we looking for this time?"

"Your own backsides I expect, but if you could spot any Adoo stragglers prowling about out there then you have my permission to shoot them a bit."

The Sergeant grunted and sloped off towards the men.

Deacon watched the men being roused from their half-slumbers under the canvas sheets that stretched between the vehicles. They gathered their guns and hats and emerged shirtless into the sun; a yawning, moody parade of tanned, muscled shoulders, broad chests and smooth trooper-bodies. The men steamed and glistened in the lime Tihammah light. Deacon felt a tightness grip his skull and the burn of his blood rushing in veins. It was a sensation he tried to curb but it spiked within him unbidden. The same passionate sensation born and released by the half naked Mr. Havers in the after hours school room and from whose guilt he had been trying to flee ever since. He had flown to hide in the army, covering his shame and disgust in the uniform of duty and servility. But it still spiked, letting him know that he hadn't run far enough and that it still lurked in his shadow. The troop began pulling their shirts over the glistening flesh. Deacon pulled his gaze away sharply. At the corner of his eye he saw that Lockett had been watching him. The corporal quickly diverted his interest to the horizons, his face impassive. Deacon ignored him.

"Shaw!"

Shaw muttered as he clicked off his radio and unwound it from the truck cab bonnet. The men pulled on their shirts and hitched their guns. They grumbled among themselves and then sauntered out into the desert.

"Ta, Harry. More frying and fucking rocks," said Shaw, almost privately.

Harry was the men's name for him. Deacon liked it. It kept him from being who he was.

Deacon took his compass and map from the jeep seat and checked his grids. He felt Lockett at his usual shadow stand.

"Not out for a nice afternoon walk with the others, corporal?"

"Someone has to stay and watch your back, sir. Short straw again."

"I suppose they will all hunker down behind some rock and fag the time out?"

"They are British soldiers, sir!"

Deacon looked at Lockett who grinned back at him. "Then let's fix a brew and really piss them off," said Deacon.

They sat in the truck's shade and rested their backs against the comfort of the mortar bags. The billy-can tea was thick and comfortingly tasteless. A Wessex helicopter drummed somewhere in a far sky. A pair of vultures soared. They always did on the Tihammah.

"What on earth are we doing here?" asked Lockett.

"They threaten our canal so we kidnap Aden. Because of the oil. It's always oil. It's why we are here and why the Adoos like shooting us."

"Oh, I know all that. I mean here. The Tihammah. Why are you so interested in mapping it? All those grids and compass readings. Even when we were chasing the Adoo. There is a stark beauty to the place but its just sand and rocks. What's so interesting about the Tihammah?"

Deacon sat himself up and pointed off towards the far mountain peaks. "Rivers start up there. Big ones. But by the time they get here they have evaporated. In just a few score miles. This sun drinks them dry. Sometimes they flood and carve new gullies. Big enough to hide a camel train. But mostly they just dry out. Rivers that never get to reach their sea."

Lockett gazed towards the unseen coast and the crescent bays of the Gold Mohur. "Lonely rivers that flow to the sea. Just like on the radio."

"What?"

"Like on Shaw's radio, sir. You know, that song. Righteous Brothers. Lonely rivers. Open arms of the sea."

Deacon groaned. "Not that bloody song again!"

"So not lonely rivers then, just dry ones. Why is the army interested in them?"

"If I told you I would have to shoot you."

"You already shot me this morning, sir."

"Then you are beyond caring, aren't you?"

"I reckon it's something to do with the Adoo using the dry river-beds to move their guns and supplies. In secret. Across the plain."

"Fetch my pistol, corporal. Head or the heart?"

"The heart, sir. Always the heart. That's the one that never hurts."

"It always hurts, corporal. The trick is not to feel it."

Deacon stood up on stiff knees and walked across to the jeep canopy. He pulled the binoculars to his eyes and scanned the eastern sector.

He saw it almost immediately, like a half-seen ant on a distant white wall. A fleeting shape that moved and was gone and might never have been at all. He steadied himself and looked again. Two small shapes moved along a sunken dry wadi. They were about half a mile away. They were moving with ease and economy as if on a long afternoon walk; two red-chequered Arab head-dresses pulsing between rocks. Deacon marked them against a stunted distant peak and a compass bearing and quickly scanned for other shapes in front or behind them. There were none. He returned to the mountain and found the Arabs again quickly. Deacon wondered if they were spotters for the rebels in the mountains. In another ten minutes or so they would see the truck.

"Corporal, run west and get the men back. Do it now."

Lockett was soon beside him.

"No smart words corporal. Just get the men back here. Very quick and very quiet. Do it now."

"Sir."

Lockett took his rifle from its lean by the radio and ran crouching out into the western plain.

Deacon watched the moving Arabs grow slowly in his lenses and felt the shiver of knowing that he was now alone. He looked quickly at his watch and at the fast disappearing speck of Lockett among the rocks.

Deacon's mouth dried. His decision to try and take the Arabs himself was instant and unwavering. It was what an officer would be expected do and it was better than just waiting. Waiting got you killed.

He checked his Browning 9 millimetre pistol and headed towards the cover of nearby scree. He stumbled over the rocks and arced back behind the Arabs using the wadis and boulders as cover. The sun scorched all the way. He was soon drenched in sweat and his mouth felt cavernous and parched. He took a moment to calm himself and to wipe the wet from his gun hand. He studied the Arabs who now walked ahead of him. They seemed oblivious to anything but their footing as they stumbled silently among the stones. Deacon took a deep breath and jumped into the dry wadi a few paces behind his quarry.

"Halt!"

The two Arabs spun round, saw the gun and cried out in

alarm. The older one with a greying beard dropped the rifle from his hand and held up his palms, his eyes wide and yellow. The other Arab was young, not even out of his teens. He held his arms outstretched as if pleading on a cross and his pale, almond face was a rictus grin of panic. Both Arabs began to edge away from Deacon, the old man jabbering like a Sterling gun.

"Stop! Or I'll shoot."

The old man fell to his knees and rocked in manic prayer over the dirt. As Deacon moved forward he saw the man leap to his feet and his hand shoot out. Needles of grit stung into Deacon's face and eyes and he choked on hot dirt. He spat his mouth clear and wiped his eyes and saw the two Arabs as a blur running away down the river bed. Deacon braced his feet and raised a sighting arm across his watery gaze and brought his pistol to a rest on his forearm. He fired two shots, one at each retreating, mirage figure. He heard a groan and saw one of the shapes stagger and fall. It was the young Arab. The older Arab took one quick glance at his comrade and disappeared under a flap of robes into the rocks.

Deacon stood over the boy who was in lip-clamped pain and holding his leg stiffly in clawing hands. The bullet had hit somewhere just above the knee. Deacon searched the boy with his boot, his pistol in both hands and pointed at the boy's head. The boy gazed up at him, wide-eyed and petrified. Deacon holstered his pistol.

"It's okay, son. Not an execution day today."

Privates Shaw and Murdoch carried the wounded Arab back to the truck. Deacon picked up the Arab rifle, an old and worn Kalashnikov. The magazine breech was empty and its sun-baked metal was too hot to touch. The young Arab struggled and screamed the whole way back to the truck. They got him into the shade and Private Ambrose inspected the wound while the other men held the wailing Arab down.

"Can he travel?" asked Deacon.

"Lower part of the thigh," said Ambrose. He was the

patrol medic, a tall Canadian who wore a smouldering roll-up permanently at his lips. He claimed it kept the bastard mosquitoes away. "Need to get it out if we are going to get the bugger back to Aden in any shape to sing."

The Arab boy bleated against his pain, his head thrashed the air.

"Lift him," said Private Murdoch. He was a small, solid New Zealand commando with the leathered face of a veteran. He was known as Kenny to all in the company because he looked like Kenneth Connor from the Carry On films.

Everyone was someone else in Aden.

Shaw and Ambrose hoisted the young Arab upright. He screamed. Kenny stepped up and pistoned a short, sharp fist into the Arab's jaw. The boy crumpled, instantly limp and silent.

"Can't do with that bleeding noise all the way back to Aden," said Kenny. "Flick the bullet out and let's get going."

Deacon bounced in the jeep as it reared across the plains. Lockett sat beside him, wrestling the steering wheel as if on a rodeo bull. Behind them the truck and machine-gun jeep groaned and screeched in the wake of their dust. Lockett had to shout to make Deacon hear him.

"You shouldn't have gone after them on your own, sir. Against all the orders."

"Using my initiative, corporal. What they pay me for."

"Dying is no pay, sir. They might have been desperate, or had grenades."

"We are all desperate, corporal, or we wouldn't be here. Bear right at the next gully."

"Impressed the men though, sir."

Deacon sat silent and watched the sun melting the plains to liquid caramel. At the distant curve of the world the mountain's ice caps flickered like candles in a cage.

"Sergeant McNish reckoned it was just a lucky shot but Kenny wouldn't have it. Proper soldier, is Kenny. The men listen to him. He paced it out. Eighty yards. He said it was good shooting. The lads know it too."

Deacon continued to gaze.

"Just thought you would like to know, sir."

They made fast way through the flat, brush-scrubbed sands of the Hodeidha Plain and it was late afternoon when they swung up onto the tarmac of the Aden road and were waved through the sand-bagged outer perimeter posts.

They sped on past the Khormaksar Airfield where toad-bellied planes squatted in shimmering lakes of vaporising fuel, and on past the blurring mesh and razor-barbed fences of the transit camp. The low white stone buildings and road-side stalls of outer Aden began to slide by. In the near distance Deacon could see Crater, the old port city of Aden, lying in its extinct volcanic bowl like a half-chewed meal. To the east the oil refineries and docks of Little Aden ghosted their skeletal derricks and the fat insect tankers queued in hover above the rippling skyline. By day Aden was all mirage; at night it was a cold and starlit well.

A group of soldiers waved them down as they sped through the narrow streets. Deacon brought the convoy to a halt and stepped out to meet the lance corporal who ran towards him and skidded to a stop on a sharp salute.

"Andrews, sir. Second company. Red Wolves been at it again, sir. Bodies in the alley up there. No Brits, by the look. Need an officer, sir."

"Where is Major Ross? He's your officer."

The lance-corporal hesitated. "Er. The Major is indisposed, sir. In the truck."

Deacon followed his gaze to a truck parked a little way down the street.

"How far gone this time?" asked Deacon.

"Two Gordons and a Johnnie Walker that we know of, sir. He's beyond waking."

Deacon clipped the lanyard to his pistol. Sergeant McNish appeared from the truck.

"Three men with me, Sergeant. Rest guard the transport and

prisoner. No-one past. Right, Andrews, you had better show me."

They made their way slowly along a baked dirt track between squat white buildings. The local Arabs had vanished, even the young street urchins who materialised to beg cigarettes whenever a soldier appeared.

A baleful quiet began to ooze and crush. Deacon heard the low drunken drone of flies and then saw the long shadows of feet stretching out from a nearby alley. He nodded "back watch" to Kenny. Kenny acknowledged with a raised thumb and dropped to his knee and shouldered his Sterling machine-gun to sweep their rear. Corporal Lockett strode forward towards the alley. Deacon noticed the oil barrel standing in the corner shade.

"Halt, corporal!" he bellowed. Lockett stopped as if he had hit a wall. "Don't move." Deacon crabbed lightly to the entrance of the alley and stood beside Lockett. He scanned the alley. Several bodies lay on their sides like felled skittles in the dirt. Scarves of brown blood entwined them. Flies frenzied above it all.

He counted three Europeans and four Arabs. All had their arms outstretched behind them. The European's throats were cut. The Arabs had been luckier – shot in the back of the head. The Adoo Red Wolves had called again.

Deacon bent down in the dust and probed his hands forward. After a few moments he felt the cotton wire that stretched across the alley at shin height. He traced it with gossamer care back to the barrel. He removed the pin and tossed it to Lockett.

"Keep your care, corporal."

Lockett relaxed with a shiver. He looked at Deacon

"I do," he said.

They checked the alley for further traps and then pulled what papers they could from the bodies. A letter or two, a club token, but the passports and wallets were gone. The Arabs had no pockets to search.

Sergeant McNish dredged some bile from deep and spat it over the nearest Arab.

"Fucking Adoos!"

"No. These are our Adoos, Sergeant." said Deacon. "Yemeni Arabs. Our friends. The bad Adoo are Egyptian Arabs. And any other Arab sod with a mind to kill us invading infidels."

"Aye. And using our own fucking British guns to do it!" said the sergeant.

"Yes. A delicious irony I agree. But look on the bright side sergeant, it means that we will be slaughtered under two British Standards. That's quality dying, that is." He heard Lockett laugh behind him. "Radio it in sergeant and set a guard. Tell all the men not to touch anything. It might save their balls."

"Maybes best if we wait for the booby squad. They'll know what they are doing."

Deacon eyed McNish. "I have given you an order, sergeant. And radio HQ and let them know our prisoner is delayed."

Sergeant McNish shuffled to a vague attention. "Sah!" He turned on his heels and began shouting at the men.

Deacon holstered his pistol and sat on a low wall to wait for the mortuary squad. Lockett returned from up the street with two cans of warm Stim. They drank the sugared lemon fizz in silence.

Deacon watched the Aden night begin to swallow the squat houses and streets about him and listened to the buzzing flies and the hollow groans of the young Arab who was now coming to in his own little hell in the back of the truck. Somewhere a wild piard dog barked over the rooftops like a seven-spray mortar.

The city was closing in again. Deacon shut his eyes and wished for the comfort of the clear, white scorch of the Tihammah. The faint strains of *Unchained Melody* drifted to him in the gathering dark.

"Corporal!"

"Sir."

"Go and shoot Private Shaw."

"Head or heart sir?"

"Start with his balls."

*

They pulled up in front of the Battalion Command HQ a little after twenty hundred hours. The brightly lit old colonial villa glowed like Christmas under the Yemeni night sky. A Military Police sergeant checked them through the razor-wired gates and on past the machine-gun emplacements. A captain and two lance corporals met them at the top of the long sweeping driveway and directed them into a large flagstoned square. The captain was young and slim, his Sam Browne belt shone brightly in the courtyard lights and his cap peak shielded his eyes like a metal visor.

"Captain Ashley. Internal Security. We'll take your prisoner. Give you any trouble?"

"No sir."

"Pity. That means it will probably be a long night. Fetch him, boys. Sign this."

Captain Ashley presented a clip board in one hand and a pen in the other. Deacon signed the form. The young Arab was dragged from the truck and hung limp between the strong arms of the two tall lance-corporals. Deacon's men jumped out of the truck and watched, blank-faced. Captain Ashley scanned slowly across the men and came to rest on the Arab.

"He has been no trouble," said Deacon.

Captain Ashley turned to Deacon. "They are all trouble, lieutenant. Pity you couldn't manage a gut shot. They squeal like pigs with those. A leg is never so persuasive. They know it's all hospital sheets and hot goat curry. They won't give up their kin for a leg shot. But we'll give it a try." A lamp of teeth lit under the cap and was then switched off. "You need to make a contact and full patrol report. In the Duty Watch office. And that Arab rifle needs to get to ATO. Do it before you go off duty."

Deacon was aware of the shuffle of discontent among his men. They were already overdue for their end of patrol beer at the Troy.

"We have just finished a five day patrol up country," said Deacon. The captain looked at him and then at the men.

"Your patrol isn't finished until the paperwork says it is finished, lieutenant. Take the prisoner on!"

Captain Ashley turned on a sharp heel and marched at stride after the escort. The Arab boy's legs hung limp, his feet floating above the flag stones. Deacon watched him disappear through one of the arched doors.

"Fucking army," said Private Lee. He was a thin, young soldier, hardly out of his teens. His pinched face and yellowed teeth gave him the look of one of the Aden rats that scurried among the rubbish mounds that piled on every street corner. "We should have left the bastard to bleed and bake. Fucking Arabs. I've earned my beer."

There was a murmur of agreement from the men.

Deacon searched in his pocket. "Sergeant, get the men down to the Troy and I'll catch up with you later. I'll file the report." He handed McNish a few pound notes. "Mine's a Tusker," Deacon said. "Make sure it is cold."

"Sah!" McNish saluted while pocketing the notes.

The men were already clambering back into the truck. "We'll make sure no-one pisses in yours, sir" said Shaw, firing up the engine.

Deacon watched the small convoy disappear along the lanterned driveway until they were swallowed by the Aden night. He turned and found Lockett standing beside the jeep.

"You still here, corporal?"

"I'm your driver, sir."

"I can drive myself, you know. I am not completely useless."

"Not completely sir, no."

"I can certainly type a report, corporal. Might take a couple of hours though. You better stay with the jeep. Get a coffee in the canteen."

"Prefer a Tusker in the Troy in about an hour, sir."

Deacon picked up the rifle and gathered his maps. "An hour! You'll be lucky, corporal. Nothing speeds army paperwork that fast."

Lockett held out his hands to the night air as if he were about to play a tall piano. His fingers rippled silently over unseen keys.

"Sixty words per minute does," Lockett looked at Deacon and grinned. "But forty for dictation."

*

Deacon checked the Kalashnikov and the metal coin into the Ammunition Technician's Office. An overweight, smoke-eyed lance corporal at the desk picked up the disc and inspected it with vague interest.

"What is this?"

"Don't know. But I found it in an Adoo scratch camp on the Tihammah. Might be something."

"Or nothing," said the lance corporal. He sneezed into a large red hanky and his eyes watered with the onset of a bout of Aden flu. "Zign here. And here."

Thanks largely to Lockett's typing skills, Deacon completed his patrol report efficiently and they were in the jeep and speeding for the Troy Hotel within the hour.

Deacon let the cold Aden night stream into his face. He felt a weariness gnawing on his bones and the blissful relief of a finished patrol ached hard in his guts. In the distance white spotlights arced across the bay of Little Aden and yellow, tiger-eyed work lamps glowed among the forests of oil storage silos and quay-side cranes. The oil work never stopped in Little Aden. Somewhere in the night the muffled sound of small arms fire sounded for a few seconds and tracer bullets fire-worked into a far night sky. The air thrubbed with the faint sound of helicopter blades somewhere over the bay. Aden never closed.

Deacon's need for a beer was almost lust. He had thought about the first taste of a tall, cool pint of Tusker from the first night of the patrol. And he had tasted it every hour since. The imagined gorge of the first swallow, of the scorch of cold glass in his sand blasted palms.

"We are here, sir"

Deacon came out of his drift in the Troy Hotel car park. They were checked in by the armed guards at the door and then made their way across the polished tiled floor and into the crowded and raucous bar.

The air-conditioned rooms of the Troy Hotel was a popular oasis for the garrison troops of Aden. It was one of many bars in the city but was favoured by Deacon and his men for its laxity of dress codes, the range of its beers and for always being open. It also served the best chips in Aden. The Hotel bar was a bright-lit series of large rooms cooled by slow turning ceiling fans the size of wagon wheels. It was always full of soldiers, Royal Navy seamen, commandos, RAF groundcrew and merchant seamen washed in from every colonial ocean. There were sometimes WRAFs from Khormaksar airfield or nurses from the RAF military hospital. But mostly, there was beer.

The men were at a corner table in the Wellington Room. They were in high spirits and had already laid waste to several rounds. They raised their glasses to Deacon in bleary-eyed welcome.

"Hope you got my name right, sir. Shaw. My Anita always wanted me mentioned in despatches."

"Got a light, sir? Hobson's fucking drowned the matches."

Deacon reached into his pocket for more money.

"Her Majesty's round lads," he said.

"But she has a fair pair of knockers," said Private Lee. He giggled into his glass.

"Will she stretch to a few chips, do you think, sir?"

The table was littered with empty bottles and small pyramids of smoking ash trays but there was a full pint of beer standing in its centre. Lockett made space on the bench beside him. Deacon slid in and took a long moment to stare at the brimming amber pint on the table. His men fell silent and watched him. Deacon took his cold beer and took it in one ecstatic gorge. He banged the empty glass on the table and savoured the explosion of wet fire in his throat. He wiped his mouth of froth with the back of his hand and lapped it off.

"Your piss has never tasted sweeter, Shaw."

The men laughed.

"Where's Sergeant McNish?" asked Lockett.

"Bought himself a couple of beers and fucked off up Maalla," said Kenny. He was grinning through a small platoon of empty bottles, his eyes drifting on a happy glaze.

Sergeant McNish was a regular customer of the brothels in the Maalla district. The platoon rumour was that he had promised marriage to at least two of his fancies.

"Hobson's been telling us about London, sir. Says all the girls have gone sex mad," said Shaw.

"I only telling 'em what I saw," said Hobson. He was a tall, slim young man with oiled hair that was slicked and parted to a precision. He had recently returned from home leave and was enjoying the momentary envy of his mates. "Mini-skirts everywhere. All the girls are wearing them. And wild parties and marijuana and everything."

"How mini?" asked Ambrose.

"Well," said Hobson, "all I can say is any shorter and they wouldn't be necessary."

It took a while for the table to gauge Hobson's measure.

"And we're stuck here in fucking Aden!" said Shaw.

"Maalla pussy is just as sweet," said Private Lee. He grinned yellow teeth around the table. "And a fucking sight cheaper."

"Yeah, they must queue up for you," said Shaw.

There was a quietening of the bar noise about them. All eyes were turned to the television in the corner of the room. The screen flickered the sight of heavy-packed young American army troops shoaling in file towards the whale jaws of two planes beached on a featureless runway, their monster props purring like gun fire. The young soldiers were mostly black. Some grinned for the camera, but most didn't. The pictures were from one of the American Cable Networks. Aden was a radio war, Vietnam had the TV.

The newscast switched to the site of a jungle clearing where an American helicopter was hovering above swirling seas of tall grasses. Lime-green soldiers in large, netted helmets were jumping chest-high into the liquid green. They held their guns above their heads and waded off-camera to invade unseen jungle shores.

"Now that's how to go to war," said a tall, moustached commando sergeant who was leaning at the bar. "With a cooling breeze up your backside and a belt full of major kill armoury on the hip. Trust the fucking Yanks."

"See they were packing that new infra-red night sight?" said a captain of Infantry. "Even the coons had 'em." He drained his glass and slid it to the bar. "Same again," he said, "And we have to find our night Adoo with torches and a fly swat. No way to run a fucking war."

"Yanks always were a bit too flash," said a Royal Navy pilot joining them at the bar, "Navy'll get these in lads. Same again, barman. And turn that damn thing off. Can't hear yourself drink."

The screen blacked to a white spot. The commando sergeant flicked a packet of cigarettes among his new friends. The captain lit them.

"Hear there might be some hot new WRAFs come in," said the pilot.

"Yes. I heard that too." The captain passed the drinks from the bar. "Cadets apparently. I've been told there are some lookers among them. Might check them out at the lido. When they go on parade."

"One looks like Brigitte Bardot. So one of the RAF lads told me," said the pilot.

"Hope he wasn't from their bomber crew," said the sergeant, "Cos with their bloody eyesight she's more likely Olive Oyl."

Their laughter rippled over Deacon.

He turned back to the table to find his men asleep. They were leaned head back or drooped on their benches like a ragged sweep of scythed corn. Ambrose slept with his cigarette still glued to the bottom lip of his open, rasping mouth. Kenny was snoring loudly into the table top, the reverberations purred under Deacon's palm.

Deacon sipped his beer and gazed at his sleeping men. He was too tired to sleep. He sat in the busy, raucous bar among his men and knew that he had never felt more alone. It was a thought that often ambushed him when he was least able to fight it, but his fatigue had made him vulnerable. Deacon knew that he was always going to be alone and remote from the world. Remote from his men because of his education and rank, distant from the officer classes because of his lowly background, and forever at odds and uncomfortable with the world and society because of his nature and the feelings he could neither deny or ignore. He stared at his life as it was and how it was destined to be and knew he was to be always alone and forever hiding; that he would never be free to experience the joy of true, passionate companionship or to share his life and his heart's beat with another. Deacon knew he would never know such love. The knowledge ate at his insides like a cancerous worm. His life was to be hollow, painful and loveless and there was no escape and no hope that it might ever change or be otherwise. There was only the soldier's uniform and duty and the desert.

Deacon sat numb and detached while the busy bar laughed and echoed about him and he felt his fatigue of pity and lonely despair begin to prick to tears in his eyes. He felt the slow, liquid trickle burn hot and heavy on his cheeks. He was too tired and forlorn to wipe it away.

TWO

Deacon rose early after a night of fitful sleep. He seldom slept easily in the city. He showered and shaved and put on the pressed and laundered uniform that Lockett had hung ready on the back of his door, sometime during the night. The men would be unlikely to rise much before noon. It was their post-patrol perk. Even Lockett would not surface for a while. Deacon welcomed the prospect of a little quiet.

He picked out a book at random from the box under his cot and headed out for the coffee house gardens. It was barely nine o'clock but the sun was already white and heavy with heat. The garrison enclave was busy. Brisk, trotting soldiers hurried about their tasks, motorbike couriers whined and wove among them and canvas covered trucks rumbled in low-geared convoy to the dock yards and warehouses of the old steamer port. A distant arrowhead of helicopters pulsed softly out over the blue mirrored bay and an ambulance wailed up the hill. All was hurry. Deacon enjoyed the luxury of his stroll. He had two days off duty and he was going to savour them.

He made his way to the gardens and took a seat at a table in the shaded corner of the scissor-cut lawns. Bougainvilleas and roses battled in the flowerbeds and cast fragrances over the fumes of diesel and fried decomposition that always hung in the Aden air. Many of the garden tables were occupied by officers and nurses trying to unwind with end-of-duty coffees or losing themselves in the three-day-old newspapers from home.

A small, elderly Arab man in a smart red jacket and tasselled cap flicked a palmed horse-hair brush over the linen clothed table. Deacon gave his order for English tea and toast.

He picked up his book and lost himself in a slow and lazy breakfast.

"Have you been in Aden long?"

Deacon looked up from his reading and shielded his eyes. A young and slender woman stood before him. She was wearing a wide-brimmed hat and a blue cotton dress and had a white glove on one of her hands. Her round, elegant face and pale, soft complexion immediately marked her out as newly arrived English.

"Only I was wondering. Do you know what it is that all the Arabs chew?"

She switched on a smile, pulled out a chair and sat opposite Deacon with quick grace. She placed the camera she had been carrying on the table beside her and rested her forearms to the table. The warm smile drifted away as her large brown eyes quickly scanned the gardens and the tables about her. Officers in dappled shade sat watching over lowered papers with encouraging smiles. The young woman pretended not to notice the looks. She turned again to Deacon.

"Do you know, by any chance?"

Deacon closed his book and studied his unexpected visitor for a moment. He was not use to bold young women who took their own seats. She had engaged him with a casual and confident familiarity, as if she had known him for years. Such was her confidence that Deacon half-wondered if they had actually been introduced before, but he knew that they hadn't. He was sure he would have remembered her.

She smiled encouragingly at him, her face unadorned by make-up. Deacon felt wariness churn with fascination. He smiled.

"Its khat. From a local plant. A relaxant and a mild narcotic. Even the women chew it," he said.

"Oh. I see."

She cast her eyes about her again, her movements small and stiff. She laughed distractedly.

"Just like in the Kings Road." The fingers of her un-gloved hand flickered on the table's edge. "Except they smoke it there, of course. I think. In the Kings Road. So I'm told."

"Is everything all right?" asked Deacon. "Is there something I might do for you?"

The young woman looked hard at Deacon, her eyes judging him. "What's your book about?"

Deacon looked at the book in his hand. "Aden," he said.

"Oh. Of course," she said. She seemed disappointed. "Quite. After all, why not? I mean, you're here, aren't you. Does your book make any sense of this place?"

"Perfect," said Deacon.

He tossed the book onto the table. It was *Alice's Adventures In Wonderland*. She looked at the book and then at Deacon. She laughed.

It was a strange laugh. One that Deacon had not heard in many months. Almost forgotten. It was a laugh of warm, self-deprecating amusement that just seemed to ripple.

She settled herself on her forearms once more, looked quickly about her and then leaned forward.

"I think I'm being followed," she said after some moments. Tension seemed to melt from her shoulders. She half turned in her chair and nodded behind her. "That old Arab man. See him? With the stick. I noticed him just outside the hospital. And he's followed me all morning. I went up some streets to try and shake him off. But he is still there. And now I have no idea where I am. I have got myself lost," she laughed.

"Wait here," said Deacon.

He walked off in the opposite direction and long-arced back to the corner where the old man sat in the shade of fig trees. He stood up quickly as Deacon appeared before him, but he did not run away.

"What is your business?" asked Deacon.

The old man gabbled and bowed and fished inside his jacket and pulled out a lady's white glove. He gave it to Deacon, then bowed again and limped quickly away on his stick.

Deacon returned to his table.

"Well?" asked the young woman.

"You dropped your glove. He was just returning it." Deacon handed her the glove. The young woman looked at it and then at Deacon. She deflated into laughter again.

"I am a such a complete ass! Just so off the boat, aren't I? A perfect fool! Please believe me, but I am not usually so fraught. It's this place. Aden is almost too much. The heat and the dust and the guns. It's so fascinatingly terrifying. All the time. You must think me very silly."

"Not at all. In Aden, suspicious is good."

She reached into the canvas bag at her feet and rummaged for cigarettes and her lighter, which proved elusive. She shook the bag out onto the table. Sun cream, a small cosmetics bag, rolls of film, another camera, mosquito spray, notebooks, salt tablets and sunglasses were quickly sifted and re-packed but no lighter was found. Deacon pulled his own and lit her cigarette. She leaned back in her seat and pulled in the smoke with almost violent relief.

"Thanks. God, I needed that! Sorry, most rude. Would you like one? I'm Clemmie Ross."

Deacon took the proffered cigarette.

"I am curious," he said. "Why choose me?" He looked around at the tables, several of whose occupants were still trying to catch the young woman's eye. "Others are much closer."

"But you were the only one reading a book," she said. "It seemed a good sign. Have you been in Aden long?"

"Care for some tea?" asked Deacon.

"Prefer a gin and bitters," said Clemmie.

Deacon learned that Clemmie Ross had been in Aden a little over three weeks. She was paying an extended visit and working as a part-time auxiliary nurse at the RAF hospital for a few hours a day.

"I'm only here a few months, so I may as well try to make myself useful. Never seen gunshot wounds before, let alone bandaged them. Quite dreadful. And the grenade victims. So awful. Those poor boys. And children too."

She had made her way to Aden in an RAF cargo flight from Cairo after a three week ocean voyage from Southampton on a cruise liner. She had spent most of her ocean time being sick in her cabin and all of her air time being buffeted about by netted crates and unsparing cross-wind turbulence.

"The plane was great fun! Like a four-hour dodgem ride in an oven. Luckily I had nothing left in my stomach. I lost four pounds getting here." She tucked into the toast and Deacon poured more bitters.

"Not a journalist, then?" said Deacon. Clemmie looked up puzzled.

"Oh, the camera! No. Nothing like that. A hobby of mine. I did some photography at art college and got the bug. Couldn't not bring my camera with me. I take a few pictures and send them to some of my arty girlfriends back in England. I have hopes of a gallery show some day. There are just so many pictures here. Aden is just too strange."

"And dangerous," said Deacon.

"There is that. But good pictures."

"Good pictures of war?"

Clemmie laughed. "I haven't got close to war yet! And I'd probably faint or be sick if I did. But there is so much else going on here. Have you seen Little Aden? Well of course you have. I'm an idiot. The shapes! Like sculpture. And the people. All the piles of rubbish in the street. The mountains. And the light here. It is so harsh ..."

Deacon leaned forward and held up a hand.

"Sh. Quiet, Miss Ross."

Clemmie sat stilled in mid-flow, her face showing mild concern as Deacon stared past her at nothing. At nearby tables, papers had been lowered.

Deacon heard the soft *woomph, woomph, woomph* of a mortar spray pumping off from on the other side of the city, like someone punching a pillow in a distant room. He strained forward and listened for the sound of explosions. He heard four rumbles and what might have been a crack. Then there was silence.

"I heard seven sprayed and four definite explosions," said Deacon loudly.

A merchant seaman at a nearby table took out his pipe. "Confirmed. I heard seven launch. But I only heard four drop."

"No, it was six explosions," said a Royal Artillery officer from across the lawns. He was packing his papers hurriedly into a briefcase. He downed his orange juice in one and picked his cap off a chair. "Two simultaneous hits. Means one is unexploded."

Clemmie reached for her camera. She turned back to Deacon and shrugged her hands.

"Where?" she asked.

Deacon smiled. "You don't see our war, Miss Ross. You hear it."

Deacon took his notebook and pen from his breast pocket. He checked his watch."Eleven-oh-five," he said and made a note in the book.

"Bombs go off and you write the time down?" said Clemmie. "What crazy place is this?

Deacon looked up and smiled. "Aden," he said. "More toast?"

Before an answer could be given he heard a rumble of engines on the road and the sound of heavy skidded wheels. Deacon looked up to see two trucks and a jeep lurching to a stop outside the coffee house gates. He instantly recognised the soldiers under the half-rolled truck canvases as his own. Lockett sprang from the jeep and, after a momentary scan of the gardens, headed in stiff-armed jog towards him.

Lockett came to attention in the shade of the table umbrella and saluted. His face was pale, his uniform newly pressed.

"Sorry about this, sir."

Lockett seemed to notice Clemmie for first time. He stole her a side-eyed glance. He returned to stiff attention and stared into the space above Deacon's head.

"Think you had better come, sir."

"And what is so damn important corporal that it should ruin my breakfast?"

"They found Sergeant McNish, sir."

"Is that all? Is he sober?"

Lockett looked down into Deacon's face with his eyes set hard. "Very, sir."

Deacon felt his stomach ice. "Where did they find him?"

"Off the Maalla road."

Deacon picked up his cap and threw a few coins onto the table. "I'm sorry, but it seems I must leave you. If you follow the hill road up there you will get to the NAAFI and there are taxis up there. Will you be alright? It's been a pleasure, Miss Ross. All right, corporal, let's go."

They sped in the jeep towards the Maalla district. Lockett filled Deacon in on the details as he knew them.

"Commando patrol found him this morning and radioed it in. Took a while for them to identify the body. No uniform or papers."

Deacon shot a glance at Lockett who stared stone faced on the road ahead.

"Tortured?"

"Don't know, sir. But the commando patrol sergeant reckoned he died uncomfortable."

"How do they know it is McNish?"

Lockett turned to Deacon, his face in stone.

"Tattoo," he said. "*Forever Angelina*."

Deacon watched the road for a few moments and then felt himself laugh. It was an Aden laugh.

"Incredible," he said.

The convoy pulled hard up the Queen Guinea road and turned towards Maalla. In the distance they could see the massed Kochi huts with their packing crate walls and corrugated roofs spewing like raw sewage down the distant mountain slopes to pool in the rat's nest streets of the Maalla.

A commando corporal waved them down and directed them into a small and deserted square. Two other commandos stood up from their smoke in the shade.

"Body up the street," said the commando corporal, his eyes were dark rimmed and yellowed with fatigue. "Called it in and told to wait for officer release. He's a fucking mess, sir. One of yours?"

Deacon shaded his eyes and looked up the long narrow street. The sun reflected white off the low houses and bleached all sight, but the hump of body was unmistakable. It lay in the street a hundred yards off. Above the body a grey cloud of flies churned.

The men jumped down from the trucks and stood in silence. Deacon turned and found that Clemmie Ross was among them. She walked eagerly up to the jeep, her camera in her hand.

"Is everything alright?" she said.

"What the hell are you doing here!" said Deacon.

"I came with Private Shaw. He offered me a lift in his truck."

"She said you said she could, sir" said Private Shaw, appearing at Deacon's side. "She is a lady, sir."

"And I did give him a pound and twenty cigarettes," said Clemmie.

"Them as well, sir." said Shaw.

"Well you can't stay here," said Deacon.

"You can't order me, Lieutenant. I am a civilian."

"Corporal!"

"Sir."

"Place Miss Ross under arrest. She doesn't move from this spot until I say so."

"What?" said Clemmie.

Lockett stepped forward and took the camera. "Best do as he says, Miss."

There was a sound of a roaring engine behind them and a jeep came to a slurred halt by the truck. A slim, young man slid out of the driver's seat, picked up a Panama hat from the back seat and made his way up the street towards Deacon.

The man, obviously English, appeared tall and he moved with the calm purpose and lightness of a cat. His hips were narrow but his shoulders broad and he wore an open cotton shirt, casually pressed linen trousers and tasselled, brown slip-on shoes. He didn't appear to be wearing socks. His movements were calm and assured, almost lithe. Deacon's men seemed to sense the pheromone waft of casual command and shuffled back to let the man through.

He stood before Deacon and took in the scene through calm, pale-blue eyes. He let his gaze fall on Miss Ross and smiled warmly.

"Clemmie, is everything all right?"

"I think I've been arrested," said Clemmie.

The man looked at Deacon. Then he took a moment to survey the men and trucks. "Care to explain, Lieutenant?

"There is a body up the street. British soldier," said Deacon.

The man turned to look up the street. He took his hat and bridged it across his nose for shade. He had the profile and still gaze of a young Caesar. He studied the scene for a moment and then turned to Deacon.

"I'm Captain Tom Villiers of the Special Forces detachment under the command of Brigadier Jennings. Now why don't you go and get your body and we can all be away from here."

Captain Villiers smiled once again at Clemmie and offered her a cigarette from a flipped pack. His arms and face were weather tanned and his blond hair flopped long above the eyes. He finger-combed the wave back behind his ear in an unconscious sweep.

"Saw you fly past in the truck, Clemmie. Had to follow. Solve the mystery."

Clemmie blew a jet of cigarette smoke to the sky. She laughed.

"Very kind Tom, but I am quite alright."

Captain Villiers turned to Deacon. "Haven't you a body to fetch, Lieutenant?"

"Can I see your ID, sir?" asked Deacon.

Captain Villiers considered him for a while. His face was placid but his eyes were pricked in blue. He laughed amiably.

"Don't have it on me, I'm afraid. Back in my uniform. But you can be assured I am who I say I am, Lieutenant. Now I think I gave you an order."

Captain Villiers let the words drift. Deacon watched them float by.

"Corporal, this man is also under arrest. He does not step from this spot."

"Yes, sir."

Captain Villiers placed his hat slowly on his head. He looked at Deacon and smiled. "You do know who I am?"

"No. Which is rather the point, don't you think?" said Deacon. He clipped his pistol to his lanyard and checked its chamber. "No ID, so no orders. I am officer in command at the scene."

Captain Villiers took a pace forward. Deacon saw Kenny and Shaw hitch their rifles and the captain stopped instantly in his tread. He smiled and held his hands up in mock surrender.

"Steady lads. Just stretching. Leash your dogs, Lieutenant."

Deacon nodded to his men and the rifles slackened.

"No ID," said Deacon. "I am the officer at the scene."

Captain Villiers smiled. "I wonder for how much longer? Care a wager?"

Deacon ignored him.

"Corporal, I'm going for a little stroll up the street"

"Sir."

"If either of the prisoners steps out of the shadow of the truck you have my permission to shoot them."

"Oh thank you very much, sir," said Lockett. "I haven't shot an officer before. At least not from the front. Head or the heart, sir?"

"It's been such a wonderful morning so far, corporal, that I am feeling particularly bounteous. You can have one of each."

"Most generous, sir." Lockett hitched his rifle at the captain and offered him a pleasant smile.

"So what are going to do, lieutenant?" said Captain Villiers. He leaned to the truck and tucked his hat down for shade. "Now that you have command. What is your plan of action?"

Deacon looked at him.

"The usual Army plan," he said. "Just make it up as I go along."

Deacon ordered his men to wait and walked a few yards up the street towards the body. He stood scanning the houses and alleyways about him and then crouched down and sighted the body through his binoculars.

He knew it was McNish even before he had finished adjusting the focus. The body lay on its side in tattered vest and underpants with its arms pinioned at its back and its feet pointing towards him. Deacon instantly recognised the white flabbed thighs that he had last seen in PT shorts on the football field, and the belly that once flopped in the Aden Lido, but which now lay like a gutted whale in the back street dirt. He couldn't see McNish's head, it was obscured by his belly, but the feet magnified in his lenses. The fat, toeless stumps were blistered and black up to the shins.

Deacon slowly scanned the street and swept the rooftops. Nothing moved in the street but the flies. He walked back to his men at the trucks. He was conscious of Clemmie and Captain

Villiers watching him all the way. Villiers flicked his cigarette butt to the gutter.

"It's quite simple, lieutenant," he said. "You just walk up the street, shove him in a bag and take him to the mortuary. You know the drill. Why all this drama and delay?"

Deacon ignored him. "Kenny, Ambrose. Up on the roof either side of the street. Anything else on the rooftops and you shoot it dead. Right?"

Kenny and Ambrose scrambled up the truck with their Sterling guns and took kneeling watch on the nearest roofs.

"Shaw, take two men and guard the back door. No-one comes up. Rest of you watch the street and shoot anything that isn't in a lieutenant's uniform. Got it?"

"You gone and spoiled the fun now, sir!" said Gibson. He was grinning. Gibson was always grinning. He was a young, dishevelled soldier with broad shoulders and a vacant, loon face. Deacon suspected that Gibson was a true idiot. He was at home in the army.

"No one moves until I say so," said Deacon.

Lockett still held the prisoners under his rifle. He turned his head. "Have a care, sir," he called.

Deacon walked slowly up the street, scanning doorways and rooftops as he went. The high sun glared its heat down on him and sweat was soon trickling his forehead and his back. He could feel his toes oozing in his bindoo boots. He stopped a few yards from McNish, checked the street again and began a slow, wide circle about the body. McNish's head came into view. It too had been burned. It was a bloated dark ball of black and red and purple; it glistened like an autumn fruit jelly. The features had melted away and only the gaped mouth and the grinning teeth identified it as human.

Flies crashed into Deacon's face as he crouched nearer to the body and he had to scarf his mouth and nose to prevent himself gagging from the smells of putrefaction and baked shit that plastered McNish's legs. He could see no wires, no obvious booby traps.

As he was rising to return to the truck he saw a high shadow move into the street from the corner of his eye. He pulled out his pistol and shaded his eyes and looked up through haze to the roof to see the image of a raised hand on an extended arm. There was also a red and white chequered headscarf and a snarling Arab face. And a hand holding a grenade.

Deacon heard the sound of two sharp cracks. The Arab was thrown backwards off the roof as if kicked by a bull and disappeared behind the house. There was a faint crump and groan followed almost immediately by a small explosion. A pall of yellow-black smoke bloomed above the roof-top before drifting away to white.

Deacon waited crouched and primed in the heavy, airless silence. Nothing else moved. He walked back to the trucks. Kenny appeared on the roof top above him. Deacon nodded up to him.

"Fine shooting. Stay there and keep alert. No sense in taking any chances. Rest of you check door-to-door in pairs. One hundred yard perimeter. When it's clear, get Ambrose in and see if we can lift some prints from the dead Arab. Might have a finger or two left. Hobson, radio the contact in. Get the body squad and find something to cover McNish. Or what's left of the poor bastard."

The men filed away silently. Deacon watched the first few doors being booted in along the street. No-one came out. The place would be deserted for half a mile around. It was like kicking in an abandoned wasps' nest. The stupidity of it all glowed in him like hot coals. He could feel it burning him. He had to take a moment to cool himself.

He went back to Lockett and his prisoners. Deacon took the camera from Lockett's shoulder and handed it back to Clemmie. His embers still smouldered.

"Want to go and take a picture for your album?"

Clemmie took the camera and fixed Deacon with fired eyes. "Of course I don't. That's a despicable thing to say!"

"Uncalled-for, lieutenant," said Villiers. He stood up and gazed hard at Deacon. He was almost as tall as Deacon and filled his space with a solid calm.

"Suggest you apologise."

"Oh, it's nothing Tom, really," said Clemmie. "A misunderstanding, that's all."

Deacon stared at Villiers' steady, earnest and preposterously young face and almost laughed. He held up his hands.

"You are quite right. Miss Ross, it was a despicable thing to say and I should not have said it. My apologies. Corporal, you can release them from arrest and see they are escorted back."

"That won't be necessary, I'll see the lady home and safe," said Villiers.

He took a hold of Clemmie's elbow and began to escort her away.

"No," said Deacon. He stepped in front of Villiers. "I can't allow that. I still don't know who you are."

Villiers slowly removed his hat and turned it in his hands. He tapped the hat lightly on Deacon's chest. "Now you are becoming tiresome, lieutenant. What is your name?"

"Deacon."

"Well Lieutenant Deacon, it seems to me that you are now short a sergeant." He smiled genially. "Take care you don't replace him."

"I am only thinking of the lady's safety, sir," said Deacon. "I still have no verification of who you are. Corporal, make guard escort."

"Only soldierly and proper, sir," said Lockett.

"But this is silly!" said Clemmie. "I know Tom. He is Captain Villiers."

"How do you know him?" asked Deacon.

"Well. He's Tom, isn't he. Captain Villiers. He was on the same flight in as me. Up in officer class. And there was the Royal Navy party last week. He played bridge with mother. He's on Brigadier Jennings' special staff."

Clemmie thought some more.

"He rowed at Harrow with my brother!" she said.

"All right, Clemmie," said Villiers. "Satisfactory, lieutenant?"

"A soldier would never doubt the word of a lady, sir." said Deacon.

He re-holstered his pistol and stepped back to let them pass. Villiers leaned to him in whisper.

"Best not play with the matches, Deacon. Not in this heat."

"Is that another of your orders, sir?" said Deacon.

Captain Villiers smiled.

"Deacon," he said. "I'm pretty sure I know your bishop. You the praying type?"

"Only for deliverance," said Deacon. "Sir."

"I think I am going to remember you, Deacon."

"In your prayers, sir?"

Lockett laughed. Captain Villiers turned to gaze at the corporal and then at Deacon's men.

"Gods have no need to pray, lieutenant."

Captain Villiers took Clemmie's elbow and escorted her to his jeep.

Deacon watched Villiers rev the engine and pull smoothly away, Clemmie searching her bag at his side. As Villiers declutched into third, he turned a long glance on Deacon before disappearing behind white walls.

"Most bravely done, sir," said Lockett.

"Just another dead soldier, corporal."

"Oh, yes. That as well. That was brave. But not as brave as that."

Deacon turned to Lockett. The corporal was still gazing after the vanished jeep.

Deacon followed his gaze.

"As what?" he asked.

"Not as brave as having me arrest Brigadier Jennings' step-daughter, sir."

THREE

Deacon was awoken next morning by the sound of cow-bells. He raised himself dreamily onto his elbows and saw Chi standing at the end of the bed. The young boy was holding a brass ewer upright over the braced lock of his elbow. Despite his evident struggle, Chi was grinning. The ewer of hot tea was almost as big as Chi himself. He tapped an enamel mug against the side of the jug.

"Chi, Master Deacon. Today it is good. Finely hot. One dinar only. Very fair."

Through the window screens, the sun was clawing talons of light across the room as it sought roost for another day of scorch. Deacon glanced at his watch. He found some kind of focus.

"It's five o'clock, Chi!"

"Best time for Chi. Good and hot. I dhobi also. I wash your clothes. Ten piesta for every piece of clothing wash. Good price. Dhobi Master Mr. Patel says only best starch."

Chi poured a mug of tea and placed it on the table beside Deacon. The young, tan-skinned Arab boy smelt of stables and sacking cloth and his woollen hair was matted in dust and streaked in palmed tea. Chi was probably no more than eight years old. Or he could have been twelve. Chi was dressed in his one-piece rag futah held at the waist by a blue rope from which hung a dozen or so tin green mugs.

"It was five piesta last week," said Deacon.

Chi's cow-bells clattered across the room and he rummaged among a pile of clothes in the box.

"These trouser very dirty. Bad smell. Ten piesta make them good wash. Nice for the ladies."

"Just the tea, Chi thank you. How is business?"

"The war is bad for tea. And for starch also. Fucking Arabs nicking from the docks. Mr. Patel must raise his price. He says tea does not grow on trees. It is a joke. Very funny."

Corporal Lockett appeared smartly uniformed at the door, rubbing the drift of sleep from his eyes. "Sorry, sir. I asked Chi to call on me first."

Chi grinned and looked from Lockett to Deacon.

"Master Lockett right. I forgot he says. You back from good patrol? Many Adoo killed?"

"Come on Chi," said Lockett, "Leave Lieutenant Deacon to his tea and we'll do our words."

"OK. Is fine. Why is trees funny?"

Deacon met Lockett's quizzical gaze.

"One of Mr. Patel's jokes needs explaining." he said.

Lockett rolled his eyes. "Don't they all. Come on Chi. I told you no fucking, didn't I? Fucking is big no-no. Bad English word. Plenty trouble."

"You tell me about funny trees? This I must know. For my business."

Deacon watched them move through to his small sitting room and take their places at the table in front of the mosquito screen. He got up and closed his bedroom door and took a long shower. Lockett would be teaching Chi his English words and writing for half-an hour, then Chi would have to hurry away to re-fill his jug for his reveille trade. Lockett rose early to accommodate Chi's working day and Deacon was happy to sacrifice his sitting room by charitable return.

Deacon took his time shaving and dressing and emerged to find Chi had left for his rush-hour shift. Lockett was at the table, tidying papers and pencils into his case.

"Did you convince him that trees were funny, corporal?"

"I think we made some progress with the willow, sir. A definite connection." Lockett yawned.

"Your dedication is admirable, corporal. I can see Chi's progress. But have a care. Don't let it interfere."

"It doesn't, sir. Anyway I feel I owe him."

"Why?"

"Well Chi gets no cleaning trade from me. I have my own arrangements you see, sir. So I give teaching. Only seems fair."

"What arrangements?"

"My own, sir."

Deacon was searching for a response when the telephone rang. He had a short conversation which mostly entailed listening and then hung up.

"A light breakfast, I think, corporal. Old Bobby wants to see me pronto at oh-nine-forty hours." Major Robert Ford-Forrest, Old Bobby, was aide de camp to Brigadier Jennings.

"Suggest no orange in your breakfast gin this morning then, sir," said Lockett.

*

Deacon sat on a bench in the crowded long corridor at Brigade Headquarters and listened as an unseen clock chimed ten.

Clerks and couriers and secretaries busied past him on urgent errands. From the second floor window he could see the crows gathering on the highest wire of the sports field fence on the far side of the chequer-cut lawns and the white-stoned quad.

The crows gathered at their high wire perch every morning at this time. When Deacon had arrived, prompt at oh-nine-forty, there had been just a couple of them; now it was several dozen. Below them in the officers'club gardens, young starlings fluttered and feasted in a joyous twitter among the fig trees. As the chimes of ten faded, Deacon watched the crows launch themselves as one from their high roost, like a black cloak unfurling. They swooped in among the starlings and the fig trees exploded in a scattering squeal of birds.

It was over in seconds. The officer's club ran a daily book on the starling body count. This week Deacon was on four. He watched the white-liveried mess sergeant slowly walk the lawns under the fig trees scouting for the dead. After a meticulous search he turned to the club rooms and held his palm aloft with all fingers spread. A rumble of groans and cheers rolled from the bar rooms below.

Deacon leaned back on his bench and tried to relax. Old Bobby liked to keep his appointments waiting and Deacon knew he could still be there in an hour. A tea trolley was rattling its way somewhere around an unseen corner.

The corridor fell suddenly silent and the flow stopped as if everyone had walked into glass walls. Before he could react Deacon saw the bodies stiffening and parting to reveal Brigadier James Robert Jennings and his wife approaching as if through a stage curtain. Deacon joined the rest of the corridor at hasty and rigid attention.

Brigadier Jennings was a tall man with a caramel-grey moustache and lugubrious, bloodshot eyes. He strode with his stiff back slightly stooped and a cane clutched in his large and liver-spotted fist. He stared ahead, acknowledging no salutes. Mrs. Jennings, a small, heavy woman in a floral dress and abstract hat, ploughed a wide and oblivious furrow ahead of him.

Deacon held his breath and stared blankly as they passed him, but Brigadier Jennings halted two strides beyond him and turned back. Mrs Jennings steamed on up the corridor, unaware the brigadier had stopped.

"You Deacon?" said the Brigadier. His rheumy-eyed gaze fixed on Deacon's face. He braced his cane to the wall and against Deacon's hip. As if he was nursing the gate on a moorland sheep pen.

"Yes, sir."

The Brigadier looked him up and down slowly. Deacon could smell moth balls and brandy and Vicks vapour rub. The Brigadier re-braced his cane to the floor, his sheep safely penned.

"Arrested young Clementine I hear. That right?"

"Yes, sir."

"And then threatened to have her shot?"

"Yes, sir."

"But you didn't."

"No, sir."

Mrs Jennings re-appeared at the far end of the corridor.

"Jimbo! Do come along, we can't keep Ambassador Taala waiting. You know a crab buffet is never fit for long in this heat." She turned on squeaking heels and was gone.

Brigadier Jennings watched the empty space his wife had left for a few moments and then turned to face Deacon.

"Pity," he said. He gripped his cane once more and marched off after his wife.

"Lieutenant Deacon?" shouted a voice from a doorway. "Major will see you now."

Major Ford-Forrest sat behind his large, sparse and razor-tidy desk and fixed Deacon with a look of vacant un-enthusiasm. The men called him Old Bobby because he looked like the actor Robert Newton, only older and gone to seed. His body was round and compact and his head large. His uniform was immaculately pressed and his too-black moustache waxed proud under a mushroom nose and small, dull eyes. He looked up at Deacon for a long moment and then studied the single file that lay before him on the desk. He turned each page with a rigid, slow-licked finger.

Deacon heard the ceiling fan whispering above him and watched it cast manic petal shadows across the framed picture of the young Queen on the far wall. Deacon remained at attention, staring at a spot just above the major's head. The head stilled over a page in the file.

"My God! Is there a school in Croydon?" he asked.

"The secondary modern, sir."

A look of mild, confused sympathy passed quickly across the Major's face and he leaned back in his chair.

"Are you completely mad, lieutenant? Arresting Miss Clementine."

Deacon stared ahead and kept his silence.

"The Brigadier's daughter! And then threatening to shoot her! And Captain Villiers!"

Old Bobby rose up from his chair and stood bracing his knuckles on the desk. He still had to look up to find Deacon. The major pushed himself from the desk and strode the room.

"Had my way, Lieutenant, you would be back swilling the muck in the sergeant's mess. Have you lost your senses? Marjorie has been kept out of it of course Like a military campaign in itself. Many tactics deployed, let me tell you. Otherwise all hell to pay." He sat down heavily in his chair. He flicked the file shut and tidied it to square on the corner of the desk. "Well, it's not to be my way and higher orders prevail. You are off desert patrols, lieutenant. Back on city duties. Road checks. Docks. You know the drill. And you are to report to the Gallery for a refresher the day after tomorrow. You'll be reassigned additional duties after that. Let me have the paperwork on McNish. Was he married?"

"Yes, sir."

"Well, you know the drill. Line of duty, fine soldier and so on. They'll seal the box, so keep it plain. He packs out from Khormaskar at sixteen-hundred. You'd better be there. Make a show. Protocol and all that. Don't forget to sign the paperwork."

"What additional duties?" asked Deacon.

The major ranked his pencils to a precision on his desk. "Whatever duties you are ordered, lieutenant."

"And my men, sir?"

"You still have them, but God knows they don't deserve you. And they are a craven crew. Your corporal, Lockheart is it? Told him he was a sergeant, and do you know what he said? No ta.

No ta! What kind of answer is that? No discipline or respect. Army taking anyone. Well, when you fish in sewers you only land vermin. He told me he couldn't be a sergeant because he had a father! Think that was his gist. Talking like some damn Arab. Didn't understand the half of it. Your men seem as mad as you. Are you smiling?"

"No, sir."

"Damn well hope not. Your rope is so thin lieutenant that a fart could snap it. You're to make yourself available for jeep transport duties tomorrow. With a driver. Show a couple of bigwigs the sites. So don't balls it up. Had my way you'd be gutted. Now get out!"

*

The aviary made up one entire wall of the Inkerman Club. From his seat in the shade of the Club's gardens, Deacon watched the feathered blues and yellows and electric greens flare like tracers in the wired cage wall. Through the aviary mesh, he could see the fan-cooled bar crowded with the noon-day military trade.

There were almost a hundred birds in the aviary wall. Donated by visiting RAF crews or by merchant seamen, the birds came from every corner of the colonial world. Deacon often came to watch them, to see them flit and to marvel at how they still hadn't killed each other.

He returned reluctantly to the task of writing his letter to Mrs. McNish. He stared at the paper pad before him. Three drafts already lay crumpled at his feet.

He was having trouble lying. He always did. But he knew he would have to for Mrs. McNish. How the sergeant had been a steadfast comrade. A valiant soldier. A tragic loss.

"Hello again. I'm not interrupting, am I? You wouldn't be a good knight and get me a very tall and very cold lemonade, would you? They don't serve women here apparently. So Aden, don't you think? I do have money."

Clemmie Ross pulled out a chair and sat opposite Deacon. She was wearing a large and loose blue cotton jacket, a wide-brimmed hat and yellow-coloured linen trousers, like an aviary bird. Deacon welcomed the flap of wings and the promise of exotic diversion from Mrs. McNish.

Deacon summoned a waiter from his hide under the acacia tree shade and ordered lemonade. Clemmie searched in her bag.

"Thank you. I'm gasping from my walk. I was hoping to catch you earlier, to return this."

She slid the copy of *Alice In Wonderland* to Deacon.

"I thought you could slip it down your trousers before you went up before the beak. But a bit late now, I expect. Was it painful?"

"I survived," said Deacon, "But thank you for the thought."

The waiter returned with the lemonades and Deacon paid for them from his own pocket. Clemmie downed half her lemonade in one.

"I thought you handled it all very well. And Captain Villiers was very impressed," she said.

Deacon arched an eyebrow. Clemmie laughed.

"No, really. He was. He hardly mentioned you at all on the jeep ride back. That's how I could tell he was impressed."

"Do you know Captain Villiers well?"

"No, not really. The Brigadier thinks highly of him, I know."

"Ah, yes. Daddy."

Clemmie fired Deacon a quick look and then seemed to cool. "Yes, that's right. Daddy. It's never exactly a choice, is it? I expect even your father does something."

"He digs roads for Croydon Borough Council," said Deacon.

"Exactly," said Clemmie.

They sipped lemonade and watched the birds kaleidoscope in their cage.

"Why take fingerprints?" asked Clemmie.

The condensation from Deacon's glass pooled into the blue ink of his letter and the words bled on the page. He crumpled it into a ball.

"Most of the rebels used to work for the British here in one way or another. Clerks, cleaners, laundry wallahs, even administration. They slid away on the call of national revolution. But left all their records behind. The army is good at records. Fingerprints. Photo ID. So when we come across one, we check them off. If they are dead we fingerprint them. If we can."

"That's ghastly."

"That's Aden."

Clemmie sipped her drink. "Captain Villiers said that you had dogged your men. What did he mean?"

"That they obeyed, I expect," said Deacon.

The bar erupted into a roll of laughter that sent the caged birds scattering like fireworks. The cage stilled for a few moments before the tracers and trills flitted again.

"No. It was that they *followed*," said Clemmie "That's what Tom said. Like dog soldiers."

Deacon was silent.

"So what was your punishment?" Clemmie asked. "Am I allowed to know?"

"Additional duties and I have to take a couple of grand gawpers on a day tour of Aden. I think I would have preferred the cashiering."

"I've not been called a grand gawper before," said Clemmie. She drank the last of her lemonade. "And I'm pretty sure captain Villiers hasn't either."

Deacon watched the smile grow slowly under Clemmie's hat.

"The tour was my suggestion, I'm afraid," she said. "Otherwise it would have been the lash, or tied to a cannon or something. And captain Villiers is new to Aden and he wants to see it all too."

"Delightful," said Deacon.

"And Tom is providing a hamper."

"Splendid."

"Well it is supposed to be a punishment, you know."

"I'll take it like a soldier."

Clemmie leaned back and watched Deacon through round eyes. "Yes. I rather think you will."

Deacon saw her gaze turn to the balls of paper on the grass. A hand came to her mouth.

"Oh I've just realised. Sergeant McNish. You are writing a letter. I am so sorry to have barged in like this. What an idiot. I'm always doing it. You must think me very rude."

"It's quite alright, Miss Ross. You are a most pleasant and welcome distraction. I assure you. And my muse deserts me, as you can see."

"It was so awful," said Clemmie, "I mean. What can you possibly say?"

"The truth of course," said Deacon.

"Really?"

"Well, perhaps its practice."

*

Deacon stood on the concrete slab runway of Khormaskar airfield trying to hold his cap on as the propellers of the Beverley transporter plane hurricaned its winds about him. Lockett nudged him in the back and nodded towards a nearby hangar. Deacon eased to attention as Sergeant McNish's transport appeared as a shimmering mirage along the runway, like a small flight of crows coming into land. The shapes coalesced into a baggage truck and a flat bed trailer carrying a coffin. Four soldiers from the Lancashire regiment marched behind it. The truck driver came to a stop beside Deacon and handed him a clip-board. Deacon read the docket and then checked the cargo.

The crude planked coffin had been lightly nailed. It was only a transportation coffin for the leg to Cairo. When McNish's body eventually landed at Middle Wallop in two days time, it would be mahogany bound and brass handled. But his black, zipped and padlocked body-bag would make the full trip.

Deacon checked McNish's army number on the coffin luggage tag and signed the goods transfer.

"OK, corporal," he said.

Lockett nodded to the soldiers and they quickly shouldered their rifles and pointed them at the sky. "On the order. Escort. Fire."

The guns cracked. The four soldiers hitched their rifles, turned and marched off towards the canteen.

"We all done then?" shouted the baggage truck driver above the noise of the propellers. He flicked his cigarette butt into the humming winds where it danced like a crazed firefly before dying on the concrete. The driver released the brake and whined his caravan in a long arc around the aeroplane and disappeared up a ramp into its backside. Moments later the truck and empty trailer whined back down the ramp and headed back to the hangar.

Deacon and Lockett watched until the plane lumbered into the air and Sergeant McNish was a small stain in the white sky.

"Why weren't our men on escort?" asked Deacon.

"Other commitments, sir," said Lockett.

"Beyond duty orders?"

Lockett inspected his toe-caps for a moment.

"McNish owed them all money, sir." he said. "They only found out yesterday. The sergeant had been into them all. Over forty quid all told. Tenner to Hobson alone. And he was saving for his teeth. A lot of bad feeling. Not being here is like payment. Only one they are going to get."

"So who did the honour of seeing McNish off?"

"Four Lancashire lads from the NAAFI, sir. Sent him off fine, didn't you think?"

"They shot the sky with great accuracy, corporal. How much?"

"Five bob a head, sir. There's a dance tonight and they were light."

"I hear you don't want to be a sergeant," said Deacon.

For a moment Lockett seemed at a loss for words.

"Yes. Well. Who would want to be a sergeant? Have you ever been in the sergeant's mess, sir? All they talk about is football, fucking and farting. I'm just not the sporty type."

"Then you won't be up for a spot of driving for me tomorrow in the Aden tourist Grand Prix?"

"Always up for a drive, sir."

"Good. Miss Ross is accompanying us."

"Oh," said Lockett. "Right."

"And captain Villiers."

"The sun keeps on shining."

"He's bringing a hamper."

"Like Ratty, sir."

"We'll use the long-base jeep. Make sure the tanks are full. Stash a couple of Brownings in the well. Supply for the full day."

"Sir," said Lockett.

*

As they were walking out through the foyer of the airfield offices, a young army captain stepped into their path. It took a moment for Deacon to recognise Captain Ashley without his peaked cap blindfold. His blond hair was cropped to near baldness on the sides and back of his head but sprouted like a parched turf of lawn from his crown. Small, pale eyes fixed on Deacon.

"A moment of your time, lieutenant," he said. "Follow me."

He led Deacon through the foyer and across the truck park to the Security Unit. The unit was a collection of three, low-rippled Nissen huts enclosed by high razor-wired fencing. They were checked in through both the perimeter and the gate guards and led down a fetid, dark corridor to a small and tidy office. The captain beckoned Deacon in.

"Thank you, corporal," said Ashley. He closed the door, leaving Lockett in the corridor.

"Hoped you might help with the prisoner you brought in," said Captain Ashley. "He's proving a bugger to shift. Says he's innocent, of course."

Ashley laughed. He slid into a leather chair and heeled his boots onto the corner of his desk. There was no chair for Deacon. Ashley looked him up and down and then took a pistol from his drawer. He looked at it for a long moment, weighing it in his hand. Then he pulled the trigger and lit a small cheroot with the flame that sprang from the pistol's hammer.

Deacon didn't move. He didn't even allow his eye to flicker. Captain Ashley exhausted a slow jet of grey smoke and smiled.

"Innocent," he said. "And they really think we will believe them. That they know nothing. They weren't there. And twenty kids to feed. Must think we are fools. Our latest innocent claims the rifle had no bullets. It was just an old one for show. The old man found it in a wadi. Lies and fairytales of course. Was the gun empty?"

"Yes, it was."

Captain Ashley swung his boots off the desk and landed lightly on his toes. He stubbed his cheroot in the shell-case ashtray, walked slowly to the window and stared out through the mosquito screens smeared grey with grime.

"You sure about that? Take your time."

"I saw no bullets."

"Maybe he got rid of them? Difficult to see everything in heat of taking prisoners and all that. He could have dropped them when you weren't looking."

The captain turned and stared at Deacon. "Wouldn't you say, lieutenant?"

"I saw no bullets, sir."

The captain stared at Deacon for a few moments. "Come with me," he said.

Deacon followed him out of the office. Lockett was sitting stiff on a bench in the corridor and made to rise as they appeared. Deacon nodded him back down and followed the captain along a short path ranked in pale daffodils and into an adjacent hut. They were checked-in past more guards and Deacon found himself walking down steps into an underground chamber lined with solid metal, peep-holed doors. The dark, humid tunnel smelled of bleach and sweat and shit. From behind one of the doors, Deacon could hear the faint sound of rushing water, like a driveway being hosed. Muffled, rhythmic grunts came from behind another door.

Captain Ashley stopped before a door and unlocked it from a spray of keys that bloomed at his belt. He stepped back and nodded Deacon in.

The large room was dismal and humid and Deacon felt himself encased in a damp cloak of heavy air smelling of over-ripe meat and pond mud. On one side of the room two soldiers, stripped to the waist and sheened in sweat were playing cards at a table lit by a suspended, dull-wattage bulb. On the other side of the room the young Arab hung on his wrists from wires suspended from the metal beams of the ceiling. He was spinning a slow pirouette on toes that seemed to hover over a dirt floor that was scattered in broken bottles and snaked in razor-wire. Lanced sticks sprang out of the ground about him like a bamboo pasture. The sticks nearest his legs and backside were spiked in blood. The boy span lazily with his chin on his chest. His feet were tatters of flesh. He was barely conscious and groaning low as if in dreamy song. His left leg bullet wound was a glistening purple ooze.

"Any progress?" asked Captain Ashley.

One of the card-playing soldiers stubbed his cigarette under his boot.

"No, sir. Moaning like this all day. MO says he's likely gone sponge, sir. Not much longer, he reckons. Want me to wake him?"

The captain waved a dismissive hand. The soldier returned to his cards. Ashley turned to Deacon and smiled amiably. He cocked his head to whisper.

"Of course we could have him down from there like a shot if we knew that the gun had bullets. Have him a nice hospital bed with all the nice English WRAF nurses. Bathing his wounds. Might even save him. If only we knew about the bullets. Such a little thing."

Deacon watched the Arab boy. The wires had cut black bracelets at his wrists and his thigh was being pierced by a stick that he didn't feel.

"Sure you didn't see any bullets?" asked Captain Ashley.

"I saw no bullets," said Deacon.

The captain said nothing for a long moment.

"Wake him up," he barked. The soldiers let their cards drop to the table and they rose wearily. Captain Ashley began unbuttoning his shirt. "Let's go the bastard again. Find your own way out, Lieutenant."

As Deacon stepped back out into the tunnel, the metal door clunked behind him.

Deacon was silent in the jeep on the way back to the billet. He was aware of Lockett watching him out of the corner of his eye as he drove. Deacon let Aden blur past. Start the lie and it never stops to hunger for more. Deacon knew about that. A lie grows behind you like a ghouled shadow.

"Everything alright, sir?" asked Lockett.

"Just shut the fuck up, corporal," said Deacon.

They continued the journey in silence until they reached Deacon's billet. Deacon swung from his seat and walked to his door.

"Tomorrow at oh-eight-hundred, corporal," he said, without looking back. He slammed his billet door closed behind him.

FOUR

By oh-eight-thirty in the morning the Aden sun was fierce enough to curl paper. In the time Deacon walked the short distance from the sentried car park and up the steps and into the grand foyer of the Belvedere Club, he was prickling with sweat.

He showed his ID to the sergeant behind the desk and wandered into the busy, cool-tiled atrium to wait. The room was already crowded with officers and NCOs and civilian clerks waiting for appointments or orders. A bazaar of uniforms sat in wicker armchairs among the potted palm trees reading newspapers, or stood smoking cigarettes as if on a provincial repertory stage. Deacon took shelter in the shade of the gun-metal statue of a charging horse and its Hussar colonel rearing in a corner of the room. The tall picture windows looked out onto the languid blue of the bay. The room babbled with whispered conversations and the occasional burst of laughter.

Deacon waited.

The tiled-floor of the atrium gleamed like a varnished chess-board. Above him, the heavy ceiling fans purred a breeze as welcome as a summer shower. Deacon enjoyed the moment of cool. A tassel-capped waiter appeared, smiling, at Deacon's side. Deacon waved him away.

Captain Villiers and Clemmie Ross entered the room amongst a small group, strolling out from out of one of the breakfast rooms. Villiers was dressed in the newly pressed uniform of a commando captain. He was taller than Deacon remembered and he moved with a boxer's light grace over the tiles. Villiers and Clemmie were in the middle of a small group that was laughing and in pleasant spirits. Deacon noticed the Brigadier and also Admiral Le Jeune. Clemmie seemed to be amusing the Admiral with a story. There was a polite bray of laughter before the group parted and went their ways. Like the rest of the room, Deacon found himself at attention.

Captain Villiers escorted Clemmie over to where Deacon stood. Villiers smiled warmly, reached into his pocket and pulled out his ID.

"My card," he said.

Deacon read the card and saluted.

"Sir," he said.

Villiers held his stare for a moment and then burst out laughing. "No ID, no orders. Hah! Damn right. Put me in my place and no mistake. And then under arrest! You've got guts Deacon, give you that. You didn't bully either. That's good."

Deacon looked at Clemmie, who was smiling. She was wearing a loose linen jacket with the sleeves half-rolled and a blue bandana coiled about her neck. A large straw hat span slowly in her hands.

"I told you Tom was impressed," she said

Villiers clapped him sharply on the shoulder. "Ease up, man! Not going to bite. You did exactly the right thing. Like a proper soldier. Now I believe you are going to show us Aden. Clemmie's armed with her camera. Got our lunch around here somewhere."

Villiers lifted his head in summons and a waiter struggled in with a large hamper and a blue plastic cool box.

"Got it from London on my last trip," said Villiers. "One of these new cool boxes. Should be fine for the wine. Sauvignon alright, I trust?"

Villiers signalled the waiter to take his burden out to the waiting jeep and then turned a broad smile on Deacon. "Behold the power of prayer." he said.

Deacon laughed.

"That's better!" said Villiers, "It's Leslie, isn't it?"

"My men call me Harry, sir."

"Why?" asked Clemmie.

"They say I look like Harry Palmer. From the film posters. You know, *The Ipcress File*."

"Saw that in Cairo a few weeks back. At the Ambassador's." said Villiers. "Rather good."

"I can see what they mean," said Clemmie.

"No glasses of course, but a definite likeness," said Villiers. "Right, then, Harry! Show us Aden."

"What do you want to see?" Deacon asked Clemmie.

"Everything," said Villiers. "I've been here a month and haven't seen anything of Aden yet. Locked in rooms with cigar smoke and mosquito screens. Show us the lot!"

Lockett was standing to smart attention beside the jeep. He saluted.

"We'll do the full tour, corporal." said Deacon.

"Right you are, sir."

They watched while the club servants loaded the bags, parasol and boxes into the jeep. Clemmie and Villiers were in high spirits. Clemmie sat on one of the jeep's side benches.

"It's like a safari!" she said.

Villiers leapt up into the jeep with the ease of a panther taking a low tree. He took a seat opposite Clemmie.

"Come on, Harry!" he said. "Let's not waste time."

They drove out of Aden along the coast road to Maalla and on towards the Old Steamer port of Tawali. Clemmie was delighted in all she saw and found pictures in everything. Villiers watched all about him with keen-eyed interest.

Lockett kept his foot down through Maalla. It was not a place to idle. Deacon kept his eyes busy and his smile light as they entered the main shopping streets of Tawali. The roads were busy with trucks and traders and camels pulling wagons of water. Desultory Arabs trudged in the roadside dust, their backs bent under bundles of sticks and baskets of baking guava and mangoes. Brightly coloured Hillmans and Morris Oxfords and maverick three-wheeled tin trucks whined and weaved among it all. In the narrow, tightly packed streets of shops and stalls the vendors chanted their wares and trades like calling gulls above a swelling ocean. Clemmie seemed transported by the exotic bustle flowing about her and her camera clicked busily.

Deacon kept a wary watch on the crowds and the shadows. The Aden sun hurled its light against the shops and stalls like searchlights and cast massive granite slabs of angular shadow that swallowed whole sections of street. The impenetrable shadows were as deep and lightless as wells. They drove through Maalla in flashes of sunlight and long moments of dark while the street chanted and sang about them. Deacon listened for the soft click of a pulled grenade pin, or the clack of rifle bolt. He did not relax until they left the shops and shadows behind them and were making for Telegraph Bay and the relative safety of the Cable & Wireless enclave.

As they were climbing a slow rise, a large piard dog ran from out of a side alley and stopped in the middle of the road. Lockett braked and skidded the jeep to a stop. The dog did not move but continued to stare at them. It had a milk-white bone clamped in its jaws. It was a human pelvis.

"Oh my goodness!" said Clemmie. She jumped out of the jeep and began taking pictures, crouching and twisting as she did so. Deacon was soon at her side. He looked back to see Captain Villiers standing up in the jeep. He was screwing a silencer to his pistol.

"Careful, Clemmie," said Villiers. "Don't want to have to shoot it."

Clemmie and Deacon stood watching the dog. Deacon could see its ribs pumping slowly and its grey eyes fixed on him.

"What is that bone?" asked Clemmie.

"I expect it's from Cemetery Hill," said Deacon, "The Arab burial ground. Just up the rise there. You can't dig deep in these rocks. The graves are little more than shallow scrapes topped with a throw of stones. The piard packs soon have them out. When the rains come the streets can be like a flooded charnel house."

"You don't have to try and scare me all the time, Harry. It doesn't work."

For a moment Deacon was at a loss for a reply. "Scare you? Why would I want to do that?"

Clemmie turned and studied him for some time. She laughed.

"I do believe you mean it. Is death so normal here?"

"It's just as normal here as anywhere else," said Deacon. "But in Aden it perhaps has more practise and opportunity."

The dog snarled, turned and disappeared among the rocks. Captain Villiers unscrewed his silencer. When Clemmie turned and pointed the camera at Villiers, he pulled the pistol to him again and offered a grinning, heroic pose.

"One for the album. *The wild dog hunter of Aden*." he said and laughed.

Deacon then felt the camera on him. There was a click.

"I'll call it *Aden Soldier*," said Clemmie.

Deacon was aware of Lockett watching him with a smile ghosting his pale face. Deacon was also aware that he was standing somewhere close to attention and that he had swelled his chest just a little. He had even turned to half-profile for Clemmie's camera. He felt a little foolish. He turned to Lockett.

"Next time you brake for a damn dog, I'll have your stripes."

Lockett lost his smile. "Sorry, sir," he said. "Won't happen again."

They drove along the high road overlooking Telegraph Bay and stopped by the gently singing aerial masts to admire the elevated, panoramic view of the Aden peninsula. The volcanic mountains rose out of a dark green sea. The wind-borne sands lightened their lower slopes like frail skirts. Beyond the blemish of the city and the shanty scars of Maalla and Crater the crescent bays of clean white sands sculpted the shoreline under a relentless sun.

"It looks so different from up here," said Clemmie. "So peaceful. Just look at those wonderful bays and the beaches. Doesn't it just make you want to run down there and just dive in and swim in the cool of the sea? To forget about all the horror and death for a blissful moment."

"Then swim you shall, Clemmie!" said Villiers. "Sure it can be arranged, eh Harry?"

"It is not advisable," said Deacon.

"Oh Harry! Why not?" said Clemmie. "Just a paddle in the cooling sea. It is so hot. Surely you can relax enough for us to have a quick paddle?"

"Yes. Come on, Harry." said Villiers. "Not too much to ask is it? Where's the harm?"

Deacon pulled the binoculars from the jeep and handed them to Clemmie. "Have a close look at your bay," he said.

Clemmie peered through the glasses but appeared to find nothing of interest. Villiers took the glasses from her and scanned the bay.

"Try just offshore," said Deacon.

Villiers refocused his gaze. The glasses stilled and then lowered. "Are they sharks?"

"Yes," said Deacon. "You don't swim anywhere here without a shark net."

"But it all looks so beautiful. So inviting," said Clemmie.

"He's right, Miss," said Lockett. "The seas around here boil with them."

"But I only want a paddle," said Clemmie.

"The wife of an Infantry sergeant was only paddling last summer but a shark still got her," said Deacon. "She died the next day."

Clemmie turned to Deacon, her face set in anger. "Well that has certainly ruined a lovely view. Are you sure you don't enjoy trying to frighten me?"

Deacon could not think what to say.

As they were travelling along the coast road back towards the city there was a sudden bang from the front of the jeep. The jeep lurched sideways and slewed across the road but Lockett brought it to a skilled stop in the sand. Villiers was thrown to the floor and Clemmie was clutching on to a roof bar. Deacon had braced himself across the seats and against Clemmie's legs. He was alert as soon as the jeep had come to a skidded halt. He could see that no-one was hurt. Villiers was dusting himself down. Clemmie was rubbing her shoulder.

"Everyone stay in the jeep," said Deacon.

He got out and scanned the terrain. The road was wide and long and was flanked on either side by flat scrubs and sands that stretched miles in all directions. This was not an ambush. He paced back along the road to where the tyre had blown and checked for roadside wires. Then he checked ahead of the jeep. There was nothing. It was just another tyre burst. They happened in Aden, frequently. Deacon turned back to the jeep to find Clemmie taking his picture. Villiers stood beside her grinning, a rifle nestled across his forearm.

"You look like a young Alexander on the Carthage shores!" said Villiers. He jumped down from the jeep and inspected the wheel. "Bet I can change the wheel in under six minutes. Take me on, corporal?"

Lockett was retrieving the jack from its box and unscrewing the spare wheel. "Going some for six minutes, sir. I'll take the bet."

Villiers unbuttoned his shirt and hung it carefully over the jeep door. He grinned, spat into his hands, turned his cap back to shade his neck and crouched ready.

"Got a watch, Harry?" he asked.

Deacon nodded and held up his wrist.

"Right," said Villiers, "Go."

Villiers dived to with the brace and jack. The wheel nuts came off smoothly, the axle was raised and a new wheel was being shucked on in almost no time. Villiers' strong shoulders and broad back were soon gleaming in sweat but the pace and graceful rhythm of his effort didn't slacken. Deacon watched transfixed as Villiers attacked his work. His hands moved fast and sure and his muscles torqued and rippled with the effort. Villiers flicked the jack out and stamped the brace hard on the last tightened nut. He stood up, puffed his cheeks and wiped a forearm across his face.

"Now," he said.

"Five minutes fifty -one," said Deacon.

"Hah! Said so. My bet, I think. I'll have your hat, corporal."

Lockett hesitated for a moment but then handed Villiers his headscarf. Villiers folded it carefully into a square and then swabbed the sweat from his face, shoulders and chest. He mopped under his arms and then wiped his hands clean of sand and dark wheel grease. He tossed the crumpled headscarf back to Lockett. Villiers lifted a jerry-can of water and doused himself. He hand-wiped off the worst of the wet, finger-combed his hair to its wave and re-buttoned his shirt over his still damp chest.

"Where did you learn to do that?" asked Clemmie. "With the wheel."

"In my father's garage," said Villiers, "Could change sparks when I was six."

"Your father ran a garage?" asked Deacon.

Villiers seemed amused by the question.

"Yes. Well, the southern England Jaguar franchise. About sixteen of them I think. And then some in Hong Kong of course. And a few engineering factories. So plenty of opportunity to tinker. Not much else to do in a garage all day. Shall we press on Harry?"

Deacon watched Lockett climb back into the driver's seat. He was looking at the soiled headscarf that lay in his hand. He lifted it out of the window as if it were a fallen bird and then dropped it onto the road. He sat passive, waiting for instructions.

"The minaret, corporal."

*

The Aden minaret thrust from out of a square island of rocks and small trees beside the two-storey grey concrete box of the GPO building. They pulled up in the car park and stared up at the tower. It was over two hundred feet high and had seven rows of blind-stone windows encircling it up to a small, capped roof. The tower's stone was smoothly finished like plaster, and so white that it seared the eye.

"My Lord!" said Clemmie.

Clemmie shielded her gaze with both hands and studied the minaret slowly from bushed base to its tumescent domed roof in the high white sky.

"It's the last remnant of the old Manara mosque," said Deacon. He pointed up to the top of the tower at the only open window. "The Muardin calls the followers to prayer every morning from up there."

"I must take some pictures." said Clemmie. "Corporal, would you be a soldier and help me with the tripod. Lockett, isn't it?"

Lockett came to attention. "Yes, Miss. Of course."

"Well Harry and me will shade it out over there." said Villiers. "We will watch the artist at work, eh?"

Deacon sat with Villiers on a shaded, low wall while Lockett and Clemmie made their way across to the tower. Clemmie had bags over her shoulders and Lockett carried the tripod and cameras. Villiers poured two glasses of wine. He drank his in one and refilled it.

"Very attractive, Miss Ross," he said. "Don't you think?"

"Yes," said Deacon. "And very independent."

Villiers laughed. "That's Clemmie!"

They sat back and watched as Clemmie and Lockett took pictures on the far side of the square. They were laughing and enjoying themselves. Clemmie lay on her back pointing her camera skywards. Lockett was holding the parasol over her. His other hand hovered over his head for the little shade it provided.

"Her father was Lord Brockenhurst, did you know?" said Villiers. He poured himself another glass of wine and proffered the bottle to Deacon, who declined. "No? Major-General Marshalsea as was," said Villiers. "Died on the Rhine taking a bridge. There's a soldier's death, eh Harry? So her mother married the Brigadier. He and the General were old chums. Our Clemmie is really rather well connected. Top drawer stock."

"Yes. She sounds quite a catch," said Deacon.

"And she'll take some netting," said Villiers. "Girl like Clemmie. Something of a wild childhood I understand. Dungarees and ban the bomb marches. But used to her comforts, I expect."

"Aren't we all," said Deacon.

He rested his back against the cool stones and watched a group of soldiers playing football against a high shaded wall on the other side of the wide road. The men were shirtless. They played their game at walking pace and called and joked

with each other. They were all smoking. Deacon guessed they were waiting for the noon bus to take them back to Khormaskar. The bus was, of course, late. It might not turn up at all.

"Heureux, humilies comme des chiens battus," said Villiers.

Deacon turned to Villiers and saw that he had also been watching the footballers. Villiers smiled and his hand swept back his wayward fringe. Deacon could not hide his surprise. Whatever he had imagined of Villiers it was not that the young, athletic Captain would be the poetry type, and certainly not French poetry, and in French. But Deacon realised that Tom Villiers had been surprising him ever since they had met. Like the Captain's slightly broken nose it was something of a charm.

"From Rimbaud," said Villiers. "The poet. One of Clemmie's favourites, I gather. Girls seem to go for that sort of thing."

"Yes," said Deacon, "I know. From *Les Pauvres a l'eglise.*"

Villiers raised a theatrical eyebrow to Deacon. Then he raised his wine glass. "Didn't know Rimbaud got in amongst your lot at Croydon Secondary."

Deacon felt himself flush. That damn school again.

"They didn't," he said. "I had special lessons."

"I bet you did!" said Villiers.

Villiers poured himself another glass of wine. Deacon tried to ignore the recollection of Mr Havers press at his side as he slowly turned the pages of the French primer with a long-fingered hand, or the light press of his other hand on Deacon's thigh. He shook his thoughts back to Villiers.

"I'd take it easy on the wine, sir," said Deacon. "The heat. It can be a bad cocktail."

"Appreciate your concern but I am quite used to it. Been six months in Palestine. Lots of practice."

Deacon lazed back against the wall and continued to watch the footballers. Villiers' scent of sweat and wine drifted in the air.

Clemmie and Lockett returned to join them in the shade.

"Marvellous pictures!" said Clemmie. She took the wine proffered by Villiers.

"Harry here knows his Rimbaud, Clemmie," said Villiers.

Clemmie looked up with interest.

"Really? He's quite one of my heroes. A wonderful poet, don't you think?"

"Not much of a soldier though, Clemmie," said Villiers. "Deserted, didn't he?"

"Did he?" said Clemmie. Her brightness seemed to fade. "But that doesn't mean he wasn't a fine poet."

"Of course not, Clem," said Villiers. "You can clear away now, corporal."

Lockett packed the bags and tripods in the jeep. He crossed the sunlit car park with a slow tread.

"He lived here for while, you know, Miss Ross," Deacon said.

"Who?"

"Rimbaud."

Clemmie sat up.

"You know? I mean about Rimbaud being here in Aden? It was one of my interests in coming here. To find his house. And take some pictures. My secret adventure!"

Deacon shaded his eyes and pointed down the road. "His house is just up the next street. Fourth on the left, *La Maison du Rimbaud.* He was here for five years. A port trader. Before his venture in Ethiopia."

Clemmie was on her feet and starting for the house. "Up Harry! Come on," said Clemmie. She was feeding new film into her camera. "You must show me. I have to see it!"

*

The house was in a terrace of two-storey Dutch built cottages with arched stonework over the four windows and a paint peeling front door of parched green. The house walls were as thick as a thrust arm. The faded façade was grey and pot-marked and a scatter of drab flowers withered in the cracked wooden window boxes that were propped in place by upturned packing crates. Above the door there was a hand painted sign. *La Maison du Rimbaud.*

"I must get inside, Harry!" said Clemmie. "To see his rooms."

A black-bearded Arab came to the door and surveyed the group. He was tall enough to have to stoop in his doorway. His gaze seemed to linger over Lockett. Deacon saw Lockett staring at invisible space just above the Arab's shoulder.

"Ask him Harry," said Villiers.

Deacon tried his sparse Arabic. And then his French. Villiers and Clemmie chipped in with Hindi and some German. The Arab refused to understand them all. He waved his hands and backed into his house and closed the door.

"He's got to open up to us. We're the British Army!" said Villiers. "Can't let Clemmie down like this. Can't we arrest him or something?"

"It's a private house. We can do nothing but beat a tactful retreat I'm afraid," said Deacon. "We don't make sparks in this heat."

"But what a memory Rimbaud's house would be," said Clemmie. "Inside the home of the great poet. Think of it!"

Lockett stepped forward and saluted Deacon. "Would you like me to have a go, sir?"

Villiers barked a laugh. "Thank you, corporal," he said, "we'll bear the offer in mind."

Lockett stood waiting for Deacon's instruction. Deacon saw the glint in Lockett's eye. He couldn't decide if it was of fire or of ice.

"Well, nothing ventured, corporal," said Deacon.

Lockett grinned. He walked back up the street to the house and knocked on the door. There was a short, subdued conversation with the black beard and then Lockett beckoned them over. He stood to attention as they joined him. The large Arab held his door open and he gestured them inside.

"He hopes you will forgive the mess, sir." said Lockett. "Just finished their meal."

Villiers grinned at Lockett. "Touche, corporal." he said. "Smartly done. Slip him something, did you?"

Lockett seemed to find a space above Villiers left shoulder. "No sir. I just asked nicely."

Clemmie laughed. "Good for you, corporal. Manners. A master tactic."

They crowded into the small front room. The furnishings were modest and sparse. A small bookcase held a few curled paperback copies of Rimbaud's poetry and there was a brown photograph of the great poet and adventurer propped on a table. A young, straight-backed Rimbaud was standing three-quarter profile in a swept-cut jacket, a high wing collar and an extravagantly pinned cravat. His young, pale face was gazing into the invisible space above Deacon's shoulder.

In the back room Deacon could see the Arab's wife sitting in her kitchen, basking in the bright-lit cool of the wide open door of a silver refrigerator that was as big as a wardrobe. The refrigerator rumbled low like a tank on sand.

Two young girls were sitting wide-eyed and sucking pencils at an upturned packing crate in the doorway. They were no more than six years old and watched their visitors through wide and spellbound eyes. They both suddenly broke into a grin at the sight of Lockett.

Villiers and Clemmie were enthusiastically inspecting the meagre sights and the Arab invited them upstairs to see Rimbaud's private room. With space at a premium Deacon remained with Lockett in the front room. Deacon could hear Villiers and Clemmie's happy chatter in the rooms above him.

One of the little girls picked out a piece of paper from a shelf and ran and handed it to Lockett, before scampering back grinning to her seat. Lockett slipped the paper into his pocket and found interest in a grey copy of the Aden Times of March 1883 that was pinned to a wall.

"What is in the note, corporal?" said Deacon.

"It's private, sir,"

"Come on, corporal. You know the drill. Covers all communications, especially scraps of paper."

Lockett hesitated for a moment and then handed Deacon the paper. The message was crayon drawn. *Happy Birthday David by Suli and Bana,* was scrawled beside a child's drawing of a blue camel.

Deacon re-folded the paper and handed it back to Lockett. He was silent for a moment, trying to get over the surprise of learning that Lockett was David. He had somehow never remembered, or perhaps known, that Lockett had a name. That he was David.

"Sorry corporal. But you know the duties. These ladies are obviously of your acquaintance?"

"I do a little writing and words with them," said Lockett. He turned to the girls. "*From*, Bana. It's *from* Suli and Bana. Not *by*. But a very good camel."

The girls giggled.

"And that is how you got us in here?" asked Deacon.

"Ali-Sid is fine sir, really. Don't let the beard fool you. He's a pussycat. He works with Mr. Patel at the laundry. I teach his girls English. He just gets a bit tired of having people tramp around his house, that's all. Who wouldn't? And he thinks Rimbaud wasn't much of a poet anyway. But he doesn't mind for people he knows."

"I hope your friend doesn't share his poetry views with Miss Ross. He's liable to lose his tip."

"Ali-Sid knows the trade sir. Wouldn't be surprised if Captain Villiers isn't buying one of Mr. Rimbaud's personal cravats for the lady even now."

Deacon laughed. He watched the two girls at their pencil work on the small table. In the kitchen, the mother had tuned a small radio on to an American big band channel. She sat at her table gutting fish by the light of the refrigerator.

"When was your birthday?" asked Deacon.

"Last week. On patrol, sir."

"Well. Happy Birthday for then, corporal."

"Thank you, sir."

The others returned from their tour in high spirits.

"The girls back home will be so envious!" said Clemmie. "Some really wonderful pictures. Oh, you are marvellous for finding it Harry. And of course you, corporal."

"Now where shall we take our picnic lunch, Harry?" said Villiers. "The choice is all yours."

*

Deacon ordered Lockett to take them to the Tawila Tanks. They drove through the early afternoon scorch of the sun and up the deserted, winding road into the Shamsam mountains above Tawila. They parked on a high, road-side bend and gazed at the vast natural cisterns that had been sculpted like a dinosaur's heel prints down the full sweep of the black, volcanic mountain's slope.

Deacon stood at the edge of the rise, in wonder at the view.

"There were fifty-three tanks in all," he said. "In the ancient times. Wonderful engineering. Man and nature together. All interconnected and controlled by sluices. They collected the river water and stored it above the city for times of drought. When the floods came it defended the city from the worst. And this was centuries ago. Only thirteen tanks remain now, though. I have calculated that they would have held a good twenty million gallons."

Deacon turned to see Villiers and Clemmie watching him and grinning like errant and impish pupils sharing a joke. Lockett stood behind them gazing out over the valley sweep. Deacon felt himself redden.

"Sorry, didn't mean to spout."

"Very informative, sir," said Lockett. "And interesting."

"I'll say," said Clemmie. "And look at that view."

"Think nothing of it Harry!" said Villiers in good humour. "Fascinating stuff. Marvellous place! Let's get down there and take a look. Corporal, bring the lunch. We'll set up down there in the shade."

Deacon wandered with Villiers and Clemmie among the carved tanks and dawdled over the brickwork walkways. He watched Lockett bringing the hamper and cool-box down the six flights of stone steps and set up a table in the coolest shades of the mountain. Lockett had to rest several times. It was a hot day. It was always a hot day.

"Simply wonderful!" said Clemmie. She took a seat in the table shades and gazed out at the mountains. Lockett passed out the plates and cutlery. "How clever of you to know this place, Harry."

"Thank you, corporal," said Villiers. He un-strapped the hamper. "You better go up on top and guard the jeep."

Lockett stiffened. He sought Deacon's eye. Lockett looked tired and his face was pink as if lightly rouged. Deacon nodded up to the jeep.

"Get some rest."

"Sir."

Lockett turned and climbed back up the steps to the jeep parked on the road's high bend. Villiers uncorked another bottle and poured generous glasses.

"You handle your men well, Harry," said Villiers. He pulled out Cornish pasties and cheese sandwiches from the hamper, each wrapped in its own greaseproof paper envelope. "Tuck in, everyone. Saw that back in Maalla. With your unfortunate sergeant. Would your boys have shot me?"

"Of course."

"What makes you so sure?"

"You are an officer. No soldier worth his salt would pass up that order."

Villiers laughed. "You have them well leashed, I'll say that."

"Oh Tom. They're not dogs." said Clemmie. She bit deep into a pasty, cupping a hand under her chin.

"Well trained then," said Villiers. "Let's settle for that."

"Are you married, Harry?" asked Clemmie.

Deacon's cheese sandwich seemed to dry in his mouth. Clemmie had a way of asking the most direct of questions. It was like being under sporadic gunfire.

"No, Miss Ross. A soldier is not a great catch. A lieutenant even less so."

"Not all women hunt riches," said Clemmie.

"I didn't mean to imply..."

Clemmie laughed.

"Do you ever stop being serious, Lieutenant?"

Deacon thought about it. "No," he said. "I don't think I do."

"So what is it you hunt for, Clemmie?" asked Villiers. He refilled Clemmie's glass. Deacon declined his. "I rather think you would go for the adventurer type. Or a rogue of a poet. Like young Rimbaud. Or a dashing actor.

Even a pop-star, maybe. But not a soldier, eh?"

"Oh no, Tom. You'e quite wrong. I am fairly sure I will marry a soldier," said Clemmie.

Deacon and Villiers both stopped eating and stared at her. Clemmie laughed.

"Every woman wants to marry a soldier. Surely you know that. The poets and painters and pop stars are all very well, but they can never compare to a soldier. It's marriage, after all. For life. Soldiers are so much more reliable and resourceful."

Clemmie peeled her tangerine. "And they are clean, and punctual and fit. And have good manners. Generally speaking," she said.

"Dutiful and protective," said Villiers

"Quite."

"Know how to iron their own shirts and to obey orders," said Deacon.

Clemmie laughed. "That too. So what could be a better life mate than a soldier?"

"Quite right too," said Villiers. He raised his glass. "To the soldier."

While the others laughed and chatted Deacon offered his excuses and went to check on Lockett. After a long and hot climb he found Lockett sitting half-dozing in the corner of the jeep. His face was both pale and flushed, like an apple. He sat up as Deacon climbed into the back of the jeep. A plastic wrapped sandwich and a pasty landed in Lockett's lap.

"Some grub. Are you alright, corporal?"

"Thanks, sir. I'm fine. Just a little tired."

Lockett bit into the sandwich and chewed it without enthusiasm. "He called you, Harry, sir," he said. "Captain Villiers."

"Did he?"

"Not right that, sir. I mean, that's the men's name for you. Can't have just anyone using it."

"Why on earth not?"

"Just not proper, sir."

Deacon looked at his watch. It was fifteen-hundred hours. "You can reckon on about another hour, corporal. Meantime check the engine water."

"Sir."

Deacon returned to Clemmie and Villiers.

"Is he alright?" asked Clemmie.

"Fine," said Deacon.

"Unusual, your corporal," said Villiers. "Had him long?"

"Six months or so. He is very good at his job."

"Certainly follows you like a whipped dog. Take much training?"

Deacon thought about it. "None at all," he said.

Clemmie and Villiers chatted about the many sights of the day's trip. Villiers kept his wine glass filled and told amusing stories of Paris and Cairo. He told his tales well, with an easy, self-deprecating wit and warm charm. Deacon leaned back in his chair and watched the afternoon drift with the mountain shadows across the valley floor. High on the mountain's slopes, the last dinosaur heel-print was slowly swallowed.

It had been a good day, all things considered. And he had enjoyed it more than he might have hoped. Clemmie had proved a charming and enthusiastic companion and Villiers a surprising one. Deacon had passed a pleasant day. He tried to remember the last one. But he couldn't.

He glanced at his watch, but he already knew it getting on for seventeen hundred hours by the cool of the sun's shadow. He could risk another half-hour of pleasant conversation before they would have to head back to Aden. Deacon watched the mountains spark under the falling amber sun.

He became aware of movement from up on the top of the rise. He looked up towards a couple of young Arab teenagers who were high up on the still sunlit roadside and waving with all arms down into the valley. It took a moment for Deacon to realise that they were waving at him.

"Something's up at the jeep," he said.

Clemmie and Villiers immediately followed his gaze.

"Stay here," said Deacon.

"I'm coming with you, Harry." said Villiers. He had already un-clipped his holster catch.

"We'll all go," said Clemmie.

"It's too dangerous," said Deacon.

"More so than staying here on my own?" asked Clemmie.

Deacon took out his pistol and led the way up the steps. He crouched low and took them three at a time and was alone when he reached the last stone step. He felt his sweated shirt tighten across his chest. He scanned the road and then strode toward the parked jeep. The young Arab boys backed away and pointed down into the road.

Corporal Lockett was lying curled like a sleeping child in the dirt beside the jeep. He lay on his side with his knees tucked under his chin. He was perfectly still, his face as pale as parchment and he did not appear to be breathing.

Deacon felt boulders tumble in his gut.

FIVE

Deacon sat forward on the plastic chair and idled his cap in his hands. The ceiling fan hummed above him but he felt no draft from its blades. Despite the cool of the night, heat clung to him like a skin. Villiers occupied a seat on the other side of the hospital's waiting room.

It had been a fast ride to the hospital. Deacon couldn't remember driving at all. He knew Clemmie had been in the back of the jeep nursing Lockett and that Villiers had stood in the passenger-well beside him, urging Arabs and traffic out of their path with a waved pistol.

It was dusk by the time Deacon slid the jeep to a stop in front of the hospital steps. Clemmie took over immediately. A couple of orderlies were smoking by an ambulance and she summoned them to get a stretcher and carry Lockett up the steps. As Clemmie led Deacon and her small party into the hospital foyer they were confronted by two Military Police guards hurrying from their desks, and several nurses. Villiers flashed his card at the guards, who inspected it briefly, then saluted and returned to their desk.

"This man needs immediate medical attention." said Clemmie to the nurses. "I think it's heat-stroke. Take him through to Casualty ward and one of you find a doctor. Major Clark. Hurry now."

"And who are you to be giving my nurses orders?"

A senior nurse appeared in the foyer. She was tall and regal and seemed to glide across the tiled floor towards them. The nurses parted before her. She cast a quick scanning eye over Lockett lying on his stretcher, tidied a greying strand of hair into her bonnet-cap and then fixed Clemmie with a look.

"I give my nurses their duties. Because I am the Senior Nurse. We are busy with urgent cases tonight. We will attend to him when we can."

Clemmie took a moment to study the nurse. She smiled.

"This patient requires a doctor now."

"Haven't I seen you here before? Aren't you one of our new Auxiliaries?" said the nurse. She looked Clemmie up and down and seemed to find little of interest. "A cadet nurse."

"Yes. That's right. I'm cadet nurse Clemmie Ross-Jennings."

"Well, cadet nurse Ross-Jennings, you do not give any orders in my hospital. Your patient will have to wait just like everyone else. Ordering only comes from those that have earned it."

"Yes. That's what my father says."

"Your father?"

"Brigadier Jennings."

There was a silence. The nurse looked at Clemmie and then at Lockett. Deacon saw the nurse's shoulders sag. She looked tired. She nodded curtly to the orderlies who lifted Lockett onto a wheeled trolley and sped him away down the corridor. The nurse turned her gaze on Deacon, and then Villiers.

"Visiting hours are over," she said.

"I said they could wait ..." said Clemmie.

The senior nurse forced a smile. "Of course you did," she said.

She turned on a heel and glided away.

Clemmie laughed. "Aren't I naughty!" she said.

"Have you in my troop like a shot, Clemmie!" said Villiers, grinning. "Quite magnificent."

Clemmie ushered Deacon and Villiers into the waiting room. She rested a hand on Deacon's arm.

"I'm pretty sure it's just a touch of heat-stroke, Harry," she said."They see a lot of that here. Soon sort him out. You'll see."

Clemmie hurried after the trolley. Deacon sat with Villiers and waited.

Villiers came and sat beside Deacon and rested a hand on his shoulder. He laughed lightly.

"You certainly gave us a day to remember, Harry!"

Deacon continued to spin his cap.

"Rimbaud's house!" said Villiers. He leaned back in his chair. "Wild dogs. Burst tyres. Fainting corporals. Quite the tour. It's been great fun."

Deacon stared at the floor.

"Harry, come on! Don't beat yourself up like this. These things happen."

"I should have seen to it that he had a cap. And was drinking water."

"Soldier's chance, Harry. We all sign up to it."

"But he's my soldier."

Villiers let his hand fall from Deacon's shoulder.

"Your concern does you great credit, Harry. But don't lose your perspective. You can't be responsible for the whole army. He did bring it on himself, after all. All soldiering is a gamble one way or another. You just have to pick up the dice and roll again. There is no-one to blame."

But Deacon did feel the blame and the discomfort swelled within him. He was Lockett's officer and should have been more mindful of his care. The image of the hatless Lockett toiling with Clemmie's bags at the minaret, and the weariness of his tread up and down the sun-baked Tiwala steps, replayed again in his mind's eye.

He had been aware, but he had chosen to hide it away behind the pleasures of the day and its diverting company.

Beside him Villiers seemed unaware of any culpability he might own for Lockett's misfortune. His bet with the corporal had been no more than another soldier's chance in the many hundred to be faced every day. Villiers felt no blames. Deacon envied him.

Villiers put his arm around Deacon's shoulder.

"You've got to stop blaming yourself for things you can't control, Harry," he said. "Let it go and march on. Your corporal will be fine. Believe me. Like Clemmie said, you're far too serious. You've got to enjoy a bit more. Why don't you let me get you good and drunk tonight? We shall toast the great Rimbaud together."

Deacon looked into Villiers' smiling, open face. Pale blue eyes hooked his gaze. The bronzed skin of Villiers' crooked nose was lightly flaked from the sun's burn and his breath was soft with the sweetness of wine. Deacon felt the comforting press of his hand on his shoulder.

"If only I could," he said. "But I've already lost a sergeant. Duties prevail."

"Of course. I understand," said Villiers. "But a rain check, eh? As our Yank friends would say."

"I'll look forward to it, sir."

Deacon reached into his pocket and handed the jeep keys to Villiers.

"It's pretty pointless you hanging around here, sir. Perhaps you will drive Miss Ross back to her house. I'll just wait on the doctor. Then find my own way."

Clemmie came into the room. She smiled at Deacon.

"Your corporal is being well looked after, Harry. So no more worrying. Major Clark says it looks like a bit too much sun. That's all. But he'll be along soon."

"Harry has asked me to drop you home," said Villiers. "And I need to be at the Navy Bar by twenty-hundred. Shower and shave, eh?"

Clemmie eyed Deacon.

"Yes Tom, of course. Are you staying, Harry?"

"Just to make sure." said Deacon.

Villers stood up and escorted Clemmie to the door of the waiting room.

"The offer to join me and some of the boys at the Navy Bar later still stands, Harry," he said. "When you've finished up here of course. It's a late fare and they do a decent steak."

Deacon was vaguely aware of his orders to attend early at the Gallery the next morning. A long day of shooting drills in the sun beckoned. And Lockett would not be there to wake him.

He was also aware of the feeling of Villiers' arm at his shoulder. It touched him still.

"I'll try," he said.

*

It was another half hour before the nurse came for him. Deacon followed the bobbing white bonnet down the corridor and on through a close-packed ward of soldier patients, strung upright in their beds like puppets or lying prone under leg cages. He was guided into a small room at the far end of the ward where a couple of white-jacketed orderlies had wheeled Lockett's iron bed into a corner space. A shirt-sleeved major was listening to his patient's chest through an ear trumpet. Locket was lying in a tent-sized pale green hospital gown. The room was small and the sinks and mop cupboards made it smaller. It was a cleaner's room. The orderlies pressed themselves to the walls to allow the major access to Lockett. The young nurse remained outside in the ward.

"Had to bring him in here," said the major. He was still bent over his trumpet. "Busy tonight. Wards chocker. One of yours?"

"Yes, sir. Lockett. My corporal."

The major stood up. He was a tall man with a barrel belly and greying moustache. He had large, dark hammocks under his eyes but his gaze was bright and alert. He stretched his back and there was the sound of a long, tearing fart.

"Allah be praised," said the major as the last rip in the fabric faded.

The nurse lifted a hand to her rapidly flushing face and left hurriedly. The major watched her leave and shook his head slowly.

"Wouldn't have lasted five minutes at Imjin River," he said.

The two orderlies grinned. The major took his jacket from the handle of the electric polisher by the door and pulled it on.

"Well, he won't be carrying your bags for a few days, lieutenant," he said. "Been on desert patrol has he?"

"Just driving around Aden. He wasn't wearing a cap."

The major looked at Deacon.

"Ah!" he said. "Attempted suicide then. That's against all army rules, isn't it? Shall I arrange to have him shot? We could do with the bed space."

He looked at Deacon through solemn eyes.

It took Deacon a moment to realise that the major was being amusing. And that Lockett was not therefore in danger. He felt relief shiver through him.

"He'll recover then, sir?"

The major picked up a clip-board and began scribbling and ticking on it.

"He'll live. Just heat exhaustion. We've got it early. He's a fit young man. A week or so and he'll be back ironing your shorts. Can you stay around until he wakes up? A known face helps and he will be woozy for a while. Sign here. And there. Oh, and you might just try and find him a cap next time. We have enough Adoo business without adding our own."

The doctor and the orderlies marched on along the ward.

Deacon sat cramped on his chair between cupboards of bandages and leaking boxes of Vosene shampoo. Out in the ward, the lights were low and a blanket of quiet lay tucked and tight at the world's corners. It was twenty-one thirty hours and Deacon felt so tired that his legs floated. He dimly thought to rub some life into them, but he couldn't summon the effort of lifting his hand. He listened to the occasional soft squeaks of nurses shoes breaking the stillness, like calls of small birds in a night forest.

Beside him Lockett lay on his bed, asleep. His breathing shallow and soft, but regular. An ice cloth wrapped Lockett's forehead and his lips were purple-blue.

Through the open door Deacon could see a rank of striped pyjama tops and sullen faces lying in their beds, spot-lit by low-wattage lamps like exhibits in a museum gallery. He was struck by the number of leg cages on the beds. He guessed it was the blast ward. The trip-wire and road-mine ward. It was doing good business. In the furthest beds two children, swathed in bandages, hung lost and limp over their mattresses, like cocoon-wrapped flies in a spider's web.

Deacon closed his eyes and let the syrup scent of hospital pour over him. He let himself drown in it. He floated deep in the fathoms, watching the distant lights of unseen fish trace across his gaze.

When he resurfaced he found himself staring into Lockett's face.

"Thought you were gone, sir."

Lockett lay curled on his side with his head cradled on his hands and he was looking up at Deacon. He had obviously been watching for some time. Deacon creaked upright in his chair.

"No, still here, corporal. How are you feeling?"

Lockett seemed to notice the room for the first time. He raised himself unsteadily onto his elbows and stared about him.

"I'm afraid they ran out of bed space," said Deacon.

Lockett tucked his gown tight under his knees and lay back on his pillow. "I've been ill in worse, sir."

"Well the Doc says its only heat-stroke, so a good chance to rest up a few days."

"Not with McNish gone too, sir. The men will think we're jinxed."

"You're not indispensable, corporal. Whatever you may believe. The British Army can manage a day or two without you. So don't let me make it an order."

Deacon filled a beaker with water and helped Lockett to a few sips.

"Anything I can get you? Anything you need?"

"No, sir. I have everything I need."

A nurse entered the room at the sound of voices and saw Lockett awake. She hurried away down the corridor and moments later Clemmie Ross appeared.

"Welcome back corporal! Good to see you awake. You had us worried."

Clemmie was in her nurse's uniform of plain blue dress, white apron and a starched cap clenched tight over her hidden hair. Her face seemed to glow. She took Lockett's pulse with professional efficiency and checked the beeping box.

"I thought you had left for the evening. With Captain Villiers," said Deacon.

"Called back in. There's been a bad accident on the Wayim road. Truck fell into a gorge. Lots of casualties. Ghastly. So all hands to the pump. Even us cadets." She flicked a thermometer from her breast pocket and stuck it under Lockett's tongue. "Fluids every couple of hours, I'm afraid, corporal," she said. "But you can get some good sleep in between. The trick is to stay strong. We will try to get you out of this cupboard and in a ward-bed tomorrow." She smiled at Deacon. "Duty, no respecter of a girl's fun, is it?"

"Or sleep," said Deacon.

He watched her smile fade.

"You do look tired, Harry. Why don't you get along? Nothing you can do here. And isn't Tom expecting you at the Navy Bar? Go on. Go have some fun. It has been a long day."

Deacon laughed. "Yes. I did make it a bit of a bore."

Clemmie inspected the thermometer against the dull-lit bulb.

"Nonsense. I had a perfectly fascinating day. And Rimbaud's house!" She kissed Deacon quickly on the cheek and laughed. "A really lovely day, Harry. Thank you. And you of course, corporal. Now say your goodbyes. I'm officer in charge at the scene now! I'll be back in two hours, corporal."

Clemmie left to attend to her other charges.

Deacon span his cap for a moment.

"Well, you seem to be in capable hands, corporal."

"So it would seem, sir. A Lord's daughter, no less."

"Yes. I know. But quite normal in all other respects. Or so I believe."

"You are meeting with Captain Villiers tonight, sir?"

"Yes. At the Navy Club. Just a drink."

"Watch him, sir. He's a dangerous one."

Deacon laughed. "Who, Captain Villiers? You've definitely had too much sun, corporal."

"He is only for excitement, sir. That's dangerous here."

"Have a care, you mean?"

"Yes sir. Because he doesn't."

"Well, we're on road check points for the next few weeks so a little excitement might be welcome."

Lockett lay back in his pillows. Deacon stretched and tried to ease the feeling back into his legs.

"You sure there isn't something you need? Something I can get you?"

"Perhaps some reading matter, sir. That's all."

"Right. I'll see what I can do. You should not have made that bet, you know. Captain Villiers isn't the losing sort."

"It was six minutes twenty-five seconds, sir," said Lockett. His eyes were closed but he was smiling. "His wheel change. I timed it on my piece. I was accurate. You lost over half a minute somewhere. Distracted, I dare say. I won the bet."

Deacon stood and waited until Locket had fallen asleep. It was an uncomfortable wait. He knew that Lockett was right. He had lost his mark on the time. He had been distracted by the fascination of watching Villiers toil at the wheel, his muscles glistening in sweat. Deacon felt a cold fear ripple through him.

He listened until he could hear that Lockett's breathing was regular. He was about to tiptoe out when Lockett spoke.

"Don't forget your Proficiency card tomorrow, sir."

"Yes. Of course. Glad you reminded me."

He waited and listened to the sounds of groans and soft pains that had begun to grow in the ward as darkness settled in. Nurses busied themselves at the bedsides with bedpans and soothing coos. Deacon stood spinning his hat until Lockett was truly asleep. He left the hospital, looking neither left nor right as he strode up the ward past the museum-case lights.

The Aden late-night air was lightly breezed and the city was ablaze with lights. Deacon took the walk. It was four miles to the Navy Bar and he had to stretch his cramped limbs and expunge his thoughts. Deacon strode out in a march and let the Aden stink cleanse him.

It was gone twenty-three-hundred when he stood among bushes at a road corner watching the Navy Bar through its large picture windows. He could see and hear several uniformed officers and wives enjoying a spirited time at the bar. A game of bar rugger seemed to be in progress. Deacon saw Villiers standing in the centre of a small group urging the players on and laughing. He had removed his jacket and his shirted arm cradled casually on the shoulder of a slim WRAF corporal at his side. The young woman seemed to be enjoying the inattention.

Deacon turned and marched the two miles back to his billet. He fell asleep in his chair.

SIX

Deacon awoke late. He showered and shaved and hurried to the Duty Office to sign on and get his troop orders for the day. They were assigned the Number Four gate on the Dock road. A hot day of checking trucks and papers and delaying already sullen drivers. Deacon was due at the Gallery at ten-hundred hours so he just had time to gather his troop up in the truck and get them to the Dock gate. In Lockett's absence he made Hobson acting corporal for the duration.

"Ta very much sir." said Hobson. "An extra tanner a week. I'll invest it in silver polish."

"Each way on a dog more like," said Gibson. His plough-boy, lumpen body shook as he giggled silently to himself. Gibson lived in a world that Deacon had never visited. Or ever wanted to.

"Not the fucking Docks!" said Shaw. "All day in the sun breathing diesel and dust. Fucking army."

There were murmurs of agreement from the men. Deacon silenced them with a look.

"That's right, Shaw," he said. "The fucking army. And you are a fucking soldier so you will do your duty. Its your job. It's what they pay you for."

His men looked at him and smiled in mock shock. Deacon was not a swearing officer, so when he did his men hoarded the oaths like rare tokens.

"You been saving that lot up, sir?" asked Hobson.

"Look," said Deacon, "Split in two-on, two-off and two-under with one to float. Three hour shifts. Floater better be your look-out because the Red Caps will be out checking you are at your posts. Work it right and you can each get three hours' kip in the sentry hut. Watch yourselves and trust nothing. Truck. Camel. Woman. Cute kid with a runny nose. No one. Understand?"

There was shuffled assent.

"Good. Where's Kenny?"

"Drew a special duty day chit, sir," said Ambrose. "He's back tomorrow. Sniper patrol up the Wayim Pass I heard, sir. CO cleared him."

"You back Hobson up then, Ambrose. Stay alert and don't get caught. Right?"

Hobson and Ambrose grinned. "Yes, sir." they said together.

"Oh, and for Christ's sake make sure they are all wearing their caps."

"How is Corporal Lockett, sir?" asked Ambrose.

Deacon thought about it.

"Enriched by his experience," he said.

*

Deacon arrived at the Gallery with two minutes to spare. He took his place at the back of a small queue and waited in line to have his ID checked by the Military Police guards at the gate. Two other guards patrolled with panting, short-leashed dogs. The queue was a mix of soldier tunics and Royal Navy jackets and beyond the gate in the roofed, wire-mesh enclosure Deacon could see uniforms of commando and SAS milling in the shade.

A lance corporal sat at a registration table and inspected Deacon's ID and then his Weapons Proficiency card. He studied Deacon without interest and returned his ID.

"We keep the WP," he said. He placed Deacon's Weapons Proficiency card in a tin box and made notes in a large, lined book. "It'll be signed and returned after the show. Next."

Deacon moved into the shade of the Gallery pavilion and stood with about twenty others. Through the crowd he saw Kenny. Kenny grinned at him and came over.

"I thought you had pulled a Special Duty chit," said Deacon.

"I did, sir. This is it. Looks like you got one too."

They cast their eyes over their fellow chitters.

"Rather a mixed bag, wouldn't you say?" said Deacon.

"Aye. And rum too. Look at them two commando sergeants. Built like shit houses. And some slippery Navy tars too. Hear tell we're here all day. Special arrangements, like."

"Sounds like quite a party."

"Sounds like recruitment to me, sir. And not for no dance."

A corporal marched onto the veranda at the back of the pavilion, planted a heavy boot and saluted.

"King Billy says now," he barked.

He turned sharply on a heel and marched back through the pavilion. Deacon and Kenny joined the rest of the crowd and followed him.

The shooting range was a shadeless, dusty patch of scratched dirt about a hundred metres wide that stretched from the back of the pavilion and on up the lower slopes of the Shamsan Mountain. It was marshalled by high, double-skinned, razor-wire fences all the way. Bullets fired on the range would sing and crack in ricochet up the mountain's rocky slopes and send small puffs of dust into the air as they died back to the dirt. A rank of Number Twelve targets, shaped and pictured like charging Korean soldiers, were sited on poles in the range at various distances and mock sand-bagged gun emplacements were used to practice grenade and two-by-two assaults. Against a far fence, a flat-packed house leaned in readiness for the urban commando drills.

The Gallery was busy every day. Mornings would see groups of twenty garrison soldiers practising their shooting skills, while afternoons and evenings were devoted to more specialised weapons training for the commando and SAS squads. Weapons training and the ability to be able to shoot with passing proficiency was a necessary life skill in Aden. The entire garrison passed through the Gallery every six months, even the clerks and orderlies.

Deacon had been to the Gallery twice, both times for a morning pistol proficiency session to get his card stamped. He had not been invited to attend a full day session before. He was not looking forward to it. Particularly as it was to be run by King Billy.

Lance corporal William Beddowes stood in the searing sun and grey dust of the shooting range as Deacon and the others shuffled into line before him.

Deacon knew about King Billy; all Aden knew about King Billy, but the legend was something of a surprise in the flesh. Billy was not much over five feet tall. He was compact and sturdy and occupied his space like a pissed-off bulldog. He had wispy red hair and small, close-set eyes planted like currants in an almost concave face. He seemed to have no nose at all. He stood, feet braced with his fists on his hips and leaned forward as if offering his stubbled jaw for anyone's best punch. He was not wearing a shirt. He never wore a shirt in the Gallery. Despite the scorch of Yemeni sun his skin stayed pale and freckled and he never burned or tanned. Garrison rumour was that Billy grew lizard skin. His flat belly was a mass of red, coiled hair and a pistol was stuck into the front of his shorts, like a glowering black crow in a copper-wire nest.

Deacon watched as Lance Corporal Beddowes surveyed the line with a slow, disdainful eye.

"I'm King Billy." His voice was deep and gravelled. "Between the wire and the Shamsan is my kingdom. What I say goes. Here I am King. And that's higher than fucking God. Any questions?"

There was silence.

"Good. Should fucking think not. You are here to learn to shoot and to kill Adoos. And I'm here to see you do it right."

Billy had been thirty years in the army and had been promoted and demoted on an almost continual basis. He had recently been a staff-sergeant in Palestine but a bar brawl that laid out two Military Policeman had seen his stripes reduced to one. But stripes didn't matter at The Gallery. All that mattered was that Billy was the best killer in the army. And the Aden Gallery was his kingdom.

Billy consulted a clipboard that one of his acolyte corporals had passed to him. He ran his finger down its page.

"Deacon?"

Deacon stepped forward.

"Yes. Er, sir."

"Only Billy here son, nothing more. Hear you plugged an Adoo at eighty yards. Show me how."

Billy pulled the pistol from its nest in his shorts and handed it to Deacon.

"Don't worry, son, it's not loaded."

Deacon took the gun.

"As you shot him. Exactly like. Show us how you did it."

Deacon looked along the line of bemused faces. Kenny offered an encouraging grin. Deacon braced his legs, raised his forearm and rested the gun across it.

"Like this," he said.

Billy spat a laugh. He stepped up beside Deacon. "James fucking Bond! I knew it. Where do you think you are, laddie, the fucking movies?"

Deacon relaxed his stance and was suddenly aware of a sharp pain in the back of his knees, and of the sky spinning above him and then his shoulders and head hitting the ground with a heavy thud. The breath left him and his eyes swam with pastel-coloured eels. He was aware of King Billy looking down at him through swirling dust as if from a great height and of a pulsing ache in every bone. King Billy crouched down and gently relieved the pistol from Deacon's limp hand in the dirt. He lowered his voice.

"Sorry about that, son, but the army pays me to be a bastard and I have sort of grown to the task, as you might say."

He blew the dirt dust from the barrel as if whistling it a tune and then held the gun out from him in a stretched, ram-rod arm. He looked down at Deacon and winked.

The gun cracked and thirty-five metres away a target grunted and stuttered on its pole.

One of the corporals ran up to the target and inspected it.

"Upper on the left eyebrow, Billy," he called.

"Bugger," said Billy. "Going for the bridge of the nose."

Billy hauled Deacon up on a strong arm. "Back in line double-oh-seven," he said.

Deacon rejoined the line of grinning faces, his body aching and his eyes liquid.

"Thank you Mr. Deacon. Three lessons in one, gentlemen," said Billy. "Mark them. Don't trust nobody to tell you a gun is loaded or not. Check it for yourself. And if you are going to tumble don't take your gun down in the dirt with you. Keep it raised, keep it clean. Can't shoot your way out of trouble with a barrel full of dirt. And no fucking James Bonds. This is Aden and war. And we don't have time for make believe. Right, let's have your shirts off."

Deacon and the line were hesitant, none sure that they had heard the instruction.

"Only one King here, boys, and no ranks," said Billy. A couple of disparate grey teeth appeared in his mouth by way of a grin. "If your King don't wear a shirt, then neither does you. Get 'em off."

The line removed their shirts which were collected by a couple of the corporals. Deacon felt the sun's sting on his shoulders. It was going to be a long and uncomfortable day.

King Billy called the line to group beside him. He reached into his pocket and pulled out a small pin badge. It was a Robertson's Jam golliwog badge. He un-clasped its pin, pinched some skin on his chest between a thumb and forefinger and then lanced the badge pin through it. Deacon winced along with the others but King Billy just clasped the pin home and then patted the badge tidy as if it were on his dress jacket lapel. He looked up at the faces ranged around him and grinned a tooth.

"Do it right today and you get one of these," he said. "But they ain't given lightly. They is earned and earned hard. Prized, they are. Want to earn your badge, boys? King Billy will pin it on you himself if you does. Your jacket collar if you're squeamish."

Deacon laughed with the others. An Aden laugh.

Billy pointed up the range to a Korean target.

"That is a charging Adoo," he said. "Mean as a bull and crazy with it. You got to take him down, and take him down quick. No time for fancy James Bond shooting. We do it the King Billy way. Quick and mortal." Billy stopped and looked up in surprise. "Well, strike my chin. We are honoured today gentlemen. Care to show these boys how, sir?"

Billy seemed to be addressing someone behind them. Deacon turned with the rest of the trainees and saw Captain Tom Villiers standing back in the shade of the pavilion veranda. Clemmie Ross sat in a wicker chair beside him. She was in her nurse's uniform. Deacon thought she looked tired but she managed a wan smile. Villiers emerged into the sunlight, grinned and stepped lightly off the pavilion veranda.

"How could I refuse the King?" he said.

He moved with easy long strides over the dirt and stood beside Deacon. He unbuttoned his shirt and slid it off. Villiers flexed his shoulders and squinted at sight of the sun.

"Captain Villiers is an old pupil of mine. Palestine days," said Billy. "Still got your badge?"

Captain Villiers smiled and turned up the collar of his jacket. A golliwog badge glinted.

"Pride of place, Billy," he said. He tossed his jacket to an attendant corporal and turned to Deacon. "Might I borrow your gun, lieutenant?"

Deacon handed him his Browning pistol. Villiers checked the magazine and weighed the gun lightly in his hand. He winked at Deacon.

"Some room, gentlemen," said Billy.

The trainees took a couple of steps back to form a ragged semi-circle around Villiers. Deacon watched him standing tall and apart in the dust. Villiers was grinning with an easy charm that was almost insouciant. Deacon was conscious of an anxiety rippling through him. A sudden concern that Tom was going to be made a fool of, just as Deacon had been.

"Now!" said Billy.

Villiers dropped down quickly onto his knee, twisted his body, brought the Browning up in both hands with a fluid, easy motion and cracked off four shots so rapidly that Deacon could not really count them. A target twenty-five metres out in the range grunted and spat and span and then leaned back so that the Korean soldier looked skyward.

In the silence, Deacon heard the distant barking echo of a piard dog from the mountains.

"Three -and -a -half seconds." said Billy looking down at the stop watch that had appeared in his hand.

A corporal ran to the target and inspected it. "Upper left thigh, belly dead centre, right nipple and left cheek," he called.

"Hmm. Fair to middling I'd say," said Billy. "Might have stopped the bugger."

Villiers stood up and laughed. "Sorry Billy. Slightly off my game this morning," he said. "Haven't got used to this lighter Aden air." He handed the gun back to Deacon. "Thanks, Harry. Not a bad piece. Seems to pull a mite left though."

The corporal helped him back into his jacket. The group parted in silence as Villiers made his way back to the pavilion. Deacon watched him skip onto the pavilion veranda and whisper something to Clemmie. She rose on his escorting arm.

"Keep them at it, Billy," called Villiers.

He and Clemmie disappeared inside the pavilion.

"That is how you get your gold badge.,." said King Billy. "But I'll settle for tin from you lot. Just good soldier shooting. Like Captain Villiers there. Four shots, rapid fire up the target. Balls, belly, breast and bonce. Let's hear you say it."

Deacon and the others chanted hesitantly.

"Balls, belly, breast and bonce."

"Faster!" ordered King Billy.

They sang it out.

"Right. Now you are going to learn to shoot it as fast as you can sing it," said Billy. "Might save your fucking necks one day."

Deacon passed the morning target shooting and attacking the sandbagged emplacements in double-tap close combat drills. The trainees were split into pairs or small groups and undertook the drills under the watchful eyes of Billy and his corporals. Billy made notes on a red plastic clipboard that hung from the belt of his shorts like an Indian chieftain scalp. Deacon was teamed up with Alec Peterson, a tall, slim and amiable young Royal Navy Lieutenant.

The range cracked with sporadic fire and the barking orders of corporals. Deacon and Peterson were set with Browning 8mm pistols against the twenty metre targets. Corporal Adams, a burly commando with a Montgomery moustache, was their guide.

"Not like that!" roared the corporal at Peterson as his target was missed again. "Up the fucker. Not across him. Couldn't hit a building."

"Sorry, corporal," said Peterson. He stood up grinning and brushed the dust from his knees. "I think my target must have moved." He spread his hands apologetically. "Don't get much call for gun play on Her Majesty's quarter-decks."

He handed the gun back to the corporal and smiled at Deacon.

"So noisy here, don't you find? You can hardly hear yourself think."

A glaze seemed to steel Corporal Adams' eye.

"You are not meant to think, sonny," he said with slow deliberation. "You is meant to shoot. And my Granny does it better than you."

"Corporal, that does not come as surprise," said Peterson.

Deacon took the gun, stepped out and waited for Adams to finish making his notes on his clipboard. He wrote slowly and licked his pencil often. Then he took his stop-watch into the palm of his hand, looked at Deacon and nodded.

"Now."

Deacon was down, straight-backed and on his knee before he even knew it and his gun was arcing up on stretched and braced arms. He was conscious of becoming Villiers. Being Villiers. Of copying the fluid grace and steel purpose of his movements. His dance. As he steadied his eye along his sighting fists, he was aware of the slowing of his breath, of the coiling of his body and of a certainty that Tom Villiers was watching him from somewhere inside the pavilion shades.

Deacon felt his head clear of all thought. His body cooled, his eyes focused and stilled and his heart pumped out pulses of fire into the balls, belly, breast and bonce of the charging Korean soldier.

The target staggered, pinged and cracked on its pole. Deacon watched it die beyond his pointing fist. A ricochet pinballed up the mountain rocks and then fell silent back to the dusts.

The world came back to Deacon. He was kneeling in the dirt and several of the nearby trainees were watching him. As Deacon got to his feet they turned to focus once more on their own drills. Corporal Adams was inspecting the target.

"Three hits. Four seconds," he said. He pocketed his watch and pulled his clipboard and pencil out. "Average."

"Looked like damn fine shooting to me, corporal," said Peterson. "Belly and breast at the least. Way above average I'd say."

"Thigh not balls and the bonce missed altogether," said Corporal Adams. He licked his pencil and ticked. "Very average. Care to try again, Mr. Peterson?"

"Do I have to?"

Corporal Adams looked at Peterson as if a cosh itched in his back pocket.

"Yes, you fucking well do," he said.

Peterson handed Deacon a beaker of water and they wandered to the shade of the large canvas canopy. It was their first drinks break of the morning and the heat and noise of the range had brought on a thirst that cracked Deacon's throat. He drank two beakers straight off. They watched the trainees shooting on the range or re-assembling pistol magazines at a nearby table with sacks over their heads. Others were sweating in two-by-two assault drills on sandbags.

"Pretty rum crew, aren't they?" said Peterson. He held out a hand and smiled. "Alec."

Deacon took the hand but said nothing. Peterson eyed him with interest.

"Take it you're a shooter," he said.

Peterson refilled his beaker and poured the water over the back of his neck and then his head. He shook himself like a wet dog and grinned.

"Shooters, snipers and pirates. That's my take on it. The skill pool. Get the whiff of mission in the air."

"Skill pool?" asked Deacon.

"Look around you. These boys have been selected. That chap over there."

He nodded towards Kenny who was lying prone on a wooden frame and firing his rifle at the range's most distant target.

"Hasn't missed all morning as far as I can tell. That's a sniper."

"Private Murdoch. He's one of mine."

"You'd know then."

"Do you know your stoker's every skill, Alec?"

Peterson laughed. "Point taken. But look at those Commando privates. Built like Cruisers. And that chap in the kilt. Seen him before. Dropped him and a couple of his mates up the coast a few nights back. Explosives man. And there is you, of course."

"Me?"

"A shooter. Definite golliwog material."

Deacon laughed. "Outside of this Gallery I have only ever fired two shots. That doesn't make me a shooter."

"Well, you are something."

"And what about you? I must assume it isn't for shooting. Does that make you a pirate?"

"God no! Rope work and fighting and all that clenching blades between your teeth? Not my line at all. I'm the physical preservation type. Especially my own. No, I think I'm the bunny rabbit."

Deacon frowned.

"Every mission must have one. The dispensable one. The grenade magnet. A tripper of the wire. The ignoble sacrifice. Might as well pin a target on my chest and have done with it."

Deacon studied Peterson. "No. You're not fodder material. You're here for something."

Peterson grinned. "My Arabic, I expect. You'd think that they would train more of us, don't you think? Speakers of the native lingo. I've been on more dodgy missions than the tabernacle bell."

They worked around the drill stations for the rest of the morning. Deacon was engaged in two-by-two assault with Peterson when he saw Captain Villiers and Clemmie driving out through the Gallery gates and on up the Khormaskar road. The distraction made him miss his pattern mark. A short corporal with yellow teeth bellowed in his ear and made them do it all over again.

They lunched in the open under the canvas canopy. Hot baked beans and cheese and ham rolls. Deacon sat in the shade against the wire and ate without tasting. Everyone was quiet, even the corporals. It had been a long and hot morning and a hotter afternoon beckoned.

Deacon somehow got through it all. In the afternoon, there was more shooting, and head sacks and lectures on weapon drill and combat recognition. It was gone sixteen-hundred hours by the time their shirts were returned to them and they were seated in the dust before King Billy. The sun was sinking to peach and turquoise skies behind the mountains. Billy surveyed them and then studied his clipboard. After a long wait he let the clipboard fall beside his knee like a trapdoor sack. He knuckled his hands to his hips and proffered his chin.

"Right." he said. "The lot of you bugger off. And collect your chits on the way."

He turned and marched away into the pavilion, followed closely by his corporals.

The trainees queued silently in the shade behind the pavilion. They were being single-filed to a long desk where several lance-corporals where busy stamping cards and checking paperwork.

When Deacon finally arrived at the desk he showed his ID and waited while his papers were moved about. A lance corporal flicked though a small tray of letters and let his fingers stop.

"Lieutenant Leslie Deacon?"

"Yes."

The lance corporal handed Deacon an envelope. "Your orders and WP sir. Next!"

Deacon climbed wearily into his jeep and opened the envelope. Inside was a formal invitation to a Supper Dance at Brigadier Jennings' villa that evening at twenty-hundred hours.

And when he tipped the envelope up a silver golliwog badge dropped into his palm.

SEVEN

On the way back to his billet Deacon checked in on his men. Their barracks was a slab-built, single-storey, flat-roofed block with too many windows to ever lose the sun, and too many doors to ever admit privacy. Deacon's nose was always assailed on his visits and he had never got used to it. The smell of sweat, fetid rot and stale beer seemed to suck out all air. Each cubicle of head-high walls and lock-free doors had enough space for a cot, a bedside table and a soldier's kit bag. The men spent all their barrack down-time in the large kitchen area. It was more a lounge than a kitchen. Worn armchairs and sofas, radios, gramophones and refrigerators the size of icebergs crammed the space.

Deacon lurked his usual moment in the corridor outside and listened to the men's talk and high spirits. The men were laughing and shouting above the sound of the fridges that were droning like wasps in a glass behind them. The men's humour had risen on learning that Shepherds Pie and Jam Roly Poly were on the canteen menu that night, and there was also rumour of a dance down at the Quayside Club later and much talk about the new batch of WRAFs from Kormaskar making a show. Deacon never failed to admire the simple pleasures of hope his men seemed to find in their deserted and drudged lot.

He strolled into the kitchen area and waited for the bottle. It came out of eleven o'clock high. It grew in his vision. He caught it deftly one-handed. His men cheered.

"I had a shilling on you dropping it, sir," said Lee. "Reckon you'd be too shagged to see straight."

Deacon smiled. He sent the bottle flying flat out of his hand toward Shaw. It hit Shaw in the stomach and he doubled-up over on a groan.

"I saw it was you, Shaw," said Deacon. "Now slips is real catching. Not like dolly-drops from the outfield. Got an unshaken one, Ambrose?"

The men laughed. Ambrose hoisted a bottle, un-capped it and passed it to Deacon. Deacon drank it down in one. He tossed the bottle expertly into a large plastic bin in the corner. There was a short scream of shattering glass.

"Thanks, lads. I needed that."

"Had a good day, sir?" asked Hobson. "Fire off a few?"

Deacon was momentarily taken aback. He had kept his Gallery visit secret from the men. He glanced at Kenny who was sitting on the arm of a chair watching him. Kenny shook his head discreetly.

"No, just following orders," said Deacon. "It's what we do, I'm told." He nodded for Hobson and Ambrose to meet him out in the corridor.

"Everything okay today?" asked Deacon.

He learned that the day had passed without incident and no Red Caps had shown. He gave Hobson the duty orders for the next day.

"Dock Road again. Checkpoint Seven. Oh-eight-hundred. So don't let them wreck themselves tonight."

"Oh no worry about that, sir" said Ambrose, "We're all pretty skint and will soon find we've run out of obliging pals. Free rounds hard to come by on dance night. Especially with the new WRAFs in. Our boys'll be back in their cots soon enough."

Deacon reached into his pocket and counted out five pound notes.

"That reminds me. Had a word with the Adjutant," he said. "About McNish's debts. He said this was all he could allow. Army's claim on the sergeant's estate. Pound for ten is all he could do, he said. No idea what he means but he said you should have this. For the troop. In final settlement. Is it acceptable?"

Ambrose took the notes and grinned.

"We will drink to the Adjutant's health, sir."

"Just as long as you do so before midnight. Have them nested by then. Agreed?"

Hobson and Ambrose saluted.

"Yes, sir," they said and returned to the rest of the men. A moment later Deacon heard whistle-whoops coming from the kitchen.

As he left the barracks through the front doors he found Kenny at his side. They walked out to the shade of a high slab wall. Deacon took Kenny's offered cigarette.

"Do the men know about today?" said Deacon.

"Not from me," said Kenny.

"Then let's keep them in bliss. Okay?"

"Fine by me, sir. Did you get an invitation?"

"Yes. The Brigadier's Supper Dance. You too?"

Kenny chuckled.

"Oh not the Supper Dance, sir. No. That's for officers, see. The Brigadier is having us troopers hosted down at the Jubilee. Good pie and bitter, so

no complaints like. I heard tell we got the new WRAFs coming along. Should be a grand night."

"Aren't they the same WRAFs that are supposed to be at the Quayside tonight?"

"That's what the lads would like to think, sir. But the lasses will come along to us at the Jubilee. We're special, you see. Cut above the rankers like. Ladies like a bit of class."

Deacon laughed.

"Moths to your flame, I'm sure."

"Did you get a badge, sir?"

Deacon was silent.

Kenny lifted his own jacket lapel and showed his golliwog badge. It was a gold one.

"You wear it under the collar," said Kenny. He tapped the side of his nose, grinned and then returned to the kitchen on a smartly spun heel.

Deacon returned to his billet and slept an hour in his chair. He woke with aching limbs that took a long cool shower to ease. He drifted away under the needled spray and watched the liquid dusts ooze from every pore and envelop him like a body bag. He let the water drum on his head and the rivulets snake down over his body. He wished for time to stop.

His afternoon at the range had both troubled and exhilarated him. His shooting had been a complete and unimagined surprise. He wondered at himself and was not entirely sure that it had all really happened. It hadn't been him. He had hardly fired a gun before and they certainly held no fascination for him. Guns were just a functional tool of command. But the afternoon shoot had been a strangely thrilling discovery.

Deacon was also aware that Captain Villiers was pulling him along a path towards something far less thrilling, and infinitely more dangerous. He knew that he was being drawn in and could not think of a way out. He wasn't even sure he wanted out. Deacon knew he could no more resist Villiers's baited line than could a fish on a Gillie's reel. It was a duty of a kind.

Deacon blanked his thoughts out and hunted for his Number Two dress uniform. He polished his shoes, shaved and dressed and made his way to Corporal Lockett's billet. It was a room on the first floor of a two-storey, square concrete block just a short march beyond Deacon's own. The paint on the block had peeled to grey and dark stains ran like mascara tears under the square metal windows.

Deacon got the key from the guard and made his way up the concrete stairs. He had never been to Lockett's room before and was not sure what to expect. But when he unlocked the door and stepped inside, he found he wasn't surprised at all.

The room was small, compact and tidy. And remarkably clean, for a soldier. The bed was made and smooth-tucked, the uniforms and boots neatly filed and ranked in the canvas wardrobe that hung from a ceiling hook. The stone floor shone in halo around a small and colourful Persian rug. There was a small wooden table under the window, a wicker chair and a kit bag squatting neat and ready in a corner. The walls were bare but very white and a small window looked out onto the parade square. In the middle of the window-sill was a polished four-inch brass shell cartridge that sprouted a small and robust chrysanthemum with bright yellow flowers.

Deacon was surprised how comfortable the room seemed, despite its lack of furnishings or personalised possessions. It was clean and functional and somehow very private. Like a monastic cell. It was almost homely. And the yellow flowers uplifting.

As he admired the room he was also aware of a sense of growing disappointment. He had come to Lockett's room expecting to find some reading matter to take to him but the room was barren of any books or magazines. A small bookshelf held copies of the Duty Order Protocols and a Signals Manual, and on the small table there was a neat pile of Lockett's teaching papers, but that was all.

Deacon felt dismay and irritation glide through him, as if he had been deceived. But he couldn't bring himself to believe that Lockett would be without books. He saw a trunk lying under the bed. He pulled it out and opened it. He felt no guilt, a soldier's possessions were never private and always subject to random inspection. Nothing was owned in Aden. It all belonged to the Army.

About a third of the trunk's space was taken up by socks, shirts and underwear but most of it was crammed with books and magazines. Deacon fingered through them and came to appreciate that it was a small, compact and rather impressive travelling library. Novels of Dickens, Hemingway and Kerouac. Stories by Wodehouse and Twain. Poetry anthologies. Plays by Ibsen and Chekhov. A hardback copy of *The Wind in the Willows*. Several back copies of the New Yorker magazine. There were also several Spider-Man comics.

Deacon's disappointment was replaced by confusion. He was not sure what reading selection to make, or about the Spider-man comics. They seemed so out of place in the library, like brash children among thoughtful men. Deacon chose *The Pickwick Papers, The Naked and the Dead,* a collection of Kipling's poems, a New Yorker magazine and a Spider-Man comic.

He was about to close the trunk when he noticed a large sketch pad that was strapped to the underside of the lid. When he opened it up he found pages of pencil drawings of the people and buildings of Aden. Desertscapes and mountains. The drawings were small with often several studies to a page. Arab women. Ambrose with his cigarette. Lee asleep. Studies of windows and Arab market stalls. The drawings were good. Indeed, Deacon had to admit that they were very good. They seemed both free and exact. Almost alive.

He turned a page and found himself staring back. He recognised his dusted hair and sun-griddled cheeks and the alert eyes straining for everything. Lockett had caught him well. There was a small corner sketch of Deacon looking out through binoculars. Another was a study of his hands close-up and of Deacon walking among the desert rocks. He could not quite believe how good they were. Deacon closed the pad and returned it to its straps in the lid. He felt a little guilty.

He tidied the trunk back under the bed, unhooked Lockett's wash-bag from the back of the door and put a T-shirt and shorts in a pouch bag. Before leaving he went along the corridor to the washroom for a beaker of water which he trickled into the cartridge shell. He locked the door, returned the key and headed for the hospital.

It took him some time to locate Lockett. The hospital was busy and the nurses were unable to give more than vague and passing suggestions as to where he might be found. Deacon eventually discovered him in a small back-ward on the third floor. Lockett occupied the furthest of nine beds, beside a large window view of the mountains. It was Chi who Deacon recognised first. He was sitting on the bed and talking animatedly about something and laughing. It was the only sound in the ward. The other bed occupants were either asleep or staring sightless beyond the ceiling fans. Deacon entered the ward and saw Lockett sit up in his bed, as if he had been expected. Chi grinned at Deacon.

"You make him wear cap next time. Mr Patel say he is a mad dog and an Englishman. He sing it. It is funny."

Lockett handed Chi some papers.

"Go do your supper round, Chi. Here are your words for tomorrow. There may be a test."

"With biscuits?" said Chi. "The chocolate bourbon?"

"Might stretch to a digestive. Depends on your spelling. These are for Mr Patel. See that he gets them."

"Yes. I see for sure."

Chi slipped the papers in his tattered army pouch.

"I am happy you live," he said. "You good teacher and very cheap."

He slid off the bed and padded barefoot out of the ward.

Deacon drew up a chair and sat beside Lockett's bed. Lockett was certainly looking better than when he had last seen him. Colour was returning to his face but heavy shadows remained under his eyes.

"Well, you have certainly found yourself a pleasant nest," said Deacon. "It's bedlam in the rest of the hospital."

"I think Miss Ross pulled some of her strings, sir."

"Then you must have impressed her."

"I don't think it was me, sir."

Deacon gazed over at the other beds and was aware of the eerie stillness of the room, as if it was holding its breath. Out through the window the mountains chewed on the last red ribs of the sun. He became aware of Lockett watching him.

"Would you like to write to someone, let them know? Get you some paper and a pen," said Deacon.

"There's only my mother, sir. And she can't read."

"Eyes you mean?"

"No, sir. She can't read. Never had time to learn, she says. But she made sure I did."

Deacon remembered the books. "I brought you some reading," he said. "From your room. Hope they are suitable. And your wash bag and a change."

He placed his bundles on the bed. Lockett studied them.

"Just fine, sir. Thank you."

"You have quite a library."

Lockett smiled but said nothing.

"Spider-Man?" said Deacon. "I wasn't sure. But I brought it along. Do you like Spider-Man?"

Lockett turned to face Deacon. "Of course, sir," he said. "Don't you?"

Deacon didn't, but he was unsure as to how he might say it without offence. Lockett laughed.

"Don't worry sir, they are not for reading. I trade them with the oilmen and pilots for New Yorkers and paperbacks. The Americans seem to love them. Like big children most of them. But I am slowly becoming a Spidey convert."

Deacon picked up the Spider-mMan magazine.

"Really? To what exactly? It's a comic."

"Oh, the stories are dull, that's true. Very predictable. But the art is quite striking don't you think? It is so brash. So unequivocal. Spider-man is not for reading, sir. It's for looking at. And trading. How did the shooting go, sir?"

Deacon dropped the comic onto the bed and sat back in his chair.

"Fairly proficiently, I think," he said.

"Very, I heard, sir."

"Really? From who?"

"Like a Yorkshire market in here, sir. News travels faster than a pigeon. There's not much else to do but pass gossip."

Lockett leaned forward and lifted Deacon's lapel. He smiled. Deacon felt a slight flush warm at his neck.

"Silver," said Lockett. "That'll make the men proud, sir."

"They don't know about it. Except Kenny. And now you."

"And the entire hospital, sir."

"It's just a badge."

Lockett sank back on the pillows. His smile faded.

"You will have a care, won't you, sir. Nothing silly."

"It's all silly, corporal. This is Aden. It's all Robertson's Jam badges."

"Pigeons tell of a special ops brewing. New unit. With Captain Villiers. Feels like trouble. Trouble always follows badges."

"It follows the uniform, corporal."

"That as well, sir. Just ask Spider-Man."

Deacon laughed.

"In your number twos, sir. Going somewhere special tonight?"

"The Brigadier's Supper dance."

Lockett lay in thought for a while.

"Can you dance, sir?"

"I don't know."

"Better learn fast then, sir."

Out through the window Deacon watched the lights of three helicopters trace across the night sky. Down in the parade-square several army trucks were revving their engines and distant voices were barking orders like piard mountain dogs. In the ward, the lights dimmed as night stole around.

"Doc says I'll be out by Friday," said Lockett. His voice was low and sleepy. "Reckon you can dance till then?"

"You know me, corporal. I'm the can-can man."

Lockett laughed in his doze and drifted slowly to sleep.

Deacon left the hospital. He decided to walk the four miles to the Brigadier's villa.

*

The Villa was a large two-storey castle that roosted on top of high cliffs. It offered a commanding view of the city sprawl below and out across the lime glass bay of Aden and up high into the razor-wire mountains beyond. Tonight the Villa's Moorish arched windows and Arabian facades were bright with lights and Deacon could hear music and the sound of laughter coming from distant rooms.

He was checked-in and frisked at the outer gates by armed guards and escorted over the stone-flagged walkway to the sentry hut on the other side, where his papers were checked again. He showed his pass once more beneath the sweeping arch of the castle door and stepped inside the atrium. He made his way across the glare of the tiled floor and handed his ID and invitation to a uniformed corporal who sat alert and expectant behind a desk. Two tall, red-capped soldiers stood stiffly and sentinel behind him, their thumbs primed on the straps of their back-slung machine guns. They looked at Deacon through still, dead eyes. The corporal leaned back in his chair and studied Deacon's papers, then he studied Deacon. The corporal was young, well-built and smartly uniformed and exuded a confident ease that was almost nonchalance. His tan was the colour of faded sandals.

"I am Corporal Golightly," he said. He continued to watch Deacon as if anticipating a comment, or a smile. He received neither. "What's the password, Lieutenant Deacon?" he asked.

Deacon was taken aback. He had no recollection of any password in the invitation.

"I didn't know there was one," he said.

Golightly continued to gaze at Deacon through soft,grey eyes. His face was a mask of blankness. He sat perfectly still.

"That's because there isn't one," said the corporal. "Just trying to spread my little piece of excitement and fun. It is a party after all."

The corporal thinned a lip by way of a smile. He picked up a piece of paper and studied it for a moment. He leaned back in his chair. "You are expected to attend a meeting in the library at twenty-two hundred hours. Keep that news to yourself. And suggest you aren't late, Brigadier is particular about that sort of thing. Make yourself available at the Supper Dance in the meantime. Eats in the Bay Room, cards in the Blue and dancing in the Ballroom. Smoke outside. Make yourself known to Mrs. Jennings first. She's in the Big Hall. Any questions?"

Deacon could think of none. He made his way to the Big Hall and stood behind a couple of Commando Captains who were waiting to make themselves known to Mrs Jennings. The lady herself stood in blue floral creation just inside the door talking with a couple of new arrivals. Deacon saw Villiers chatting amiably with a group of high-ranking uniforms in a corner of the Hall. Villiers seemed to be telling them one of his stories. He acknowledged Deacon from across the room with a smile and discreet nod and with no break in his anecdote.

The Supper Dance was crowded with officers, wives and civilians and Deacon could see a group of young WRAFs enjoying the dancing in the Ballroom. Various young officers of land, sea and sky were enjoying it with them. They all seemed to be having a good time and the drinks were flowing. Deacon thought of Kenny at the Jubillee and the rest of his men down at the Quayside. It seemed that they were in for a disappointing night. Their WRAFs had been castled. Deacon was going to have a moody troop at call the next morning.

An Army jazz band played on a low stage. The buffet tables were piled and garlanded to excess and the bar was already crowded. Orderlies in brilliantined hair and snow- white jackets glided and weaved among it all, their palmed trays of clinking drinks and vol-au-vents surfing the party waves.

Deacon was ushered forward to meet Mrs. Jennings and he saw Clemmie had joined her mother in the reception line. Deacon thought she looked tired, her smile painted. She saw Deacon and the paint cracked a little.

"Harry, how nice!" she said.

Mrs Jennings turned to look at Deacon as he approached. She was a small, round woman and had to gaze up as he approached, her narrowed eyes searching him for hope of a vague recognition. None came, so she smiled her welcome.

"Lieutenant Deacon, Mrs Jennings. Of the Sussex Regiment," said Deacon. He held out his hand. "Thank you for inviting me."

Mrs Jennings took the hand briefly and then let it fall. She had small folds of skin holstering her neck, like rippled lava flows on a blue-flowered hill.

"You're one of Villiers' boys, aren't you? So glad you could come. Not one of the Shropshire Deacons, are you?"

"No. I'm from Croydon."

"Croydon?" Mrs Jennings thought for a moment. "Where's Croydon? Isn't that where Cousin Douglas got posted during the war, Clemmie? Scotland way, I think it was. Do you know Douglas, Mr. Deacon?"

"Oh Mummy!" said Clemmie. She stepped forward and took Deacon's arm. "He's no relation. This is Harry. And he can't answer any more of your questions because he is on one of Daddy's secret missions. He would probably be shot at dawn if he told you any more. I'll take him away and you can interrogate the next one."

"I wasn't interrogating him, Clemmie. I was just being polite. Manners is an art you might do better to learn, dear. Tell daddy I'll do another ten minutes on reception. Then I must mingle. I've promised to pair Ambassador Telah in a rubber. And I must remind Jimbo to take his pill at ten."

Clemmie laughed and kissed her mother on the cheek.

"Roger and wilco, Mummy." said Clemmie.

Mrs Jennings turned and smiled at the next couple who were being ushered towards her. She held out her hand.

"Roger," she said. "And you must be Wilco."

Clemmie giggled into Deacon's shoulder and escorted him away to the buffet.

"Have I just been rescued?" said Deacon. He handed Clemmie a cheese and pineapple stick. It looked like a small Mills bomb.

"Mummy can seem like a bit of a foolish dragon. But she's not the dangerous kind," said Clemmie.

"Like Puff," said Deacon.

Clemmie laughed.

"Not so magical I'm afraid," she said. "Most people want to be rescued from Mummy. It's one of her gifts. I think she does it on purpose. To amuse herself. Being married to a Brigadier, she needs all the fun she can get. She is a wonderful old girl really. Do you dance?"

Deacon took a moment to think.

"Not yet," he said.

"The twist looks quite fun, don't you think?"

Deacon gazed across to the Ballroom where the jazz band had been replaced by a record player on loudspeaker that was tinning out a Beatles song. The knot of young uniforms was twisting happily and energetically into the Ballroom tiles.

"How about us having a go at this one, Clemmie?"

Deacon turned to find Villiers beside him. Villiers grinned and held out a courtly hand to Clemmie.

"Fancy a bit of a twist? Have a dance while the night is young, eh? Come on. Be a sport."

Clemmie re-brushed her smile. "Of course, Tom. Delighted." She took his hand. "I might even get Harry to dance later," she said.

"Of course," said Deacon. "Look forward to it."

"Fibber," said Clemmie.

"We soldiers never lie, Clemmie," said Villiers, "Its one of the things you love about us. Remember? Come on. Let's have some fun."

Deacon watched Villiers and Clemmie slow twisting to the music. They danced rather well together. Or so it seemed to Deacon. Villiers moved with the grace and flex of a cat. Clemmie just seemed to ripple. Deacon watched Villiers as the Supper Dance drifted around him. He had to jerk himself back to the party.

He took a tall gin from the tray of a short orderly and idled among the ham rolls and chicken legs. He took the food to a corner to await Clemmie's return. He saw Alec Peterson talking with a young female naval rating and he also recognised a few faces from the Gallery mingling about. Old Bobby stood on the fringes of a small, high-ranking group gathered under a small copse of potted palms. He stood stiff, with his hands clasped behind him, and was bouncing slowly on his toes. He rose and rocked, going nowhere. He saw Deacon and gazed through him with a practised ease.

Deacon turned to watch Villiers and Clemmie again but found that they were no longer dancing. Villiers had joined with the Brigadier and other officers under a large acacia tree that ornamented the courtyard. They stood drinking and laughing together. Clemmie was doing the rounds of the guests, stopping to chat and to couple-up and replenish plates and bend an ear and generally smooth the party along.

Deacon suddenly realised that Clemmie was not going to be returning to him. He felt rather foolish. Clemmie was, of course, the hostess of the party, or at least one of them. Clemmie kept her smile warm and her voice light. She danced with a major and again with Villiers. She circled and mingled among the military and civilian guests and instructed the orderlies. She even had time to regularly check-in on her mother in the card room. She would not come over to see Deacon; he had already been done.

Deacon laughed at his stupidity. He checked his watch. There was half-an-hour before the library meeting. He went to the bar and ordered two large whiskies.

Twenty minutes later, Deacon mounted the wide sweeping staircase up to the first floor and made his way to the library along a low-lit mezzanine landing draped in oil paintings and Zulu shields. He was surprised to find carpet under his tread. Its soft give was unnerving, like stepping into mud. He could hear the music from the ballroom down below.

Two guards were standing outside the library door. One stepped forward to meet him. Deacon offered his card. The guard studied it for a moment.

"Do you have a badge, sir?" he asked.

It took a moment for Deacon to understand. He lifted his jacket lapel collar. The guard smiled. Deacon flushed a little.

"A silver. Very good, sir. Do you mind?"

Deacon felt himself being quickly and expertly frisked. He stared at the paintings of Balaclava and Waterloo on the walls and endured it as best he could.

"Thank you, sir. Can't be too careful, eh?"

The door opened, the heavy cloth curtain was pulled aside and Deacon stepped into the library.

EIGHT

Even as he took the step into the half-lit room smelling of warm leather and cigar smoke, Deacon knew that it was a step from which there could be no turning back. It was the step into another world. He remembered that late Springafternoon step he had taken with his teacher Michael Havers in the Infirmary Room of Croydon Secondary. And the step he had taken for the Army the very next dawn, leaving everything and everyone behind him. He had stepped away from his home and school, away from his mother and all her vainglorious hopes for him, and away from his bestial sins. Now he stepped again, this time striding as a soldier.

Captain Villiers was sitting on the corner of a desk, one leg slowly swinging. The Brigadier sat beside him in a high-backed leather chair. There were about twenty other men in the room, perching on chair arms or leaning among the library shelves. All seemed to have a drink in their hands and most were smoking. An Edwardian fog floated under the dim wall lamps. Deacon recognised a few faces from the Gallery.

"Harry! Glad you could make it. Take a squat," said Villiers. "Just waiting for one more. Ah, Alec! There you are. About to send a search party!"

The room laughed experimentally. Deacon found a shadow by a book-shelf and occupied it. Alec Petersen joined him.

"I hope the Old Boy keeps it short," he whispered to Deacon. "I'm on a mission with a charmer and she curfews at midnight."

"Operation Cinderella?" said Deacon.

Petersen laughed.

"Ahumm."

Deacon realised that the Brigadier had risen and was waiting to speak.

"Sorry, sir," said Petersen. "Urgent signal chat."

The Brigadier looked at Petersen, then at Deacon. His rheumy gaze slowly swept the rest of the men.

"Urgent, indeed gentlemen," he said. He took a sip from his brandy glass and let the silence settle. The Brigadier braced his cane to the floor and stood straight and tall.

"What is said in this room, stays in this room," he said.

He was about to say something more when there was a sound of a woman's voice shouting in an adjoining room and then Mrs. Jennings appeared through a back door of the library in an urgent gust of blue flowers.

"Your pill, Jimbo dear. It's gone ten and the doctor was most particular."

Deacon saw Villiers glare at the two corporals who had entered the library from the main door. It seemed that Mrs Jennings had somehow outflanked the sentries. The corporals shrugged their bafflement. The Brigadier turned to his wife.

"Not now, Marjorie! I am in a meeting. A private one."

"I know dear, but the doctor was insistent. It's gone ten. You must have your pill."

Clemmie appeared at the back door, her face a little flushed. She had obviously been pursuing her mother.

"Sorry daddy! She slipped away. Come on, Mummy."

"Not until he's had his pill, dear. It's gone ten!"

"Marjorie! This is an Army meeting."

"Oh just take the pill, Daddy, for God's sake. You know she won't let it rest."

Deacon saw Clemmie take in the front row of officers who were sitting quietly enjoying the show. She leaned forward.

"No, please gentlemen, don't get up."

Their grins faded.

The Brigadier took the pill from his wife's palm and threw it into his mouth as if it were grenade into a Philippine fox-hole. He stared hard at his wife and then hard at his step-daughter and chased the pill down with a half-balloon of Napoleon Brandy. He wiped his mouth with the back of a slow hand.

Clemmie kissed him on the cheek.

"There. That wasn't so hard was it?" she said. "Come on, Mummy. Mrs. Frobisher has brought her Lobster Bisque notes. She was in your cupboards looking for lemons."

"But I don't like lobster," said Mrs. Jennings.

Clemmie escorted her away. "Well you'll just have to pretend you do. You've had lots of practice."

The door closed. Deacon saw Villiers nod and Corporal Golightly appeared like a spectre from the shadows and locked the door. He pocketed the key and stood guard. The Brigadier settled on his cane and looked once more upon his men.

"As I was saying. What's said in this room, stays in this room," he said. He searched the library with a measured gaze. "Do I make myself clear?" There was an acquiescent silence. "Good. Then someone get me another brandy. A damn large one."

It took two brandies for the Brigadier to finish his briefing. Deacon leaned to the book-shelf and half-dozed as he listened. There was not much that he hadn't known or already half-guessed. About how the war in Aden was changing. The Adoos were leaving the plains and bringing the war inside the city. Two rebel factions, the NLF and FLOSY, had access to Russian weaponary smuggled across the plains. Mortars and grenades and Kalishnikovs. A new war was happening and the Army needed new skills to fight it. Special soldiers. Chosen for the task.

"We need city soldiers. Chaps who can fight in the streets. And that's why you're here," said the Brigadier. "To volunteer for Special Duties. I take you are all volunteers?"

He waited a moment in the silence.

"Good," he said. "I'll leave you with Captain Villiers." The Brigadier looked around the room through a basset hound gaze. "Let's give 'em what for, eh, boys?"

He turned and made his way out of the library. The room stood to attention.

The door was closed and locked behind him. At a signal from Villiers all the lights in the room were turned up. Deacon had to blink the room back into focus.

Villiers stood with his back to the black tiled fireplace and grinned at the faces in the room.

"I'm Captain Tom Villiers. But I expect you all know that."

The men laughed. Villiers strode the room.

"Look around you, boys, and get to know one another. You're all in the Special Forces Unit now. The Aden Branch. Do get comfortable, gentlemen."

The room settled to chairs and casual leanings. Villiers waited for absolute silence to settle. It did not take long.

"Well boys, you are going to be busy. Because you will be training in a special unit that will take this war to the city streets. Night time raids. Day time forays. In and out and bang and crash and all back in time for a last swim at the Lido."

He waited for the laugh. It came as sure as a salute. Villiers stood feet apart before the fireplace and waited for the mirth to ebb. His eyes were bright with energy.

"Not only bang and crash, but stop and search and bag the buggers in their own homes if we must. Under the moon and at the dawn. This is additional duty boys. No extra shillings, no net and no glory. Just duty above and beyond with a band of brothers. What more could a soldier need, eh? There is a new challenge in Aden. Together we will meet it and damn well overcome it. This is a secret unit. But a deadly and decisive one."

Villiers let his words settle. Deacon was aware of Alec shifting at his shoulder.

"So this is extra duty on top of what we are already doing? Have I got that correct, sir?" asked Alec.

Villiers turned and gazed down at Peterson. He laughed.

"Don't worry, all of your bosses know to assign you only light duties during the day. So you'll have to work off all that unused energy somehow, Alec. A few night time strolls through Crater will help keep you fit."

"But no richer," said Peterson.

A laugh rolled through the room. Villiers allowed it to fade.

"Our duty calls, boys. We're moving into a new war. We're building up good intelligence and we will act upon it. We will operate in secret and in select units recruited to the task. There are many skills in this room. We aim to use them. You will be contacted through Corporal Golightly."

Golightly stepped forward from his guard at the door and came to a smart, stamped foot attention.

"Sir," he said. The thin smile appeared briefly. On a stamp and turn Corporal Golightly stepped back to resume his guard.

"There will be only one or two operations a week but you'll get regular training. In the meantime, go about your usual business and await the call," said Villiers.

A commando spoke up from the sofa.

"What are we going to call the unit, sir?" he asked. "Must have a name."

"The Aden Raiders?" came a voice.

"No, too like a Yank football team," said another. "What about the Aden Specials. Add a touch of class."

"Bandits, more like." said Villiers, laughing.

Corporal Golightly stepped forward.

"How about Villiers' Vikings, sir? That's a fighting name."

There were murmurs of assent from the chairs.

"Yes. That's more like it."

Deacon watched Villiers struggle to resist the offer. And fail.

"Well, I suppose it's as good a name as any," he said. He raised a glass of brandy to the room. Glasses were raised in salute.

"Villiers' Vikings," he said and drained his glass.

The toast echoed around the room. Villiers stood up and straightened his jacket.

"Right, gentlemen. I believe there is still a party going on downstairs, the night is young and the ladies are missing us almost as much as the barmen. It is our duty to relieve both of their miseries. We Vikings like a party. So let's make it a good one."

Deacon detached himself from the Viking triumph as the excited crowd reached the bottom of the stone stairs. He watched the officers skidding on the polished tiles as they followed Villiers eagerly into the Ballroom bar. High-spirits suddenly seemed to have filled the air. The jazz band swung into party mood. Deacon became aware of Peterson beside him.

"Looks like a Rear Admiral has cornered my charmer," he said.

Deacon followed his gaze to a white haired, smart uniformed officer who was talking with a young, flush-cheeked WRAF by a grand piano. "Can't have that," said Peterson. "Frontal attack do you think? What are my chances?"

"None. He outranks you."

Peterson grinned and tidied his tie.

"Not at a bloody party, he doesn't," he said and strode out for the piano.

The party seemed to have swelled with people, as if they had been waiting for the meeting to finish. The orderlies were busy with trays and the bar rumbled in laughter. Deacon could see Villiers at the Ballroom bar. He was ordering a round, surrounded by an excited knot of officers. Some of the WRAFs joined them. The dance floor was alive with manic jazz.

"Parties are so hard on the feet, aren't they? I feel like I've marched to Cairo and back."

Deacon turned to find Clemmie beside him. She smelled of strawberries.

She stood gazing into the Ballroom. She slipped her foot free of one her sandal shoes and rubbed her foot against her ankle. Her hand rested on Deacon's shoulder in light support.

"We never did have the dance, did we?" she said.

"Would you like to now?"

"Do you want to cripple me? No, what I would really like is a cigarette. Can you save a girl?"

Clemmie slipped off her other shoe and gave them to Deacon. She took two drinks from a passing tray and led Deacon through the party throng and out onto the flagstoned courtyard and into a small lawned garden beyond. They sat alone at a table, looking out into the dark curtain of a night pricked by the firefly lights of unseen flotillas and myriad stars. Clemmie leaned back in her chair and lifted her ankles onto Deacon's knees.

"You wouldn't be an angel and rub them, would you?"

Deacon began to massage her feet. Clemmie leaned back and gazed to the stars.

"Ah, bliss!" she said.

She reached for her cigarettes, lit two and passed one over to Deacon.

"Long day?" asked Deacon.

"Never ending. I don't know where Tom gets all his energy. He never seems to tire. He is quite remarkable, don't you think?"

"Very."

"I do wish he would slow down sometimes though. He picked me up straight from the hospital this morning and took me to the Gallery. I wasn't supposed to be there. A civilian girl. And I was looking forward to my bed. But Tom charmed the guards and got me in. It was rather embarrassing. I felt rather awkward but Tom, of course, would have none of it. His guest, you see. Nothing ever too much trouble. Even if it is. It was interesting though. You did well, I think."

"Not as well as Captain Villiers."

"Yes. He was rather splendid, wasn't he? He said he was calling in to check on the training but I think he just wanted me to see him shoot. And then he whisked me off to lunch at the Inkerman Club with a frightful couple of colonels. Wonderful crab, though. I managed a couple of hours sleep this afternoon before seeing to the party preparations. I'm dead on my feet and Tom is still dancing. I don't know how he does it. Oh, Harry. That feels so good."

Deacon sipped his drink and continued to rub Clemmie's feet.

"Did your meeting go well with Daddy? Or shouldn't I ask?"

"You can ask, but I cannot tell. I'd have to shoot you if I did."

"Not again! Will it be dangerous?"

"It's Aden. Opening a door is dangerous."

"Do you like Tom?"

Deacon was taken unawares by the question and paused in his foot rubbing while searching for a response. Clemmie looked across at him.

"As a man I mean," said Clemmie. "Is he a good sort do you think?"

Deacon thought about it.

"He's a good soldier," he said. "But I hardly know him. He seems very taken with you."

"Yes. But Tom seems taken with everyone. He thinks you a fine soldier."

Deacon laughed.

"Then maybe his judgement is a little suspect after all," he said.

Clemmie took a sip of her drink and watched Deacon through round eyes.

"No, I don't think so," she said.

They lapsed to silence. Deacon watched the searchlights on the far side of the bay slicing the city roofs and heard the distant pulse of waves crashing against the cliff roots far below his feet.

"I'm sorry we missed our dance," said Clemmie. "I was looking forward to it, even if you weren't."

"I am not much of a dancer," said Deacon. "I don't think you missed much of a treat."

"Nor you either, it seems."

"Oh I didn't mean it that way. Well, I am sure I would have enjoyed it. If we had danced."

Clemmie laughed.

"You are always so serious, Harry! So correct. Like you're walking on thin ice all the time. Don't you ever find a crack? Let a good time out. A smile. An unguarded word. Do something reckless?"

"Like dance with you?" said Deacon.

Clemmie laughed again.

"Well, it would have been a start. Unfortunately I don't think my legs will let me stand at the moment. But thank you for asking. Be sure to do so again. In the meantime, could you get me another drink?"

Deacon released Clemmie's ankles and made his way to the crowded bar. It was noisy with party revellers. Villiers and a group of red-faced officers and rose-cheeked WRAFs were singing heartily at one end of the bar and an impromptu game of rugger was being enjoyed in the Acacia courtyard. In the Ballroom several couples circled slowly together, heads pillowed on shoulders, eking out the last moments of the night as the music carouseled around them.

Deacon saw that Peterson and his charmer were one of the couples. Peterson grinned at him over the girl's shoulder. He gave Deacon a discreet thumbs-up and nuzzled his cheek back to his partner. Deacon felt the pain of his own loneliness stab deep again.

After a wait, Deacon finally got his drinks and returned to the secluded garden. Clemmie was smoking a cigarette and watching the dark sea.

"Sounds like everyone is having a good time," she said.

Deacon noticed Clemmie's arms were goose-bumped and she was hugging herself gently against the chillness of the night air. He took off his jacket and nestled it over Clemmie's bare shoulders. She smiled up at him.

"Thank you Harry. You are always rescuing me."

Deacon sat down and lit another cigarette. "Your party seems a great success," he said. "All your hard work was worth it."

"Oh, the real hard work starts tomorrow, trying to get it all cleared up. Mother has a luncheon bridge tournament to host. Is there much mess?"

"Not that I could see."

Clemmie lit another cigarette from the stub of her previous one. She flicked the butt over the cliff wall.

"Tom told me tonight that he is going to ask Daddy formally for permission to take me out one night soon," she said. She turned to Deacon and smiled. "Not an engagement, you understand. Just a date. He said it is the proper way. Asking Daddy. Don't you think that is rather sweet?"

"Very courtly," said Deacon.

"Yes. Very. Tom seems so marvellously modern and yet so wonderfully old fashioned. Very flattering of course but it feels wrong for him to be asking Daddy before me. Don't you think?"

"And what will you say when he does ask you?"

Clemmie blew a last jet of smoke to the air and then stubbed her cigarette on the grass. She laughed lightly.

"Rather depends if I get a better offer," she said. "Doesn't it?"

"A general, perhaps?"

Clemmie stood up and leaned against the cliff top wall. She allowed the breeze to fly her hair.

"Rank doesn't enter into it." she said "Only better."

"Can't be many better than Tom, I wouldn't have thought," he said.

Clemmie gazed at Deacon for a moment. She smiled.

"No," she said. "Not many."

Clemmie picked up her shoes and slid the jacket off her shoulders and returned it to Deacon. She kissed him lightly on the cheek.

"Thank you Harry. You've been so kind. Now I must away to my bed. It has been such a long day. Let Tom know I've retired, will you?"

"I'll walk you home," said Deacon.

Clemmie laughed.

"You are a dear Harry! But I live here. Remember? That's my quarters over there."

She pointed to the lantern-lit door of a small, clay-tiled cottage that bordered one of the Villa's lower lawns.

"Thank you for my feet. And your jacket. It's been a lovely end to the day but I must get some sleep. Perhaps if you are free one afternoon you might show me more of Aden? I'll take it as a forfeit for the missed dance."

"Of course," said Deacon. "Delighted."

Clemmie walked barefoot across the grass and down the wide stone steps to the lower lawn. She waved her shoes adieu to him and walked across to her door. Deacon watched until the door closed and waited until the lights were lit. He continued his watch until the shutters were closed and the lights went off again some minutes later.

Deacon found Villiers in the buffet bar and relayed Clemmie's message.

"Thought she looked a little beat," said Villiers. "These parties take a lot of organising. Bound to tire her."

"Plus the extra hospital night shifts and Gallery visits," said Deacon.

"Of course. As I say, bound to tire her. She safely tucked?"

"Yes, sir."

"Fine. Getting her beauty winks, eh? Not that Clemmie needs them. Come on and meet some of the boys, Harry."

Deacon found himself at the bar and being introduced

to several other officers whose names flowed passed him like jetsam on the tide.

"Carter and MacDonald. Plays rugger in a kilt. I know, against all rules of sport and decency. And this is Stephens. RAF Wing Co. Just pitched up from Malta. Right Alan? Shanks and BJ from the Artemis. What's that?"

A barman in a white jacket was trying to catch Villiers' eye. He leaned over the bar to Villiers and spoke quietly.

"Er, six pounds, seven and six, sir," he said.

Villiers began handing out the squad of drinks that had appeared on the bar.

"Tab it up, corporal."

The Corporal looked up. A look of concern on his face.

"Will that be your personal tab sir? It is rather a busy one."

Villiers sipped his drink and smiled at the officers about him.

"Think we ought to start a new tab, corporal. Chalk it up to the Vikings."

The men cheered. So did Deacon. And he downed his drink and listened to Villiers work his new boys with his team captain charm. He did it well. Deacon half wanted to stay but the press of crowds always made him feel uneasy. He allowed himself to drift to the outer edges of the huddle and to eventually find opportunity and time to slip out of the bar.

A few couples still danced in the Ballroom and orderlies and jazz band players were tidying the buffet table like herons at the lake's shores. Their mouths stuffed with meringues and their trays piled high with pasties and unfinished trifle tureens.

Deacon slipped into the courtyard and took a slow smoke on a stone bench behind potted palms. He judged he had another half an hour before he could leave the party. It would be oh-one-hundred then. Go now and he would risk the raised eyebrows and cheery mockings of Vikings. It was an attention he would prefer to avoid. He was here to hide, not wave.

He walked the courtyard and strolled into the lower picture gallery until it was time to slip back into the bar to be noticed drinking. Villiers had gone from the room but the revelry was still rolling. Deacon joined in the last choruses of a bar song, drained his drink in one on a bet and, with due patting of backs with his new colleagues, he made his leave.

As Deacon walked back across the villa courtyard a car appeared at speed from nowhere and almost ran him down. He had to jump up onto a low wall to avoid it. The car slurred to a stop beside him. It was a black Wolseley with the Brigadier's pennant flying from its bonnet. Villiers was in the driving seat. He leaned out of the car window, a broad grin on his face.

"Harry! Nearly had you there. Sorry about that. Can't get used to these brakes."

Deacon recovered his calm and stepped down into the road beside the car. Villiers grew in the car window, but not big enough to fully obscure the stockinged and flat-shoed leg that Deacon glimpsed in the passenger well. Villiers saw his look.

"This is Susan, Harry. Corporal Devon. It's late so I'm dropping her off at her billet."

A young woman bent down from the shadows of the car and waved her fingers at Deacon. Villiers engaged the gears and revved the engine.

"Can give you a lift to yours if you like Harry? Plenty of room inside."

Deacon knew the offer to be a test. A Viking test.

"No, thank you, sir. Most kind. I'll take the air. A very good party, sir."

Villiers grinned.

"And only just begun," he said.

Deacon watched the Wolseley speed off to the gatehouse and then disappear along the Aden road.

He ran the three miles back to his billet because he felt like it and because by the time he reached his billet he knew he would be so tired he wouldn't have time to reflect that he was alone and that he shared his bed and companionship with no one. He collapsed across his bed as if felled.

NINE

It was Chi who woke him early in the sun's rise with a mug of hot tea and a beaker of gin and orange.

"Mr. Lockett said the gin first," said Chi grinning. "So you don't feel my tea."

Deacon rubbed the bark of sleep from his face and sat up on his bed. He blinked the day into his head, un-cramped an arm and took the beaker.

"It's taste, Chi. Not feel. Then I won't taste the tea. Corporal Lockett was making a little joke."

"I know. But my tea is fine. So it is not a good joke. It is not funny."

Deacon drained the beaker and then took the mug. He drank the tea in two gulps.

"You are right, Chi. Definitely not funny."

"Corporal Lockett said if you drink both I get biscuits."

"In the drawer," said Deacon. "Only two."

Deacon spent an hour in the Duty Office filing his reports. After that he attended the morning Officers' briefing where he was advised of the recent outbreak of syphilis in the Royal Lancashire's signal regiment, learned the new radio frequencies for night time assaults and also the winner of this week's Starling Pot. It wasn't Deacon. After the briefing, he checked his duty rosters on the board and grabbed a bacon sandwich from the canteen.

He drove down through the streets of white-box terrace housing and out along the coast road to the Dockyards. He parked up in tree shade a half a mile from Checkpoint Seven and scanned it through binoculars. He could see Ambrose and Lee slunk in chairs in the shade of the hut and Shaw lying on his back smoking a cigarette on a nearby bank of sandbags. The road traffic was quiet. While Deacon sat and watched only three trucks went past. Ambrose and Lee waved them through from their chairs. Deacon left the jeep and walked to the Checkpoint under cover of the roadside scrub and rocks. He picked up a cricket ball sized rock and made his way behind the hut. Through the window he could see the rest of the troop asleep on the benches. Deacon lobbed the rock and let it thud into the doorway dust.

"Grenade!" he yelled.

Ambrose and Lee fell off their chairs and scrabbled the dirt on all fours like electrocuted crabs. Hobson appeared in the doorway his hair awry and sleep still dulling him. Shaw had rolled off the sandbag hill and fallen among the rocks with a yelp. Someone was half out of the hut window. Deacon stepped forward.

"Didn't disturb you, did I, lads?"

"Fucking hell, sir."

"Yes. Jesus Christ, sir. Near wet myself."

"Think I broke my knee, sir."

"Outside. Troop rank. Now," said Deacon.

The men lined up in the road outside the Checkpoint hut without enthusiasm. Deacon stood before them. He tossed his rock from hand to hand. His men looked tired and bored and hot. Deacon could hardly blame them. Nor could he blame them for the surliness that seemed to envelop them all. His men would now know their WRAFs had Supper Danced last night at the Brigadier's Villa, so they had much to be surly about. They slouched before Deacon as servant cuckolds.

"Nice dance, was it, sir?" asked Lee.

Deacon ignored him. He held up the rock.

"What is the grenade drill?" he asked. "Just remind me."

There was a long silence. Deacon waited. He tossed the rock from hand to hand. He lobbed it in the air and caught it one handed behind his back. He had time.

"Turn away. Crouch and bury your head under your arms," said Kenny.

"Very good. And what did you actually do, Kenny?"

"I was asleep, sir. I got blowed up."

"What a pity. And you, Hobson. How brave of you to walk towards the bomb. Were you going to throw yourself upon it to save your mates, maybe?"

"I didn't really know what I was doing, sir."

"Allow me to admit to no surprise there, Hobson." Deacon leaned towards the line. "The whole lot of you are a fucking shambles! Stand up straight. Attention!"

The line rose and stiffened as one.

"You're supposed to be bloody soldiers!" said Deacon.

A large double-axle truck pulled up at the barrier, its brakes screeching. A thin-faced lance corporal of the Anglians leaned out from the truck window and grinned down at the line.

"Bin naughty boys?"

Deacon nodded Kenny to check the truck's transit orders. The co-driver, a sergeant, emerged from his cab and strolled around to lean on the front of the truck and watch the show. He passed his clipboard to Kenny.

"Little late for morning parade, ain't we, boys? Or have you been pissing in the officer's gin again?"

The Anglians laughed. Deacon saw his men blanch, but they kept stiff in their line, staring ahead at nothing.

Deacon strode over to Kenny and took the clipboard from him. He studied it for a moment and then checked the truck's licence and code.

"So you're down from Abyan?" he asked.

The sergeant lit a cigarette.

"Yeah. NAAFI Stores for Dock Three. And I'm late. Three sodding hours and then it's all start back and do it again. And axle loaded. Fucking Army. Caught your boys napping, did you?"

The Anglians grinned at the line. The line held steady.

"You must have come through Checkpoint Six then. If you drove down from Abyan," said Deacon.

"Yeah. So?

"So you haven't got a Checkpoint Six pass."

"They was packed up with trucks and the guard was on a shit so he waved us through. The dock storehouse closes in an hour. Just tick us off and get us on our way, eh sir?"

Deacon handed the clipboard back to the sergeant. He had never been an officious type, but no one got away with ridiculing his men.

"You have no six stamp, sergeant. So no Seven pass. Not from Abyan. Orders, sergeant. You know them. Suggest you turn your truck around and revisit six."

"But that's twenty minutes back where we come from!" said the lance-corporal from the cab.

"Then you'll know the way," said Deacon.

He smiled. The sergeant didn't. He hurled his cigarette to the dirt and climbed back into his cab.

"I will hope to see you again in about forty minutes," said Deacon. "Do drive safely."

The gears growled under kicking heels and the truck backed up in an arcing wheel-spin of dust. The sergeant gave Deacon a stare, spat dust from his mouth and roared back down the road. Deacon turned to find the men still stiff to attention, but grinning as one.

"That showed 'em, sir," said Shaw.

Deacon stepped forward and looked slowly along the line. "Shambles!" he bellowed. "Bloody amateurs."

He strolled away and stood for a moment in the road. Liquid tarmac stretched to dry scrub land and low hills in both directions. Beyond the hills to the north the quayside derricks herded the skyline like skeletal herons paddling a lake's shore. Down the long straight of tarmac road, the Anglian's truck was just a black fly buzzing in the distance. Deacon dreamed of a cold Tusker.

He returned to stand before the line. To help them once again to survive their miserable lot.

"Drill, boys. You've got to do the drills if you want to stay alive. It's got to be instinctive. The Army knows drills. It's being doing them since Crecy. And that is a long time drilling. Drills work. That is why they are there. So learn your drills, lads. Do you want to fly back in a bag like McNish? Grenade drill. Tell me. Lee."

"Turn away, sir."

"And?"

"Run, sir?"

"And how far do you think you could run with pieces of grenade blasted into your spine, your legs and whatever it is that you use for brains?"

"Not very far, sir."

"Barely a step I would hazard, Private Lee. So a better plan would be?"

"Er. Hit the floor and bury your 'ead, sir?"

"Top of the Class, Private Lee," said Deacon.

Private Lee beamed. Deacon held out the rock and dropped it at his feet.

"Grenade!" he shouted.

A small troop of arses, haloed in a cloud of swirling dusts, greeted his gaze.

"Splendid, lads," he said. "Now, shall we have a brew?"

The men were quickly on their feet and dusting themselves down.

"We got coffee, sir," said Ambrose.

"And custard creams," said Lee.

"What a treat. Hobson, take the jeep and get two bags of chips from the REME kitchens."

"What jeep, sir?"

"Half a mile down the road. In the shade," He tossed Ambrose the keys. And then a sixpence.

"Divvy the rest of the bill among the men. I want my chips hot mind. And plenty of vinegar."

Hobson was already running down the road.

"Lee, you go on the barrier. Think of it as another drill. One that stops the Dizzies bombing your favourite bar. Shaw, Ambrose, make the coffee. Gibson on watch first fifteen. Kenny, go back to sleep. Then relieve Gibson. Anyone got a smoke?"

Ambrose and Shaw proffered packs. Deacon took one from each. He pocketed one and lipped the other.

"Thanks, lads."

"So what were the girls like, then, sir?" said Lee.

"Bridget Bardot we heard, sir," said Shaw. "A real looker, like."

"Well," said Deacon. He let a jet of cigarette smoke take its time. "I didn't see them all, of course. But I would say that the most beautiful WRAF I saw last night very much reminded me of that woman in the film, From Russia With Love."

The men thought hard. Then smiled.

"You mean that Daniela Bianchi?" said Shaw. "Cor!"

The men grinned lupine leers at each other.

"No," said Deacon. "I was thinking more of Rosa Klebb."

Lockett would have laughed at that. But the men took a few moments longer to find it.

"Very funny, sir," said Shaw. "When is the Corp back?"

"Any trouble?" asked Deacon.

"Oh no sir. It's just. Well. It's not the unit without the Corp is it?"

"He should be back in a couple of days."

"Good. Been missing the little bugger," said Ambrose.

While Deacon drank his coffee in the shade of the hut he was surprised to find that he had too. He had certainly missed Lockett's laugh.

*

Deacon spent the rest of the duty checking truck papers, lifting barriers, organising the men and sweating in a plastic chair. Aden, like any war, was mostly boredom. The only way through was to take the small victories when you could. Like a bag of noon-day chips. A grenade drill. A pissed-off Anglian sergeant. But mostly it was just routine boredom and sweating. Deacon kept the men busy. He knew that boredom was the devil's only friend.

The monotony of the day was relieved momentarily by the arrival of two seconded privates from C Battalion and a short visit by Captain Villiers. The two new privates, Doyle and Ably, brought a truck with them. They were replacements for McNish. There were no sergeants available so, by logic of the Army, Deacon had received two privates in exchange. Doyle was thin and his face was a flowerbed of purple sprouting acne. Despite this impediment, he was a smiler. Ably was squat and square and Welsh, so he smiled less. Deacon checked their papers, welcomed them to the troop and passed them over to Ambrose and Shaw for induction. He knew this would consist of the men taking the new recruits around the back of the hut and quizzing them until their ears bled while scrounging all the ciggies they could. They would all be best mates in a couple of days. In the meantime, they were on the barriers.

Captain Villiers arrived in a jeep driven by Corporal Golightly. Deacon went out to meet them. Villiers leaned out of the jeep window.

"Harry. Thought you might be interested in this."

He flicked a coin towards Deacon, who caught it in his palm. It was the silver disk he had found in the Adoo scratch camp up on the Tihammah. Deacon tried to remember how long ago that had been, but he couldn't. He had grown an Aden memory. He could see far back and out beyond the horizon with an absolute clarity, but the yesterdays and the days before were always a little miraged.

"You carried it back for four hours in your pouch, I understand," said Villiers.

"Yes." said Deacon.

Villiers laughed. Golightly sat stone faced.

"It's a bloody mine, Harry!" said Villiers. "A little PacVac pressure mine. Step on it and bang! No foot. Czech apparently. That's a dud by the way. You were damned lucky, Harry!"

Deacon handed the mine back to Villiers.

"Ingenious, ain't they?" said Villiers. "And quite a few are turning up in Aden. Live ones. Silver coin mines and seven-spray mortars. Got a Viking meeting of brains planned for tomorrow. Care to join us?"

"Oh-ten- hundred at the Inkerman Club," said Corporal Golightly. "I take it you will be available?"

"Of course," said Deacon

"Then the major will be expecting you."

They stood looking at each other for a few moments.

"The barrier, lieutenant?" said Golightly.

"Sorry," said Deacon.

He lifted the barrier and the jeep sped away. It was only when it was well down the road that Deacon realised he had just apologised to a corporal. And that Villiers now wore a major's crown on his shoulder.

They were relieved in the late afternoon by a troop from the Lancashires. After the usual shared jeers and jibes, the men piled into the truck and Private Doyle drove them back to the barracks. Deacon took the jeep, drove a couple of miles to a small cove in Fisherman's Bay and parked up. He ran down the steep, rough-hewn stone steps carved helter-skelter into the rocks and out onto the small, secluded beach. He scanned the narrow bay for sharks, undressed quickly and slid into the water. The feel of liquid sizzled over his body. His brain cooled. He swam hard and strong and fast in four short bursts across the inlet and then got out. Deacon never gave himself more than five minutes. That was his shark limit. He dressed while still wet and smoked a cigarette in the late afternoon sun, letting its heat bake and cleanse his sandy feet.

Half an hour later Deacon was driving back to Aden along the Mallaa road when he heard a soft and distant boom. Noises were not uncommon in Aden and Deacon had learned most of them, but this one eluded him. It didn't sound like any ordinance he knew. Rounding a bend on the bay road he saw in the distance, above the sprawling township roofs of Crater, a plume of grey smoke rising like a small toadstool above a leaf-littered forest floor.

Deacon drove on for several minutes until he came to the street nearest the smoke. It was an area of houses and shops. Several people were in the road talking excitedly and staring up one of the narrow, twisting alleys that led back up into the warren that was Crater. Deacon slid out of the jeep and took a sighting of the smoke against the sun and mountains. He unclipped his holster flap and went into the alley. It was busy with knots of people in states of fear and confusion. Deacon could hear army trucks up ahead and the sounds of shouting British voices. A woman came running down the alley, wailing. Mothers were dragging their children inside, others were calling theirs in a frenzy, like ocean gulls over fish.

Deacon followed the smell of cordite up the steep hill and through into a wider street where a large, silent and inquisitive crowd was being held at easy bay by a troop of commando soldiers.

Deacon rested his hand on his gun and pushed his way through the crowd. Beyond the perimeter line of soldiers he could see an area of deserted street, and then more soldiers holding back crowds in the streets beyond. In the middle of the cordoned off area a stone brick corner house no longer had a corner. Or much of its roof. Through the smouldering and gaping hole in the stonework Deacon could see a fallen wooden beam with a tongue of the upper floor lapping over it. Below it half a bed was piled among a scatter of broken furniture. Small flames licked blackened shutters, hanging limp from one of the remaining walls. The stones that had once been the corner walls of the house now splattered like vomit across the street in chunks of rock and dust. A brightly coloured bed cloth and children's clothes peeked amongst the debris. It looked like the house had sneezed itself into the street. A thin, grey funnel of smoke rose lazily from the blackened roof.

Deacon pushed his way to the front of the crowd. A commando sergeant was patrolling behind the line of soldiers. Deacon showed his ID.

"Just passing. Saw the smoke. Everything OK?"

"Reckon we got it ringed, sir. Got here ten minutes ago. Sealing the area. The tecs are in there now. More boys coming up. But don't think they'll be needed. Leave it to us Lancs, sir. The natives seem quiet enough."

The crowd jostled behind Deacon. He could hear whispers about him.

"Not to my ears, sergeant. Suggest you widen your perimeter and start breaking them up. Any casualties?"

"One dead Adoo woman. The Grandma apparently. No other casualties. My major has it sorted, sir."

"I'm sure he has. One of our bombs?"

"Word is we had no Ops scheduled here. Nor did the fly boys or the Specials. We reckon it was an Adoo bomb-making house. I saw coils of wire in the back room. And I can smell blackcurrant jam. Sack of clocks in the back room. Reckon this one blowed itself up."

"Tell your major..." said Deacon.

But he didn't say any more because he saw Clemmie in amongst the crowds on the other side of the cordoned off area. She was crouched down with her camera, taking pictures of the house and the crowds and the streets around her. Deacon could see the crowds closing in, watching her.

"Tell my major what, sir?" asked the sergeant.

"Widen perimeters and break them up. And do it now."

As Deacon forced his way through the crowds, he was aware of being jostled. He raised his gun and the press around him eased. He made his way around and behind Clemmie and then waded into the back of the crowd and grabbed her arm.

"Oh, Harry! It's you."

"We must leave now."

"Isn't it awful?"

"Now," said Deacon.

The crowd about them began to murmur. A shout went up from somewhere near. Deacon pinned Clemmie's arm to her hip and hurried her out of the crowd and into the street.

"Harry, not so rough! Are you trying to frighten me again?"

A rock landed at their feet. Pebbles started raining about them. A section of crowd had broken away and was following Deacon and Clemmie down the alley. Deacon heard shouts behind him. He stepped into the street to face them and levelled his gun. The crowd stopped and stilled. Deacon guided Clemmie down a winding street and into an alley. Heads ducked back into doorways as they ran past. Deacon could hear the shouts of soldiers and revving engines behind him and guessed that the major was widening his perimeter. The streets and alleys became crowded with stampeding people. Deacon pushed Clemmie along and emerged onto the street leading back down to his jeep. Looking back up the hill, Deacon could see a large group of young Arab men. They saw Deacon and Clemmie and began to jeer and run towards them. Deacon turned to find Clemmie squatting on her knee, taking pictures of their pursuers. He pulled her up and pushed her ahead of him down the slope towards the jeep.

About half way down the hill, the rocks and bottles began to fall and shatter at Deacon's heels and he could hear the feral whoops louder at his back. Clemmie seemed to become suddenly aware of the seriousness of the situation.

"My God. They mean it, don't they? What do we do, Harry?"

Ahead, Deacon could see the tarmac of the main road and his parked jeep. Clemmie now ran stumbling at his side down the hill, her camera bag clutched to her stomach and her face pale. Deacon realised that they were not going to make it to the jeep unless he stopped, turned around and shot the pursuers to a stop. At least Clemmie would get away. He checked his gun as he ran and he was about to stop and turn when he saw Corporal Lockett loom up from the ground before him. A moment later, the shapes of Kenny, Ambrose and Shaw joined him. The troopers had rifles shouldered.

"Above their heads, lads. On the order. Fire!" said Lockett.

The rifles cracked above Deacon's head. He turned to see the crowd duck and stop as one.

"And another to tickle the Queen, lads. Fire!"

The crowds scattered back up the hill and into the alley crevices.

"Tidy them away, lads," said Lockett.

Shaw, Kenny and Ambrose walked up into the alley with their rifles hipped. Other troops were coming down the hill and the road was suddenly busy with trucks and machine-gun mounted jeeps. The Arab crowds had disappeared as if they had never been.

Clemmie stood panting with her hands on her knees by the jeep.

"I think I'm going to be sick." she gasped. She coughed and panted for a moment and then slowly straightened herself. Her face was blushed with exertion, her lips pale with fright. She wiped her forearm across her mouth and laughed weakly. "No I'm not. Anyone got a cigarette?"

Lockett offered her one from his pack and flicked one for Deacon too. Deacon holstered his gun. Lockett lit him up. Deacon was conscious of his hands shaking and of a rivulet of sweat snaking cold down his spine. He took a long pull on the cigarette.

"Aren't you supposed to be off dying somewhere, corporal?" he said.

Lockett grinned. "I'm dying everywhere, sir. So I though it might as well be here."

"How did you know where to find us?"

"I got back a couple of hours ago. Lads saw the smoke. So we came to investigate. Saw your jeep parked up and empty. So I got the lads to take a stroll to find you."

"Are you quite recovered, corporal?" said Clemmie. "Did they discharge you?"

"I sort of discharged myself, miss. I'm fit enough not to take a bed."

Clemmie watched him for a moment.

"If you are sure. I can't say we are not thankful. You arrived like the cavalry."

Clemmie placed her camera bag on the jeep bonnet and busied herself in changing the films in her two cameras.

Deacon scanned the streets and alleyways for signs of trouble and found none. Troops from the Lancashires were being deployed to all points by a balding and barking major. Deacon turned to find Lockett watching him. His face was calm, his cheeks were pinked and he stood unusually still. He looked tired and drawn but content. Deacon felt it too.

"I could die for a coffee," said Clemmie and swung her bag into the jeep.

They drove in silence until Lockett pulled the jeep to a stop outside the lion-plinthed gates of Queen Victoria Park. Lockett turned off the engine and waited for Deacon and Clemmie to disembark.

"You must at least let me buy you coffee, corporal." said Clemmie. "I am sure Harry won't mind. It's not everyday that one's life is saved."

Lockett sought Deacon's eye. Deacon nodded.

"Of course, Miss Ross," said Lockett. He got out of the jeep. "But really, there is no need for reward."

"Oh do call me Clemmie, corporal. I think you've earned that."

Deacon saw Lockett hesitate for a briefest moment before he smiled.

"Thank you for the honour, Miss Ross," said Lockett, "but I don't think that would be right. It would be, well, uncomfortable. You are the Brigadier's daughter. And I am a corporal."

Clemmie watched Lockett for a moment. "Oh, I think you're more than that," she said. "But I wouldn't want you to be uncomfortable."

Deacon tugged his jacket smooth. "It's Aden, Clemmie," he said. "We are all uncomfortable. Shall we get some coffee?"

Deacon sat at a table in the Queen Victoria Park coffee shop watching the sheets of baize-green lawn turn to glistening tar under the gathering night. Yellow-sparked shrubs loomed from the nearby flower-beds. Out beyond the wrought-iron park gates, Deacon could see trucks and jeeps busying along the main road, their blazed headlights fencing with the dusk.

The park was almost empty. A steel-spined colonel was trotting his horse up and down a distant sanded lane and a young uniformed couple, lost in each other, ambled hand-in-hand along one of the park's shadowed pathways.

The wooden pavilion coffee shop was bright with the lights of Indian lanterns that hung from the awning and cast small pools of blue light onto the surrounding tables. A REME major with a plaster cast on his foot sat engrossed in his paper at one table. Two white-capped and grey-cloaked nurses chatted with bowed heads and low whispers at another. The rest of the tables were empty. A white-jacketed waiter brought coffees and a doilied plate of Jacob's assortments.

"Biscuits complimentary," said the waiter. "Five and six please, sir."

Deacon paid before Clemmie had found the bottom of her bag.

"Well, I'll pay for the biscuits," she said, smiling, and bit into an orange cream.

Deacon cradled the hot coffee mug in his palms and watched the park. The colonel's horse ran a final short canter, the sand spitting from its hooves. Then horse and rider trotted primly out of the park and clattered away down the tarmac road. The ambling couple had stopped beneath the stone bowl fountains and stood facing each other, their gazes locked. Deacon knew it was a parting. He averted his stare to the dance of lights waltzing across the distant bay.

Clemmie offered cigarettes from her pack. Deacon took one but Lockett hesitated.

"It's not a name, corporal," said Clemmie. "Only a cigarette. You can take that, surely?"

Lockett stood up and a lighter flame appeared in his palm. He lit Clemmie and Deacon's cigarettes and then clicked the flame dead. He placed his cigarette between his lips and clicked his palm alight again. He sat down. Deacon sipped his coffee and smiled to himself. Even in the Victoria Park, Lockett wouldn't give light to a third soldier in the trench. That was the light with your name on it.

Clemmie span the cigarette pack idly in her hand. "Are you going to have to do an official report about this afternoon, Harry?" she said. "I mean the bombed house. And our being caught up in the riot."

"Would you prefer to keep it secret?" asked Deacon.

"Well no, of course. Not if it's important. Wouldn't ask you to fib or anything like that. But I would rather Daddy didn't get to hear about me being out and about in it. Thinks it's dangerous. Unladylike. He's forbidden me to take my camera out into Aden. He would explode if he knew."

"He is rightly concerned for your safety," said Deacon.

"It's a camera, not a gun, Harry."

"Not here, it's not. In Aden, only the spies have cameras. And they take pictures of faces and bombed houses. People here are suspicious of cameras. They can get angry. Like this afternoon. The Brigadier has a point. A fatherly one."

"Do you know he even tries to hide my cameras?" said Clemmie. She lit another cigarette and summoned the waiter. "Three more coffees, please. But for a Brigadier, he's a poor thief. He hides them in really the most obvious places. Absolutely no imagination."

"A luxury of rank," said Deacon.

Lockett spluttered in his coffee. To Deacon, it was like hearing a returned friend.

"And I can't get my films processed anywhere," said Clemmie. "Only one shop here in Aden and they refused point-blank to serve me. I'm sure Daddy told them not to. Will you do a report?"

Deacon wasn't sure. He thought a while in silence.

"It was a Lancs show, sir," said Lockett. He sugared his coffee and stirred it slowly. "They were the unit on the scene. They get the paperwork."

"Yes," said Deacon. "True. But there is still our truck. You and the men must have signed it out. We can't say we weren't there. And the Lancs major must have seen Miss Ross. And her cameras."

A silence sank over them.

"Looks like I'm up for one of Daddy's rants then. And another week grounded," said Clemmie.

"I'm afraid I forgot to sign out the truck, sir," said Lockett. He took a biscuit. He smiled. "I was in a bit of a hurry, like. Sorry about that. Won't happen again, sir. I'll be sure and fill in the transport chit when I get back. Troop out for a chip run. That should do it. The men did chip-up on the way back, sir, so no lie. You know the men won't talk, sir. Half-crown for a wet and they will swear up to Cairo."

Deacon laughed. He fished in his pocket and passed Lockett a half-crown.

"What about Doyle and Ably?" said Deacon.

"They'll ride along, sir," said Lockett. "The men will see to that. And I wouldn't worry about that Lancs major. He was sweating out the gin too hard to have noticed much of anything, let alone remember it. He won't report it. And I know his staff sergeant, anyway. Won't be any mentions, sir."

Clemmie looked from Lockett to Deacon.

"So no report?" said Clemmie.

"No," said Deacon. "Not from me."

Clemmie reached forward and took Deacon's hand. And also Lockett's. Then she released them and sat back.

"You are real friends. Thank you. And I promise to be more careful with my camera in future. This afternoon was quite a shock. How can anyone get so angry about a camera? It is only showing what is there. What is real."

"But nothing is real in Aden, Miss Ross," said Lockett. "So any picture of it is a lie to someone. Wars and cameras don't mix very well."

"Well, they should," said Clemmie.

"They already are," said Deacon. "I saw a three camera platoon loading up with the Yank infantry troops on television the other night. Vietnam will be your picture war, Clemmie. Jungle and napalm are so photogenic. In colour, too. But we don't do cameras here in Aden. Ours is an old-fashioned war."

"The more people who see a real war, the better," said Clemmie. She stirred her coffee vigorously, her eyes glowed as her passion rose. "It's so important, don't you see? To show people what really goes on. What war means. Its awful effects on people. Their lives. Our lives. On children. In the hospitals.

On the streets. That is the only way to stop it happening again. The camera doesn't lie. People must face up to how awful war really is." She sat back. "But you are soldiers. You would not understand. You have stopped seeing it because it's around you every day. You are immune."

Deacon gazed at Clemmie. She was now tilted forward in her seat, stabbing her half-finished cigarette out in the coffee saucer. Deacon sat back and lit himself a cigarette. He tossed the packet across to Lockett.

"All cameras lie, Clemmie," said Deacon. "That is what they were invented for. To capture the lie. Pictures of fairies at the bottom of the garden. Which lie just depends on where you point the lens. And when you click. All pictures of war are propaganda. For one side or another."

Deacon was aware of Lockett watching him from over the rim of his palmed coffee cup. His eyes were round and he seemed to be sipping Deacon's words.

"I knew you couldn't understand," said Clemmie, "That's just an excuse for doing nothing at all."

"No," said Deacon. "It's the excuse for having a care about who you are shooting, and with what. And a care about yourself too."

"I have care enough, that's why I must take my pictures. Are you saying I am being selfish?"

"No. I don't think you are. I think you are an adventurer. An explorer. But an untrained one."

"I am not a soldier, Harry," said Clemmie.

"But out here everyone is a soldier, Clemmie. Even you."

"I can look after myself."

"Today would indicate otherwise," said Deacon.

They were silent for a while.

"It's just being a bit smarter, Clemmie, that's all," said Deacon. "Learning some of the tricks to live a little longer. Simple things. Shoes that you can run in. Street maps in your bag. Whistle in your pocket. Modestly dressed. Coins to barter or throw. Cameras kept hidden."

Clemmie watched the park for a while.

"I was a bit naïve, wasn't I?" she said.

"Enthusiastically so," said Deacon. He smiled at Clemmie. "But what hasn't killed, teaches. Right?"

Clemmie laughed. "Okay, Prof," she said. "I promise more care with my camera. But no-one is going to stop me taking my photographs. I'll just have to be more discreet."

They sat in silence for a while. It was Lockett who eventually spoke.

"I can probably get your films processed, Miss Ross," he said. "If you wanted. Half-crown a film."

Clemmie sat forward eagerly. "Really? Yes. Of course. Wonderful. Thank you, corporal. But where?"

"Professional, I assure you," said Lockett. "Same as the shops. Better even."

"Who?" said Deacon. "Would I be right in guessing Army, corporal?"

"Rather not say, sir. Best that way. Take a few days."

Clemmie was rummaging in her bag. She pulled out a clutch of films and piled them on the table before her like casino chips. From her purse, she found two pound notes and she placed them on the hillock of films. She pushed the lot across the table to Lockett.

"You are a true friend, corporal. Harry, rather embarrassing. I'm afraid that was the last of my money. Can you settle the bill for the coffees?"

TEN

Deacon was woken by Lockett's gentle cough.

"Time to get up, sir."

Deacon rose on his elbows and through sleep-dulled eyes saw an empty room and his pressed uniform swinging from its hook on the back of the door. He showered and shaved and listened to Lockett and Chi at their lessons through the door while he dressed. They were discussing Fagin. Chi liked the Dickens stories because they had the best devils. And in the Artful Dodger, a true Chi hero. But the concept of London was proving difficult.

"It is a very big city," said Lockett. "In this story it is biggest city in the whole world. Many people. But not many policemen. A dangerous and exciting city. Lots and lots of houses and streets and horse-drawn carriages and drinking places and shops."

"Sell tea?"

"Some."

"Hot tea?"

"Not as hot as yours, Chi."

Deacon waited in his room until Chi had left and Lockett had set the breakfast.

"Morning, corporal."

"Sir. Toast and jam this morning. Busy morning, sir?"

Deacon started on the toast and gulped a mouthful of warm, thick tea.

"Meeting with Captain Villiers at ten hundred. Finished by lunch."

"It's Major Villiers, sir."

"Yes, of course. God, how did you know, corporal? Villiers can only have sewn his crown up last evening."

"NAAFI pigeons, sir. Fastest of the lot, they are. Afraid I've got a driver training call, sir. Three hours this afternoon."

Lockett slid a form and uncapped pen across the table. Deacon glanced at the paper and signed it.

"What sort of training?"

"Advanced, sir," said Lockett.

Lockett took the form and folded it into his jacket pocket. "I enjoyed my coffee last night, sir. Miss Ross is interesting company."

"Yes. Not many dull moments with Clemmie, are there?"

"Do you really think all pictures of war lie, sir?"

Deacon looked up from his toast. Lockett had his back to him, busy mixing the gin and orange. Deacon poured himself more tea from the billy-can.

"Photographs certainly do," he said.

He saw Lockett nodding slowly.

"But," added Deacon, "I think perhaps art is quite another matter."

He saw a blush light momentarily at Lockett's collar. Lockett finished his mixing and began collecting the plates and jam pots from the table. He looked up and held Deacon's gaze. He smiled.

"Yes sir. Quite. Will you be requiring the jeep?"

A taciturn and stone-faced Corporal Golightly met Deacon in the foyer of the Inkerman Club and led him up the two flights of carpeted stairs to the Private Rooms. Two guards stepped aside and Golightly tapped on the door. He opened it and nodded Deacon in. The door clunked shut behind him like a rifle bolt locking.

Major Villiers was seated in a large leather armchair in a circle of large leather armchairs. He was in discussion with a Lieutenant Colonel of Commando and a Naval Commodore. Through the tall, ceiling-high windows the sun threw a checkerboard cloth over the floor. Books lined a far wall. A painting of Rorke's Drift hung over the mock fireplace. Scarlet-uniformed soldiers with spear-long bayonets standing island proud among a sea of Zulu corpses.

A dozen chairs ringed the room and a ripple of conversations and hushed laughter bubbled gently. Deacon saw majors and captains compassed about the circle. Whisky bottles and tumblers crowded the tables and cigar smoke drifted the room like Flanders gas.

Deacon took the only unoccupied chair. An orderly appeared at his side and handed him a tumbler of whisky from a small silver tray. Deacon saw Lieutenant Peterson seated across from him. Peterson was talking with a kilted major, the same explosives man he had dropped on the moonlit beach.

Corporal Golightly came into the room as a distant clock chimed ten. He locked the door behind him and nodded to Major Villiers.

"Right, gentlemen," said Villiers.

The room immediately hushed. Villiers reached down beside his chair and tossed a silver coin onto the rug in the centre of the circle.

"PacVac mine," he said. "Blow your leg off if you stepped on it." He gave the circle of chairs a moment for imagining. "This one's disarmed, of course."

He waited for the room's laugh to settle. Then Villiers reached behind his chair and gently lobbed a four-inch mortar shell onto the rug. It landed with a thud that Deacon could feel reverberate up through his boots.

"81mil mortar bomb.Also disarmed," said Villiers.

The laughter stuttered and then died.

"And if I had a disarmed grenade I'd chuck that in the pot as well," said Villiers. "But this will have to suffice." He pulled an orange from his pocket and dropped it on the rug.

"Mines, mortars and grenades, gentleman. Damn Adoo are playing a game and it isn't cricket. And they are doing it on our doorstep. It has got to stop. We must find their mine factories. We have to stop these damn mortar attacks. And we have to kill them before they can throw another grenade. This is an open session. Mines, mortars and grenades. Right now these are the priority. We are looking for answers. Any ideas, gentlemen?"

Deacon was surprised by the sudden animation in the chair circle. Everyone seemed to have something to say. Villiers calmed the rush with raised palms and began to weave some order into the forum discussion while tumblers were emptied and more cigars were lit. Deacon sat back and sipped his whisky and listened to the theories and suggestions and hypotheses that came from all points of the leather compass.

The discussions went on for some time. An agreement was eventually reached that the only way to tackle the PacVac mines was to spring surprise night time sweeps into the Crater district, sector by sector. The only hope was to find the mine warehouses. It was a needle in a desert's hope, but it was the only way. Grenade attack solutions were less pragmatic but it was agreed that a new sniper unit would be set up on the lower mountain slopes and take out any Adoo that appeared on the rooftops of Aden. Searchlights would keep the roof top sweep going through the night. The seven round mortar problem, however, remained unresolved.

"Pretty sure the Adoo rebels are Russian trained and armed," said the kilted major. "Ivan always trains his mortar troops in the seven-spray pattern. And we know Adoo squads have been recent customers of the Reds training. So bound to copy 'em. Use their weapons. So Russian mortar we reckon. But we've never found a damn launcher. They move them about. Do they move them in parts and assemble them, fire them, dis-assemble them and take the bits away? How do they fire them? We just don't know for sure."

"Damn mortar is still a weight even if it is in bits," said Villiers. "A patrol would have seen something by now. A mortar base plate couldn't be easily carried."

"Camel?" suggested someone.

"We check them," said the kilted major. "And everything else that walks, wheels or floats. The Adoo isn't going to be stupid enough to chance running into one of our patrols with a mortar base plate hidden up his britches."

"Well they are doing it somehow, Tosh," said Villiers. "And we have got to find out how. And fast. Our people are relying on us."

The room became silent. Villiers leaned back in his chair and looked towards Deacon.

"Any thoughts on our mortar problem, Harry? You've been unusually quiet this morning. Not like you. Cast any light on how the Adoo fire seven bombs into our city and under our very noses and without us ever seeing them?"

Deacon was aware of a roomful of faces turning to look at him. He felt his collar burn and his head ice for a moment. He carefully placed his tumbler on the floor and tried to order his thoughts.

"Perhaps they do it at night," he said.

There was a moment of silence. Then a couple of laughs were stifled somewhere and Deacon heard the soft farting sound of several humid backsides shifting in leather and an amused murmur started to simmer about him.

"Night?" said Major Macintosh. He knuckled his kilted thigh and laughed. "The mortars go off in the day, laddie!" he said.

"Exactly," said Deacon.

More laughs rippled.

"That is an interesting idea, Lieutenant Deacon."

A thin faced captain leaned forward in his chair and studied Deacon. He was Captain Banks. Like Deacon, he had not spoken in the meeting until now. He had watched proceedings from the deep of his armchair, his gaze as keen as a bird's. Deacon knew him to be attached to Army Intelligence. The room seemed to quieten on the captain's interest.

"Care to elaborate?" said Captain Banks.

"They place the mortars at night. It is a possibility, sir."

"But the damn things are fired all through the day, laddie!" said Major Macintosh. "In the daytime. Not at night!"

"Well, lieutenant?" said Captain Banks.

"The very fact that they aren't firing them at night seems odd, don't you think?" said Deacon. "Night or day makes no difference to a mortar bomb. It still blows up, it still kills. Why aren't they firing them at night? We are sleeping ducks then. Under cover of dark there is much less risk of discovery than day-time firing. And with respect, Major Macintosh, they are not firing all through the day. The mortars only fire between oh-ten-thirty hours and twelve-hundred hours. Never in the afternoons."

Deacon was aware of a heavy silence pressing him into his chair.

Captain Banks smiled at him. "And how do you know this, lieutenant?" he said.

Deacon pulled the notebook from his jacket pocket. "I've kept a noted record of every mortar attack for the last three months, sir. Eleven in all. And every one explodes within the same hour and a half."

Captain Banks's pen drummed lightly in his hand. "That is interesting. We had not seen that. Yes, that is interesting. May I? I shall, of course, return it."

Captain Banks began to leaf through the note book.

Villiers poured whisky into his tumbler and passed the decanter on.

"So, come to any conclusions, Harry?" he said.

Deacon was aware of the orderly bending down beside him and pouring more drink into his glass on the floor. Deacon picked up the glass and took a quick pull. The whisky burned in his throat.

"They transport the mortar at night. No need for assembly in the dark. Who is going to see them? They position it ready somewhere where it stays hidden during the day. The mortars are set off by a timing device. Car battery, clock, candle and rope. I don't know. But a timing trigger that is simple and dependable and set to go off during the day. Always late morning. No one need be around to actually set it off. Bombs already loaded and primed. Just needs that reliable timing trigger. The mortar launchers are retrieved the next night from wherever they've been hidden."

"But where could they hide a seven spray-mortar launcher in broad daylight in the Aden streets without us knowing about it?" said Captain Banks.

Deacon drank the last of his tumbler and watched the glass sparkle in his hand for a moment. He turned to Captain Banks and smiled.

"I'm afraid all I can think of," said Deacon, "is that it must be somewhere where we haven't looked yet."

Deacon was aware of a stillness in the room. It seemed to last a long time.

"Thank you, gentlemen," said Villiers. "A good morning's discussion. The Vikings are now on the march."

The meeting broke up. Deacon headed for the door but was waylaid by Corporal Golightly, who stepped into his path.

"We'll wait for the others, shall we, sir?" he said.

Deacon stepped back and let the other officers pass. They crowded out of the door, several of them glancing at Deacon as they left. Peterson grinned at him as he passed by.

"A pirate all along," he said. "Hope it's not the plank."

Deacon saw Villiers and a colonel talking with Captain Banks by one of the tall windows. They seemed to be talking about him. As the last of the officers left, Corporal Golightly closed the door and turned to Deacon.

"There is a show tonight and you are in it. I take it you have no objections sir?"

Deacon, unable to find sensible words, shook his head.

"Good," said Corporal Golightly. "Small operation. A seven team. Truck will pick you up from your billet at twenty-two hundred hours. One hour briefing. Quick show and back by oh-two hundred latest."

"Fine," said Deacon. He didn't feel it.

"Night sortie drill. But we march on rubbers and coon-up. Work yourself a couple of hours sleep this afternoon, it might be a long night. Any questions?"

Deacon could think of none. There were too many to choose from.

A moment later he was outside on the carpeted landing listening to the rifle-bolt clunking home in the door behind him.

*

Deacon took a quick lunch at the NAAFI, checked the bulletin boards in the staff office and then drove through the dusty haze of Aden to checkpoint seven. He spent the afternoon being baked by the sun and grilled by the tarmac road while his men checked dockets and goods with surly drivers. The traffic on the road was heavy and the barrier was kept busy. The trucks were moving stores and guns in earnest and the men knew that kind of heavy traffic only meant trouble. They were more curmudgeonly than usual and, Deacon thought, also looking a little shifty. He ignored his curiosity and let it ride. Experience had taught him that whatever his men were hiding, it would soon make itself known. And it was too hot a day to go hunting for it.

Lockett returned from his driver training shortly after fifteen-hundred hours. Ambrose saw him approaching along the Dock Road.

"Corp's back!" he said. The troop gathered outside the hut and watched the truck advancing up the road at speed. Deacon rose from his chair in the shade and joined his men at the roadside.

"Three foot for a Tusker," said Ambrose. He removed the roll-up from his mouth and piffed a tobacco crumb from his lip.

"One-and- a-half feet," said Kenny.

"Four," said Shaw. "He won't risk it with Harry here."

The truck roared towards them. Less than a hundred yards from the checkpoint the truck turned suddenly and smoothly across the road and onto the dust strip leading up to the hut. The truck was moving fast in front of a cloud of dust and spitting road chips. Lockett hit the brakes forty yards out and controlled the crunching skid to a stop within inches of the concrete bollards.

Lockett jumped down from the cab amid a swirl of dust balloons, grinned at the men and went to inspect the front of the truck. "Anyone have nine-inches?" he said.

Ambrose re-lipped his roll-up.

"Shit," said Shaw.

"Call the men in line, Ambrose," said Deacon. He wandered over to Lockett by the truck.

"Training go okay?" said Deacon.

"Fine, sir. We did emergency braking."

"That was lucky. Do you know how much a four-ton army truck costs, corporal?"

"Are you buying or selling, sir?"

"Stop showing off with the army's expensive toys, corporal. It sets a bad example for the men."

"Sorry, sir."

"Your punishment is looking after the troop for the rest of the day. I'm on a duty tonight so I am getting my head down for a couple of hours. Truck the men back at sixteen-thirty hours when you are relieved."

"Viking duty, sir?"

Deacon looked at Lockett. "Line up the men, corporal."

The men were lined up in front of the hut. Deacon walked

across and stood before them. Lockett took his place at his side.

"Let's have them tidy, corporal," said Deacon.

"Ten-shun!" said Lockett.

The line straightened their backs, stamped their boots and stared ahead. Deacon looked along the line. He was still aware of a shiftiness behind the blank stares. He saw the small figure of Ably at the end of the line. One side of his face was red and grazed and his lip and left eye were swollen. He was staring ahead, immobile. Beside him Doyle was also standing to attention. A scar of dried blood stained under his reddened and swollen nose.

"What happened to you two?" asked Deacon.He could sense the line tensing.

"Walked into the hut door, sir," said Ably. "Wasn't looking, like."

Deacon turned to Doyle.

"And you?"

"Tripped over a rock, sir. Fell on my face. Very clumsy."

Deacon looked along the line. The faces stared ahead at nothing. "What happened here?"

The men were silent and stiff.

"I mean it, gentlemen. Don't make me do something you will regret. What happened?"

Lockett coughed lightly at his side and spoke softly. "Might I have a word, sir?"

They moved away and stood by the truck. Lockett offered his cigarettes and then lit them.

"Well, corporal?" said Deacon.

"If you were asked for a couple of our men to second to another unit, who would you send, sir?" said Lockett.

Deacon thought about it. But not for long. "Gibson and Lee, probably. Why?"

"Because Ably and Doyle is another unit's Gibson and Lee, sir. That's why we got them. Seconded troopers are always trouble. In one shape or another. Drunks. Shirkers. Weeds. Take your pick. Ably and Doyle are magpies, sir. Lift anything that isn't nailed down. That's why they were kicked our way. Lads found them going through Ambrose's locker sir. They sort of persuaded them not to do it again. Soldier justice, sir. Nothing more than that."

"I can't have bad blood in the troop, corporal."

"You won't, sir. All over and done with. Ably and Doyle won't try it again. They may be magpies, but they won't be stupid enough to piss in their own nest again. They are OK lads really, sir. Just need a little guidance."

"We are not running a reform school, corporal."

Lockett looked up at Deacon, his eyes wide and round in surprise.

"Well, that is certainly news to me, sir."

Deacon laughed. It felt good to have his shadow back.

*

The six-wheeled Saracen Armoured Personnel Carrier came to a stop at the roadside outside Deacon's billet and rumbled at the kerb. It was just after twenty-two hundred hours and the night was bright with stars. A warm diesel breeze rolled in from the bay and the blackness purred with distant helicopters.

Deacon shouldered his pouch, closed his billet door and climbed into the back of the Saracen truck.

"Ah! The Pirate King!" said Peterson. He made room on the bench seat. "Thought we might be seeing you."

Deacon took his seat in the fetid, sweaty dimness of the Saracen's troop pod. It smelled of diesel fumes and deodorant. The back door was clanged shut and the gloom was pricked by the soft blue glow of two bulwark lights. The Saracen revved hard and lurched forward. The sound of the grinding gears screamed inside the riveted steel plates of the sealed box.

"Carter and McFadden," said Peterson. He shouted above the noise and nodded towards two soldiers sitting on the opposite bench. "They are the watch boys on this one."

Corporal McFadden and Sergeant Carter offered a weary hand of greeting.

"And Sergeant Myers and Golightly are up front. Quite a gang, aren't we?" said Peterson.

They drove to a remote, guarded hut on the north side of Kormaksar airfield where Major Villiers and a couple of staff officers gathered them around a briefing table of upturned motor oil crates. A street map of the Crater sector had been spread out over it. Villiers greeted his Vikings with a brisk nod. The guards were re-posted and Corporal Golightly secured the hut door. Villiers was dressed in a dark overall and wore a black woollen hat. A shaded light-bulb on a long ceiling flex hovered above the map. Villiers lit a small cigar and looked at the faces around the table.

"Going to be a simple sortie," he said. He stabbed a finger at the map. "We will ride up to the outskirts of Crater and park up in a dark alley. A raid party of me, Deacon, Myers, Peterson and Golightly will make their way to a house in the back streets that Intelligence has confirmed as a front for an NLF operational centre. Myers and Peterson will break into the house and destroy the offices and equipment. Peterson will graffiti the walls with pro FLOSY slogans and drop some leaflets. Deacon and I will be the guard. Golightly will ride piquet."

Villiers slapped a palm hard down on the map table. He smiled at the faces about him. "We blow the house and make it back to the Saracen where Carter and McFadden will be waiting. Then all get the hell out of it back to the bar and enjoy a pint and the prospect of fisticuffs and mayhem erupting between the FLOSY and NLF Adoos."

Villers let his plan sink in. "Vikings are fighting behind the lines, gentlemen. And under them." He said, "This is a new war.

It needs every weapon we've got. And Vikings were always good for a bit of skullduggery, eh?"

The Vikings laughed.

They studied the map and rehearsed the signals. They blacked each other up. Villiers turned to Deacon and wiped a smear of tarred fingers across his forehead. Then he flicked his fingers down Deacon's cheek and across his chin.

"Can't go to the party improperly dressed, Harry," he said and grinned.

Deacon felt his face flush as Villiers' soiled, strong fingers smeared across his cheeks and nose. "Now do me, Harry."

Villiers watched him steadily through clear blue eyes as Deacon rubbed tentative strokes of blacking onto his face. Deacon felt the amusement behind Villiers stare, as if a dare had been thrown. Deacon finished with a flourish and then helped Peterson with his camouflage.

"Very Hiawatha," said Peterson.

An over-the-top spirit fired among them and Deacon could feel the adrenalin burning against his artery walls. He laughed to hide the heat of his fear. Only Golightly remained apart. He stood in the corner of the room in a dark overall and black balaclava hat. A 9mm Browning, two grenades and a couple of knife sheaths hung from his belt. He coughed lightly. Villiers looked at him, then at his watch and nodded.

"Let's get this done, gentlemen," he said.

Deacon stumbled from the comforting, humid womb of the Saracen and stepped down into the still blackness of the Crater streets. He squatted by the truck with the others searching the streets for movement or noise. Deacon could hear his heart pumping hard and his breath came shallow and parched from his burning lungs. The streets were quiet and empty and, as his eyes became accustomed to the dark, the shapes of houses and roofs began to silhouette under the starlight. The raiding squad moved off with Villiers at their head. They ran at a crouch along the dark lanes and alleyways, stopping occasionally to recce and to check the map under a pencil-thin torch light. By the time they reached the jump-off rendezvous-point Deacon was sweating hard. They squatted in a huddled group under a low archway and scanned up the street towards the NLF house. It looked no different from all the other ramshackle houses that jostled along the street. A small, squat, two-storey building with shuttered windows and drab, patched stonework. But they could also see that a blade of light still shone from under its front door. It was the only light in the street.

"They are working late tonight," whispered Villiers. He grinned, his black-smeared face catching starlight like a Swanee minstrel. "They will be gone soon. Take up your positions. We go in at the stroke of midnight. Meet back here, okay?"

"Where's Golightly?" said Deacon. The corporal seemed to have vanished.

"Don't worry about him, Harry. He's about. Let's go."

Myers and Peterson moved ahead. They were both carrying large pouches, one full of explosives, the other clunking with paint canisters. Peterson grinned at Deacon from a blackened face.

"Avast, me hearties!" he whispered and ran off after Myers.

Villiers and Deacon made their way up the street and crouched in the dark against a low wall from where they could see the front of the house and have firing sight up and down the street. Myers and Peterson hid in an alleyway opposite the house. They crouched and waited.

Several minutes later the blade of light under the door switched off and an Arab came out of the front door of the house. He locked the door, rattled it and then disappeared down the street. After more long minutes of panted waiting and the constant checking of his watch dial, the luminescent green hands finally came together on midnight. Deacon saw the shadows of Myers and Peterson emerge onto the street before the house. Myers went to the door and jemmied it open. There was a sharp wail of splintered wood and Myers and Peterson were inside.

The door closed to black. From his crouch by the wall Deacon could see the dance of torchlight flicker at the shutter's cracks as Myers and Peterson moved about inside.

Deacon cradled the Sterling machine gun across his thighs and tried not to see shadows moving in the street about him. His breathing was tight and strained and his legs were beginning to turn numb as he braced himself against the hard shelter of the wall. Villiers was pressed beside him, his shoulder solid and still as he watched his side of the street. Inside the house, the torchlight danced on.

"Taking Clemmie out," said Villiers. His voice was whispered but had no trace of anxiety. "Got the Old Man's nod. Thought I'd take her to the Inkerman for a spot of lobster and peach melba. Do you think she will like that?"

Deacon turned to look at Villiers. He was squatting back against the wall as if relaxing on a country walk. He grinned at Deacon.

"Have to make the right first impression, you see? Do you think the Inkerman will suit Clemmie?"

Deacon could not concentrate on what Villiers was saying. He wondered if he had heard it at all. He sat silent, pressing his back to the wall and wishing the dancing torchlight would stop.

"Only I wondered if it was really Clemmie," said Villiers. "Her sort of thing. I mean, she likes poetry and I have to confess that I'm not really a poetry man." He grinned wider. "I'm afraid I cribbed the Rimbaud to impress her. Rather convincing, wasn't I?" He laughed. "But not sure I know what she will find to her taste. For going out, I mean. Aden is rather a small place. You seem to know about these things, Harry. Poetry and women and all. Where do you suggest I take her? Will the Inkerman do?"

Deacon laughed softly. He couldn't quite believe any of this conversation or his current situation and wondered if he was actually in a dream. The dark, oppressive stillness seemed very familiar.

"I suspect something a bit more romantic might be more in Clemmie's way," he said.

"Romantic? The Inkerman is very top drawer."

"But rather familiar for Clemmie, don't you think? It will be full of brass hats and officers' wives. Daddy's circle. People she sees and lunches with every day. Top drawer maybe, but not exactly romantic. Not very special."

"So what do you suggest?"

Deacon tried to think. To imagine Villiers on a date. "A moonlit table for two on the beach perhaps. A long walk by the shore."

"Think that will do it?"

"Better chance than the Inkerman, I would think," said Deacon.

Deacon was aware of a discomfiture aching his body and his mind. He could not quite believe the conversation he was having or the part he was playing in it. He felt a guilt ooze through him. He felt he was somehow selling Clemmie, and doing it cheaply.

Villiers thrust an arm across him and pressed a finger to his lip for silence. Deacon followed his gaze up the night street and saw an Arab shuffling towards them. The Arab was old and slightly bowed but was moving along the street quickly. Villiers and Deacon pressed themselves back into the shadows.

They could hear the Arab muttering to himself and as he shuffled nearer. As he passed the house he turned, stopped and peered at the house. He looked up and down the street and then edged forward to investigate the light. Deacon un-clasped his holster and rested a hand on his pistol. Villiers reached across him and placed his hand on his shoulder to prevent him drawing his gun. He looked at Deacon and winked.

Deacon saw a shadow emerge into the street behind the Arab. He recognised the silhouette of Golightly. The shadow crept silently up behind the Arab, who was now peering in through one of the windows. Deacon saw Golightly's dark shape merge silently with the stooped old man. There was a glint of metal and a short, wistful sigh and the Arab collapsed into the shadow's arms. Golightly laid the Arab gently in the street and crouched beside the body.

Deacon tried to convince himself he hadn't seen it. He felt a shiver of bile rippling his guts. A shock of murder icing his mind.

Villers continued to watch the street beside him, seemingly unconcerned.

The door of the house opened and Myers and Peterson emerged. They glanced quickly at Golightly and ran on back to Villiers and Deacon at the wall.

"Seven minute fuse," said Myers.

"And the NLF are all women and goat lovers," said Peterson grinning. "What a wonderful thing a Cambridge education is."

"Well done boys," said Villiers. "Get yourselves back to the archway. Harry, go help Golightly. We've got five minutes."

Corporal Golightly was beckoning from beside the dead Arab. Deacon ran to him.

"Let's put the bugger in the house," said Golightly. He was wiping his knife on the Arab's headcloth. The balaclava hat was pulled down over his face and Deacon could only see him through the eye holes and the gap for his mouth. The mouth hole smiled like a macabre doll.

"Couldn't you have just clubbed him, corporal?" said Deacon.

Golightly's grin switched off. "You telling me my fucking job, sir?" he said. "Get his feet and keep that gob of yours shut. Sir."

They lifted the Arab and hustled him in through the doorway of the house. When Deacon made it back to the wall he was sheeted in sweat. The three of them made their way back to the archway where Myers and Peterson were waiting. They crowded in the shadows and watched the house from the safety of distance. After several minutes they saw a sheet of green and orange flame vomit from the windows of the house. It was instantly followed by a booming *woomph,* several sharp cracks and then billows of tumbling brown smoke. As the smoke lifted they could see the front of the house spewed into the street and fire was leaping from what remained of its upper floor. A distant pack of piard dogs barked in alarm from the mountains.

Villiers slapped a wall in pleasure. "That'll fix the buggers," he said. "The Vikings first strike, lads. And they'll be plenty more. Now let's get out of here and back to the truck before the streets are full of angry Adoo!"

They rode back in the Saracen in high spirits. Deacon was light-headed with relief and adrenaline and horror. He grinned along with the rest of the raiders while the tin box of the Saracen screamed at him. Villiers, his face tiger-streaked with sweat, pulled out a bottle of malt scotch from the trucks tool-box and they drank to the success of the raid. Deacon drank deep. By the time he was dropped back at his billet his head was spinning and his stomach was cramping. He stumbled out of the Saracen and down onto the road outside his billet in grateful relief.

"Great job, Harry!" said Villiers and the Saracen door was clanged shut.

It was oh-one thirty and the night breezes cooled his sweat to a chill.

Deacon waited until the Saracen had disappeared around the corner and then threw up in the road. After some moments of deep breathing, he opened the door to his billet and collapsed exhausted in his chair. He unhooked his collar and gazed around the room. Even in its swim he was aware of something different but he couldn't tell what it was. His bed was made and tucked down. His laundered uniform hung smart on the back of the door ready for the next day and fresh towels had been draped over the shower rail. A tumbler and bottle of scotch stood ready on his bedside table. Deacon poured himself a large one and drank it slowly. As he drank he glanced over at his window.

In the middle of the sill was a three-inch brass mortar shell with a small yellow chrysanthemum flowering from it.

ELEVEN

Major Ford-Forrest sat behind his desk reading the contents of the thin file with meticulous attention. He flicked his tongue on a rigid finger and turned the pages slowly, arranging them into a neat and exact pile at his elbow. A lance corporal with blue eyes and razor-cut hair stood stiffly to attention beside the desk with a leather file case tucked under his arm. Deacon sat in his chair and waited for the major to finish his papers.

The room smelled of lavender-oil and whisky. Out beyond the grassed quad and the parade-ground Deacon could hear the bells of St.Thomas's church tolling. He realised it must be Sunday morning. He had lost some days somewhere, or had muddled them up. The monotonous days at Checkpoint Seven had melted into each other and he couldn't quite believe that his Viking sortie into Crater was now four nights ago. For three days he had been checking trucks under a scorching sun and hearing the sound of the Old Arab's last wistful sigh, like a distant sea in a shell pressed tight to his ear. He felt his tiredness eating him.

Major Ford-Forrest unscrewed a large fountain pen and signed the last paper with a stuttered flourish. He handed the papers to the lance corporal.

"See that Stores gets a double duplicate and get the slackers to sign for it. Can't have a Waterloo Ball without bunting. Mrs. Jennings likes a good show of flags. And make sure it's all Union Jacks this time. None of that Frenchie Tri-colour arse-wipe like before. Diplomatic coves had a blue fit."

"Sir." said the lance corporal. He saluted, gave Deacon a wink and marched from the room.

Major Ford-Forrest took another file out of his drawer and placed it carefully on his desk.

"And what on earth are we going to do with you, Lieutenant Deacon, eh?"

It was what Old Bobby always said when starting his fortnightly duty meeting with Deacon. Deacon always remained silent. The major opened the file and read the pages with slow care. When he had finished he sat back and studied Deacon without interest.

"Well, it seems you haven't shot anyone this week. Or wrecked any of Her Majesty's transport. What's this request for a sergeant?"

"We don't have one, sir."

"Well, neither do I. So you'll just have to make do. There is a war on your know."

"I did hear a rumour, sir."

The major eyed him. "Got a truck?"

"Yes, sir."

"Then you are running stores for a few days. Khormaksar airfield depot. And make sure your men don't get light-fingered. Lost a crate of Rothmans and ten of single malt last week. Ranks nothing but a bunch of thieves and shirkers."

The telephone on the desk rang. The major answered it. There was a moment of listening.

"From the Brigadier's office?" said the major. He sat up in his chair. "But I am the Brigadier's office. What's that? Yes, he is. Are you sure? This is highly irregular."

The major looked at Deacon and handed him the phone.

"A call for you. From the Brigadier's office. I am not a public pay phone, Lieutenant Deacon. Make it short."

Deacon took the phone.

"Deacon." he said.

A male voice sounded distant down the line.

"Putting you through now, sir."

There was a clunk on the line as if the phone had been dropped. Then Clemmie's voice sounded.

"Is that you, Harry?"

"Clemmie?" said Deacon.

Major Ford-Forrest looked up suddenly from behind his desk.

"Clementine?" he said. "Is that Clementine Ross-Jennings? What are you doing talking with the Brigadier's daughter?"

Deacon cupped a hand over the mouthpiece.

"She has called me, sir."

"Thank God, I've caught you," said Clemmie. She sounded a little breathless. "I need you to rescue me again Harry. I'm desperate. There has been some mix-up over Sunday lunch. The Clancys have the flu, Colonel Richards has been called back to Cairo and we somehow seem to have got landed with the SAS Padre. We now have thirteen at the table and mother is getting into one of her states about it and insists on another chair. So I thought of you. Say you can come."

"When?" asked Deacon.

"As soon as you can. At the Villa. We dine at twelve-thirty on the dot. The Brigadier likes his Sunday roast punctual. We have drinks from eleven-thirty. I know it's short notice but you would be my shining knight if you could come. Say you will."

"Of course," said Deacon. "Delighted. I can probably make it by noon."

"Wonderful. You are a true soldier, Harry. Is Old Bobby huffing?"

"Rather."

"Put him on."

Deacon handed back the telephone to the major who took it with a snatch. He settled his face to a smile and spoke into the phone.

"Miss Clementine. An unexpected and delightful pleasure. The Brigadier is .... Yes. Of course. I understand. Assignment?

I haven't been… Well, of course happy to accede to the Brigadier's… Yes. I understand. Kind of you to keep me informed, Miss Clementine. I wonder if I might …"

The line had gone dead. The major cradled the phone and stared hard at Deacon for a while.

"I'm watching you, lieutenant," he said. "Like a bloody hawk. Some may find you interesting, but a barrow-boy with pips is still a barrow-boy. You would do well to remember it. If any stores go missing on your watch you'll be back in the gutter. Dismissed."

Deacon stood up and saluted. Major Ford-Forrest was already busy with another file.

Deacon returned to his billet. Lockett, as usual, was waiting for him. Deacon told him the new orders and duty rosters.

"Stores transport. That'll please the lads, sir." said Lockett. "A few days of sit and snooze."

"There's been some pilfering. So the watch is on. You might let the men know that, corporal. Help them resist any temptations."

"Don't worry sir. They won't get caught."

"That's not what…Well, just make sure they aren't. What are you and the men up to this afternoon?"

"We're all going down to the bay, sir. Some of the Navy boys getting a net out. So we thought we'd join them. Bit of relaxation after finishing Checkpoint Seven. Got plenty of beer sir. Care to join us?"

"Perhaps. I've been asked to attend the Brigadier's Sunday lunch. Any idea what I am supposed to wear?"

Lockett looked up. "The Brigadier's Sunday, sir? You?"

"You don't have to sound quite so surprised. I am only there to make up the numbers."

"Off-duty casual, sir. No uniforms at the Brigadier's Sunday, sir. Might I suggest the blue Oxfords and the linen jacket. You'll need a tie. Brigadier's idea of casual, isn't. I believe you are permitted to remove the tie after pudding. You have not attended one of the Brigadier's Sunday lunches before, sir?"

"No."

"Oh. Well, good luck then, sir. Shall I run a shower?"

Deacon parked his jeep among the staff cars, Jaguars and Rovers that gleamed in the Villa's driveway. He showed his ID to the guards and was met by a relieved Clemmie in the atrium. She was in a slim dress patterned with blue cornflowers and her hair was tied back. She greeted Deacon with a wide smile, locked an arm in his and escorted him down the passageway towards the dining hall.

"So glad you could come. And you look quite the thing. Clever of you not to wear your uniform. I quite forgot to let you know we are casual for lunch. One of the Brigadier's foibles. He thinks it makes him very modern. Now don't talk army or religion, quite taboo at lunch, but anything else is fair game. Oh, and daddy will have his rant at the Labour Government, he always does at Sunday lunch. I think it aids his digestion."

Clemmie guided him out onto the terraced lawns where drinks were being taken in the shade of acacia trees. The sun was glaring white and out beyond the wide-striped lawns Deacon could see the blue-glass of the bay stretching to a haze at the horizon and the mountains herding the sprawl of Aden into its ragged pen on the shores. Mrs Jennings came over to meet him and took his hand.

"Lieutenant Deacon. You are a saint to make us fourteen. I was quite at my wit's end. Now we can sit and enjoy our lunch. Jimbo, this is Lieutenant Deacon. He is a friend of Douglas."

The Brigadier offered Deacon a cursory nod and returned to his conversation with a lieutenant colonel, a tall man in a smart blue blazer. Clemmie quickly pointed out the rest of the guests, most of whom were playing croquet or swinging lazily on the canopied swing seats. A table bar of drinks had been set up in the shade of the trees and several white-jacketed orderlies were busying themselves with trays of glasses and canapés.

Deacon saw Major Villiers on the lawns. He stood with a mallet, demonstrating the correct croquet grip to a couple

who Deacon understood to be Mr. Fanshawe, an executive from the oil company, and his wife. Another dark-suited businessmen and his wife were relaxing with a balding but trim SAS Padre and a thin-faced colonel of Artillery in seats by the bar. Deacon saw Captain Banks standing with a tall, slender woman in a plain blue dress and Grecian sandals. Captain Banks nodded a greeting to Deacon and introduced him to his wife, Grace. Grace Banks looked at Deacon and smiled.

"I hear you have saved the day, Mr. Deacon." she said. "Clemmie said you would not let us down. We shall lunch after all!"

An orderly appeared at Deacon's shoulder.

"Drink, sir?" he asked.

Deacon quickly scanned the rest of the guests. He was relieved to see that both the Brigadier and Lieutenant-Colonel had beer glasses in their hands.

"Beer will be fine," said Deacon.

When his drink arrived, Captain Banks caught Deacon's eye and beckoned him over to the shade of the hedge. He offered Deacon a cigarette and they stood for a moment, watching the guests on the lawns. Clemmie was ushering her mother towards the guests on the swing seat. Major Villiers was standing with one foot resting on two wooden croquet balls. He swung his mallet in an easy arc and then brought it to a crack at his heel. A wooden ball shot along the ground as if from the mouth of a howitzer. His small audience clapped. Beside the canopied bar the Brigadier seemed to be demonstrating a slow and arthritic golf swing to Lieutenant Colonel Foster.

"We make a strange troop for war, don't we, Lieutenant?" said Captain Banks. He smiled. "Could you be free for a couple of hours tomorrow morning? Around ten, say?"

Deacon was momentarily taken off guard. He had rather hoped for a long sleep–in and a leisurely breakfast.

"Yes sir."

"Good. Got something brewing that might interest you. At least I think I have. Unfortunately I can't confirm if the show's on until early tomorrow morning. That all right?"

"Yes, of course."

"You'll just be along as an observer. Nothing dangerous, I assure you. My man will pick you up. Should have you back by lunchtime. Oh God! I think Grace is going to show Foster the correct golf grip. And he is so proud of his back swing."

Banks grinned and set out to rescue the lieutenant colonel from his golfing tutorial. Grace Banks was standing on the grass beside the Brigadier and demonstrating a fluid and graceful golf swing over an orange that was placed on the ground before her. The Brigadier and Lieutenant Colonel Foster seemed unconvinced.

Deacon gazed through the large French windows into the dining hall and was momentarily stunned by the opulence of the table. High-backed chairs ranked around a long dining table lost under a glitter of cutlery and china place settings and small forests of glasses and sauce boats and rolled napkins in silver collars. The table looked like a Dickens Christmas. A large floral spray bloomed from its centre and chandeliers hung from the cavernous roof spaces in cobwebs of pearls.

Deacon had not expected such formality or grandeur. He became aware of his guts knotting as he realised he was not sure he knew how he was to eat at such a table. He did not know its rules. Deacon was suddenly fearful that he was going to make a fool of himself. That the common barrow-boy would out.

Voices sounded behind him and he turned to see Clemmie ushering the guests into lunch. Deacon stepped back to allow them to pass and then followed in to the room. Clemmie busied herself with guiding people to their seats. Deacon stood in the cool shadows of the room waiting to be seated and realised that he still held his half-finished pint of beer in his hand. All the other guests had left their drinks outside. Deacon was not sure what to do. He had just formed the idea of gulping the beer down and hiding the empty glass behind a nearby bronze figurine of Wellington, when an orderly coughed discreetly at his elbow. He offered Deacon a sympathetic smile, took the glass from his hand, and slid back out through the French windows and onto the lawns without anyone noticing.

Deacon found himself seated between one of the business wives and Grace Banks. Even as they sat and un-choked their napkins the conversations began to bubble about the room. Two orderlies appeared with plates of prawns and lettuce and another uncorked bottles of wine at a mahogany sideboard as big as a cathedral organ.

Deacon studied his guests for napkin clues. Grace Banks smiled at him and placed her napkin in her lap. Deacon gave himself a moment or two before copying her.

An orderly appeared at his shoulder. "Wine aperitif, sir?" he said.

Deacon took one of the glasses from his crystal copse and held it up for the wine. "Yes. Thank you," he said.

The orderly took the glass gently from him and replaced it back to its setting. He picked up a small, fluted one and poured the wine into it.

"And for you, madam?" he said turning to Grace Banks.

Grace reached out and took one of the larger glasses from her setting and held it up for the orderly. He looked at her and seemed about to say something. Grace Banks offered him a spark-eyed look that seemed to dare him to. The orderly filled her glass and passed on.

Deacon tried a laugh.

"I'm afraid I'm not much practised in glasses," he said. "As you have seen."

Grace Banks smiled.

"Fancy glasses have their place perhaps, Mr Deacon," she said. "But they are hardly of importance. I'm more interested in its arrival rather than its mode of transport. I've always thought that champagne tastes so much nicer out of a china mug." She looked across the table at her husband who grinned back.

"Especially a chipped one, eh Grace?" said Captain Banks. They both smiled at some shared memory. Grace turned to Deacon.

"Peter tells me that you are interesting man, Mr. Deacon. Do you feel interesting?"

"I'm afraid not," said Deacon.

"And he says you are clever."

Grace laughed as her husband rolled his eyes in mock horror.

"Quite clever, I think I said, Grace," said Captain Banks. "Don't embarrass the man. More importantly, don't embarrass me." He laughed. "Sorry about this Deacon but I'm afraid my wife has an independent spirit and she likes to exercise it occasionally."

"It's why you married me, dear," said Grace. "Were you at University Mr. Deacon?"

"No." said Deacon. "I joined the army straight from school."

"In the ranks?" said Grace.

"Yes. I was seventeen."

"And now you are a lieutenant. I think Peter must be right then. You are definitely interesting. Will you make captain, do you think?"

Deacon sat looking at his lettuce-bedded prawns and the armoury of cutlery that paraded before him.

"I'll be happy to make it through to the cheeseboard, Mrs Banks," he said.

Captain Banks and his wife laughed.

At the top end of the table the conversation seemed less animated than around Mrs. Banks. The Brigadier and the lieutenant colonel had not quite settled to the presence of a padre at their table, and having him so close to their elbows.

When Mrs Jennings asked the Padre, Major Cullen, to say Grace, the light in the Brigadier's eye seemed to dim a little further. Major Cullen smiled. He was a young man to be so bald but he carried his domed-burden with a calm and easy detachment.

"Of course, Mrs. Jennings." he said and inclined his head. Deacon stared down into his lap.

"Thank you Lord, for all that you bless," said Major Cullen.

There was a long silence.

"That it?" said the Brigadier.

"I don't think He would ask any more, do you?" said Major Cullen.

"No. Don't suppose He would," said the Brigadier. "Just a bit short-winded for a parson, that's all. You chaps usually talk the barn down. Padre and SAS, eh? Quite a combination. Seen any action?"

"Jimbo!" said Mrs Jennings. "Thing to ask a Padre!"

"It's quite all right, Mrs Jennings. It is a rightful question," said the major. He smiled around the table. He took a sip of wine. "I was attacked by an Arab wielding a machine-gun once. I was alone on the street with a badly wounded comrade. Poor fellow. Gutted by a Spandau burst. I was giving him the last rites. Then an Arab bandit came running at us out of nowhere, blazing away with a machine gun while I was sitting in the dust, cradling a soon-to-be-dead soldier's head in my lap. And I only had one bullet left. Tricky choice."

He reached out and took another sip of wine. The table fell quiet. Everyone knew the codes of the SAS and dying comrades. Pop them and go. They turned to stare at him.

"So what did you do?" asked Clemmie.

The major smiled. "What could I do?" he said. "The SAS way. I had to shoot the poor fellow."

A brittle silence fell. The Major plucked a tear of roll and ate it slowly. He looked around the table of hesitant faces and grinned.

"The Arab, of course," he said.

The Brigadier laughed the loudest and slapped the major on the back.

"That's the stuff, Padre," he said. "Fill the major's glass somebody. Let's get down to lunch!"

The conversations bloomed once again around the table and laughter rippled.

The prawns were followed by a terrine and then Dover Sole and by the time two orderlies brought in the log-sized roll of beef on a silver platter Deacon had drunk from all his glasses. The food was excellent and plentiful and Deacon allowed himself to gorge.

The pleasant atmosphere of the table conversations was momentarily broken by the sound of the Brigadier's loud voice. Mrs. Fanshawe, one of the businessmen's wives, had made an innocuous comment about the scarcity of good Arab gardeners. It seemed enough to launch the Brigadier on what was obviously a regular and practised tirade.

"And do you know why, Mrs. Fanshawe?" The Brigadier waved the carving fork before him as if charging an Omdaman plain. His eyes bulged. "The damn Labour Government, that's why! Telling the Adoo we will be leaving in 'sixty-eight. What mad fool thinking is that? Might as well tell all our friendly Arabs to scarper over to the other side now because we won't be around to protect them for much longer. That damn Foreign Secretary! Ought to be shot as a spy. And his rabble couldn't govern a school. Need a soldier or two in the Cabinet to tell them what's what. Labour Government? Hah! Nothing but a bunch of college boys with pipes."

The table fell silent.

Clemmie leaned forward and patted her father's hand. She smiled at the rest of the table. "Daddy failed his interview for the Diplomatic Corps. It still rankles."

The guests laughed. Even the Brigadier found a slow smile.

"Just speaking as I find, Clemmie. Nothing wrong in that. Who's hoarding the buttered swede?"

"How are you finding Aden, Clemmie?" asked Mrs Banks. "Still taking lots of pictures?"

Deacon was aware of Villiers and the Brigadier sharing a discreet look.

"Oh, Aden is fascinating," said Clemmie. She smiled. "So much to see. But Daddy has forbidden me to take any more pictures."

"I haven't forbidden you, Clementine," said the Brigadier. He carved a large slice of beef and rested it on Major Cullen's plate and then forked a roast potato into his own mouth. "I'm not Stalin. You can take all the pictures you want. But I don't see the point if you can't get them printed."

"Oh, I can get them printed." said Clemmie. She grinned at her father. Deacon saw the Brigadier share another quick look with Villiers.

"You can?" said the Brigadier. "How?"

Deacon was afraid that Clemmie would glance his way, but she remained unmoved. "Oh, a friend," she said.

The Brigadier grunted and returned his attention back to his plate. Clemmie stole a quick look towards Deacon. As she did so Deacon saw that Villiers was still watching her. Deacon immediately found interest in Mrs. Fanshawe's conversation at his side. He felt rather than saw Villiers's gaze upon him.

Mrs. Fanshawe was still in the middle of describing the gardens of her newly acquired summer cottage in Devon when Deacon heard the faint sound of a distant rumble. Mrs Fanshawe did not hear it and carried on with her conversation but Deacon was aware of others pricking their ears around the table.

"That was an explosion," said Grace Banks.

"Sounded like it came from Maalla way," said Villiers.

The Brigadier pushed back his chair and headed out through the French windows and onto the lawns overlooking the bay.

"Fetch my telescope and some glasses, Ralston!" he called to an orderly.

The rest of the guests joined him at the cliff-top walls. Across the far side of the city sprawl, Deacon could see a small plume of smoke snaking lazily into the sky from one of the Arab quarters by the quayside. An orderly came out with a large telescope and tripod and several pairs of binoculars. The binoculars were soon in use.

"Looks like a fire's broken out," said Captain Banks. "Near the Victoria Depot."

"Mortar attack?" said the Brigadier.

"No. Don't think so. It's in the wrong place," said Captain Banks.

"Blast it, Ralston, the thing's broken!" said the Brigadier. He was crouching over his telescope, peering into the eyepiece and twiddling knobs.

Ralston stepped forward and removed the lens shield.

"No, it's alright, Ralston. I've got it." said the Brigadier. "Who's got that sector today?"

"The Scots Guards, I think, sir," said Villiers. "Colonel Merchant."

"Binky eh? Well, he'll soon have it ordered," said the Brigadier.

The distant sounds of sirens could be heard drifting in on the bay breezes.

"Looks like several buildings damaged," said Captain Banks. "I'd better make a call."

He returned a few moments later.

"Small bomb gone off near the Edward Road sub-station," he said. "Local damage only. Several Arab casualties. No British personnel involved. It looked like a bomb has gone off in transit. I'd better get down there. Your permission, sir?"

The Brigadier was still crouching over his telescope. He looked up momentarily and nodded.

"I'll come with you," said Major Cullen. "I have some SAS troops billeted that way."

"You'd better come too, Grace," said Captain Banks. The Brigadier looked up from his crouch.

"Eh?" he said.

"Grace speaks Arabic better than any of us, sir. And there are women casualties."

"Ah, yes. Of course. Well get going, Peter."

"Shall we?" said Captain Banks. He offered his elbow to his wife.

"Of course, dear," said Grace Banks. "But only on the condition you let me drive."

"Nothing above sixty," said Captain Banks.

"But this is an emergency, Peter," said Grace. They thanked Mrs Jennings for a wonderful lunch and left with Major Cullen.

Clemmie went back into the Villa to call the hospital. The remaining guests followed the Brigadier back to the dining hall and sat back at the table. Clemmie returned within moments.

"I'm afraid I will have to dash, Daddy," she said. "The wards are all on Sunday short-staff and need auxiliary support. I'll be back as soon as I can. "

The Brigadier looked around the remnants of the table.

"Another lunch ruined," he growled. "And we had roly-poly and custard for pudding."

"Well we can have it later, dear," said Mrs. Jennings. "Why don't you have your meeting with your oil friends now in the library, while we ladies take to the gardens. Then we can all have tea on the lawns later. With roly-poly."

"We do need to discuss the pipeline security issue, Brigadier," said Mr. Fanshawe. He cast his napkin onto the table and straightened his tie knot to smart.

"And if you don't need Harry anymore, we can let him get back to his men," said Clemmie.

She slipped her arm into Deacon's and guided him quickly from the room. Villiers rose from his chair and seemed about to say to something. But he remained silent. As the door closed behind them, Clemmie laughed.

"And now I have rescued you for once, Harry!" she said. "Are you grateful?"

"Very," said Deacon.

Clemmie kissed him on the cheek.

"Thanks for everything," she said. "But now I must to get changed and get to the hospital. You run along and enjoy the rest of your day."

She ran up the sweep of the atrium stone stairs and waved him goodbye from the landing.

Deacon drove back to his billet feeling bloated on rich food and heavy with wine. The sun scorched all the way. He entered the cool of his rooms and flopped down in his chair. He stared about him. The room wobbled at its edges and his head ached. Outside the world was Sunday afternoon quiet. He heard the revs of a distant truck, a faint pulse of helicopter, but that was all. Deacon tried to think of other things but the richness and splendour of the lunch would not leave him. The first sight shock of it through the French windows.

His mother loomed into his thoughts. It was a rare and an unwelcome visit. His mother would have delighted to see her Leslie dining in such splendour. At such a grand table and under chandeliers. She would have marvelled at all the silver and finery. A wish come true. Her blue-collar boy at luncheon with the class where he belonged. With servants and silver-ringed napkins. It would have made all her sacrifices worthwhile just see that. All the hours she had put in on Deacon's education. Standing over him at the kitchen table while he drilled on extra algebra and modern history. The additional overtime hours at the factory to pay for private Latin. A sacrifice that Deacon had spurned and turned his back on and to which he had never returned. He had left and never looked back. The guilt of Mr. Havers, his mother and his blighted sins had stayed with him despite his smothering them under the army uniform and casting himself to the other side of the world. His sins followed him like an indelible stain. Running and hiding had been the only way and he had not spoken to his mother and father for nine years. He could sometimes almost believe he had succeeded in forgetting them, but the grandiose luncheon had conjured his mother like a ghost. Deacon washed thoughts of her away under a stinging hot shower.

He changed into his swimming costume and shorts, packed a beach bag, watered the yellow crysanthmum and headed for Fisherman's Bay.

Deacon drove the jeep up the final rise of the pass and heard the beach before he saw it. A gentle cacophony of calling gulls, childish voices, tinny pop-music and the drum-brush of surf rolled up the road to engulf him. He crested the rise and gazed down onto the beach. The pale yellow sands curved in a gentle arc under the skirts of grey mountains and the still sea sparked in violent blues. The beach was busy with off-duty soldiers. Deacon could see small groups lying in the shade of makeshift canopies, others were playing football, some were trying to fly kites. At the far end of the beach some soldiers were jumping motorbikes over the dunes. A stick of soldiers were tug-of-warring on a rope in the sea's shallows. Everyone was either in shorts or swimming costumes. Every hand seemed to hold a bottle.

Out in the bay Deacon could see the reassuring presence of the shark net. Within its safe and cordoned waters small shoals of soldiers were leaping and splashing like trawled fish. Others swam or just floated. A couple of daffodil-yellow rubber boats paddled amongst them. Some soldiers just idled the shoreline kicking waves.

Deacon parked up the jeep and went looking for his troop. He found them under a stretched awning of canvas surrounded by a cache of crated beer bottles, stacked and ranked like shells before a bombardment. His men looked up as he approached. As always, Deacon was surprised by the easy warmth of his welcome.

"Hey up, sir," said Shaw. "You came, then. Two pound in the kitty. Grab a neck." He was bouncing a plastic football on his thigh. "Twenty-five. Twenty-six."

"Only twenty-three," said Lee. He was official counter for

Shaw's attempt at the troop record. "Beer's over there, sir. Help yourself. Twenty-seven. Feeling faint, Shawy? Eighty-seven's long way off mate. Thirty."

Corporal Lockett emerged from under the awning. He blinked into the sun and grinned at Deacon.

"Well, we seem to have been lucky with the weather, sir. Going to be a fine afternoon."

He handed Deacon an uncapped bottle of beer. It was cold in his palm.

"Borrowed Major Villiers's cool box for the afternoon," said Lockett. He pulled a bottle to his mouth and drank deep. "No chit, I'm afraid, sir. But it'll be returned unmissed."

Deacon raised the bottle to his lips, closed his eyes on the sun and sucked in the cool wetness. He took off his boots and shirt and sat with his men in the shade. Ably and Doyle slept under the truck's wheels. Ambrose and Kenny were somewhere in the sea. Gibson waddled lobster-red along the beach ploughing a kite into the sands behind him. A couple of navy boys from the HMS Ajax slept on the shaded sand beside them.

"How was your lunch, sir?" said Lockett. He uncapped another bottle.

Private Lee took two bottles from a crate and palm-slapped the tops off against the metal spike planted for the purpose. A litter of bottle caps sparkled on the sands about it, like silver leaves under an autumn tree.

"Very rich and plentiful," said Deacon. He took out his cigarettes and offered one to Lockett. Privates Lee and Shaw appeared beside him.

"Ta, sir!" they said in unison and took a cigarette. They flopped down in the shade and settled for a smoke. They watched the beach while Shaw's transistor radio tinned in the opening lines of *I can't get no satisfaction* throbbed in the breeze Deacon saw his men grinning at each other. Shaw turned up the radio. A couple of soldiers idling past on the beach stopped. Then, as one, every soldier sang out to the sky *and I try* in a rising crescendo until it roared *satisfaction.*

Deacon joined in. He sang at the top of his voice. He felt his blood race through him.

When the Stones were done, the soldiers resumed their shaded rest or idling walks. Lockett took a couple more bottles out of the cool box and palmed them on the spike. He handed one to Deacon. They sat back in the shade and watched the sea.

"Did you know there is a special fork for prawns?" said Deacon.

Lockett laughed.

"That's fucking toffs for you!" said Lee. He flicked his cigarette butt towards a sailor who was being sick in nearby rocks. The sailor had a large, blue snake's head tattooed across his back. The snake arched and retched with him.

"So long as it keeps the Sheffield steel boys in beer and ciggies who gives a fuck," said Shaw.

Deacon smoked and drank and wondered what kind of fuck he gave. He was surprised to find it wasn't much of one. The lunch still gnawed and rumbled in him. It wasn't so much the rich food and wine, it was the realisation he just hadn't enjoyed it or been impressed by it. The Brigadier's Sunday lunch and its world was just not for him. The Bankses had been kind and Deacon felt he had acquitted himself without mishap or disclosure. But he had not liked it, and he knew he never would. And he knew that his mother would never get her silver napkin ring.

"Anyone fancy a swim?" asked Deacon.

"Yeah!" said Lee and Shaw. "Coming, corp?"

Lockett grinned. "Sure."

The men finished off their beers and shucked out of their shorts and boots. Lockett pulled off his T-shirt and folded it to a square on his bag. He placed his boots upside down on two sticks lanced into the sand for the purpose and then rubbed sun cream along his arms and legs.

Deacon noticed that despite Lockett's smaller stature his

body was tightly formed. Deacon had never seen Lockett bare-chested before and to see him now was a surprise. Deacon had expected thinner arms and ribs. Less muscular legs. And he had certainly never imagined the small dark triangle of tufted hair that marked the centre of his chest, like a brand.

"Let's take the footy," said Shaw. He stood in his lurid-coloured swimming trunks with the ball under his arm.

"If it goes over the net, I ain't dibs," said Lee. His trunks were so brief and red it looked like he had sat in a ketchup pool. He was lighting the remnant of the fag that would see him to the waves. "Come on then!"

Deacon ran to the sea and thrashed himself into it. He ducked and swam and breached and threw ball with Shaw and Lockett. He let the sea scour him. He tasted its salt tang in his mouth and let it crash over his shoulders and head. He plunged among the waves and let them punish and cleanse him. And when he had no more energy to give he lay on his back and floated under a grilling white sun.

The afternoon grew. They played football on the beach against the Artillery and sat in the shade drinking beer. Late in the afternoon they got Gibson on the back of a motorbike and saw his kite finally flutter into the air. The boys from HMS Ajax built a fire of empty beer crates, and sausages were cooked on corrugated metal sheets. As the evening rolled in the troop packed the remaining beer crates into the truck and headed for the REME canteen. Deacon went in the truck with them. They took their fish and chips to the old wooden jetty at Steamer Port and ate them gazing out over the glow-worm ships, gliding and hooting in the bay. From there, they had ventured to the Troy for drinks and then to the Chinese take-away before returning to the Troy for more drinks.

They dropped Deacon back at his jeep in Fisherman's Bay a little after o-one hundred. He had jumped down from the truck on unsteady legs and he was conscious that his head was swimming and the world blurred at its edges.

"You okay, sir?" asked Lockett. "I can drive you if you like." He sat in the passenger seat of the cab, his face reddened by beach and beer.

"Fine, thank you, corporal," said Deacon. He could feel the pleasure of his afternoon draining from him like a sluice. He knew he was drunk and he could feel his day churning within his gut.

"Wonderful afternoon, lads. Thank you."

A line of grinning, vacant faces glazed back at him from the truck. The night was dark and starlit and Deacon could hear the sounds of the surf brushing the sands below.

"And you, sir. Thanks for the Chinese," said Shaw.

Deacon waved a dismissive hand and stumbled a little.

"Pleasure," he said.

"You sure, sir?" asked Lockett.

"Fine, corporal."

Deacon waited until the truck disappeared back down the hill and then he turned and threw up everything he had into the night.

TWELVE

Tom Villiers was speaking to Deacon in a dream.

"Hello. Are you supposed to be here?"

Deacon's mind was lit by a watery sun and he could taste sand in his mouth. He could feel a skin of sweat ooze over him and his mind and heart raced as he sought some answer to Villiers's question, to keep himself hidden and undiscovered. Tom Villiers spoke again.

"Looking for Lieutenant Deacon."

The voice was muffled as if from a far room. Deacon lay still on his cot and realised Villiers was taking to someone in the next room. He let his heart settle and ewas fully awake by the time the knock at his bedroom door sounded. He struggled onto his elbows. Corporal Lockett's face appeared around the crack of the open door.

"Sorry to wake you, sir, but Major Villiers is here to see you."

Lockett slipped into the room and closed the door.

"And Captain Banks called sir. Says it's on for ten. Something I should know, sir?"

"What time is it?"

"Oh-eight hundred sir."

"Give me five minutes."

Deacon dragged himself to the shower and tried to baptise himself into the day. His head felt like a stone weight and every bone seemed to ache. He wondered how he had driven back to his billet. He couldn't remember the drive at all. But he remembered the beach, it was still in his ears. He finished his shower, dressed himself quickly and listened to the murmur of conversation coming from his sitting room. Major Villiers had obviously arrived in the middle of one of Chi's lessons. He could hear Chi's laugh and Lockett's nervous talk through the door. Deacon went out to join them.

Major Villiers was standing with some of Lockett's teaching papers in his hand and Chi stood before him, spelling him words.

"Ah! Morning, Harry," said Villiers. He grinned at Deacon. "Sorry to break into your slumbers. Thought you were the early riser type. You certainly get a morning crowd."

"C.A.M.A.L.," said Chi. "See, I learn good."

"Very close!" said Villiers. "Quite a spark, this one, isn't he?"

He rubbed Chi's head. Chi grinned up at him.

"The corporal has my permission sir," said Deacon. "He is teaching Chi English."

"Oh quite commendable, I'm sure. Admirable. As long as it doesn't interfere with duties."

"It doesn't sir." said Lockett. "Just some early mornings. I think that's all for today, Chi. Time you were off."

Villiers kept a hand on Chi.

"Don't stop school because of me, corporal. I have only come to take your Lieutenant out to breakfast. You haven't breakfasted yet have you, Harry?"

Deacon shook his head. He felt nausea rise like a pebble balloon in his gut.

"Good. Now young man," Villiers retrieved a sixpence from his pocket. "Willing to test your spelling for this?"

Chi's eyes widened.

"I'd rather not encourage Chi with money rewards, if it's all the same to you, sir," said Lockett. He began tidying his papers. "It upsets the teaching."

Villiers laughed and flicked the coin in the air and caught it deftly. Chi watched spellbound.

"It's only sixpence, corporal. Hardly going to corrupt him now is it? So Chi. Will you spell for sixpence?"

"I fine spelling," said Chi grinning.

"That's the spirit!" said Villiers. He laid the sixpence on the small table beside Chi. "Now let me see. Ah! I know. I am an officer. Can you spell officer?"

Chi's grin widened with confidence.

"Yes. Fine. O.and F with I and S...I.. R. .?"

"Bravo!" said Villiers. "As close as makes no matter." He rubbed Chi's head again and flicked him the sixpence. "You are doing a fine job, corporal. Most commendable. Don't let me interrupt the good work. You and Chi carry on while I take Harry off and get some coffee into him. Looks like you had a rough night, Harry!"

They breakfasted on the lawns of the Officer's Club. The jeep ride had helped clear Deacon's head and by the time they sat down he was still feeling fragile, but at least he was awake. Villiers ordered a full English fry-up. Deacon settled for coffee and toast. Villiers talked enthusiastically about his plans for the Vikings while he attacked his plate of eggs and bacon. Deacon drank his coffee and tried to avoid the sight of the black pudding floating on its violent pool of baked beans. He gazed about at the other tables until Villiers had wiped the last slither of egg from his plate and sat back in his chair.

"Sorry to wake you so early, Harry. I was ravenous and didn't think."

"Quite alright sir."

"Your corporal is an interesting fellow. Presume you have checked out the boy?"

"Yes sir. His file is clean. He is one of Mr. Patel's young workers. Tea and laundry boy. We don't think he has any local family."

"We are all bastards of war, Harry. But you can't help feeling sorry for the lad."

They drank coffee in silence for a while. Deacon watched as the first of the crows took their perch on the high wire fence of the sports field. Below them he could see the first flutter of starling wings catching the sun among the fig trees.

"Clemmie mentioned yesterday she was getting her films printed by a friend," said Villiers. He watched Deacon through a steady eye. "That friend wouldn't be you, would it, Harry?"

Deacon held his gaze.

"No," said Deacon. "It's not me."

"But you know who it is?"

"Yes."

"Who?"

"One of my men."

"Can you be more specific?"

"Someone under my command, sir."

Villiers eyed him for a moment and then smiled. "Of course, Harry. Quite understand. But, as you say, under your command. I am afraid I'm going to have to ask you to get the films back from him, whoever he is. Awkward thing to ask but it does come down from the Brigadier. I am sure you will understand his concern. All to be done quietly of course. No fuss. Just bring me Clemmie's films and the Brigadier and I will take it from there. Clemmie need never know."

Deacon stared at his coffee cup.

"I would rather not make it an order, Harry," said Villiers. He smiled and poured more coffee into Deacon's cup.

"But why?" said Deacon. "They are just Clemmie's adventure photographs."

"Because she is sending them back to some of her political chums in Cambridge," said Villiers. He cast his napkin to the table and sighed. "Clemmie has got in with some University crowd and sends them her pictures. Despatches from the front line. And Clemmie, well you know Clemmie. Very determined, but easily led. We need to save her from herself. Keep her out of trouble. And the Brigadier away from the firing squad. You do see?"

"But they are just pictures of Aden. Rimbaud's House. The mountains. You and me," said Deacon.

"And Adoo riots and bombed houses," said Villiers. "Can't have them getting into the Daily Mirror, now, can we? Especially from a Brigadier's daughter. Press would have a field day. You can see why it has to be done. Clemmie doesn't know we know, of course, and we must keep it that way. She means no harm by it. Fighting for her cause and good for her, I say. But not here. Not in Aden."

"But she will know. She won't have any pictures."

"Oh, we only want to intercept them and check them over. Make sure there is nothing too embarrassing. You know, diplomatically. We'll print up what we can and return them to Clemmie. She'll be none the wiser."

"But she'll know some are missing surely?"

"Oh, overexposure, problem in processing, chemical bleaching. I'm sure you, or your mystery man, can come up with a good explanation. I am sure he must be resourceful. And of course, under your orders."

Deacon sat watching more crows gathering on the distant wire. "Of course, sir. I'll do as you ask," he said. He knew he had no choice but that didn't stop him from loathing himself for his cowardice and betrayals. Once sin had you it just grew, rotting everything inside you like a cancer.

Villiers smiled. He leaned forward and patted Deacon on the shoulder.

"Thank you, Harry. I know I can rely on you."

Deacon drained his coffee and stood up.

"Thank you for breakfast, sir. But I must be away. I have an appointment with Captain Banks."

Deacon saluted and strode away and didn't look back. He marched the two miles back to his billet with his mind burning all the way. He felt disgust in the deceits he was being forced to play. A disgust in himself. He was going to have to lie to Clemmie. Worse still, he was going to have to make a demand of Lockett. He couldn't understand why that thought troubled him so much.

When he arrived back at this billet a jeep was waiting in the road outside. A portly but fit-looking sergeant with a Clark Gable moustache slid out of his seat on Deacon's approach.

"Lieutenant Deacon, sir?" asked the sergeant.

"Yes."

The sergeant smiled. "I'm Captain Banks's man, Sergeant Allenby, sir. Your card?"

Deacon showed him his ID. The sergeant saluted and slid back into the driver seat. Deacon sat beside him. His guts lurched as the jeep lunged from the kerb and headed towards Crater.

They parked up in the derelict walls of an old warehouse and two soldiers gave Deacon escort through the back streets and alleyways. The warren air was cool and the alleys quiet. Deacon stumbled past shaded houses often only a shoulder's width apart. Deacon felt the menace of the rat's nest all about him. It smelled of goats and khat. The warren seemed to gather over him leaving only a thin blade of sky above. Deacon couldn't quite believe that people lived here.

They came to a small courtyard where two more soldiers were waiting in the shadows of a smooth stone tower. The top floors of the tower were missing and it stood stunted and scarred on the corner of a small square. One of his escorts nodded Deacon towards the door in the base of the tower. On the far side of the courtyard a soldier was crouched with his Sterling across his knee and beckoning Deacon on.

Deacon crouched low and ran to the door. It opened as he arrived and the two soldiers followed. They locked and barred the door. Two soldiers stood guard while the other took Deacon up the wide stone steps that spiralled up the inside of the tower's walls. Another soldier met them at the third floor and, after checking IDs, opened a heavy wooden door. Deacon stepped into a large space of room with a view of the streets of Crater displayed as if on a large, curved cinema screen before him. It took Deacon a moment to realise that the view was real. At the back of the room, behind the door, a row of soldiers was sitting quietly smoking in the dark shadow. Captain Banks nodded to Deacon and indicated the only vacant seat.

There were four chairs, the others were occupied by a couple of corporals with several cameras hung around their necks. They offered a cursory greeting to Deacon and continued to watch the screen of Crater before them. Deacon saw that the view was actually through three large windows that spanned a one-hundred and twenty degree curve of the tower's wall. The windows had no glass and their frames were broken and buckled from a past explosion. The view looked out onto the neighbouring roof tops, streets and houses and out beyond to the kochi huts that grew like fungi up the slopes of nearby mountains.

Captain Banks leaned forward and whispered, "What do you see?" he said.

Deacon took in the roof tops and houses and streets and rubbish piles and goats and dust. "Aden," he said.

Captain Banks grinned and leaned back in his seat, sucking dryly on a dead pipe. A soldier with a Sterling machine gun was crouched under one of the windows watching the flanking rooftops with a metronome eye. Deacon waited in silence and watched the film with the others. After a while he became aware that the streets were quieter than they usually were at this time of the morning. A few Adoo scuttled the streets and the tin trucks whined occasionally but it was not the usual pre-noon bustle. That late-morning Aden scurry before the sun becomes to hot to move. Deacon also became aware that the quietness seemed localised to the area around the tower. In distant streets he could see Crater busy about its business, but in the streets below there was quiet.

He turned to find Captain Banks smiling at him. Captain Banks reached into his pocket and passed something over to Deacon. It was a small nugget of hard, golden wax. Captain Banks leaned back in his chair and continued watching and sucking on his pipe.

The door opened and Major Villiers walked in. Deacon sought to rise to offer his seat but Villiers waved him down and settled himself to a lean on the back wall with a cigarette. The room continued in its watchful silence. It watched for some time.

Deacon saw thin trails of white smoke scratch up the screen in front of him. *Woomph. Woomph. Woomph.* The noise startled him. It seemed loud enough to be in the room. Captain Banks and Villiers ran to the window. Deacon joined them. He saw parallel trails of smoke arrowing up into the sky and then stall and fall back towards the ground. They were homing back to their launch site. Deacon gazed at the streets below him. Up the road he saw the walls of a squat, grey house swell as if suddenly inflated and then erupt in a volcano of stones and tumbling smoke clouds. There was a reverberating crack and a boom followed almost immediately by three other explosions somewhere close. A donkey flew through the sky in a gentle arc, scattering confetti lemons as it sailed. The sounds of screams and cries of alarm rose from the streets. A woman staggered blind into the road, her shawl on fire. A couple of children ran, wailing in confusion. People were emerging onto the streets from nearby houses and running towards the stricken homes. In the far mountains, Deacon heard piard dogs barking.

"That was rather close," said Banks. "That wasn't supposed to happen."

Villiers turned and grinned at Captain Banks. "Had the boys make some fine adjustments, Peter. Sorry to go over your head. Needs of war and all that. No use sending them into the sea. Give them a taste of their own medicine. Make them think twice, eh?"

They stepped away from the window and returned to the shade at the back of the room. The two soldiers with cameras moved to the sides of the windows and began firing off shots like semi-automatics. Captain Banks looked down to the mayhem on the streets. He seemed confused by what he saw.

"Well done, Peter," said Villiers. He beamed his satisfaction. "Fine intelligence work. Finding the mortar. First class."

Captain Banks blinked. "I couldn't have done it without Lieutenant Deacon, sir. It was his idea. I just followed it."

"Of course, of course," said Villiers. He slapped Deacon on the back. "Well done too, Harry! Now I'd better get back to battalion HQ and await the damage score. Get a report to me as soon as you can Peter. Good work. The Vikings are marching, eh?"

He laughed and left the room.

"Here they come," said one of the camera soldiers. He and the other soldier crouched and bobbed at the windows, photographing the scenes and people below.

Deacon crept to the edge of the room's shadows and peered down. Several Arab men were arguing in the small square. After a few moments they moved their argument over to a rubbish pile.

"In the rubbish!" said Deacon.

"I wondered how long it would take you." said Captain Banks. He offered a pale grin. "Somewhere where we haven't looked yet. Remember?"

The soldiers continued clicking their cameras. Down in the street more people were beginning to emerge into the small square. Deacon heard a woman wailing somewhere and goats bleating.

Captain Banks refilled his pipe from a leather pouch that he finger-stroked like a kitten in his palm.

"A soldier happened to see some young kids playing in the rubbish pile," he said. "Found out they had built tunnels in it. Proper tunnels. Engineered. With an open chamber to the sky in the middle of it. So I had a discreet watch put on it. The Adoo came and set the mortar up in the rubbish last night. And it went off at oh-eleven sixteen this morning. Just as you said it would."

Deacon pulled out the nugget of wax and rolled it in his fingers. It had become sticky. "Beeswax?" he said.

"That, Lieutenant Deacon, is your timing device. So wonderfully simple. Wax plug in a metal clothes peg. Attach the wires to a car battery. And?"

"Wait for the sun to shine," said Deacon.

"Exactly," said Captain Banks. "Wax melts, peg snaps shut, circuit made, car battery sparks, mortar fires. Simple and quite brilliant."

"But they sent the mortars the wrong way," said Deacon. "They've bombed their own people."

Captain Banks looked out onto the streets, his eyes glazed. He gave Deacon a thin, nervous smile.

"So it would seem," he said. "We paid the rubbish another visit last night and, er, re-set the mortar. Out over towards the sea. Or so I thought. But Major Villiers obviously had other plans."

Deacon looked out of the window towards the small plumes of grey smoke that ghosted over nearby roofs.

"But they're civilians," he said.

Captain Banks lit his pipe and sucked the embers to a small glow. He took the pipe out of his mouth and held his thumb over the bowl.

"There are no civilians in Aden," he said. "You rather it were us? Wars are for winning, Lieutenant. Any damn way we can. Major Villiers was right. This will make the buggers think twice about setting their mortars on us. Maybe even stop them. Saves lives either way. Worth the toss of fate, I'd say. Come on. We'd better get out of here before the crowds get too nosy."

They went back down the sweep of stone steps and halted at the first landing. The two soldiers guarding the door had their faces pressed to the window cracks and held up their hands for quiet. Outside in the street, Deacon could hear the scurry of running feet and angry voices shouting nearby.

Captain Banks tapped Deacon on the shoulder.

"Do you play tennis?" he asked.

Deacon almost laughed. He was conscious of his hands sweating and of the sound of people chattering excitedly on the other side of the tower's walls.

"Not very well," he whispered.

"Well Grace and I like a game. Why not come around tomorrow afternoon? Around sixteen-hundred. My backhand is wooden but the gins won't be. Sort of a thank you for helping with my mortar problem. How about it?"

"Of course," said Deacon. "Delighted."

"Excellent. Corporal, this waiting is getting tiresome. Why don't we just shoot our way out?"

The corporal waved for a few more moments of patience and then lifted the door bar.

"All clear., he said. "They are in the square out front. One every five and keep your fucking heads down. I'll be behind you so you better move fast. I'm a fucking cheetah, me."

Deacon crouched low and headed out across the street five seconds after Captain Banks. Sergeant Allenby appeared from the deep shadow of a doorway and covered their retreat as they burrowed back down through the alleys to the derelict warehouse. Deacon found the cool of the dark, silent alleys almost a comfort and he was disappointed to reach the open sunlight of the warehouse street. A Saracen rumbled in its shade and they all scrambled in. They journeyed back in the half-dark of the Saracen's womb. They were silent.

They dropped Deacon back at this billet. Captain Banks leaned out of the cab.

"I'll let Grace know you're coming. Don't worry about racquets. War's hell, eh, lieutenant?"

The Saracen roared away.

Deacon eventually found his men parked up in two trucks on the far side of the dock's transit yard. He had expected to find them at Khormaksar depot and it had taken over an hour to trace them. The trucks were parked in the shade of a high brick wall that formed part of the dock's outer defence line. Some of the men were playing cards on an upturned crate in one of the trucks. In the other truck, various bodies slumbered and snored. Shaw's transistor radio hung from the roof and pop music floated through the air.

"Hey up, sir," said Shaw. He grinned from behind a fan of cards and cigarette smoke. "Crane's fucked." He slapped a card on the crate. Corporal Lockett laid his.

"Shit," said Shaw.

"It's true, sir," said Lockett. He picked up the loose cigarettes in the middle of the crate and settled them in his breast pocket. "Number Five crane is out. They reckon a couple more hours at least. Can't get the cargo off or on. Major Dolby's orders. We're posted here on standby. Ciggies in, lads."

"Not fucking fair," said Lee. He shuffled the cards with frozen hands, as if making snowballs. He flapped the cards out slowly to the crate. "I only got three ciggies left."

"Then that'll just about see you through this hand, won't it?" said Lockett.

Private Lee studied his fist of cards and then contemplated the three remaining cigarettes in his carton. He put one in his mouth, one on the crate and one in his pocket for later. Deacon leaned into the back of the truck, retrieved the transit dockets and studied them while the card game continued.

"Fucking knew it!" said Lee. He slapped his last card down and kicked the side of the truck with his heel. "Of all the shit luck. How about I owes you til Friday, corp? I'm good for it."

Lockett leaned forward and took Lee's last cigarette from his pocket. Lee watched it leave him like a lost love.

"What have I told you about gambling, Lee?" said Lockett. He carefully placed the cigarette with its troop in his own pocket. "What lesson are we learning?"

Lee sulked in the shades. "Don't gamble if you can't afford to lose," he chanted.

"And give up smoking," said Lockett.

"You fucking smoke!" said Lee. "That ain't fair."

"Yes. But I haven't got a baby and a young wife back home. You going to smoke all your money away, Lee? Or just gamble it maybe. Got a present yet for your Alan? Isn't it his first birthday next month?"

Lee slumped against the truck. "Yeah. So what. I ain't got no fucking money."

"Then stop gambling," said Lockett. "Because, Lee, you are rubbish at it. And quit smoking. Then maybe you can send some housekeeping back to your Carol."

Lee stayed silent in the truck's shadow.

"How do we get the call-up?" said Deacon. He returned the file to the back of the truck. He noticed two card-playing soldiers he didn't know.

"These are lads from the depot stores, sir," said Lockett. "Crane stopped them too. They'll sound two bells when they need us at the docks."

The two men nodded to Deacon from the truck's shadows. Deacon noticed two half-empty bottles of single malt whisky standing to attention on the tool box.

"Splendid," said Deacon. He looked around at the wall and the couple of concrete hangers and the vast expanse of dusted tarmac that stretched for hot and idle hours ahead. "We couldn't have chosen a nicer spot."

"Deal me out, lads," said Lockett. He jumped down from the truck and fetched two bottles of beer from the cab. He palm-slapped the tops off against the tailgate and gave one to Deacon. They sat in the shade of the wall.

"Did you hear the mortars sir?" said Lockett.

"Yes."

"Not like the Adoo to bomb themselves. Maybe we will win this war after all."

Deacon took a long suckle on his beer. He watched Aden and the mountains fracture and hover in the distant haze.

"No one wins in Aden," he said. "I'm invited to the Banks's tomorrow afternoon. Tennis and drinks. I thought the cream shorts."

Deacon watched the liquid distance.

"Not shorts," said Lockett. "Not if you're going to cocktail on the veranda after. The linen trousers are more apropriate, sir. Shorts a bit risky on garden chairs. Take it ladies will be present, sir?"

"Where did you learn all this stuff, corporal?"

"Life University, sir. Joint honours. Can you play tennis?"

"Not a chukka."

Lockett laughed. "Another one betting more than he's got then, sir."

Deacon smiled. "Yes. Quite. And I serve like Lee deals cards," he said.

Lockett turned to him and grinned. "Well, we're stuck here for a while. Why not practise?" Lockett shouted up to the truck. "Nobby, you got a tennis racquet and balls in PACIT?"

Deacon raised a curious eyebrow.

"Property awaiting collection in transit, sir" said Lockett. "One of the services from the stores boys. Nobby has most things in PACIT. Golf clubs. China sets. Nice bit of curtain cloth."

"And single malt whisky," said Deacon.

"Perks," said Nobby jumping down from the back of the truck. He was a slim young man with dark, oiled hair. "Malt whisky is duty perks. Might have a tennis racquet awaiting collection. Dare say they won't collect it for it for an hour or so. What do I get?"

"My undying gratitude not enough, Nobby?" said Lockett.

Nobby grunted.

"One free laundered uniform then," said Lockett.

"Two," said Nobby. "Got a dance coming up."

"One uniform and a dry-cleaned jacket," said Lockett.

Nobby grinned, softly slapped Lockett's raised palm and slid into his jeep. He roared off towards one of the distant concrete warehouses. He returned in a cloud of dust some minutes later and handed over a tennis racquet and six canary yellow tennis balls in a blue plastic net. Lockett handed Nobby a card.

"Give this to Mr. Patel. Tell him the deal. You pay for your own starch."

Nobby inspected the card. Then he reached over and took two cigarettes out of Lockett's top pocket.

"Insurance," he said.

Nobby jumped back into the back of the truck.

"Okay. Nobby's back in the game," he said.

Lockett led Deacon further along the wall and handed him the racquet and a ball. "Let's see a serve then, sir," he said.

Deacon was aware that some of his men were watching from the truck. He bounced the ball, eyed the wall and then threw the ball up into the white and swung at it. The ball hit the rim of his racquet and looped away a few yards from him. He heard laughter from the truck.

"Oops-a-daisy, sir," said Shaw.

"Don't mind them, sir. Try another," said Lockett.

Deacon slapped the next one into the ground. The third he missed altogether. He handed the racquet back to Lockett.

"Perhaps I'd better shoot myself in the foot. Or break a leg or something," he said.

Lockett took his jacket off. He eyed the wall, bounced a ball at his feet a few times and then gently lobbed it into the air. Deacon saw Lockett rise on to his toes, arch his back and swat the ball with an easy grace. The ball sang off the racquet and hit the base of the wall like a yellow tracer. Applause sounded from the truck. Lockett turned to Deacon and grinned.

"It's all in the timing sir," he said.

"Where on earth did you learn to play tennis, corporal?"

"Here and there, sir. Now, shall we try again?"

Deacon practised his tennis with Lockett as his guide. After a couple of hours, Deacon's serve had improved to the point of being able to hit the wall with some degree of accuracy and both his forehand and backhand shots passed a kind of muster. In the frequent breaks for beer and shade, Lockett apprised him of the basic rules of the game. Lockett was a patient and diligent coach and while Deacon took pleasure in the progress his game was making, he could find little pleasure in the shadowed prospect of having to order Lockett to hand over the films. As Lockett curled Deacon's fingers around the racquet handle to show him the correct grip, or demonstrated the backhand chop shot, Deacon paid only half a mind. The other half was trying to work out a way of giving the order. He knew he would have to broach the problem sooner rather than later, but every option he considered seemed unpalatable.

He was still considering the problem when a shirtless soldier roared up on a motorbike and skidded to halt beside the truck. His dark hair was slicked back and a thin cigarette hung from his lip in the Marlon Brando style. The effect was ruined by a falsetto Glaswegian accent.

"Crane's oot. S'al fucked. Yees back on in the mornin. Major's orders."

He roared off on his motorbike. Deacon watched him until he was a speck. He turned to find his men watching him from the truck. An expectant silence was heavy in the air. Deacon looked at his watch. They still had two more hours on the duty shift and should be reporting back to Checkpoint Seven as standby relief. The sun promised to burn all the way.

"You got two crates of PACIT beer, Nobby?" he said.

"Maybe. What you offering?"

"How about my silence on malt whisky matters?"

"Told you. Them's perks. One crate."

"Two dozen by the neck and the crates thrown in. And it's *sir.*" said Deacon.

Nobby thought about it.

"And a pair of dry cleaned trousers?" he said. "Sir?"

Deacon looked at Lockett, who was grinning. Lockett nodded.

"Done," said Deacon.

Nobby sped off to get the beer. Deacon turned to his men. They were looking a little downcast.

"At least the fucking barriers won't be so bad with a beer," said Ambrose.

"No, not so bad," said Deacon. "But I was thinking of drinking mine on the beach. Perhaps you'd care to join me?"

They spent an hour lazing with beer on the beach and paddling in the sea's warm shallows. There was no shark net so the larks remained knee high and vigilant. After the beach they got a fish and chips take-away and ate it in the truck overlooking Telegraph Bay. The sliding clutch of the late sun scratched pastel colours across the sky and sparked off the mountain top Cable and Wireless pylons like Christmas lights.

After a drink at the Troy, the men returned in the truck to their barracks and Lockett drove Deacon back to his billet in the jeep. Deacon fetched his linen trousers and handed them to Lockett.

"I'll have them back in an hour, sir," said Lockett. He grinned and drove off. Deacon knew Lockett would be putting in a half-hour teaching visit before he returned with his laundered linen trousers. Probably with Mr. Patel's young workers. Or Ali Syd's daughters. Lockett had an energy that Deacon could only envy and admire. He did not know how he could give him the order.

Deacon took a long shower and then flopped in his chair and picked up a book. He let Alice's adventures float before him. But he couldn'tt read. He got up and fixed himself a large whisky. Through his window he saw Lockett standing to attention in the road with a plastic laundry bag hooked on a finger at his shoulder.

Corporal Golightly was talking with him. They conversed for a moment and then Golightly turned towards Deacon's door and, moments later, knocked on it and let himself in.

"Corporal Golightly. What a pleasure," said Deacon.

Golightly slowly turned his head and scanned the room. He didn't seem impressed. He adjusted his stance slightly in the doorway and proffered a shoulder. Deacon noticed the three bright stripes of a new sergeant.

"Sergeant Golightly," said Deacon. "Congratulations on your promotion. Are you coming to join us as our new sergeant?"

Golightly offered a thin-lipped grin. "I'm the major's man. A fighting sergeant. Not nanny to a stores troop."

Golightly relaxed his shoulder and heeled the door closed behind him.

"A Viking sortie going out Wednesday oh-eight-hundred and you are on it. Meet at the Troy. Pack for two nights. Duty's been covered. Any questions?"

Deacon could think of none.

"Should think not," said Golightly. "You're navigator. Bring your compass and glasses. Patrol kit. Don't be fucking late."

Golightly turned on a smart heel and left. Lockett came in with the laundry and began unpacking the linen trousers.

"I think he is definitely thawing, don't you, sir?" he said.

Deacon took his drink down in one and then poured two full glasses. He knew he had to do it now or it would never be done.

"Sit down, corporal," he said.

Lockett stopped in his brushing down of the blue cotton jacket and looked across at Deacon. His eyes seemed suddenly wide and his face pale. He sat down slowly.

Deacon took a mouthful of whisky. He suddenly felt very tired.

"I'm afraid I'm going to ask you to do something you won't want to do, corporal," he said.

Lockett reached out and drank a little of his whisky. He held the glass tumbler in both palms.

"Not a transfer, is it, sir?" Lockett said. He tried a smile.

"What?" said Deacon. "No. Not transfer. Whatever…? Oh, never mind."

Lockett eased back in his chair.

"I have to ask you to give me Clemmie's films."

Lockett stayed silent for a moment and then laughed softly.

"Miss Ross's films, sir?" he said.

Deacon finished his drink and poured himself another. Lockett declined a refill.

"Yes," said Deacon. "Want you to give them to me. Not Miss Ross."

"But Miss Ross asked me," said Lockett. "She has paid me, sir."

"I know," said Deacon.

Lockett was silent for a while.

"Is it an order, sir?" he said.

"Would I ask you nicely otherwise?"

Lockett smiled. "Then of course, sir. I will have them for you in a couple of days."

Deacon looked up from his glass.

"That's it? No protest? No moral outrage? Just, of course, sir?"

Lockett said nothing. He just shrugged.

Deacon flicked Lockett a cigarette. Deacon lit them and pulled the smoke hard into his throat. They sat. Out beyond the yellow chrysanthemum on its sill Deacon heard a marching band and a drill sergeant's piard bark sounding somewhere in a far distance.

"I'm going to be away for a couple of days on a sortie," he said. "Viking call. Start Wednesday morning. You'll be okay to run the men?"

"I'm afraid not, sir." said Lockett. He stubbed his cigarette, got up from his chair and drank the last of his whisky. "I'm afraid I'll be on away on a two-day sortie too, sir."

Deacon looked up, puzzled.

Lockett grinned and saluted smartly. "Corporal Lockett, Advanced Driver Grade One reporting, sir! Sergeant Golightly was good enough to invite me along. Well, order actually. They need me as a Viking driver. But Ambrose will act up in our absence. Will that be all until the morning, sir?"

Deacon saw Lockett's grin, just as he saw Lockett open the door and close it behind him, but it didn't quite register. Deacon sat sitting in his chair staring at the door, trying to gather his wits. A leaden weight seemed to grow in his gut. He had felt many things while in Aden, but a dawning worry for Lockett was a new and troubling one.

THIRTEEN

Captain Banks and his wife lived in a pink-stoned villa that stood in two acres of lawns and flowerbeds halfway up the Telegraph Hill road. Its gardens were enclosed on three sides by trees and mountains but the open view from the terraced lawns looked down upon the blue of the Aden bay and the grey scum of the city that foamed at its shores. The portico and windows of the house were arched in the Moroccan style, but the design was large bungalow. As Deacon parked his jeep on the cobbled driveway, Indian music snaked out on the sea breezes to greet him.

Grace and Captain Banks arrived with the music and met him at the front door. Deacon was relieved to see that the couple were both wearing white linen trousers and cotton shirts. Grace Banks had a brightly patterned sweat-band headscarf tied across her brow, like a Comanche brave.

"Harry! Glad you could make it," said Banks. "Grace was beginning to think she'd have to play doubles on her own."

"Don't listen to Peter," said Grace. She took Deacon's arm. "He's just trying to soften us up before the game. Playing his Intelligence mind tricks on us. It's the only way he can win."

"Remind me, Grace, how many games am I beating you by?"

"Two. But a gentleman wouldn't have counted my games with the flu."

"Since when has tennis been played by gentlemen?" said Captain Banks.

They escorted Deacon through cool, light rooms furnished in the oriental style. Grace explained that the house had been built by a spice merchant at the end of the last century. He had brought the bungalow design from Kashmir, the arches from Arabia and the gardens from the pages of English Country Life.

They stepped out onto the wide lawns and made their way past a small cherry orchard. Deacon could see the fence of a tennis court peeking out through trees on a lower lawn.

"Now, it's Peter and Grace, ok Harry?" said Banks. "Leave ranks in the jeep."

"You can return to bowing and scraping before Peter tomorrow," said Grace. "But Peter is quite right. We are very informal. Like gypsies. You know Clemmie, of course. And we have Alec Peterson and Lizzie to make up the party. You know Alec? Splendid. Clemmie! We've found a partner for you at last!"

Clemmie was sitting at a garden table under a large, tasselled umbrella. She grinned and waved as Deacon approached. She had her camera in her lap. She clicked Deacon's arrival. Peterson stood up, beaming, and shook Deacon's hand.

"May I introduce WRAF Corporal Elizabeth Benson," said Peterson. "Watch this one, Lizzie, he's a pirate."

A young, attractive woman with dark curls and slim limbs smiled and held out her hand for Deacon. It was the same young woman Peterson had prised away from the Rear Admiral at the Viking party.

"Anyone not in the Navy is a pirate to Alec," said Lizzie. "All that sailing the ocean waves. Bound to make you crazy."

Peterson laughed.

"Whereas flying imaginary skies keeps you sane, eh Lizzie? What do you think, Harry? I'm on Frigates and Lizzie is pushing her model planes around on a desk. Sea and sky. They just don't mix. I just can't see any hope for us, can you?"

Deacon watched Lizzie giggle beside Peterson. They were both wearing tennis shorts and cotton shirts. Lizzie's limbs were tanned to a cob-nut brown and her face was bloomed in youth. They had eyes only for each other. Deacon felt the pangs of envy stabbing through him.

"There's always aircraft carriers," he said .

Peterson and Lizzie looked at each other. Peterson grinned and turned to Deacon.

"Now why didn't we think of that?"

"Because you're both besotted," said Grace. "And can't think past your noses. A good set of tennis will see you right. Burn off some of that ghastly energy you young people have in so much abundance. Come on, Peter, let's leave Harry to rest a while. We'll take the bay end."

Deacon sat with Clemmie under the umbrella. She looked through the long lens of her camera at the tennis game, her eye squinted and her lips apart. She clicked her shutter on more pictures that would be secretly taken from her without her knowing. Deacon sat in his chair and felt the camera shots punch into him like hot, tiny fists.

Deacon gazed about him. Tall carafes of iced water and gin stood to attention on a nearby table with small bottles of Schweppes tonic and orange juice trooped about them. On another table linen cloths covered small hillocks of unleavened bread, cheeses and fruit. Clemmie poured Deacon a tall gin and tonic and they settled in the shade to watch the game.

Clemmie explained that Alec and Lizzie were staying as the Banks's guests for a few days. They had the lodge cottage beyond the rose garden. Grace worked with Alec Peterson in the translation unit and they had become friends. Lizzie was ending her WRAF tour at the end of the month and returning to Kent. Grace and Peter had offered them the lodge for their last few days.

Deacon watched Alec and Lizzie laughing and shouting as they broke from each other's shadows to return a shot or to cry out in delight as another sun-high lob was teased up by Peter Banks. Deacon didn't recognise their love. He could not imagine what it must feel like. To be so joyously caged. And so wonderfully free.

"Tom took me out the other night," said Clemmie. "Guess where."

Deacon sipped his cool gin.

"The Inkerman?" he said.

"That's exactly what I would have thought," said Clemmie. She laughed. "But he took me for a dinner on the beach. Table and umbrella by the shore. We had lobster and champagne in the moonlight. Tom is always so surprising. It was a lovely evening."

Deacon could think of nothing to say. They watched the game. Banks's lob had just been called long. Deacon saw Grace slap the net with her racquet.

"Four – two," Grace called. "Come on, Peter! We can't let young 'uns beat us!"

"You do like me, don't you, Harry?" said Clemmie.

Deacon's glass slipped in his hand. He recovered it before it spilled.

"Yes, of course," he said. "Have you any reason to doubt it?"

"No. But then you like everyone. So it's hard to know who you *really* like. It's part of your charm. You like Tom, though, don't you?"

"He's difficult not to like," said Deacon. "There aren't that many Toms around."

Clemmie sucked hard on a cigarette and blew a gentle, smoke jet.

"Yes. That's true," she said. "But maybe that's because he doesn't give anybody else much room. Tom is always so much the centre of things."

She stubbed her cigarette and smiled at Deacon.

"The dinner on the beach was a lovely surprise though. Even had a wind-up gramophone playing Caruso. Hadn't seen that side of Tom before. You know, romantic. Quite disarming."

"It was probably all that Rimbaud," said Deacon. "Bound to have its effect."

Clemmie looked at Deacon. They both laughed. Their good spirits were maintained as they successfully contrived to lose a vigorous tennis match with their enthusiastic hosts. Deacon even managed to hit a few shots himself.

That evening they ate at a large table in the conservatory overlooking the lawns as the sun sank under lavender clouds. The meal was a simple one of rice and lamb with salads and breads. Deacon was relieved to see only one knife and fork at his setting. The night was falling fast over the bay and the lights of ships sparked like fireflies in the picture window frame. Alec Peterson and Lizzie joined them at the table. They looked fresh and flushed, even a little younger.

"Everyone just tuck in," said Banks. He took a serving spoon and scooped some rice onto his plate. "Wine or beer on the dresser. Help yourself. Maybe we should get out the champagne, eh Grace? Celebrate our win."

"I think Alec and Lizzie have shown themselves perfect guests by letting us win," said Grace. She smiled at Deacon. "That is definitely worth some champagne!"

Banks fetched a couple of bottles from one of the tall refrigerators that stood in rank in the nearby utility room. The bottles popped amid much laughter.

They talked of the recent tennis games and of the problems of getting good pipe tobacco in Aden and of the arrival of HMS Valiant in the docks that afternoon.

"Heavy cargo, I understand," said Banks.

"Yes," said Peterson. He took a sip of wine. "Trucks and munitions, I believe. And they brought in the Lancashire's relief. Valiant takes the Lancs boys back in a couple of days."

Deacon saw Alec glance at Lizzie, almost as if he halfexpected her not to be there. Lizzie was staring deep into her wine glass.

"So what are you two love birds going to do?" asked Grace.

"Do?" said Clemmie. She poured herself more champagne.

"Alec and Lizzie, dear," said Grace.

Clemmie laughed lightly.

"I have no idea, Grace," said Alec. He cut a wedge of cheese and put in on his plate. "Haven't had time to plan anything."

"Alec has six more months of duty tour before he can come back home," said Lizzie.

"But six months will soon fly by," said Clemmie. "I'm sure, Lizzie. You'll see. Six months is hardly anything."

Lizzie looked up through wide, steady eyes. "It's time enough," she said.

She smiled at Alec. Deacon saw Lizzie break a little. Her hand came quickly to her nose and it seemed to stifle a small whimper as it sought escape. Lizzie turned in her chair and then stood up. Alec was at her side with his arm around her shoulder. He looked toward Peter and Grace. They waved him be gone with understanding smiles. Alec escorted Lizzie out onto the lawns and down to the cottage. Lizzie's head burrowed hard into his shoulder all the way. Deacon watched them to their far front door. He watched it close. He envied them their love so much it hurt.

"Well, if it's love, it will find a way," said Grace. She plucked a couple of grapes from their cluster and dropped them into her mouth.

Peter smiled.

"It usually does, my dear," he said. He patted Grace's hand.

Silence drifted about them.

"You're out with Captain Villiers tomorrow, aren't you?" said Grace.

"He can't possibly tell you that. Grace!" said Banks.

"Don't be silly, dear, there are no secrets here, it's Aden. But just be careful Harry. That's all I was going to say. Captain Villiers is rather a wild one, I fear."

"I'm sure it will be fine," said Deacon. "There is more trouble in the Brigadier's cheeseboard."

Banks laughed but Grace and Clemmie didn't. A silence descended. Deacon tried to avoid Clemmie's eyes. He gazed out into the darkening skies and seas.

"Harry and Clemmie," said Grace, "it's been a pleasure today. Can't quite remember when I have enjoyed myself so much. Thank you both. But I know you are on hospital call tomorrow, Clemmie, and Harry has, well, other duties to attend. So why don't you both run along, eh? Get some good sleep. Better than hanging around with us ancients. Now, go on, shoo!"

Deacon drove the jeep with care along the coast road towards the Brigadier's villa. Clemmie was animated in chatter beside him and the champagne evidently still bubbled within her. She held up her palms to the jeep's night airs and let her hands surf them.

"Peter and Grace are wonderful, aren't they? Look at the lights on the bay. We played very well to lose, didn't we! What a lovely afternoon."

Deacon drove up to the villa gates and showed his ID to the two guards. The guards grinned at Clemmie.

"Hello, Sam," said Clemmie. "And Tommy, isn't it? Keeping me safe?"

Deacon nursed the jeep up the sweeping driveway and pulled to a stop before the small bridge. Two more guards waited on the other side. Clemmie stepped out of the jeep and draped her shawl across her shoulders.

"Now you will pay heed to Grace, won't you? No silly heroics."

"I'll probably be sitting on a mountain counting camels for two days," said Deacon. "Not heroic territory."

"Stop being so damn British about it, Harry!" said Clemmie. The words had snapped from her. She ruffled her shawl at her shoulders and took two cigarettes out of her bag and lit them. She passed one to Deacon. "Things always seem to happen around

Tom. And it's never camel watching. Just be careful, that's all. Now promise."

"I will."

"I do care about you, Harry. You do know that, don't you? And Tom, of course." Clemmie flicked her barely-smoked cigarette into the night. "I don't want to see you as one of my ward patients."

She smiled at Deacon. "I might have to give you bed baths."

Deacon laughed. Clemmie kissed him on the cheek.

"Thank you, that was a wonderful afternoon."

She pulled her camera bag from the well of the jeep and slung it over her shoulder. She patted the bag at her hip.

"An afternoon to remember," she said.

Deacon drove back to his billet by way of the beach. The half-hour of sitting in the jeep staring at the night sea made him later than he would have wished. He had an early start in the morning and he needed sleep. But he needed to clear his head more. It didn't work. Driving back to his billet, Deacon couldn't remember what he had thought at the beach. It was just surf and the drum-brush tide. A thirty-minute mind-wipe.

Deacon finally closed his billet door behind him a little after twenty-two-hundred. He switched on the light and hung his cap and jacket on the hooks. The room was clean and ordered. It looked like it had been recently swept and dusted. His uniform for the sortie and his patrol bag were on the bedroom chair ready for the morning. His cot had been tucked down, a fresh towel placed on the shower rail and the small bedside alarm had been thoughtfully set for oh-five-hundred hours. Beside the alarm clock sat a tumbler half-full with brandy.

Deacon lay back on his cot. In a night of strange dreams, he slept it like a bear.

FOURTEEN

Despite the sun's rise behind distant mountains, the early morning light in the large tent was grey and almost chill. A thin veil of slate clouds peeked over the far horizon. It was an unusual sight in the Aden skies. Rain was brooding somewhere close. Inside the tent Deacon felt like he was inside a Tupperware box.

Major Villiers stood in combat fatigues at the head of a long trestle table. He wore a bush hat and had his shirt sleeves rolled to the elbows. There were several large maps spread on the table before him. There were six soldiers in the tent. The tall, kilted Major Macintosh stood beside the table trying to get his pipe to light. A young, smartly uniformed SAS captain called Daniels stood with him, studying the map with intent. The sergeant standing next to Deacon flipped him a cigarette from his pack and nodded a grin. He introduced himself as Sergeant Lamb, the sortie's Arab interpreter. Sergeant Golightly stood stiffly at guard by the tent flap. Outside with the trucks were Lockett and six SAS soldiers, smoking themselves awake.

Villiers explained the sortie.

"We travel north through Lahij and over the mountains to the Yasim Plain. Intelligence has confirmed that a camel train will be heading out from Dhamar bound for Al Sah, a small village on the Yasim road. The train will be carrying four crates of PacVac mines and detonators." Villiers let the information sink in for a moment. "The mines are coming in through a Czech arms agent who is in Al Sah and waiting for his shipment to arrive there sometime tomorrow morning. He plans to sell them to the Adoo in Ta'izz . But we gentlemen, we will change his plans." He grinned at the faces gathered around the table. "We'll be there this evening. We're going to catch the shipment coming into Al Sah. And we're going to get those mines off our Czech friend before he can sell them to the Dizzies and we're going to bring them back here. Then give the Adoo a taste of their own PacVac medicine, eh? That means we have to travel nearly one hundred and thirty miles by tonight." Villiers stabbed a finger on the map. "Reckon you can navigate us to Al Sah by tonight, Harry?"

Deacon studied the map. He didn't need to. In Aden, all maps were wrong. He had been driving the deserts too long to ever trust them. Deacon recalled his patrols through the Shasam mountains and the dust of the Yasim Plains, trying to remember the passes and the terrains. He made some quick calculations of journey speed and distances.

"What are we taking?" he asked.

"Two trucks and a long-base jeep," said Villiers.

Deacon gazed at the maps before him.

"By sunset might be possible. We'll have to eat on the move. No more than ten minutes rest in every two hours."

"How are we going to get the Czech to hand over the mines to us?" asked Captain Daniels.

"We'll barter them," said Villiers. He nodded towards a large metal box that stood on the ground beside Golightly's glinting boots. "A few thousand in gold sovereigns. And if that price isn't acceptable, we'll just have to take them for free."

Deacon saw Villiers glance at Golightly. The sergeant grinned. Villiers turned to back to the table.

"Those mines cannot get to the Dizzies. Is that clear gentlemen?"

The tent was quiet.

"Then let's get on with it," said Villiers.

They drove the road to Lahij and were through its sprawl of grey block buildings and knock-down huts a little after oh-eight-hundred. Only the camels, lying squat on the dirt and chewing air, saw them pass. Deacon was in the lead truck with Golightly driving. Villiers and Macintosh were following in the longbased jeep and behind them Lockett was driving Captain Daniels and the rest of the men in the troop truck. The grey light had been scorched away by a rising sun but Deacon could still see the thin charcoal line of clouds pencilled on the far horizon. The clouds seemed to be heading north and away from them. The threat of rains diminished.

The rise up into the Shamsan mountains was slow and heavy going. Golightly jerked the gears and stamped the pedals and swore loudly at the truck's every grind and lurch. Golightly didn't drive the truck, he fought it. It was not a comfortable ride. In the wing mirror Deacon could see Lockett driving his truck with an easy skill, laughing with Captain Daniels about something. Deacon's truck lurched again as Golightly attacked the gears and the truck groaned up the steep winds of the mountain road.

They stopped at midday on a high pass looking down on the arid scrub land of the Yasim plain that stretched out below them to the white, glared horizon. The plain was flat, rock-strewn and smudged in khaki-coloured swathes of brush. Dark scars of dry river beds scratched across the plain like cats' claws on a slate. Deacon studied the plain through his binoculars and studied his maps and compass while the others brewed up and checked the vehicles.

"See no ships, sir?" asked Lockett.

He appeared beside Deacon and offered him a mug of tea and a cheese roll. Deacon let his binoculars fall and took the tea. It was heavy and sweet with rum.

"They forgot to pack the sugar, sir," said Lockett. He grinned. "No way to run a patrol."

Deacon bit into the roll. "No chutney, corporal?"

"There is a war on, sir." Lockett stared to the far horizon where the clouds still lingered. "Don't see many clouds out here, do we? They look ominous. Not heading for trouble, are we?"

"Of course we are, corporal. The British Army never heads anywhere else. We follow a noble tradition."

"And always led by donkeys, sir. More tea?"

Deacon watched Lockett turn and wander off to replenish his mug. Lockett stopped and then retraced his steps. He looked a little sheepish. He grinned up at Deacon.

"Didn't mean to suggest you for a donkey, sir. I meant the Generals. You know. Not the real soldiers."

Lockett made his escape back to the tea kettle. Major Villiers was sitting around the primus stove with the SAS soldiers, laughing and smoking. Major Macintosh slept open-mouthed in the jeep and Sergeant Golightly stood sentinel at Villiers's shoulder, demolishing a cheese roll with savage bites. Captain Daniels was staring down at the plain through binoculars. Deacon gave them ten more minutes and then signalled time to leave.

As they drove down the narrow, twisting roads off the Shamsan mountains, Golightly managed to slew the front wheel of the jeep into a roadside gully and it went down into the ditch with its back wheels off the tarmac, spinning in air. The skewed jeep blocked the road and the rest of the party were soon gathered on the roadside watching Golightly trying to back the jeep out of the gully. The jeep whined and screamed and rocked and dust clouds billowed but Golightly couldn't get it up onto the tarmac road. The SAS soldiers enjoyed the spectacle. Villiers was becoming impatient.

"If needs must we'll transfer the load to the truck and boot this one into the ravine," said Villiers. "Can't waste time here or we'll jeopardise the mission. Come on, Golightly! Pull your damn finger out."

Golightly was red-faced and cursing as he tried to move the truck. He ignored the cheery advice and encouragement of the soldiers.

"I'll get the bastard," said Golightly and stamped on the pedal. The jeep roared and spat dust but didn't move. Villiers kicked the road.

"Get out, Golightly. That's an order. Unload it."

"I'll have a go sir," said Lockett. He stepped forward and called across to the soldiers who were squatting with a smoke on the road bank. "Fancy a free fairground ride, lads?"

Lockett got a few of the men onto the back of the jeep while he took over from Golightly in the driver's seat. He revved the engine and shouted to his passengers. "Bit of bounce boys!" The soldiers began to sway and swing with the revs and lurch of the jeep and laughed on its ride. As the back wheels found purchase, the jeep reared up and rocked backwards. Lockett slipped the gears and the front wheels bit. Amid grinding metal and dust, the jeep spat itself onto the road. The riders cheered.

"Troop dismount!" ordered Golightly. "At the double." His face was flushed and sheened in sweat. "Move it!"

The soldiers jumped down and loitered to a casual line at the roadside, grinning at Golightly. Lockett parked the jeep and checked the front wheel and axle. There was no major damage and the truck was driveable.

"Good work, corporal," said Villiers. "Now let's get going. Don't jeopardise the mission again, Golightly."

Golightly fumed and swore beside Deacon for the rest of the day, his fists clutched tight on the steering wheel and his heels stamping hard.

It took almost four hours to drive the forty miles to Al Sah. There were no straight paths over the Yasim plain. The track led them across many shallow wadis but where they had been sculpted into deep, dry river beds they were forced to travel laterally along them until they could find a place to cross. They drove sixty miles to make forty and swirling dusts, a scorching sun and arid scrub land kept them company the whole way.

As they neared Al Sah, hillocks of rock and scree began to ripple the grey dirts of the plain and the mountains rose higher into the sky about them. Deacon led them up a low rise and parkedup in the lee of a bank of scree. He jumped out of the jeep and crabbed his way up the loose rocks and dusts of the hill. He scanned the view through his binoculars. About a mile away Al Sah lay like a throw of small stones on a low flat plateau rising from the grey cloth of the plain; a desolate collection of stone huts and concrete-slabbed buildings, seemingly in the middle of nowhere. Deacon could see a few people moving about, some tethered goats and thin smoke hazing from a couple of chimneys. The road in and out of Al Sah was empty of traffic except for a man leading a laden donkey. Deacon watched until the man and the donkey disappeared behind the buildings.

Deacon slid down the embankment. The whole party was there to meet him.

"Well?" said Villiers.

"Al Sah is a mile beyond the rise," said Deacon. "Everything seems quiet and normal."

"Well done, Harry!" said Villiers. He slapped Deacon on the shoulder. "Let's have a look."

Villiers, Macintosh and Daniels scrambled up to recce the village themselves and returned after some minutes.

"Right, we camp here," said Villiers. "Keep watch on the road for traffic. Two on in two-hour rotating shifts. Sort it, Sergeant Golightly. Right, let's radio back to base."

Sergeant Golightly turned to the group of soldiers who were huddled by the truck smoking.

"Right lads," said Golightly. He grinned thinly. "Lockett, you been sat on your arse all day. You can take the first two hour watch. And you too Private Robson."

One of the SAS soldiers hurled his cigarette to the rocks at his feet. He had been one of the soldiers most amused by Golightly's accident. Robson hitched his gun and spat a tobacco crumb into the gathering night. Golightly ignored him.

"Styles, Makepiece and Rogers. Fix the tents. Towser and Dyson, camp sentries. Move it!"

The soldiers drifted to their duties.

They kept watch on the road and pitched the two troop tents as the night settled about them. No camel trains came along the Dhamar road and the village of Al Sah remained quiet under the distant, faint glows of scattered rush lights and home fires. Villiers returned from one of his regular visits to the top of the rise.

"Right, let's get some chow. Lamb, get the stove going. Brought some brandy in the jeep too. See everyone gets a tot. Going to be a chilly night!"

"The stove is not advisable sir," said Deacon.

Villiers eyed him, but remained silent.

"The light, sir. From the stove. Seen for miles out here."

Villiers waited a few moments and then smiled.

"Quite right, Harry," he said. "But I can't do without some hot chow. We'll park one of the trucks in that dry river bed down there and canvas her in. Won't see the light from our stove then."

Deacon peered down into the wide river bed already being swallowed in night. It was deep enough to hide a truck.

"It's best to keep out of the river beds sir." said Deacon. "There might be rains."

"I saw the clouds Harry, but they disappeared this afternoon. There is no rain. So we'll stove it in the truck."

Golightly snapped to attention.

"I'll see to it, sir."

Golightly drove his truck down into the river bed below the tents. Sergeant Lamb organised the stove and canvas roof and they were eating hot stew within the hour. Villiers sat around the truck stove with Deacon, Daniels, Macintosh and Sergeant Lamb. A map of the village was brought out and the plans for the next day were briefed. They would go in at dawn from the east and do silent house-to-house until the agent was found. Make him the offer and then wait for the shipment to arrive. They would take possession of the PacVac mines and then skedaddle back to Aden. They would move out an hour before dawn.

"So let's get some good sleep," said Villiers. "Daniels and Lamb in the camp truck. The men in the tents. Tosh will sleep in the jeep. Harry, you can bunk with me here in this truck. Now, where's the brandy?"

They drank and talked in the truck through the two-hour watch. Daniels then left and scrambled up the side of the river bed to the camp to organise his men. Soon after, Sergeant Lamb headed for his tent and Major Mackintosh yawned like a bear and made for his jeep.

Villiers poured another brandy for Deacon. Sergeant Golightly had stretched out on the front bench seat of the truck cab with his bedding roll and was already snoring softly. Villiers and Deacon doused the stove and cleared the truck for sleep.

Deacon lay in the dark with his feet pressed against the tailgate and his head resting on his kit bag. Villiers lay still beside him with the metal sovereign box close by at his elbow. The ink-black sky was pricked with stars like a first fall of snow on a winter's night. Deacon could hear the sentries chattering in low voices and the scrape of their boots as they patrolled the camp rocks above them. The sounds seemed to echo in the river bed about him, as if from a deep well.

"Good work today, Harry," said Villiers from out of the dark.

"Thank you, sir."

Deacon was conscious of lying very still beside Villiers. He could not see him but felt Villiers' shoulder pressed at his. Their boots were almost touching. Deacon tried to breathe normally, but he felt too alert.

"Think Clemmie liked our dinner on the beach." said Villiers. "The Caruso touch worked wonders too. Brigadier's suggestion.

Said Clemmie liked that kind of thing. Italian, you know. Pictures being dealt with?"

"All in hand, sir."

"Good. It's best, for her you know."

"I know."

Deacon kept himself awake by staring at the snow-flaked sky. He dare not fall asleep. If he did, he knew that he might drift away. That he might turn in his sleep and lay an arm soft across Tom Villiers' slow breathing chest. That his head would find a pillow on Villiers's shoulder. And he knew that if it did, he would be lost. Forever.

Deacon stared into the night, his body hard as iron. He could feel Golightly's snores rumbling softly through the truck floor from the front cab. The air smelt of warm stove gas, sweat and cigarette smoke. Villiers lay asleep beside him, his breathing low and regular and sweetened with brandy. Deacon was able to relax a little. But he placed his holstered gun at his back for discomfort. He didn't want to fall asleep.

Villiers's hand fell on Deacon's thigh. It was so sudden in the dark that Deacon almost jerked. But he managed to keep his calm. Villiers was still breathing softly and evenly in the dark. He was still asleep and the hand had been unconscious. But it lay heavy and uncomfortable on Deacon's leg. He let it rest there for some minutes wishing it not there, and almost thrilled that it was. Deacon carefully felt for Villiers' sleeve and raised the hand from his thigh and placed it on Villiers' own. Villiers snorted softly, but slept on. Deacon quietly eased himself out of the truck. He scrambled up the dry river bank and took watch on the cold rocks at the top of the rise. He was sweating.

FIFTEEN

"Still no sugar, I'm afraid, sir." said Lockett. He squatted down on the top of the rise beside Deacon and handed him a steaming mug. It was approaching dawn.

"Double duty, corporal?" said Deacon.

"Couldn't sleep sir. Mattress full of rocks."

Lockett lit a couple of cigarettes and passed one to Deacon. Deacon could feel his fingers on fire around the mug. The rocks and air were cool as the night began to slip away. The mountain shapes beyond Al Sah began to ghost their dark teeth at the horizons and the rocks and scrubs of the plain loomed to khaki greys.

"Not exactly Piccadilly Circus, is it?" said Lockett. "Any traffic at all?"

"Just a donkey," said Deacon.

Lockett flushed a little. They watched the village in silence for a while.

"Just doesn't feel right, this one," said Lockett. "I mean why here of all places? This hole in the middle of nowhere? Makes no sense."

Deacon laughed. "Sense, corporal? This is Aden."

"Sorry, sir. Silly of me."

They watched the low plateau of Al Sah take shape in the pre-dawn salmon light and smoked their cigarettes.

They heard it together. A low, faint sound in a far distance. It was like the soft galloping of hooves. Deacon kneeled upright and scanned through his binoculars. Lockett crouched beside him.

"Horses?" said Lockett in a whisper.

"No," said Deacon. "That is not the sound of horses."

Deacon trained his glasses beyond Al Sah to the edge of the plain where it met the mountains. Through the dim light he saw what appeared to be small grey clouds rushing along the floor of the plain towards Al Sah. Like a rolling bank of smoke hugging the ground.

He turned and looked at Lockett. "The rains!" he said.

Deacon ran down the rise, his boots skidding on the scree and rocks. Lockett was beside him. They bellowed the alarm and ran to wake the men. The soldiers stumbled half-asleep from their tents and then heard the distant rumble. They were suddenly fully awake. Deacon ordered them up the rise and Daniels went to rouse Macintosh from the jeep. Deacon ran to the edge of the river bed and saw the other truck below him. He gazed out onto the plain and saw the low clouds rolling brown and grey towards him. He scrambled down the river bank and roused Villiers from the back of the truck.

"Rains, sir!" he said. "You need to get out of here and up on the rise!"

Villiers was instantly awake. The rumble was now turning into a roar. Villiers jumped down from the truck beside Deacon and without a word they ran for the bank. A stiff breeze had sprung from nowhere and dust and grit stung their arms and face. Villiers stopped his run and seemed to be in two minds. He glanced back at the truck and then at the advancing roar.

"The metal box!" he said. "In the back of the truck. Get it, Harry!"

Deacon found himself returning to the truck before he really knew what he was doing. He hauled the heavy box under his arm and scrambled back up the river bank and onto the flat below the rise. Villiers took the box from him and put in the back of the jeep and covered it in a canvas sheet.

Deacon stood and watched the advancing cloud part and roll around Al Sah and speed on towards him. The roar became deafening and the smoke cloud turned into a brown surge of slurried water that crashed and pulverised its way along the river bed channels. Stones and rocks careered and cracked on the bow-wave like ricochets along the the dry wadi below his feet. Behind the gunfire, a raging flood of foaming sludge and water roared and rumbled along the river bed, devouring everything in its path. Deacon watched the wall of liquid desert tumbling before him with a sense of utter detachment that only real fear could bring. He could see that the water would not get up on the rise where they stood and he was only conscious of the sheer power of the sight before him, and of the head-splitting noise about him and of Lockett's hand holding lightly onto his belt.

Villiers turned to face Deacon. His eyes were wide.

"Golightly!" he shouted.

The words were almost lost in the roar. Deacon felt ice flush through him. He turned to look down at the truck. The stones and boulders of the river flood's bow-wave were already cracking into the back of the truck. Seconds later the tumbling, surging flood waters passed under where Deacon and Villiers stood and lifted up the back of the truck as if it were a toy. The back wheels rose in the air and the truck was momentarily aloft and groaning on a slow spin before it was carried away on a rage of rushing water like a piece of driftwood on the tide's rip. The truck bobbed and span in the torrent and clouds of spray for a moment and then it disappeared beneath the raging caramel waters and was carried away.

It was two hours before the waters subsided to a knee-high stream and another hour before they became ankle high rivulets. The flood waters were gone as quickly as they had come. Another hour later and the plains were scorching once more under the parching sun.

Villiers spent much of the waiting time in close and private conversations with Macintosh and Daniels and at a distance from the rest of the party. They had the radio pack and held several long conversations with base. Deacon ordered Sergeant Lamb to do an equipment check and to send a scouting party down the river bed.

"Looking for his body?" asked Robson.

"And for any kit that was in the truck." said Deacon. "We might need what we can find. Half an hour, then turn back."

Deacon scrambled up the rise and trained his glasses on Al Sah. The village remained untouched by the flood waters. He was aware of Lockett beside him.

"Is the village alright, sir?"

Deacon smiled.

"Yes. It's not in the middle of nowhere. It's in the middle of somewhere particular. A low rise in a flood plain to be precise. And probably has been there since the time of Noah."

"Smart buggers, the Adoo," said Lockett.

The soldiers returned from their patrol of the river bed. They had found only Sergeant Golightly's kit bag.

Villiers called the party together. He was stern-faced and businesslike, his voice hard with frustration and fortitude.

"Well, it's rotten luck but without the truck and equipment, the sortie is a bust. A truck has gone along with several rifles, machine guns, diesel, the second radio and the stove. We have also probably lost a damn fine soldier."

Villiers let the thought linger for a respectful moment. "The floods will have put paid to the camel train too. So nothing we can do but cut out and pull back to Aden as soon as we can. Nothing to be gained by staying. A party will take the jeep down the river bank to search for the truck and Sergeant Golightly. The rest pack up the camp in the remaining truck and keep watch on Al Sah and the road. The jeep to return after two hours. With or without Golightly."

Villiers led the jeep party of Deacon, Lamb, Robson with Lockett as the driver. They followed the dry river bed accompanied by a relentless sun and persistent dusts. After a little less than an hour they found the remains of the truck wedged into the bank on a sharp bend in the river bed. The truck was on its side with its back wheels in the air but the cab and the front half of the truck were buried under a dune of dry silts and rocks. It looked like the truck had been speared into the river bank from the sky. The canvas and roof stays had gone and the body of the truck was bent and crumpled like a crushed tin can.

Villiers took off his jacket and threw it in the jeep. He began rolling up his sleeves.

"Stay with the jeep, corporal. And guard the box. Right, gentleman, let's find the worst."

Deacon went with the rest of the party to inspect the wreckage. They found a trenching tool still latched to the side of the truck and used it to dig the loose sand and rocks from around the cab. Eventually they managed to find the cab door and Sergeant Lamb wrenched it open. Sand sluiced from the cab and pooled about Deacon's legs. He waited for the flow to ease and then began to burrow into the remaining cab sand with his hands. They discovered Golightly lying along the cab floor entombed in silt. He lay rigid with his arms straight and stiff by his sides as if the river's sludge had engulfed and pinioned him before he was able to react or move. His eyes were open and white with a sightless terror and his grit-filled mouth was open wide as if frozen in a scream.

They dragged Golightly out and laid his body on the rocks. Deacon stood gazing down at the carcass. It looked like the shrivelled pupa of an insect.

"Damn fine soldier," said Villiers, almost in a whisper. "Rotten bad luck. Let's get him in a bag."

Deacon and Villiers looked on as Lamb and Robson zipped Golightly into a body bag. Villiers kept up an unconvincing morale-boosting chatter as the jeep headed back to camp, emphasising the bad luck of events, the rotten fortune, the unlucky Golightly but Deacon knew it had not been anything to do with luck. It was bad and reckless soldiering and poor leadership. Villiers had thought more of saving the metal box than he did his sergeant. It was gone midday by the time they arrived back at the camp.

The camp tents and equipment had been stored and the soldiers were squatting on their haunches and smoking on the river bank. They watched silently as the body bag was carried from the jeep and placed in the back of the truck.

Villiers, Macintosh and Daniels walked a little way out onto the plain and discussed plans. Villiers made several more radio calls.

Deacon waited in the shade of the truck, too tired to care or think much about anything. Eventually Villiers called them all together.

"Nothing for it but to make out way back to Aden as best we can," he said. He plucked a small cigar from his pockets and lit it. Deacon saw that Villiers's hands shook. "Afraid Tosh and I will have to leave you on your own to make it back, though. A helicopter is on its way to take us back to Aden. Need to report in as quick as we can. Don't want to leave you but I've been given my orders. We'll take Sergeant Golightly with us in the chopper. Only right. Just bad luck boys, that's all. But we won't go back with our tails between our legs. RAF are going to be paying Al Sah a visit in a couple of hours. Leave a few Viking calling cards after all, eh? Teach the bastards to harbour Dizzy agents."

Villiers looked around at his troop. He grinned. "Even when down and cornered the Vikings can still pack a punch, eh gentlemen?"

The soldiers stared back at him in silence.

They stored the last remaining equipment away in the truck. Golightly's body bag had to be taken out to accommodate the packing. It lay on the slope of grey scree. The soldiers kept away from it. A meal of dry biscuits and brandy was shared in the shade while they waited for the helicopter to arrive. The mood was quiet and subdued.

Villiers took Deacon aside.

"You'll have to lead the men out, Harry. Daniels doesn't know the desert like you. But I couldn't leave the men in better hands."

"Aren't we going to warn Al Sah about the planes, sir?" said Deacon.

Villiers stared out into the desert plains beyond the village. "No time for that, Harry. Those courtesies belong to older wars. Al Sah has to take its chance like everyone else. When do you reckon you can get back to Aden?"

"We should get to the mountains by nightfall. Back in Aden by tomorrow afternoon."

"Fine. But take care, Harry. Don't want any more bad luck on this trip. I'll report to the Brigadier as soon as I get back. File the report. See to Golightly. Make sure it's all done right. Proper and fitting arrangements. Now, I want you to report to me personally the moment you get back to Aden, understand? We'll have steaks at the Troy. The whole troop. My treat."

Deacon sat and smoked cigarettes with Lockett in the shade of the jeep. The sun baked the air about them as they watched two vultures gliding the thermals in lazy coils high above them.

"Can you smell it, sir?" said Lockett.

"What?"

"It's all around us, sir," Lockett flicked his cigarette butt to the sun. "It's the unmistakable whiff of donkey shit."

Deacon smiled.

"Yes. I do, now you come to mention it. Good to see the traditions haven't been lost."

"Why did you join the army, sir?"

Deacon stared out at the parched grey rocks of the Yasim plain. He could hide for days out there; no one would ever find him. "Fear," he said.

Deacon heard the sound of distant purring and moments later a helicopter appeared as a small black fly moving in fast and low over the desert. He shaded his eyes and watched it come in and land on flat dirt nearby. Whirlwinds of gritted dust erupted around it and then fell away as the blades idled and then stopped. It was a small Westland Siuox scout helicopter, only able to carry two passengers. But Deacon saw it also had a couple of stokes litters on its runners, special metal cradles for evacuating casualties. Sergeant Golightly would be travelling in style.

They loaded Golightly's bag into the cradle and the helicopter pilot strapped him down. Villiers went round to each of the men with handshakes and words of regret and encouragement. The steak dinner promise was repeated.

"Fetch my kit, corporal," said Villiers. The metal box, wrapped in a ground blanket, was already under his arm. "Ready Tosh? See you in Aden tomorrow then, Harry."

Villiers climbed into the helicopter. He offered a brief nod to the men and then sharply tapped the pilot on the shoulder. The helicopter lurched and then rose in another cloud of dust and noise and banked away into the scorching,white sky.

Deacon and the men watched until its speck disappeared over the far mountains. Deacon turned to find the men all watching him. Lockett came and stood beside him.

"They really going to bomb Al Sah, sir?" he said.

"Apparently," said Deacon.

Sergeant Lamb stepped forward. "It don't seem right, sir. Just bombing a village. For no reason. Not without a warning. Women and kids, we should give 'em a chance to get out."

Deacon looked to Captain Daniels. He was standing with his men. The captain smiled and shrugged.

"Not my idea of soldiering," he said. "Killing civilians. Bombing homes. But what can we do? We have our orders."

Deacon went to the top of the rise and scanned the village through his binoculars. He could see people moving about among the squat stone huts, tending to their goats and camels, checking their hovel homes for flood damage. Two young children played football against a stable wall. Deacon checked his watch.

"Fancy a little drive out in the jeep, corporal?" he said.

Lockett grinned. "It's a nice day for it, sir."

Deacon turned to Sergeant Lamb. "Care to join us?"

"Delighted," he said.

Deacon took out the map and went over his plan with Captain Daniels. They would take the jeep to the east of the village and drive through it. Captain Daniels was to take the rest of the men in the truck and head west out over the plain and meet them on the Yasim road. They would then cross the plain and camp overnight in the mountains.

"You're taking a risk, Harry," said Daniels. "But I'll have the men ready to come in if you get into trouble."

Deacon, Lamb and Lockett set out in the jeep. The recent flood had reshaped and deepened the wadis and it took them almost half an hour to position themselves on the road outside the village. Deacon checked the village through his binoculars. Everything seemed as normal as it could be after a flash flood. He saw the truck heading away across the plain to the other side of the village.

"Are you in good voice, Lamb?" Deacon said.

"Yes, sir. What should I say?"

"Just tell them that a plane is coming to bomb them in less than an hour and to drop everything and go hide out on the plain."

They drove slowly through the village. Deacon kept his Browning pistol to hand and Lamb stood up in the back of the jeep shouting his urgent news. The young children fled back into their houses as the jeep approached but a few curious villagers appeared in doorways to investigate the noise. Lamb kept up his Arabic shouting while the jeep moved slowly past the village huts. An old man came out into the street and called up to Lamb and a short conversation ensued. Other villagers came out and Lamb gave his warnings again. Lockett kept the jeep moving.

Deacon looked back as they left the village. He could see people standing in the road arguing and gesticulating. They drove on and met Daniels and the truck a mile along the road.

Daniels was standing on the cab roof looking back at the village through his binoculars.

"They seem to be moving about," he said. "Taking their goats out onto the plain. Think you've done the trick, Harry. We best get out of here."

They drove fast down the Yasim road and then Deacon headed them onto the tracks across the plain that led them back to the Shamsan mountains. Moments after they had left the tarmac road Deacon heard the low drone of the planes. Two Bristol Brigand bombers appeared in the sky flying low and slow over the plain. Deacon watched the planes pass over Al Sah and then bank slowly in the sky and return. Deacon tried to see through his binoculars but the village was masked from view by the intervening rocks and scrub of the plains. He saw the four bombs drop through the sky and the small eruptions of black and grey smoke spurt beneath them, followed by the sound of faded booms. The planes flew on across the plain and disappeared over the far mountains.

SIXTEEN

They arrived back in Aden in the early afternoon. Captain Daniels shook Deacon's hand on parting in the car park of the Troy Hotel. The rest of the soldiers tumbled out of the truck, offering silent nods to Deacon as they headed for the bar.

"Can't say it's been a pleasure, Harry," said Daniels. "But war is not supposed to be, is it? Just another cock-up in the hen house. Bad luck followed this one like a smell."

Deacon said nothing.

"See you around again, I hope, Harry. But now I need a beer." Daniels left to join his men at the bar.

Deacon and Lockett drove to the duty office and signed in. Lockett disappeared for a few moments and returned with two bottles of beer and a small,brown paper parcel. He handed the parcel to Deacon.

"Miss Ross's negatives and films sir. As requested."

Deacon took the parcel. "Thank you, corporal. We best pay our respects to Major Villiers."

They drank the bottled beer as they drove up the long, wide, snaking boulevard of Victoria Drive to the high grounds above the bay. The trim, leisurely ranks of large, detached, pastel coloured houses and painted lawns looked more like toys than homes. They were separated by tall hedges and stone walls and each nestled back from the road at the end of long, tree-shaded drives. Deacon showed his ID at the gate and they were nodded through. Villiers's house was a two-storey villa of orange and white stone work under a Tuscany-tiled roof. The lawns and fruit orchards in the grounds were marshalled by troops of large earthen pots sprouting palms and shrubs and small lemon trees. Deacon could see table umbrellas and sun loungers on an upper balcony viewing deck that stretched along one side of the house overlooking the harbour.

A young, teak-tanned man dressed only in army shorts and boots sat on the front-door steps of the house. He was leaning back against one of the portico pillars with his eyes closed and holding a curved sheet of aluminium under his chin like a silver fan. He was slim, and his smooth skin shone with oils and sweat. His hair was dark and long to the nape and swept back, slick over his head, as if he had just emerged from the water after a dive.

"Looking for Major Villiers," said Deacon.

The young man squinted a lazy eye open without disturbing his fan. He looked Deacon slowly up and down and then did the same for Lockett. He closed his eye.

"Tommy? Around somewhere, I dare say. If he's not swinging the MacGregor down in the golf net, he's probably up on the sling-deck with a gin. Up the stairs. Wander. Can't miss it."

Deacon and Lockett made their way up the wide stairway and onto a landing of open-doored rooms. The sun-deck was empty.

"Major Villiers?" called Deacon. There was no answer. Lockett checked a couple of rooms and then Deacon pushed open the door of a bedroom. Crumpled sheets lay unmade on the large bed and the French windows were open to a small balcony and a view of a blue satin sea. Deacon heard the sound of a shower and a low voice singing from the en-suite bathroom.

"Major Villiers?" he called. "Lieutenant Deacon, sir."

The sound of the shower continued but the singing seemed to slow. A moment later Deacon was taken aback to see Chi appear from the bathroom. He looked at Deacon and then at Lockett as if they were not there. He walked calmly to the other side of the room and picked up his tea urn from behind the door and two coins from the dresser.

"What are you doing here, Chi?" said Lockett.

"Bring Tom his tea," said Chi. He gazed out at the sea view. "Good business."

Villiers appeared at the bathroom door. "Harry! Good to see you back. No problems?"

Villiers was rubbing his wet hair with a towel. Another large towel wrapped around his midriff and covered him down to his calves. Deacon noticed the tightness of the towel and tried not to notice the fading bulge at its crotch. Deacon was aware that Lockett had noticed it too. Villiers strode across the room, rubbing his hair busily.

"Thank you, Chi," he said. "Fine tea. Same again tomorrow, eh? But bring both your urns, I've got a couple of Generals in from Cairo and they'll have thirsts like camels."

Chi hitched his urn to his shoulder. He didn't look at Deacon or Lockett.

"I go," he said and padded hurriedly away.

Deacon saw the hem on Chi's futah was rimmed with wet and small beads of water glistened in his dusted hair like beads. A trail of his small wet footprints traced his exit across the tiled floor.

Deacon shared a look with Lockett. Lockett's face was pale, its skin tight.

"I'll see him out, sir." Lockett said and hurried away after Chi.

Villiers sat on the edge of his bed guiding a palmed comb through his hair and smoothing it on a deft pat. He looked up at Deacon, watching him through steady eyes for some moments.

"Nothing wrong is there, lieutenant?" he said.

"No, sir," said Deacon. "I'm here to report. As ordered. And to give you this." He handed over Clemmie's films.

"Well done, Harry. Good work." Villiers began to look through the prints. "Your report?" he said.

Deacon gave his debrief while Villiers continued to study the photographs. He reported how they had camped overnight in the Shaman foothills and had set out for Aden at first light. That there had been no hostile contacts, no incidents to report.

Deacon came to the end of his report with their arrival back in Aden. He stared through the window at the sea and waited while Villiers finished with Clermmie's pictures.

"Fine, Harry," Villiers said at last. He grinned. "Fine picture of you here. The day of Rimbaud's house. Remember, Harry? Say this for Clemmie, she takes a good picture."

Villiers stuffed the pictures back in the envelope.

"Not much to worry us, I think." He handed the parcel back to Deacon. "I'll hold a couple." He slid some prints into his briefcase. "Your man can return the rest to Clemmie tomorrow. Is that the lot?"

"Yes sir. All that she gave my man."

"Well, we'll check for others back at the villa. So, everyone's happy and no harm done, eh?"

"No sir."

A silence fell. Deacon continued to watch the sea.

"Golightly got a proper soldier's send-off," said Villiers. "Saw to that. All the paperwork, rifle salute and so on. Tried to get him a medal. Do you know what, Harry? They don't give any medals in Aden. We are not an official war. Not officially combative. Did you know that?"

"Yes, sir."

Deacon felt Villiers watching him.

"Well, I told them it felt pretty combative from where I was standing. Now don't forget I'm standing all the boys a steak dinner tonight. Just put it up to my tab."

"They are looking forward to it sir."

"Okay, Harry. Now bugger off and get some well deserved kip and I can finish dressing. Taking Clemmie to the Artemis Ball tonight. Need to look my best, eh?"

Deacon sat on a rock at the roadside of Victoria Drive and waited for Lockett to return with the jeep. He was too tired to order the images that floated about him into any semblance of comprehension and too afraid to let them linger long. He was just aware of a deep feeling of disgust gnawing his insides. Disgust at himself. For saluting. And saying sir. And saying nothing else, doing nothing else. It was easy to persuade himself that there was nothing that needed doing, that nothing had happened. Nothing he could do or say. Chi was bringing tea like he did with Deacon most mornings. Nothing untoward. He was in the Army and under orders, but such excuses offered few comforts. He knew it was all a lie. Everything. He had let the lie wrap itself around him like a body bag and he had zipped himself up in it. To preserve his own lie, to stay hidden at all costs. But the cancer worms gnawed. Deacon felt like screaming.

Lockett eventually arrived with the jeep. He was silent, hard faced and distracted. He didn't look at Deacon when he took his seat.

"Where to, sir?" Lockett said.

"The Depot," said Deacon. "Better check in on the men."

They drove in silence for some time.

"How is Chi?" said Deacon.

Lockett took a moment to answer. "Chirpy," he said. "But very evasive. I took him back to Mr. Patel."

"Did he say anything?"

"Only tea business."

"How did he get himself all the way out to Victoria Drive?"

"By an officer's jeep, sir," said Lockett. "It was sent for him."

They drove to the depot and found the men. They were running stores from the dock. A steamer from India with holds full of cement and wire and a freighter laden with kerosene and wood had recently docked and stores transit was running on double time. The men had been kept at it all day and the usual doze and game of cards in the truck denied them.

"Fucking dockers, that's all we are," said Shaw.

"Not on one-and-six a day we ain't," said Hobson. "We're fucking coolies."

"You wish," said Ambrose.

The troop were shuffling in a ragged line across a concrete dockyard that rippled like water in the afternoon glare. They were moving bags of sun-hot cement from a row of palettes and then fast-striding them on their shoulders across the yard to heft the bags onto a flat bed trailer parked against a far wall. Then they idled back to the line to do it again. They were shirtless in the heat but wore rag epaulets to prevent the cement bags grilling the flesh from their shoulders. The men ignored Deacon's arrival.

"Keep it going, lads," said Kenny. "Bring the beer closer."

Deacon got back in the jeep and drove it up to the flat bed trailer. He backed under it, jacked the trailer wheel off until it rested on the jeep and then slowly pulled the trailer from the wall and parked it in front of the cement palettes. He jumped out of the jeep and re-jacked the trailer wheel, then he drove the jeep out and parked up.

"Right," he said. "Four on the bags and four on the trailer. Just swing them up and on. Stack them well. Get more on that way. Rest of you find shade. Beer if you've got it. Fifteen minute turn-around shifts. Should have it done in half the time."

The men looked at the cement palettes and at the trailer parked beside it, now just a short heft away. They seemed to droop a little. Shaw took the rag from his shoulder, wiped the back of his neck with it and threw it to the concrete.

"Fucking officers," he said and swung himself wearily up onto the trailer.

Deacon stayed with the men until the cement had all been loaded. Lockett worked with them but said very little. He just heaved-to with the heavy and hot cement bags until the sweat was dripping off him like rain. They had a short break of shade and beer before moving off to the dock side and unloaded wire and wood for another hour.

Deacon dismissed the men at sixteen-hundred hours and returned to the duty office with Lockett. He filled in his duty report, checked the rosters for the next few days and then had Lockett drive him back to his billet. The jeep slid to a stop outside his door and Deacon climbed out on stiff limbs.

"Suggest you get some sleep, corporal," he said.

"No thanks, sir," said Lockett. He stared ahead to a vague distance. "I'll drop the films off to Miss Ross then I'm going to get me some beer. Wash the taste and memory away."

The jeep revved hard and Lockett pulled away on screeching tyres.

Deacon showered and tried to get some sleep, but he dozed only fitfully. By twenty-two-hundred he was up and in his chair reading Dickens by lamplight, with a tumbler of whiskey at his elbow. Herbert Pocket was just explaining to Pip the etiquettes of eating peas when there was the sound of a sharp knock on Deacon's door and Corporal Lockett opened it almost immediately. He stepped into the room, closed the door behind him and stood almost to attention.

"Saw your light sir," he said. "So I thought I'd report that Miss Ross has her photographs. She seemed happy with the service. Shame about the exposed Crater film though. And the other two missing prints. One of the ships in the bay and the other a picture of you. Coming back from the dog. *Aden Soldier* Miss Ross called it. Remember, sir? I explained about the over-exposure. A faulty lens connection maybe. She gave me an extra half-crown for my trouble. Nice lady, sir."

Deacon closed his book and looked up at Lockett. He could tell by the flush on Lockett's cheek and the flint of his eye that he was a little drunk.

"Yes, very," said Deacon.

Lockett set his face to a smile. "Not taking advantage of the Major's steak dinner, sir?"

"It's been a long day."

"What are you going to do about Chi, sir?"

Deacon placed his book on the table and poured two tumblers of whiskey. He gestured for Lockett to take a seat.

"Prefer to stand, sir," said Lockett.

"Sit, corporal."

"Is that an order sir?"

"Yes, Lockett, it is."

Deacon watched Lockett hesitate for a moment before he relented and took a perch on the edge of the chair. Deacon pushed the whisky glass towards him.

"Do what, exactly?" said Deacon. "About what in particular?"

Lockett was about to speak but Deacon did not let him.

"Has Chi said anything? Made any complaint?"

"Well, no, not yet but how could he?"

"Then what can we do? We didn't actually see anything, did we? We have no evidence or proof that anything untoward has actually happened."

Lockett spat a laugh."Untoward!" he said.

Deacon ignored him. "And against Major Villiers. Of all people. Think about it. We would be clinked and laughed back down to the ranks. And we don't know if anything happened at all. It could all be perfectly innocent."

Lockett leaned back in his chair and watched the space before him through blazed eyes. He drank the tumbler of whisky off in one and refilled his glass from the bottle.

"So we just let that bastard..."

"Be careful, corporal. Remember where you are."

"So we do nothing?"

"What can we do?"

Deacon heard Lockett's short, grunted laugh. Lockett was watching him with soft eyes ringed hard with disappointment.

"Yes, that's right," Lockett said "See nothing. Do nothing." Lockett drained his tumbler and stood up on slightly uncertain legs. "That's all you ever do, isn't it sir? What you are good at."

Deacon stood up and faced Lockett. "Have a care, corporal."

Lockett laughed. A small Aden bray.

"Have a care!" he said. "That's exactly what I do have. But what about you? You just going to look the other way? That what officers do, is it?"

"What do you expect me to do?"

"We can't just do nothing!" said Lockett. His voice was rising and quivering in anger. "Pretend we didn't see what we both know we saw. We have to do something to protect Chi from that bastard. We know what Villiers is. How he uses people. We've got to try and keep Chi away from him."

"And how do we do that?"

"I don't fucking know!" Lockett was almost shouting. His face was reddening and he was swaying slightly. "I just know we have got to try. You're the officer. The one with the clever ideas. Fucking well think of something."

"I wish I could, corporal, but I really don't know what I can do."

Lockett drained the last of his whisky and placed the tumbler with care on the table. He shucked his jacket smooth and fixed Deacon with calm, sad eyes.

"Do?" he said. "Well how about you step out and stop hiding behind that damn convenient uniform of yours and start acting like a real human being for once? You know, like a real man."

Lockett turned suddenly on his heels, marched to the door and slammed it behind him on his exit.

Deacon felt the door's slam cut through him. He knew Lockett was right. He was hiding and Lockett was aware of it and had now shamed him for it. Deacon felt his betrayal of Lockett and Chi gnawing in his chest. He felt unclean and cowardly. He sat in his chair for long while, staring at the night walls.

SEVENTEEN

The day after a lengthy patrol was usually one of rest but Deacon felt compelled to check on the men and then to complete his patrol report at the duty office. He saw little of Lockett when he made his morning rounds and when he did it was always seemed to be at a convenient distance. Lockett worked with the men on the depot runs and busied himself with the many tasks, duties and comings and goings of a good troop corporal. But he didn't bother Deacon.

Deacon was content to ignore it at first but a nagging discomfort grew in him during the morning. It was disconcerting not to have Lockett at his shoulder, quipping, or sharing an observation. Sometimes even laughing. Deacon felt like his shadow had escaped him. The feeling unnerved him.

Deacon spent his lunch typing his patrol report in the duty office. It was a short report but typing made it slow going. The office telephone rang, and it was Clemmie.

"Harry! I heard you were back from counting camels. Are you all in one piece?"

"Mostly."

Deacon heard Clemmie's laugh ripple through the wires.

"Good. But I must see you for myself. To make sure. You're off duty now and you've had your morning nap and lunch, so you can take me to the Tiwali Tanks this afternoon. I want more pictures. It was so beautiful. It'll be fun. About time you had some of that. The Brigadier has approved, as long as I go with a responsible adult. Says you'll do fine. So say you will , Harry? I'll treat you to afternoon tea. Pick me up at two?"

Deacon gazed across the office to the duty corporal who sat behind the telephone board watching him. He had a head-phone clamped over one ear. He was a young, thin-faced soldier with acne. He grinned and began pumping a pencil up and down through a circle of his fingers. Deacon turned his gaze to the window and the parade ground.

"Delighted," he said.

Clemmie was waiting outside the Villa gates, sporting a wide straw hat and dark sunglasses. She grinned and waved as Deacon drove up. Clemmie swung her large blue camera bag into the back of the jeep and slid in gracefully beside him. She pulled her sunglasses up and studied Deacon from head to boot.

"Well, still in one piece, I see," she said. "Had to check. Tom seems to break an awful lot of his toys. The poor sergeant. But I'm glad you're here and answering the call."

She kissed him on the cheek. "A true soldier, Harry," she said. "Now get me to the Tanks before the light's gone."

They drove up the hill out of Aden in the scorch of the early afternoon sun and spent idling hours wandering among the shaded cisterns and canopied walkways of the Tiwali Tanks. Clemmie took many photographs and was bright with chatter and wonder at everything she saw. The afternoon was fading by the time they came to sit at the Tanks cafeteria. They ordered coffee and crumpets and gazed upon the mountains. So few other customers were present that Deacon felt alone with Clemmie.

"It's been a wonderful afternoon, Harry. Thank you," she said.

"Some wonderful pictures. And good memories."

Deacon said nothing. But he smiled.

Clemmie took off her sunglasses and turned to gaze at the setting sun. She watched for some moments.

"Tom is going to ask me to marry him," she said. "So he says."

Deacon could think of nothing to say.

"So like Tom, don't you think?" said Clemmie. She smiled. "Going to ask Daddy for permission to ask. Channels and protocol. Not quite the Rimbaud, is he?"

"No, he is a soldier," said Deacon. "And my superior officer, Clemmie."

Clemmie continued to watch the mountains. "Are you ever going to ask me out on a date, Harry?" she said.

Deacon was momentarily at a loss for a response. "Aren't we on one now?" he said.

Clemmie looked at him. "Not when I'm paying for the coffee, Harry, no. Are you never going to ask? You said you liked me."

"But you're with Tom," said Deacon. "And I'm in the Army."

Clemmie turned to gaze steadily at Deacon through wide, brown eyes. She lit a cigarette and smoked a moment or two. "Why ever did you join the Army?" she said.

Deacon leaned back in his chair. The last of the customers had left and he and Clemmie were now truly alone on the veranda of the cafe. The night was beginning to roll up over the Tiwali valley and the dinosaur heel prints of the tanks were being swallowed one by one. Deacon felt the weight of the last few days beginning to drain away through every limb, as if releasing him from its cares. He was tired and trapped, yet he felt reckless. As if he wanted to just step out from behind his rock and take the bullets. He felt his heart still.

"I had an affair with a teacher," said Deacon. "I ran away to the Army to avoid the scandal."

Deacon watched a vulture sailing high before the clouds of night as if trying to out-fly them.

"I was seventeen," he said.

Clemmie laughed. Cigarette smoke clouded around her. She waited until it had drifted away.

"An affair's hardly murder," said Clemmie. "Young men and older women. Love's young infatuations. It is nothing. It happens all the time."

"The teacher was a man, Clemmie."

A silence stretched between them. Clemmie lit a cigarette from the butt of one she still held. She flicked the fire-fly stub to tumble in the darkness.

"Was it love?" she said eventually.

Deacon laughed. "Love?" he said. "No it wasn't love, it was far worse than that. It was passion."

Clemmie fell silent long enough to finish her cigarette.

"Life isn't all passion, Harry." she said. She smiled a sharp smile. "It doesn't have to be. It's not everything. Not if we don't want it to be."

Deacon took a mouthful of coffee and let it warm in his mouth for a moment. He looked across at Clemmie. She was hugging herself from a slight chill air and was watching the mountains.

"But it can't only be foot rubs either, Clemmie," said Deacon. "You know that too. In your heart, you know it. In the end it would be bound to stifle us. Our friendship. As slow and sure as bindweed on the rose."

Clemmie sniffed and Deacon could see a glint of tear appear fleetingly in her eye. She shook it away in a toss of her head and grinned at Deacon. She gazed at him for a moment and then stroked his cheek with her fingertips.

"My very own Rimbaud," she said. "Lost him again, it seems."

They drove back to the Villa in silence. Deacon parked the jeep on the road outside the gates and escorted Clemmie past the guard posts and on through the Villa to the rear gardens. A couple of white-coated servants dusted and mopped in various rooms but the Villa appeared quiet and empty. They came to the lawns above Clemmie's lodge and stopped at the low wall overlooking the bay. Clemmie lit a cigarette and stood watching the flickering lights out at sea.

"Does anyone else know? Besides me?"

"No," said Deacon. "Only you."

Clemmie turned and kissed Deacon lightly on the lips. "You do me a great honour. It is safe with me. We will stay best friends, Harry, won't we?"

"Always," said Deacon.

Clemmie smiled and turned away. When half-way across the grass, she held her arm aloft and spread her fingers on a blind wave. She did not look back. Deacon let her disappear in through her front door and then waited for several minutes until the lodge lights fell to darkness.

Deacon stood on the cliff top and gazed out into the night, the low wall pressing at his knees. He had hoped he might discover some relief in having confessed to Clemmie, but salvation's relief proved elusive. He only felt that he had hurt Clemmie. Worse than that, he had perhaps betrayed her. He had confessed, but he hadn't guided. He knew he should have said something to Clemmie about Villiers, to put her on her guard. To forewarn her. But what could he say? Saying anything would only hurt Clemmie twice over.

Deacon gazed out into the darkness and listened to the sea brushing against the shore rocks far below. He knew that he had failed Chi too. And he had also lost his laughing shadow, perhaps forever. Deacon felt his loneliness envelop him like a shroud. Wherever he looked or reached out to touch, there was blackness. He also recognised a fear in that darkenss. The fear that came from confessing something to someone else and which he had kept so secret for so long, even half from himself. In confiding to Clemmie he had said too much, given too much away and his cloak of invisibility and respectability was now in tatters. He knew Clemmie would keep his secret. At least until the time came when he knew she wouldn't.

A cooling, sea-smelling breeze filled Deacon's nostrils and its fingers fussed at his hair. A starlit night unfurled like a carpet before him. He wondered what it must be like to fly.

He stood tall on the cliff top and spread his arms sky-wide to embrace every star.

EIGHTEEN

Deacon woke suddenly from his dream of flying and sat up sharply. The sensation of falling faded as his room swam into focus. His sheets were damp from sweat and he shivered in the cool air. He sat in his bed and watched the talons of dawn's light take roost again in his rooms. Another day.

He took a long shower and an early breakfast in his rooms. Lockett arrived while he was dressing. He gave Lockett his troop duty orders for the day.

"Just keep them out of trouble."

"Means I'll have to lock them up, sir."

"Tight and sober," said Deacon. "How much money do I have in the rainy-day fund, corporal?"

Lockett took a moment to pour Deacon's tea. Deacon saw him watching in the mirror, a look of mild concern on the corporal's face. "About sixty-five pounds, give or take a goat. Any special reason, sir?"

"You teaching over at Mr. Patel's tomorrow?"

Lockett looked a little taken aback. "Well, I'm not sure…"

"It's a Thursday afternoon, don't you do an English class?" said Deacon.

"Well, yes. But I didn't think that you…"

"Good. Like a chat with your friend Mr. Patel. Think you can arrange that with him? Tomorrow at sixteen hundred would be convenient."

"A chat? Can I tell him what its about, sir?"

"No."

Corporal Lockett seemed momentarily lost for words. "Can you tell me then, sir?" he said. "So I know what it's about."

"Of course, corporal. I'm thinking of going into the slave trade."

He left Lockett to sort the men and made his way to the duty office. The bulletin board was full of the usual pinned papers and notes that littered it like leaves. Notices of personal effects sales. Benefit for the widow in Dorking. Missing ginger cat answers to Tigger. Lost much-treasured monogrammed hip-flask. Missing portmanteau bag. Hillman California for sale, driver grounded for the duration.

Deacon found and read the duty orders under the foliage and then checked his mail-box. It was empty. It usually was. He took a quick pie and tea at the canteen, checked his jeep out from the troop motor pound and made it to the Viking briefing in good time.

The meeting was being held in the Sports Hall of the Aden Officers Club. Deacon showed his ID at several guard points before he was admitted into the hall. About thirty Vikings were already seated in plastic chairs ranked on the polished cedar wood floor of the room. Various ceiling ropes and vaulting mats and pummel horses were tethered to the wooden-barred walls. Deacon took an empty seat.

Moments later Major Villiers and a couple of Colonels entered the room. There was a scraping of chairs on polished floor and the room stood to attention.

"At ease, gentlemen," said Villiers.

The briefing lasted over two hours. It was a report on the recent night-time forays into Crater, a new tactical approach that involved troops marching in and surrounding a patch of city and then searching every house, room and cupboard within the cordon. It had been tried a couple of times and had offered good results. Many rifles, a known fugitive and several likely suspects had been netted in the trawl.

Villiers commanded the room with an easy charm and a soldier's light steel. There were even a few jokes to ease and bind the mood. Villiers was casting his spell upon everyone in the room. But it was no longer creating its magic on Deacon. He was watching a different Villiers from the rest of the audience. His was a Villiers who would also seek to command young tea boys. Deacon continued to stare at Villiers and felt the distaste pool in him. Villiers, still speaking to the room, happened to turn and lock gazes with Deacon. Deacon held the pale blue stare for a long, steady moment and then he simply closed his eyes. He heard Villiers's voice momentarily catch before returning to drift with easy charm over the room.

"We've had possible word of a Pac-Vac warehouse in north Crater," said Villiers, "and the Intelligence boys are following it up. Should know in a couple of days. Then the Vikings will march. Those that are called. So be prepared, boys. Briefing over, gentlemen."

Deacon opened his eyes and walked out.

Deacon called in at the duty office to pick up the troop mail and literally bumped into Captain Ashley in a corridor. He bent to help Captain Ashley retrieve the papers fallen from his zip-case. It was impossible to avoid conversation, so Deacon decided to start it.

"Did the Arab boy talk?" he said.

Captain Ashley gathered the last of his papers and they stood facing each other. Ashley's stare was set hard but he switched on a friendly grin.

"Couldn't stop the bastard," said Ashley. "Talked the hind leg off a camel, in the end. Confessed to everything. Insurrection, bombs, murder, plotting to assassinate the Queen. Everything. All a pack of lies of course. He was an Arab, what can you expect?"

"Was?"

"Boxed and despatched him yesterday. Or was it the day before? Difficult to keep track these days. Planning on sending flowers were you?"

Captain Ashley smirked, turned on a sharp heel and marched on down the corridor.

Deacon checked in on the men at the Depot and then spent an hour with the Stores commander checking inventories and batch plans. He did not manage to extricate himself from the pedantic major until fifteen-hundred hours.

He saw the men finish their duty and then packed off back to their barracks in the truck before he took his jeep and headed for his appointment with Mr. Patel.

The Aden Laundry (and Associated Services) Company occupied a large stretch of coastal plain beyond the Khormaksar airfield. As Deacon drove past the endless grey slab of razor-wire topped fences and out onto the hard dirt road he was greeted by the sight of a vast forest of drying laundry flapping in the sea breezes, like the flags of all nations. It seemed to stretch to the far mountains. And when Deacon drove nearer he could see that all the lines of laundry were slowly moving, as if on a lazy pulley. Jackets and trousers and undershirts and sheets were slowly marching along in the Aden airs.

Deacon called in at the office reception and was advised by the smartly dressed young Punjabi behind the counter that Mr. Patel was out on-site and would return in half an hour. He was courteously offered a seat and coffee for the wait but Deacon decided to clear the stale airs of the briefing and wandered outside.

He strolled and smoked and passed the time watching the laundry company teem about him. The laundry seemed to stretch as far as his eye could see and a pungent smell of starch and soap and the sulphurs of burning volcanic rock scraped at the nostrils. Arab boys and young men scurried among the fields of fluttering clothes or in the many outbuildings scattered over the site. Everyone was busy. Pulling large trolleys of sheets, staggering by under huge shells of uniforms on their backs, or pegging sheets as big as sails to the conveyor belt line. It was an impressive operation, not only in scale, but in ingenuity. The moving lines of washing were operated by a volcanic rock-fired engine house that spewed grey steam clouds to the skies. In the main yards there were eight huge concrete bowls, each twenty yards across, which held the soap and rinsing waters. The bowls were stirred by a mechanical paddle operated by a team of workers on a treadwheel,while the heat for the bowls' waters was provided by nests of volcanic rocks glowing tangerine-hot beneath them. Further up the road, Deacon could see several trucks being loaded with clean laundry and through the doors of a low, huge warehouse he could see more workers on steam presses and sewing machines.

"Like a beautiful machine, is it not, Lieutenant Deacon?"

Deacon turned to find Mr. Patel at his side. Deacon had the impression he had been there for some time, watching the laundry with him. Mr. Patel was slim and dressed in an immaculately laundered dark suit, a crisp white shirt and a blue tie with a small gold pin lancing its windsor knot. His oiled and scalpel-parted hair shone black above a trimmed black moustache and his deep brown eyes were wide in welcome and warm pride.

Deacon knew that Mr Patel was at least forty, but he looked fifteen years younger. Being a Pakistani he was a well-known and exotic figure in the Aden community. His laundry had made him rich and his Army contracts had made him powerful, but he never allowed either to make much show. He stood beside Deacon with a quiet, unhurried calm and spoke in impeccable public school English.

"Did you know that this," Mr. Patel cast a shy hand over his laundry, "is the largest independent trading company in the whole of the Arabian southern peninsula? By turnover and workers. Think of that. Here in Aden. We employ over two hundred people. Four thousand transactions a day. This wonderful machine works twenty-four hours. It never stops. The people work. They have money. Spend at the local shops. It is good for Aden. Sound economics. People are happy. And it's all thanks to the Aden Laundry Company."

"And the eight thousand garrison troops it has as captive customers," said Deacon. "Plus the sole trader contract that goes with it."

Mr. Patel leaned back a little and allowed a laugh to escape. He smiled at Deacon and laid a friendly hand on his sleeve.

"I am so glad you understand Business, Lieutenant Deacon. Shall we adjourn to my office?"

As they entered through the glass reception doors, two young Arab boys rushed forward with rags in their hands. Mr Patel stood dutifully while the boys dusted the sand off his black brogue shoes and brought them to a mirror shine.

Mr Patel smiled at Deacon and shrugged apologetically. "A good laundry manager must always be laundered." Mr. Patel grinned. "It is good for the customers, good for business, good for young workers. Harib, have you done your school today?"

One of the boys grinned and nodded. Mr Patel put a hand in his pocket and tossed two sweets into the air. They were deftly caught. The two boys ran off laughing.

"My young employees are always the most enthusiastic," said Mr Patel.

Deacon was guided up the stairs to the first floor and into a large, window-walled office. An impressive desk and a suite of comfortable chairs dominated the room. Through the glass Deacon saw dozens of clerks and typists busy in the rooms about him. The offices were full of filing cabinets and desks and large charts festooned the walls. A ceiling-high picture window along one wall looked out onto the laundry works and to the sea beyond.

Outside, down in the shaded courtyard Deacon could see Corporal Lockett with his class. A dozen children were seated on rows of packing crates before him. Chi was standing by a black painted door propped against a wall. The makeshift blackboard had a large outline drawing of a child chalked on it. Lockett was leading the class in song and tapping his head and shoulders and knees energetically. Chi was pointing to the chalk drawing for the benefit of the younger ones who were sitting cross-legged on a mattress at his feet. Deacon heard the singing chants of the children drift up through the open window.

Head and shoulders, knees and toes
Knees and toes
And eyes and ears....

Lockett looked up and saw Deacon watching him. He nodded and sang on. He signalled five minutes with his hand.

"I like to hear the children sing. And in English. David is a fine teacher," said Mr. Patel.

"A school in the laundry?" said Deacon.

"Of course. It is safer here for the children. Aden is a dangerous place, as I am sure you are aware, Lieutenant. May I call you Harry? Please call me Sebastian. But the children, even in these dreadful and dangerous times, they must still learn their writing and numbers somewhere. Why not here? Some children have relatives working here. And our many widows are caring teachers for those less fortunate children. We all look out for the children."

"Rebels get everywhere," said Deacon.

Sebastian leaned back in his chair. "Doubtless they do, Harry. But this laundry is a business. Commerce takes no sides. We contract with the Army and employ many Arab locals. We are Switzerland. We are neutral. We are not interested in politics, only in business."

"And in schooling," said Deacon.

"Yes, schooling. Education is a right of every child. Don't you think? And good health. We have a dispensary here and a nurse. Hot food in the canteen. And children's play rooms so that mothers can work. And grandmothers to sing to them and sew a few buttons. This machine is not made of metal, Harry, it is all flesh and bones."

Lockett came into the room, followed by a servant with a large tray of coffee. Mr Patel indicated Deacon and Lockett to the settee and sat in the armchair opposite. The coffee was placed on the glass-topped table before him. Mr. Patel poured three cups.

"So, Harry," said Mr Patel. "What is it that I can do for you?"

Deacon sugared and stirred his coffee. He smiled at Mr. Patel. "I'd like to buy Chi from you, Sebastian."

As Deacon sipped his coffee, he was aware of a silence in the room, but the typewriters continued to clatter softly from the nearby offices. Lockett was staring at Deacon, his head cocked slightly to one side. Deacon noticed that Lockett always did that when surprise fell on him. It was a rare sight and it never lasted long.

Lockett quickly returned to corporal watch. Mr. Patel studied Deacon for a long time.

"David tells me you are an honourable man, Harry. Is this an honourable request?"

"Fifty pounds honourable," said Deacon.

Mr. Patel nodded slowly. "Is Chi in danger?" he asked.

"This is Aden. We are all in danger, Sebastian."

Mr. Patel nodded again. He took a sip of coffee and leaned back in his chair.

"Interesting as your offer is, Harry, I'm afraid I couldn't possibly countenance such a business. Chi is an employee in my care and a very promising one. An excellent tea boy."

"I assure you my intentions are honourable."

"I'm sure they are, Harry. But Chi is not mine to sell. I am not a slaver."

"But you hold his papers?"

"Of course," Mr. Patel wafted a hand towards the outer offices. "All our employees' papers and records are kept here. We are most thorough."

"Then I will buy his papers. And his tea employment contract," said Deacon. "And draw up papers to make me his guardian. Then I'd like to offer a bursary to the Aden Laundry Company to employ Chi as a school assistant."

Deacon was aware of Lockett sitting up in his chair and cocking his head once again.

"Generous indeed, Harry," said Mr. Patel. He smiled and shrugged. "And in normal circumstances I would be happy to discuss your offer. But these are not normal times. Your British pounds are not what they once were, Harry. Paper is fine for contracts but for money it is different. Even the British sterling. These are uncertain times. Sterling notes and cheques are not to be trusted. This is no disrespect to your country or currency, Harry. And of course its quite magnificent soldiers. But a paper promise to pay the bearer loses its value in war. Especially when the bearers will be shipping out soon. I am sorry, but your fifty pounds sterling will not buy Chi."

There was a small silence before Lockett stood up. He reached into his pocket and pulled out four large coins and laid them on the glass table before Mr. Patel. They were golden sovereigns.

"These might."

Mr. Patel stared calmly at the coins. Deacon saw a flash momentarily light across Mr. Patel's dark brown eyes, like a goldfish darting in a muddied lake. Lockett placed a finger on one of the coins and slid it forward across the glass. "One for papers." He pushed the next coin. "One for employment." He pushed the last two coins across the table. "And, of course, expenses."

Mr. Patel carefully took one of the coins and weighed it gently it in his palm. He studied it up close under a lamp light for several moments and then replaced it back on the desk. Mr. Patel undid the bottom button of his suit jacket, leaned back in his chair and smiled.

"To business, gentlemen," he said.

Three hours later Deacon was back in his billet and Lockett was folding three new towels into the chest drawer. The towels were an insistent gift from Sebastian. Deacon was also the official guardian of a ward. Chi was his, at least on paper. Deacon suddenly realised the commitment he had taken on. A responsibility and the duty of protection for another person. Someone who would rely on him. He also realised that he was no longer alone; that Chi would now share and be part of his life. The idea made him light-headed and weighed in his chest like a stone.

Lockett busied himself about the room. "Well done, sir!" he said. "Very clever. Chi out of harm's way and safe in a nest and under your care."

He poured two whiskys and they saluted the day. Lockett stared into his glass. "You've got Chi now," said Lockett. "Sort of like being like a parent. Don't you think?"

Deacon sipped his whisky. "They wouldn't have been Viking sovereigns, would they, corporal?" he said.

"No, sir."

"Are you sure? I mean you didn't slip them out of the metal box while we were busy digging Golightly out of the truck? For instance?"

"Can't be those coins, sir, because they don't exist."

"But I saw them, corporal, with my own eyes."

"The heat and all that excitement, I expect, sir."

"Are you telling me I imagined it?"

"Yes, sir. You must have done because the metal box was swept away in the flood with Golightly. At least that is what Major Villiers put in the official patrol report. So my sources say. No sovereigns came back, sir. They were all washed away in the sudden floods. Rotten luck apparently."

Deacon stood watching Lockett for some time. He knew the metal box had been real. He could feel the weight of it as he pulled it out of the back of the truck with the river floods roaring in his ears. He could see it, under Villiers's arm as the helicopter took off in a cyclone of dust. Villiers had been stealing it away. But Lockett had somehow dipped him first.

Lockett grinned at Deacon and downed his whisky. "Afraid I'm just a common thief, sir," he said. "But it was a safe chance and I reckon the bastard owed me. Four days of hospital food for a start. So I slipped some. Then I found out he had stolen them himself. So I can't have taken anything. I've got gold that doesn't exist. It's Wonderland, sir."

Deacon laughed. "How many did you slip?"

"Not nearly enough," said Lockett.

As he shaved the next morning Deacon could hear, through the bedroom wall, Lockett explaining the new arrangements with Chi. Deacon bent his soaped cheek to the door and listened. The idea was taking some explaining but it was evidently being received with a cautious welcome, of a kind.

"Lieutenant Deacon own me?"

"Not quite Chi. More like an Uncle. Like Sami Al Mustaf is to Harib."

"He beat me?"

"No. Of course not."

"I am not tea and dhobi boy? I work all time at school?"

"Yes."

"For money?"

"Yes. A little."

"With you?"

"When I'm there, yes."

"I think about it."

After breakfast, Lockett took Chi away to the laundry to finalise the arrangements with Mr. Patel. Deacon went on the depot shift with the troop. It stretched into a long, hot day of driving trucks of stores from the quayside docks to the various garrison warehouses.

On their last run in the late afternoon, they were driving through the Aden streets when Deacon noticed Clemmie walking along the road. He was in half a mind to pretend he hadn't seen her. To save them both any embarrassment in remembering their last meeting. But he also knew that Clemmie shouldn't be walking the Aden streets alone. Deacon called the truck to a stop and leaned out of the window as they came up beside her.

"Need rescue or transport?" he said.

Clemmie stopped and looked up, shielding her eyes with her hand.

"Oh, Harry! It's you. No, I'm fine. I'm just making my way to Alice Brewer's sixth birthday party. You wouldn't care to accompany me, would you? Tom is busy soldiering. Birthday parties are so much more fun with someone to share. I can promise jelly and cakes."

Deacon was aware of Hobson and Doyle smirking beside him on the front seat of the truck, and of the troop of ears that were straining inches behind his head. He was also aware that he was a British officer. He jumped down from the cab.

"Take the truck on and see the men home, Hobson," he said. The truck roared off and Lee and Ambrose's Cheshire cat grins faded away down the street.

Deacon walked with Clemmie to the Tardyne district, where the birthday party was being held. Tardyne was a quiet suburb of wide roads, parched grass walkways and close ordered, semi-detached homes and three-storey flats. This was where the middle-ranking military families had their homes. The junior officers had acacia trees in their gardens, the senior NCOs had deckchairs in the block's communal yard. Some people were strolling in the shaded areas of the streets but most were indoors avoiding the hot scorch of the afternoon sun.

Deacon was relieved to find that Clemmie seemed happy to ignore the awkwardness of their last meeting. She chatted to Deacon about the heat of the day, and her recent photographic trip to Telegraph Bay and about Alice, the birthday girl, who was the daughter of Staff Sergeant Brewer. Clemmie didn't know the family personally but Sergeant Brewer was one of Daddy's boys and she just happened to be out this way today.

Deacon knew that Clemmie's visit was really an act of Aden charity. The women's charity which knew children's birthday parties needed all the help they could get in Aden. To try and make them fun and help the children forget, even if only for just a couple of hours, that real war was being played in their back gardens. Army children grew up hard in Aden and the opportunities for fun were rare. All the women gave what support they might and young women who could blow up balloons, pass parcels or nurse grazed knees, were particularly prized. Clemmie was doing her bit.

They found the street and saw rows of bunting flags pinned around the gate of the Brewers's house a few doors down. Two girls in party dresses were playing skipping rope in the shaded side of road. A boy was practising skid stops on his bike. Music was coming from the back courtyard of a squat, single storey house and the sounds of a children's party tumbled over the walls.

"Alice is getting a Dansette for her birthday," said Clemmie. "So I bought her a record." She pulled a flat, small gift-wrapped parcel out of her camera bag and grinned. "The Beatles. I played it safe. Thought she might be a bit young for the Rolling Stones."

They walked down the street to the party.

The shock of the explosion was sudden and startling. A gush of hot wind barged Deacon backwards. A flash of light and a sound, like tube trains roaring angrily from tunnels, swept over him. He found himself lying on the ground. He saw dust swirling in clouds above him and heard the soft patter of shrapnel-rain tap-dancing on the road about him.

Deacon picked himself up and checked on Clemmie. She was sitting on the grass embankment, a little dazed but otherwise unharmed. Her face was pale and her hands fussed busily at nothing.

"What happened?" she said.

Down the street, Deacon could see a section of still smoking courtyard wall had spewed into the road. A car opposite had been flipped onto its side and was cast in dust, like sprinkled sugar on a cake.

"Grenade attack," said Deacon.

And he had seen nothing. But at the outer wash of the blasted debris he could now see a large doll in a chequered yellow dress lying still in the middle of the road.

Deacon ran to the girl as others began to stumble through the settling dusts. Children staggered up slowly from various parts of the road. They stood trembling and ashen. Cries of alarm and panic were beginning to sound from the party home and the houses about. Some of the children began to wail.

Deacon knelt beside the young girl. She lay on her back staring out through glass-cold eyes into the white heavens above. Her arms lay easy at her side and her ankle socks were crossed casually above scuffed brown shoes. She lay as motionless as a mannequin, her yellow party dress blown up her legs and exposing her white-pantied crotch. Deacon instinctively flipped her dress to decent.

Deacon knew she was dead. He checked her pulse as others began to gather about him.

"That's Susan Collins, isn't it? Oh God."

"Fucking bastards!"

"Where's my Danny? Have you seen Danny?"

"Someone telephone the hospital. And get the duty troop down here fast!" shouted Deacon. The party goers and neighbours began to gather up and comfort the rest of children and run for telephones. Deacon reached out and closed Susan's eyes. It was the least he could do for the parents.

A couple of soldiers emerged from nearby houses and Deacon ordered them to collect some men and check the nearby streets. The grenade thrower could still be around.

"Don't go too far!" yelled Deacon after them. "It might be a lure trap."

Clemmie knelt at his side in the road and looked down at Susan. She reached out a slow, shaking hand and straightened

Susan's pigtails and smoothed the dress hem down to scabbed and nut-brown knees.

"She's dead, isn't she?" she said. It was almost a whisper.

"Yes," said Deacon.

"But there's not a mark on her," she said. "Not a blemish."

A woman emerged from a nearby street and wailed at the sight of Susan. She ran towards her and collapsed sobbing on the dirt beside Deacon. She was screaming and shaking the limp body, telling it to get up, shouting that the *Beverly Hillbillies* was on the television. Others quickly came to gather her up and help her away and the street was a confusion of angry shouts and sobbing.

Deacon backed away to the shade of the wall. Through the crowds, he saw a young girl come skip-running out of the party house and then head for the noisy crowd gathered around Susan and the rubble. The girl was wearing a green party dress with an *I am six* badge and she held a plum coloured ice-lolly in her fist. Alice Brewer. The birthday girl ran up to the knot of people and peered between them. She looked down and became still. Deacon saw her back out of the crowd as if dazed. She stood for a long moment, her eyes wide with horror. The ice-lolly fell softly from her hand. She doubledup in search of air and then she screamed. A shrill scream that didn't stop. She screamed for the shock of it and for the sheer horror of all her birthdays to come. It was an Aden scream.

Alice was enwrapped in arms and guided away by the women. Troops arrived in trucks to seal and search the area and to herd the people into some kind of order. Deacon sought out Clemmie from the crowds. He found her wandering in the house courtyard. She was clutching the wrapped record in her hand and was walking unsurely, as if lost.

"I must leave her present," she said. "It's her birthday. I can't go without leaving her the present."

Deacon guided her into the party room which was crowded with people.

Alice was lying curled on the settee with her back to the room. Several women were fussing over her. Groups of men were talking angrily around a table of coloured balloons and small hillocks of fish paste sandwiches. Deacon guided Clemmie to a sideboard covered in cards and wrapped present to add hers. She turned to Deacon. Her face was very pale.

"I think I'm going to be sick," she said.

Deacon took her back out into the air and they sat on a shaded grass embankment. Clemmie breathed slowly and deeply, waiting for her feeling of nausea to pass. They sat and watched the bustle about them, trying to recover from themselves. A woman neighbour gave them mugs of hot, sweet tea. They watched the ambulance back up to the debris pile and the soldiers strap the small load to a bagged stretcher. The bag was zipped and the ambulance whined away up the road. Deacon could hear sobs trickling from a nearby house.

Deacon felt his world jolt. As if the two hemispheres had been gripped and twisted. Turned a notch so that they no longer fitted and patterned as they had before. And he was in another world.

He looked out on the rubble of the courtyard wall and the scurrying of soldiers and kind neighbours passing out mugs of tea on bone-handled trays and he realised that he didn't recognise any of it. He couldn't understand it. The wanton stupidity of it. This Aden. He couldn't understand what on earth he was doing here. Or how he could get out.

Clemmie sat beside him, gazing out at the street. She lit two cigarettes. Her hands trembled. She held them up and watched them quivering before her with a mild interest, like a tired assistant watching laboratory rats. She passed one of the cigarettes to Deacon.

"Does the shaking last long?" she said.

"Forever," said Deacon.

Clemmie let her hand fall to the grass and sucked deeply on her cigarette. Soldiers were shovelling the remains of the wall into the bucket of a dumper truck. A group of women stood huddled in close-headed whisper on a far street corner. Smoke and the smell of cordite still stung the air and a pall of silence had fallen around the party house. Over the rooftops Deacon could see the sun sliding to treacle on the bay.

"Tom has asked me to marry him," said Clemmie. She bayonetted her cigarette into the grass and lit another. "Or says he's going to ask me to marry him. At the weekend. He was preparing me. Tom is a great planner."

Deacon watched the skies melting and said nothing.

"I'm thinking of saying yes."

Clemmie turned and looked at Deacon. "Eventually." She tried a smile. "I think its good to keep a future husband dangling a bit, don't you? Ruffle his best-laid plans."

"A wife's duty," said Deacon. Clemmie laughed. She lay back on the grass. "So you do approve?" she said. "I'm doing the right thing?"

Deacon saw the glass eye of a doll staring at him. "No," he said.

He was aware of Clemmie rising up onto her elbows and looking at him.

"Why not?"

Deacon stared at the courtyard wall down the street. It looked like someone had taken a huge bite out of it.

"You're too young to get married. You haven't lived yet. There is more life to explore. More pictures to take."

Clemmie sat up and watched the road.

"This isn't living, Harry." She lit another cigarette. "Tom's tour here is only short. He plans to be back in Surrey by the spring. He wants a summer wedding. Military bands and marquees. Won't that be lovely?"

"What about your photography? The Gallery shows?"

Clemmie flicked her cigarette into a gutter drain. "Had a letter from my Cambridge chums the other day. Apparently they couldn't use the last prints I sent them. Aden is not the vogue.

But they were kind enough to say my pictures showed some promise. I can't settle for some promise, Harry. So I've decided to settle for a soldier."

"But you don't have to marry one, Clemmie, at least not yet. Aren't there more adventures waiting?"

"Tom is an adventure. And so is marriage. A whole new life."

"What's wrong with the life you have?" said Deacon.

Clemmie gazed at the street. "It's been blown away, Harry. And I'm just too tired to run after it."

"But it's only been a couple of months. To take a husband. You hardly know Tom."

Clemmie gazed at him. Her eyes were wide and round, the shocks of the day still drifting across them.

"Not like you do, Harry. That's true. But you will always see a different Tom to me, won't you? Tom really is quite magnificent. The Brigadier and mother think the world of him. We are to get their place in Esher. So it's pretty well all decided anyway. Tom says he's going to try for politics. And Esher is strong rugger country apparently."

Deacon stared at the distant sky that was as yellow as Susan's dress. He knew he could say no more. Perhaps Clemmie and Villiers might make a go of it and what right had he to seek to deny Clemmie any chance of a loving, life companionship that he himself could never know. It was best to keep a friend's silence.

Moments later Lockett appeared, driving his jeep in swerves around soldiers and trucks and skidding to a halt beside the embankment. He jumped out and quickly took in the scene.

"You alright, sir? Miss Ross? Lads said you might be up here. Can I give you a ride home? Not much use staying here any more, sir. Only in the way. Let's get the lady back. Only cure for today is rest, and plenty of it."

They drove back to the Villa in silence. Deacon and Lockett

saw Clemmie into the arms of her mother and left to the sounds of barked orders for baths, beds and the Brigadier.

"Take the coast road," said Deacon as they climbed back into the jeep.

"That's the long route, sir."

"I know, corporal. Can't you just obey one of my fucking orders for once?"

They drove the coast road in silence. Deacon let the salty breezes shower over him. He just sat and stared ahead at nothing. He couldn't think. He couldn't feel. He couldn't move. Everything was numb.

And then he felt a burn of wetness bite at his cheek and drip to his throat and he realised he was crying. He sat perfectly still and calm and just let leak what little he had. His well soon dried. Deacon was aware of Lockett watching him out of the corner of his eye. He didn't care.

NINETEEN

Deacon heard the distant bells of St. Thomas drifting in over the parade ground and realised, with some surprise, that it was Sunday again. Major Ford-Forrest sat at his usual place behind his desk studying a file with silent and steady sloth. His head, his body and his uniform were all exactly where Deacon had seen them last. It was as if the major hadn't moved since last Sunday. Or was it the perhaps the Sunday before? Deacon could not recall. Nor did he want to. He could tell by the pink flush rising up the major's ears he was about to get angry.

Major Ford-Forrest closed the file and pushed it away from him. He gazed at Deacon through small black eyes and his neck ripened.

"You almost got Clementine Ross killed! Are you stark, staring mad? Do you realise how much work you have put me through? And poor Marjorie, well...Any reason why I shouldn't have you shovelled out of here a shit private?"

Deacon remained silent. Major Ford-Forrest flicked open the file and slapped one of the papers with a palm.

"And you never saw it! Didn't see a thing. Fifty yards away. No Arab. No grenade. What kind of officer are you, Deacon? Blind or just incompetent? Are you going to speak?"

"Miss Ross asked me to accompany her, sir, and the grenade was thrown from the cover of ten-foot high walls. As I mention in my report."

"Yours is not a report, Lieutenant Deacon. It is a farce."

Major Ford-Forrest rose up from behind his desk and began to pace the room as if trying to dissipate his anger through his glistening tan boots. His voice had risen with him. "To endanger the Brigadier's daughter! Wanton irresponsibility. Poor Clementine to choose you for an escort. God help her! Miracle she wasn't badly hurt. And she's laying none of the blame on anyone but herself. She just went home, got changed and went out and took her duty shift at the hospital. Couldn't stop her. There's a proper lady for you! Had my way you'd be stoking your passage back to whatever slum you call home. Flush you out and away like a turd."

The Major returned to his seat. He picked up the file with evident distaste and placed it in a desk drawer. He leaned back in his chair and gazed coal-eyed at Deacon.

"But Clementine insists on bailing you out. Refuses to bring charges. Against my better advice. But she is the Brigadier's daughter. And I know my duty. Doesn't mean to say I like it. But at least there was no lasting damage done. You have all the luck of a snake, lieutenant."

"Yes sir. Unlike Susan."

"Who? What Susan? What are you blathering about man?"

"The girl who died, sir."

"Oh yes. Of course. Susan..."

"Collins, sir. One of your trooper's daughters."

"Yes I know. And I don't need telling from you, lieutenant. Remember your rank. Because that's exactly what you might be doing."

Deacon stayed silent. Major Ford-Forrest pulled another file out of another draw and placed it before him. He read the pages with slow, finger-licked deliberation. Across the quad, Deacon could hear a soft-swelling wave of baritone voices rumbling from a distant congregation.

Bring me my bow of burning gold
Bring me my arrows of desire

Bring me my spears o'cloud unfold
Bring me my chariot of fire...

Major Ford-Forrest snapped the file shut. "Better warn your men to be on the look out for Pac-Vacs. Adoos been spraying them in the sands apparently. All over the place. Nine soldiers already in hospital and only two pair of feet between them. Tell your men to keep to the roads. Those are orders from the Brigadier's office."

"I'll tell my men to keep a special watch on the sand, sir."

Major Ford-Forrest ignored him. "Oh, and the Sussex regiment's tour of duty has been extended three months. Leave it to you to pass the good news to your men."

"Can I tell them why, sir?"

"Yes. Tell 'em there's a war on."

"Do I get a sergeant?"

"No."

The Major leaned back in his chair and smiled. "But some good news, lieutenant. Seems the Vikings don't think any more of your soldiering than I do. There's a big Viking sortie tomorrow night and you're not in it. You and your troop will be standby unit instead. Safe and cosy in the wings while the real soldiers show the way. You're on duty from twenty-one hundred till whenever you are relieved. Don't get blown up by a grenade, lieutenant. You are dismissed."

Deacon drove the longer route back to his billet, out along the coast road. His head was hot with anger and he needed the jeep breezes and the feel of speed to cool himself. His meetings with Major Ford-Forrest were never uplifting affairs and this last had plumbed even deeper. The news that the Sussex tour had been extended another three months had not surprised Deacon. He knew that the garrison was stretched thin for the needs of a war now come inside the city walls and every soldier would be needed. Back in Whitehall, the Government could not send more troops lest it be seen as panic. They would just stretch what they had a bit further. But the news of the extra tour months would not go down well with the troop. Nor that they were going to be running as standby unit for the Viking sortie. It would mean the whole troop getting into full night-kit and blacking, beer would be off-limits from lunch time and then they could look forward to sitting in a fetid truck all evening in a dark Aden back alley. This was to be done on top of a day's duty shift at the depot. And being only standby, and therefore officially off-duty, the long truck hours would not count on the trooper's duty log. They would be soldiering in their own time. The British soldier might endure many affronts, but giving his labour for free wasn't in the canon.

And of course, Deacon would also be sitting in the truck all night with them. Giving away his duty hours. He knew that it was Major Villiers who had put him there. It was Tom's show and he would have picked and deployed the squads. Deacon had been dropped from the team, and he had taken his troop down with him. Villiers was playing it rough. Teaching Deacon the penalty for playing with matches.

Deacon pressed his leg stiff to the floor of the jeep and let it speed the wide coast road.

When he arrived back at his billet he found Shaw parked up in a jeep outside his door. Shaw was leaning back in the passenger seat with his feet resting high on the windows. He gave Deacon a smile and a vague salute.

"Sir."

"What are you doing here, Shaw?" said Deacon.

Shaw remained lounged and just shrugged his shoulders. "Taxi for the Corp, sir."

Deacon entered his billet and found Corporal Lockett in the sitting room with a grin on his face. Lockett held up his hand.

"Lieutenant Deacon, it is my pleasure to introduce you to the new Aden Laundry School teaching assistant. I give you, Chi. Ta-raa!"

Chi stepped out from Deacon's bedroom behind a wide, self-conscious grin. His hair had been washed and now hung in ringlets to his shoulders. He wore a bright red T-shirt and a pair of smart khaki shorts. He was shaking with glee.

"Look, Mr. Deacon," said Chi. He thrust his fists deep into his shorts. "I have pockets!"

Deacon had to sit down. It felt as if all the blood in his body had fallen into his boots. His head was light. It felt as if Chi had physically stepped inside of him. Taken nest in his guts. He couldn't think what to say. In the corner of his eye he saw Lockett stir the air with his finger and Chi did a slow twirl. His grin returned to face Deacon. It was like electricity.

"Very smart, Chi," said Deacon. "Very smart indeed. Everything sorted?"

"Chi has a bed at the laundry, sir," said Lockett. "Over the sewing room."

"I have locker!" said Chi.

"There's plenty of widows over the way so he won't want for fussing. Breakfast and evening stew every day in the workers' hut. Year's rent paid. Mr. Patel was very generous."

Deacon went to his trunk and pulled out a dog-tag chain. He took his spare door key from his drawer and hooked it on. He placed the chain around Chi's neck and handed him the key.

"My spare key, Chi. To this place. If anytime you ever need anywhere to go. Day or night. There is always here. Understand?"

"Even when you not here?"

"Especially then. I'll need you to guard the biscuits."

Chi wriggled the key down inside his T-shirt. "And water flower," he said.

"Time you were off, Chi," said Lockett. He ushered him towards the door. "Shaw kindly offered to give him a lift, sir. So Chi could arrive safe and in style."

"Shaw let me toot horn," said Chi.

They went outside to wave Chi off. Chi scrambled into the jeep beside Shaw and they drove away. Around the corner the horn honked twice.

When he returned to his rooms, Deacon saw the tray laid up for brandy bombs. Lockett knew that Deacon's meeting with Old Bobby invariably required a pick-me-up. Somehow he had known today's meeting had been bad enough to warrant the brandy bombs. One part brandy, one gin and one vodka and a small tonic splash for the gulp. The drink looked like cholera, smelt like paradise and kicked like a bull. It was just what Deacon needed.

They sat drinking at the table and Deacon shared the warnings of the Pac-Vac mines and the bad news about the tour extension. Lockett just shrugged.

"Not a real surprise, sir. We've seen the troop shipments. We can do a little maths."

"Won't the men be angry?" said Deacon.

"Of course they will sir. True British soldiers. Always got to be angry about something. But it won't be real. Most of the men would welcome a few weeks extra away from their missus. Or the rent man. Or the kids. But there's trouble brewing. Poor Susan Collins is all over the garrison. Men are rumbling."

"They're not the only ones," said Deacon.

"Lee's fuse is particularly short, "said Lockett. "He was looking forward to getting back home. Seeing Carol and his Alan. News might push him a bit, sir."

"I'll think on it. I wouldn't blame the men if they were angry. I know I bloody well would be."

"They are British Tommies, sir. Happy and humble, just like beaten dogs."

Deacon raised an eyebrow and looked at Lockett. He poured a couple more drinks. "Was that Rimbaud, corporal?"

"Miss Ross was so keen on him, sir. So thought I'd take a look."

"And?"

"Not exactly a soldier's poet is he sir?"

Deacon smiled. It was his first of the day. He undid his collar button. "I'm afraid there's more good news. The whole troop is up for standby duty on a Viking sortie tomorrow night."

"Standby? Now that will make them angry, sir."

"Then they will have to join the queue, corporal."

Deacon told the men in the late morning when they were loading crates of fence wire into the truck. The day was griddle hot and the shades scarce. The men were shirtless and sheened in sweat and their hands and arms were dark smeared with packing greases. They worked in heavy silence. Deacon could feel the menace that brooded beneath it.

"Nothing but fucking slaves," said Shaw.

"Treated worse than building-site Micks," said Ambrose.

"Fuck, sir!" said Lee. "I was going home."

The dark mood lasted well into the afternoon. It cast a dragging weight to the day. Deacon tried not to think of anything, but the doll-like face of Susan Collins flickered in him like a shorting-bulb. Staring up from the docket, peering from the street crowds. She was everywhere.

Deacon waited until they were on their last delivery before he told the men about the standby duty for the next night.

"Fucking limit," said Lee. "So unfair, sir!"

"Worse than dogs," said Hobson.

"This ain't right, sir," said Kenny.

"We're just a fucking sideshow!" said Doyle. "We should get at the bastards. Killing our children. In our fucking streets!"

The men rumbled in menace and assent.

"Yeah. While Adoo orphans play football and get jeep rides and new shorts," said Shaw.

"Careful, private," said Deacon.

He saw Shaw turn to look at him. Shaw's face was a rat like sneer.

"Pay much for him did you, sir?"

"Shut up, Shaw," said Lockett. He stepped up and shoved Shaw back. He glowered at the rest of the troop. "You don't know what you are talking about. You forgotten it was the Lieutenant that found Susan? Shame on you, Shaw. And the rest of you. Fight the children now, do you? You're soldiers. This is the British Army. We are in Aden. And this is a fucking war. But we never do children. Now tuck it in, the lot of you. "

The troop climbed into the back of the truck, ready for departure. They muttered and kicked things and lit fags for the journey. Deacon shut the tailgate and leaned on it. A cloud of cigarette smoke and disgruntlement enveloped him. He let it drift.

"I know it's hard," said Deacon. "And confusing. And we certainly know that none of it is fair. Or right. But losing your heads and mouthing off won't solve a damn thing. Just get you killed quicker. So we take it on the chin because we are soldiers and that is all we can do. Get your heads down tonight because you'll need it the next. We'll do slow duty tomorrow. Corporal, I noticed the truck is running ragged. Bearings maybe. Better have it checked over at the depot garage. That should see you the morning through. Get some rest tonight men. That is an order."

Deacon locked the tailgate and slammed his palm hard against its hot sheet metal. The truck roared away and Deacon stood in a hive of diesel fumes.

He took the jeep and the fresh air and headed for the Maalla shopping district. He was running low on billet provisions and needed to stock up. Whisky, cigarettes, razors, shampoo and extra biscuits. It was a convenient diversion from having to go back to the garrison, at least for another hour or so. A mood of heaviness had descended across the docks and barracks since the news of Susan's death. For many the blow had come like a slap. The men were muttering insult and murder and the officers whispering revenge.

Deacon diverted himself in shopping. He found it strange to be standing before the biscuit shelves of the crammed and cramped grocery store trying to guess which might be Chi's favourite. Deacon was suddenly aware of having much new to learn.

Like the sensation of guilt that lurked at the back of his mind. He was simply buying biscuits for Chi but was aware that the purchase, like others, might be misconstrued if viewed through a distorted or venal lens. Shaw's sneer had struck deep. A man he thought he knew had surprised him with the venom of his bite. His hints about Chi almost feral. Deacon knew Shaw had a young daughter back home. His rage and fear had spewed and Deacon just happened to be the first thing in its path. But Deacon was aware of the suspicion now cast on his shadow. The world would be watching him.

The world, he thought, could go hang. He chose the custard creams and paid for his purchases with a soldier's straight back.

As he was walking back to his jeep he saw Clemmie and Major Villiers coming up the street towards him. They were side by side, Clemmie's hand held lightly in Villier's arm. Villiers was talking and in high spirits. Clemmie drifted at his hip, watching the shop fronts glaze by. She saw Deacon, even as he saw them. There was a momentary hesitation in Clemmie's face before she shone a smile and hurried her step to greet him. Villiers followed her.

"Harry! How lovely. Tom and I are out prowling the shops."

Clemmie took Deacon's arm. "We are hunting hats."

"Under protest, Clemmie," said Villiers. He laughed. "Out on your errands too, eh Harry?" He glanced into Deacon's bag. "Essential provisions, I see."

"Don't be rude, Tom. One's shopping is private, isn't it, Harry?" said Clemmie.

"Like a confessional," said Deacon.

They stood for a moment in awkward silence. Villiers broke it.

"Look, I'll just pop in up the street to see if they have my compass fixed. Two minutes. Okay, Clem? Harry?"

Villiers disappeared into a nearby shop. The streets were busy with shoppers and traders. Deacon guided Clemmie into a shaded doorway. She lit two cigarettes. Her hands were still trembling. She saw Deacon looking at them. She laughed.

"I try not to think of her," she said, "but it's all I do. See her. You know?"

"It will ease in time," said Deacon. "The shakes need rest. That's all."

"I know. But they can't shake away the awfulness of this place. Living like this. Feeling so vulnerable all the time. Out of a clear blue sky. How do we protect ourselves from that?"

"You send for a soldier," said Deacon.

Clemmie puffed a laugh of cigarette smoke and turned to look up at Deacon. Her eyes were wide but sunken in wearied hollows.

"That's exactly what I've done, Harry," she said. "Sent for a soldier."

Deacon was silent.

"A strong one," said Clemmie. "I think Daddy is right. I need protecting."

"From who?"

Clemmie laughed, "Myself, I think."

They saw Villers emerge from the shop. He was holding his compass aloft.

"Beat the bugger back a pound!" he said. He pocketed the compass and smiled at Deacon. Villiers became aware of a stopped conversation. There was a moment of silence before Villiers turned to Deacon.

"Look, sorry, you are only on standby duty tomorrow night, Harry. But remember the reserves are just as important as the team out on the field. We all know that. And have to give all the boys a crack. Only fair. You understand?"

"Yes, of course sir."

"He must come to the party though, Tom," said Clemmie.

Villiers smiled at Clemmie. "Of course, my dear. I was just about to ask. If you are free Friday night, Harry, we are having a little do at the villa. Clemmie and I. Small party. Come as you are. About twenty hundred hours?"

"Delighted," said Deacon.

"Lovely," said Clemmie. She stamped her cigarette out under a grinding foot. "Now Tom and I have hats to hunt."

Villiers laughed and rolled his eyes. Deacon watched them walk away down the crowded street, Clemmie leaning into Villiers elbow. She was not wearing her camera bag.

The Aden night streets were dark and very quiet. As always in the Arab sector of the city. Inside the truck Deacon sat with his men in a moody fug of cigarette smoke and fetid breath. In the gloom of the truck, the cigarette embers glowed like fireflies swimming in a tank of liquid night.

The men muttered. The truck space was cramped on the bench seats and the row of butt-down rifles glinted like moonlit saplings along the truck floor. Lockett backed the truck to a stop in the alley darkness and radioed into Command that Standby Two was in position and then switched the engine off. The sudden silence was shocking. The night enveloped them.

Deacon leaned forward on his bench seat and tried to tune his ears into the silence. He listened for echo, for the slow slide of sandal on cobble, for the unnatural click. He heard nothing but the sounds of backstreet Aden going about its usual evening business. Which was nothing. The streets and alleys were deserted, as they always were at this time. He could hear the sound of distant voices coming from the market square several streets away. The women and children of Crater were locked safe indoors but the men would be gathered at the late night coffee shops and cafes of the square, chewing the day out on khat and bravado. Deacon could see a dome of lemon light hovering in the sky above the square. But everywhere else was a sheet of dark.

"Kenny, Ambrose," whispered Deacon. "Back and front guard. We'll half hour rotate. Corporal, have a man with the radio at all times." Deacon looked at his watch. The luminous hands grinned at him. "Show won't start for an hour. So let's eat."

Deacon pulled a box from under his seat and passed out cheese rolls to the men. The men took them with suspicion and some surprise. An unexpected and free picnic was always welcome, even in deep grudge. They tore and wrenched the rolls like dogs on a T-bone. A couple of the men nodded perfunctory thanks.

"And there's a crate up front for when we finish," said Deacon. "But not before."

"That could be fucking hours away," said Ambrose from the dark.

"And we're sat here while the Lancs get really stuck in," said Doyle.

"They'll kick it up tonight," said Shaw. "For Susan."

The men grumbled in outrage and envy and attacked the last of the rolls. A few slurped on their water bottles. They listened to the silence of the Arab streets sliding about them.

"Your Carol. A game girl is she, Lee?" said Deacon.

He said it quietly, almost in whisper. Lee's gaze froze, his mouth open on the last of his chew. The rest of the troop turned to look at Deacon.

"Eh, what, sir?" said Lee. He gulped his cud, the wad sliding down inside his thin throat like a mortar bomb through a sock.

"Is your Carol the spirited type?" said Deacon.

"Na. She likes a sweet cider. Why you asking, sir?"

"Is she a proper trooper then? Reliable?" said Deacon

"Eh, sir, now what's this all about ..."

"Writes letters, does she?"

Lee was silent for a moment. So was the rest of the truck. Lockett had turned in his driver's seat to watch.

"Every week. Mostly. Why, sir?" asked Lee.

"Because she is going to write to you telling you she is going off to live with her mother and is taking young Alan with her. And that all the rumours about her and the fancy man are a tissue of lies and you are not to believe them."

Quiet oozed in the truck like tar.

Then Corporal Lockett laughed. It was a short laugh. He turned back in his seat and laughed again.

"What, sir? Saying my Carol got a fancy man?" Lee's voice was hesitant, anxious.

"Of course not, Lee. Do you think so little of your Carol? But it's what she will write. If you tell her to. Then you'll show her letter to me and I'll have to send you back home on a Pash. An emotional domestic. Reckon we can swing you a fortnight for that. Enough time to see your Alan. Just get Carol to write a letter."

The truck was silent.

Deacon leaned forward. "Just think of it,Lee. Your first true fatherly act will be to defame your wife and cuckold yourself, to stain your son's family name and to perjure the whole British Army. Young Alan will be so proud."

Deacon could feel Lockett laughing silently in the driver's seat. The springs squeaked softly.

"Write a letter, sir?" said Lee.

"Like you did at school," said Deacon.

"School, sir?" said Lee.

"Christ, Lee," said Kenny from the dark. "You smoked your brains away boy? The lieutenant is trying to get you two civvy weeks back in Peckham to see your Carol and the baby. Just get Carol to write a letter. Like he suggested."

"What letter, sir?" said Lee. The truck groaned.

"It's alright, Lee," said Lockett. "Come see me tomorrow. We'll sort something. Get you two weeks holiday."

Deacon saw Lee's quick glance at Shaw. Shaw hardly nodded at all.

"Right. Ta, corp," said Lee.

Lee sat back and lit a cigarette. A moment later he flicked it to the floor and stamped it under his boot. The embers fireworked in the dark.

"I'll get to see Alan," said Lee.

"And your Carol," said Ambrose.

"All of her most like," added Ably.

The men laughed softly. So did Lee.

A half-hour later they heard the sortie go in. The night was ripped awake by a crack of a whistle blast a few streets away, followed immediately by the sounds of roaring trucks and army boots running on cobbles and corporals shouting sharp orders. The noises shrilled and wild dogs barked into the night and searchlight trucks cast white ghosts in the sky. Deacon could hear distant shouts of menace, the shrieks of eviction, and the drums of gun-butts on doors sounding like machine gun fire through it all. Deacon could hear the extra menace of it. Of angry soldiers doing their job with vengeful efficiency. For Susan.

Sitting in their side alley a few streets away, Deacon and his troop could see nothing of it. They could only hear it. It was just noises in the dark, like a raucous Guy Fawkes party in the next street. Across the road a few windows shone brief blades of lights but they were soon sheathed back to dark behind tugged shutters. Nothing moved in the streets about them.

They sat and waited. Listening with intent through the noises of partying soldiers and splintering doors for the single sound of the radio's green-light buzz.

It never came.

It was a long time before the nosies of the Viking sortie began to ebb away and finally die to a silence. Deacon was aware of the men watching him. They were embittered by the day and cramped from their waiting. It had been a wasted night and all just wanted their cots and a wall to kick. Deacon glanced at his watch; it was almost one-hundred hours. He heard the sound of an approaching motorbike and moments later the alley was lit and blinded by the arc of its headlamp. The motorbike came alongside the truck and a young lance corporal in flying goggles shouted in.

"Ops all done and dusted. You're relieved of standby. Major's orders."

He revved the engine and lurched up the alley and away down the road. A heavy silence fell.

Lockett switched on the truck's engine. Its sudden close roar made the men start. They pulled up the tailgate.

"Fucking army," said Shaw. "Someone neck me a beer from the crate."

The next two days drifted past on the dull routine of stores duty. The whole garrison had been routined. Orders from on high. It was the army's way of calming the bubbling waters. Routine kept the men busy. Kept their minds off Susan Collins.

Deacon didn't mind, he savoured the calm days of routine. They were as precious as sleep. He could go through the motions of command and allow himself to drift a little. To torque down and re-charge his batteries. To think about nothing. Except Susan. And Clemmie and Villiers's party.

As he signed dockets or bounced in the truck through the scorching Aden streets, he was aware of the party hour looming closer. Deacon knew that Tom and Clemmie were going to announce their engagement and he wasn't sure he wanted to be there when they did. He would, of course, have to go to the party, but he would do so with troubled feelings. Certainly reluctance and rage simmered in his bones. But guilt was there too. Deacon knew he wouldn't enjoy the party.

On the Friday afternoon he arrived back in his billet and found Chi working at the sitting room table. Chi's daily visits had become another welcome routine for Deacon. Chi would get the laundry bus to the garrison every afternoon when his school job was over for the day and would work an hour or two on his English in Deacon's rooms.

Deacon hung up his cap and loosened his jacket collar.

"School go well today?" he said.

Chi continued to write on the paper before him. His head was bent over in concentration and he pencilled his letters with slow care.

"Big animals have long English words. Small ones have little words. See. Elephant. Very big word. Ant. Little word. I learn my animals. Corporal Lockett say clean towel in bathroom."

"Cow is not a big word," said Deacon.

Chi sucked on his pencil with his forehead propped on his palm. He considered for a while. "Not work all the time. Men play football tonight?"

Chi played football with the men in the quad before he went home, but since Susan the men and the games had disappeared. They didn't feel like playing with an Adoo boy.

"Not tonight. They're tired. You can catch the early bus at the gate. A tuppence by the flower for chips." He placed a coin on the window sill. Chi watched him.

"Are you my uncle?"

"No Chi. I'm your guardian. Until you are eighteen."

"Shaw say you tell me about birds and bees."

Deacon was taken aback only for a moment. Certainly not long enough for it to show. Shaw was having his rat fun.

"What is birds and bees?" asked Chi.

Deacon sat on the chair and poured himself a whisky. He poured a lemonade for Chi.

"It is an English phrase for sex, Chi. Between a man and a woman. Making babies. You know?"

Chi nodded. "I know man and lady thing. But it is not birds and bees. They do not sex. The bird get sting, the bee gets eat."

Deacon laughed. "That's about it," he said. "I'm off for a shower. Then I'll walk you to the gate."

"Bee is little word," said Chi. "And bird is not so big."

Deacon watched Chi ponder on his thought, his feet in pendulum under his chair and his pencil idly knitting in his hair.

"What about whale?" said Deacon. And went for his shower.

When Deacon returned from seeing Chi onto the laundry bus, Lockett was in the sitting room tidying away the last of the homework papers into his case.

"Keep Shaw away from Chi, corporal," said Deacon. "That is an order."

Lockett looked at Deacon and smiled. "Already fixed sir,"

"How?"

Lockett zipped his case and pulled his jacket even tidier. "Because the men now know that if any one of them as much as bad mouths Chi and I will kick them to fucking dirt, sir."

"Did they quiver at this prospect?" said Deacon.

Lockett grinned. "Visibly sir. Wiped the smile off Shaw's face. Off to a do, sir?"

Deacon was putting on his Number Two dress jacket.

"A party," said Deacon.

"Is that Miss Ross and Major Villiers engagement party, sir?"

Deacon turned to face Lockett. He raised an eyebrow.

"Grapevine pigeons, sir," said Lockett. He grinned. "Fastest of the lot, they are. Will you be requiring the jeep?"

"Yes."

"Driver?"

"No. I don't plan to stay long. Just raise my glass to the happy couple and then slip away."

"Like a beaten dog, sir?"

Deacon wasn't sure.

TWENTY

There were over one hundred people at the party, most in uniform. It was certainly not the small do that Deacon had expected. The ballroom of the Brigadier's Villa was crowded with guests and its walls gleamed golden and bright under the electric chandeliers that floated under the roof beams. Officers and ladies stood chatting amiably in clusters and couples about the room. Orderlies in white jackets wove among them on urgent errands of drinks and canapes. Deacon saw Clemmie and Villiers talking to a group by the high garden window. The Brigadier and Mrs. Jennings were with them. Clemmie looked pale and tired beneath her fixed smile, but she laughed often and easily among the party guests. Villiers beamed at her side, his booming voice and laughter firing over the room like mortar blasts.

Across the room, Deacon saw Major Ford-Forrest standing beside, and a little apart from, a group of senior officers huddled in conversation by the potted bay tree. The Major held a drink in one hand and a sandwich on a plate in the other. He gazed from one hand to the other as if considering an unexpected dilemma. He rose and fell slowly on the balls of his feet in aid of contemplation. Peter and Grace Banks were also there, and Alec Peterson was in the crowds.

An orderly had just handed Deacon his beer when Villiers and Clemmie appeared before him. Villiers grinned. He stuck out a hand of welcome. Deacon had to swap his pint of beer to his other hand to accept Villier's strong and gripping welcome.

"Good to see you here, Harry, glad you could make it," Villiers said. He dropped his grip and nodded to the room. "Guest list got a bit out of hand I'm afraid! But reckon we have drinks and grub for all."

"I'm so pleased you came, Harry," said Clemmie. She linked arms with him. "It couldn't have been a party without you."

"There's Colonel Michaels, Clemmie." said Villiers. His gaze had drifted to the next group on the round. "With Isobel. We must say hello. Be sure to snout at the trough, Harry, and order any drinks. The boys will have it all bottled somewhere out back. Mickey! Lost a few pounds by the look of it!" Villiers laughed and guided Clemmie away.

Clemmie looked back over her shoulder at Deacon, her smile still fixed. She raised a trembling fingered wave to him before turning her smile in greeting to her new friends.

Deacon felt guilt surge within him. He knew that he should run after Clemmie and tell her not to go through with her engagement to Villiers. To warn her of his character and plead with her to change her mind. To save herself.

But his feet would not move. He could think of nothing to say that might be persuasive or believable. Nothing that would not seem to be petty and spiteful. He had no evidence, only suspicions and circumstantial maybes. And perhaps that was all they were. Maybe Clemmie would change Villiers and settle him to a loving life in Surrey. Deacon doubted it. And still his feet wouldn't move.

He stood and watched Clemmie and Villiers continue their tour of the guests, their laughter grating like pieces of glass through his guts.

Deacon drifted to the walls and let the party bubble about him. Alec Peterson appeared at his shoulder.

"Duty sortie coming up in two nights' time." said Peterson. His words were hushed and discreet. He took a large bite out of a vol-au-vent. "And you're in it. We all are. Officers' briefing tomorrow afternoon. Thought I'd tip you the wink."

"A Viking show?" asked Deacon.

"Yes. Together with half the rest of the garrison. Going to be a pretty big show. Busting down more doors in Crater I think. But I'm going to duck out of this one. I plan to be elsewhere."

"With Lizzie perhaps?" said Deacon.

"It will be our last night before she sails for home on the Princess and buggered if the Vikings are going to spoil that. Think I might twist a knee."

A bell sounded in a doorway and orderlies appeared with trays of champagne. The room fell quiet as the Brigadier climbed slowly up onto the small one-step stage. He gave a short speech of welcome and a long one of ramble before handing over to Major Villiers. Villiers stepped up with Clemmie at his side. They couldn't stop smiling. Clemmie stood happy before them in a sleeveless blue gown and with her hands clasped together before her. Deacon had never seen Clemmie stand like that. Her arms still, her hands encradled. A new stance to control her shaking hands. She almost made it look natural.

Villiers announced the engagement and the room pretended to be surprised and delighted. Clemmie made a smiling, hand-clasped little speech about how Tom was blissfully unaware of what he was letting himself in for and Villiers winked at the room like a vaudevillian Max. A toast had been raised and glasses drunk and the party had begun in earnest.

"Time I slipped away," said Peterson. He crammed a few rolls into his pockets. "This is Lizzie's almost last night and the Lodge is ours for the taking."

"How do you know about tomorrow night's show?"

"Brigadier's administration staff are highly corruptible. So that helps."

"How do you plan to slip the party?" said Deacon.

Peterson grinned. "You want to sneak out too? Stuff your pockets and follow me."

Deacon discreetly grabbed handfuls of buffet to his pockets and slipped out with Peterson through the garden windows and over the dark lawns to the tennis courts. A path led up the hill to the back of the car park. They shook hands on parting.

"Sorry about your knee," said Deacon. "Do you think it will hurt?"

Peterson grinned. "Been thinking about that. Reckon I might have the runs instead. Bound to forget to limp and give the game away. The shits are easier to handle, don't you think?"

"Have fun," said Deacon.

"Feel guilty about ducking the show though," said Peterson.

They drove their jeeps to the gatehouse and were checked out. Peterson headed out for the hillside Lodge with a final wave.

Deacon took the coast road and hit seventy on the long sweeping stretches. He didn't head for his billet. As it was not yet late, he made for Lockett's rooms, to forewarn him about the coming sortie.

The lights were still on in Lockett's room. Lockett seemed surprised to find Deacon at his door when he answered the knock. He was barefoot and in his shorts and a T-shirt. Deacon could see that Lockett had been drawing. A radio on a shelf was playing pop music and Lockett's sketch pad was open on his table.

"Trouble, sir?" asked Lockett. He switched the radio off.

"No, just a drop by. Not disturbing you am I?"

"No. Of course not, sir. Sorry. Would you like a drink? The gin is open."

"Why not," said Deacon. "I have brought a buffet. Slightly dented, I'm afraid."

He pulled some pasties and rolls from his pockets and looked for somewhere to place them. The sketch pad and pencils lay on the table. There was a large and detailed drawing of a smokey street and a wall with a bite taken out of it. Soldiers and civilians roamed as if in a ghostly daze. It was so real and vivid that Deacon felt himself flash back to the moment. To see it again.

He stood transfixed, unsure what to do, unable to take his eyes from the picture.

Lockett quickly closed the pad and moved it off the table. He poured a couple of drinks. "Sorry about the mess sir. Just sketching. Not expecting visitors."

"It's very good, corporal. You have a wonderful talent."

Deacon saw Lockett's face flush momentarily before he busied himself with finding plates and cutlery. Deacon divided up his food. Lockett sat on his bed while Deacon took the only chair. He undid his jacket collar and buttons and Lockett refilled his glass.

"Nice party, sir?" asked Lockett.

"Lots of fun. And I bring news of another Viking sortie." He stared at the two pasties on his plate. "Any ketchup about?" he said.

TWENTY ONE

Deacon peered into his bathroom mirror and studied the stranger. The face was leathered, tanned and beaten. It looked donkey old. He stared in wary exhaustion at the impostor, expecting him to laugh. But he didn't.

He dunked his head in the sink and shook himself awake under the water's slap. He soaped himself for a shave and watched a white beard grow on the donkey. There was a knock on his door. Expecting it to be Lockett back with his laundry, he was surprised to find Major Villiers standing on his doorstep.

"Morning, Harry!" said Villiers and stepped into the room.

Deacon wiped his jaw on the towel at his neck. "Good morning, sir." he said.

Villiers looked about the room, his eyes amused and alert. He grinned. "Hope I haven't dropped by too early, Harry," he said.

"No, of course not, sir," said Deacon "Coffee?"

He found another mug and poured the coffee. Villiers wandered the room and studied the pictures pinned up on the wall. They were Chi's drawings of planes and ships and camels. Chi had signed and annotated them in his careful, curled script.

"Hope you enjoyed the party, Harry," said Villiers. "Great fun wasn't it?" He sipped his coffee and then brayed a laugh. "We made quite a night of it I can tell you! Massed rugger on the villa lawns and had to send Tosh home on the flat-bed. Clemmie said you left early."

"Yes. I had some reports to write. It was a fine party. And, of course, many congratulations on your engagement, sir."

Villiers unpinned one of Chi's drawings from the wall and looked at it for a while. It was a picture of Deacon in a jeep. The crayoned annotations said so.

"I hear our tea boy has new masters," said Villiers. He turned to look at Deacon. Deacon remained calm.

"A new position with Mr. Patel, I believe," said Deacon. "We must wish him well."

"Indeed," said Villiers. "I am sure we must."

Villiers dropped the picture on the table and sipped his coffee. He looked at Deacon. "The grenade attack has been a great shock for Clemmie," he said, "I am sure you know this, Harry, and seen it for yourself. She put up a bloody brave show for everyone last night, but I could tell. As I am sure you could too. Sort of things we friends just know. I'm afraid poor Susan's death has affected Clemmie badly. Shaken her up."

Deacon could think of nothing to say. He removed the towel from his neck and began putting on his shirt. Villiers wandered to the window and stood gazing out. Deacon could see squads of soldiers drilling on the far reaches of the square. He saw Villiers cast his gaze down to the yellow chrysanthemum in its brass-shell pot on the sill.

"I want you to know, Harry," said Villiers, "That I do intend to try my damndest to make Clemmie happy. Very happy. Look after her. It's what she needs. I know she is a friend of yours. You understand what I am saying?"

He turned and gazed at Deacon through pale and earnest blue eyes.

"Of course, sir," said Deacon.

"Good. I wouldn't want there to be any doubts. It's for the best. Poor Clemmie has been through a lot these last few months," said Villiers. "And seen far too much. Aden has been quite a shock. She needs a strong arm about her. And comfort and calm in her life. I can give her that. She deserves that, don't you think?"

"Yes, sir."

"I'm glad we agree, Harry," said Villiers. He smiled. "After all, a soldier's first duty is to protect the weak."

The door swung open and Corporal Lockett entered with a laundered uniform finger-hooked at his shoulder.

"Mr. Patel says the jacket stitches will..." Lockett stopped on seeing Major Villiers. He came to a quick attention. "Sorry, sir. Didn't see...."

"That's quite all right, corporal," said Villiers. "Just come to tell your Lieutenant here about the sortie briefing. Have you got wind of it, Harry?"

"Only that something is on, sir," said Deacon.

"Yes. Briefing this afternoon," said Villiers. "But thought I'd drop by to let you know that there is a special place on the team for you this time, Harry. Can't say more at this stage. Wait for the official briefing. You were stuck in the wings on our last show, so only right you have front seats for this one. You too, Corporal."

"And my troop, sir?" said Deacon.

"They will get the chance to kick down a few doors too, Harry, don't you worry. Everyone will have some fun, eh!" Villiers laughed. "Officers' briefing at the Inkerman at fourteen-hundred hours."

He pinned the drawing back onto the wall. He looked at Deacon and then at

Lockett. He flicked his fingers to his cap, grinned and strode from the room.

After a moment of silence Lockett looked at Deacon. "Fun, sir?" he said.

"With front row seats, apparently," said Deacon.

Deacon tasked Lockett with getting the men and the truck over to the garage yards for its bogus check-over. The men would spend the morning playing cards with the mechanics in the cool of the REME canteen and it was a safe bet that they would still be there come lunchtime. Today the canteen rumour was shepherd's pie, treacle tart and custard and Deacon knew there would be no complaints.

"Get them back by fourteen-hundred, corporal," said Deacon. "Quiet rest for the afternoon. No booze. Kit and weapons check for sixteen hundred. We go in seventeen thirty. It could be a long night."

"And you, sir?"

Deacon picked out a book at random from his shelf. "I am going to have a long and quiet coffee," he said.

The coffee garden was still busy with late breakfast trade and the tables under the shade were already occupied. Even the unshaded tables on the sun-soaked lawns were busy. The café customers were mostly couples or small parties but Deacon saw Peter Banks sitting alone in a distant shade at the only table with an empty seat. Banks was studying papers in a thin leather file case lying open on the small table. A pot of coffee crowded at his elbow. He looked thoughtful and a little pale, his face lined with tiredness. Banks looked up and saw Deacon. After a moment's hesitation, his face stretched into a warm smile and he pushed the empty chair out with a foot.

"Harry! Looking for a breakfast perch?"

Deacon took the seat and laid his book aside. A waiter appeared and he gave his order for coffee and scrambled eggs.

"Just waiting on Grace," said Banks. He tidied his papers into the file and poured himself a coffee. "Gone shopping with Clemmie. A husband's obligations are many, but shopping has never appeared on my list. I only get in the way."

The waiter arrived with Deacon's coffee.

"I expect you are on tonight's sortie?" said Banks. His voice had become light and discreet.

"I understand there is a rumour, sir," said Deacon, "but nothing official. Not until the briefing."

"Of course. Absolutely." said Banks. "Quite." He offered a weak smile, his fingers tap-dancing the leather file. "Keep a watch out on this one, Harry."

Deacon stopped sipping his coffee. A waiter arrived with his scrambled eggs and there was a moment of china and cups and the space clearing of files before his breakfast was laid and the waiter gone.

"Are you expecting trouble?" said Deacon. He buttered his toast. Banks leaned back in his chair and gazed into the café crowds about him.

"No, not expecting," he said. "Just fearing." He turned to Deacon, leaning forward on his elbows. He smiled again. "Me being silly, I'm sure. A kind of hunch, that's all. This place gets to you after a while. Addles the brain."

"Hunches are good," said Deacon,"Especially here."

"It's the intelligence," said Banks. "On the ticket, I'm sure. And it's a good plan. Villiers certainly knows his stuff. But the intelligence hasn't been verified. You know, second-sourced. Checked. And we always verify. Especially before a big show. But time is against us on this one. We will go in on unverified information. A silly hunch. Nothing more."

Deacon saw Grace and Clemmie making their way through the crowded tables of the café garden. They were being followed by two waiters, each carrying a chair. Grace waved on sighting Peter and the small convoy headed for their table.

Grace and Clemmie were in high and happy spirits,the shopping trip had been a success. They chattered of purchases and small adventures and attacked the coffee when it came. Through the talk Deacon came to understand that Grace had been buying furniture from the market for shipment back home to England.

"Are you leaving Aden?" said Deacon.

"Of course, Harry, you wouldn't know," said Grace. "Forgive my rattlings. Yes. Peter and I are on our way. We ship back to England next month."

Deacon looked at Banks.

"Getting too old for this intelligence work, Harry," said Banks. "And I always get itchy when I stay in one place too long. I'm missing Wiltshire. It will be good to get back to green hills. Grace has been offered a job at the University of Southampton. Didn't even know Southampton had one! Good post though. Suit Grace. So I thought I'd finish my tour early and go back with her. To England. Enjoy the garden for a while. And Lizzie will be there."

Deacon learned Lizzie would take rooms at the Banks's house and stay with them until Alec Peterson returned. Captain Banks was to take up an instructor's post at the Tidworth barracks.

"On Wiltshire's rolling plain. Teaching the officers the tricks of the trade," said Banks.

"But mostly sitting in the garden and reading books," said Grace.

"Officer perks, dear," said Banks.

"And I promise to visit the moment you are back," said Clemmie. "I can be your welcome home party." She was smoking a cigarette. Deacon saw that her hand hardly shook at all. She smiled at Deacon.

"It will be so good to get back to normal," she said. "And out of this awful sun. The thought of an English summer shower. Heaven."

And in her smile Deacon realised that she was leaving too. He knew he should be happy for her but could not help feeling a sudden sense of loss for himself and sadness for Clemmie. Life with Villiers would not be smooth and the vitality and curiosity which made Clemmie so compelling would be worn away by the duties of her new Surrey life.

"In a couple of weeks," said Clemmie. "I'm going to help Lizzie settle in. And get the house ready for Tom. I shall be kept busy."

"Sounds very sensible," said Deacon.

"Very," said Clemmie, "I shall hate leaving the hospital, though."

"I expect you'll be going home soon too, won't you Harry?" said Grace.

"My tour has been extended. A few months more."

Grace studied him. "Well, take care, Harry. Are you getting any closer to that cheeseboard?"

Deacon laughed. "No. But I think I can smell it."

Grace held his gaze. "That's the thing with cheeseboards, Harry," she said, "It's the smelly ones that you learn to avoid."

There was a small silence. It was broken by Grace."Well, you will have to come over for another tennis party before we go, Harry. Give you a chance for evens. So look after yourself. Don't do anything silly. And we'll have a return set in Wiltshire. Come on Peter, you've got to come and sign some shipping papers."

The Banks's offered their farewells and were soon lost in the café crowds. Deacon sat with Clemmie under the cool shades of acacia trees. He watched the uniforms, bright-coloured doll skirts and white jackets effervesce and glide in the gardens about him. The still airs smelled of coffee and diesel and cigarette smoke. High on the rock bluffs above Telegraph Bay, the sun glinted off the radio towers like mirrors. Out at sea tankers queued along the horizon like shy fairground ducks. They smoked, sipped coffee and gazed.

"You will get in touch, won't you, Harry?" said Clemmie eventually. "When you get back to England. We shall be true friends."

Deacon buttered another piece of toast, spread some scrambled egg on it and offered it to Clemmie. She bit into it eagerly.

"Of course, Clemmie," said Deacon. He smiled. "Always."

He walked her to the bus stop. As the bus came in Deacon handed Clemmie his book. It was *Alice's Adventure in Wonderland.*

"My wedding present to you," he said. "With wishes for a wonderful life."

Clemmie looked at the book in her hand. She looked at it for some time. Then she placed it carefully in her bag and looked away towards the mountains.

"Thank you, Harry," she said and stepped on board the bus. When the bus drove off, she did not look back.

Deacon returned to his billet. He lay on his bed and tried to capture a litle sleep before the briefing. But sleep eluded him.

The briefing room of the Inkerman was crowded with officers. The tall curtains had been drawn closed against the afternoon sun and a sepia light oozed through the room. About thirty officers, all smoking, talking and laughing, were seated at the rows of plastic chairs. Deacon took a seat and made soldier chat with a lieutenant from the Signals Corps seated in front of him, whom he vaguely knew.

Major Villiers entered the room at a brisk stride and the chatter died to a silence. Seats were hastily sought. Villiers stood, legs braced and faced the room. He nodded to the wall and a single light came on. It was the light directly above him.

Villiers gave a clear, confident and lucid briefing. He fixed his earnest gaze upon his men and told them what was going to happen, and when and how. He held his audience transfixed, as he always did. But he no longer held Deacon.

It was to be an ambitious sortie. A Viking Villiers special. They were going to raid deep inside Crater and kidnap Alim Said Becha. The senior rebel leader of FLOSY was known to be on a fleeting visit to a house in Crater. Alim Becha was rumoured to be the organiser behind the grenade attack on Susan Collins. His bandit rebels, who acted as his travelling armed bodyguard, were billeted for the night with families in the Al Malah district. The families had no choice in their overnight guests, but they would still welcome the honour bestowed. Alim Becha would be away from his bodyguards' protection during his late-afternoon visit to his see his granddaughter at the family house in the

Backlar district of the city. Back in Al Matah his bandits would be indoors enjoying the delights of solid mud walls and stove-cooked meals after months stalking the hard and dusted desert plains. It was an opportune moment. A Viking moment.

A brigade of troops was to encircle the small Al Malah sector and flush out every occupant and weapon. Troops from the Lancs and Anglians would establish encircling clear ground in the streets about. A small raiding party would then go on up the hill to the house in Backlar, arrest Alim Becha and fetch him back for questioning.

Villiers lit a small cigar and puffed its smoke to the ceiling fans. He grinned.

"Everything clear so far, gentlemen? Any questions?" The room was silent and still. Deacon raised his hand.

"Am I to understand that we will be raiding into Crater in daylight, sir?"

The room murmured, as if recognition had just sunk in. Villiers chuckled.

"I thought it would be you, Harry," he said. "Yes. Going in in daylight. An hour before dusk. Catch them unawares. At supper."

"But Alim Becha will hear it, won't he, sir?" said Deacon, "The Backlar house is only a few streets away. It will be his alarm."

"Which is why we will do it quietly," said Villiers. He turned his gaze across his men, his pale blue eyes bright with mischief. "No Alam Becha alarm bells will ring, gentlemen, because we go in very, very quietly. Like a shroud. Rubber-soled and silent. We do every Al Malah house. But no crashing and kicking of doors. We do it quiet. And we do it firmly. We gag and bag and truck the lot of them. Women and children too. And the bandit bodyguard. Any protest, then we have the boot and the rifle butt. Once the bodyguard is out of the way, it's on to the house and Alim Becha won't have heard a thing. So we nab him and bring him back to justice."

The Vikings rolled a murmur out across the floor, like a ripple of rising tide under longboat seats. Deacon saw grinning, excited faces about him. The Vikings were on a promise of pillage.

There followed a briefing on the troop deployments and radio frequencies and then the men were broken up into their action units for further operational instructions. On consulting the bulletin board, Deacon was not surprised to discover he had been allocated to the kidnap squad. He would be part of the Alim Becha house raiding party. Hunting into the streets of Crater with the night gathering fast about them. And he would have Major Villiers, Corporal Lockett, Alec Petersen and three privates of Commando in company at his side.

TWENTY TWO

When Deacon returned to his rooms he found Lockett already there. He was rinsing out two mugs under a steaming kettle at the sink. The coffee pot on the small camping gas burner bubbled a fragrant aroma into the room.

"Or gin, if you prefer, sir," said Lockett.

"No, that's fine. Coffee is what's needed."

Lockett looked at him.

"That bad, eh?"

Deacon briefed him on the sortie while Lockett made the coffees. They sat and drank in silence.

"Smell that, sir?" said Lockett, sniffing the air.

"The coffee?"

"No sir, the donkey shit."

Deacon leaned back in his chair.

"That'll be our transport arrived then," he said.

Lockett laughed.

"Tell the men I'll brief them at sixteen hundred. Have them ready."

"Of course, sir," said Lockett. "More coffee?"

Deacon kept his briefing short and to the point. His men wouldn't remember, let alone understand, too many instructions. Simplicity seemed to work.

The sun beat hard and the troop scattered at his feet in the shade of the latrine building in the barracks courtyard, sitting or lounging in their combat kit in a ragged semi-circle, smoking and listening to Deacon with quiet and fixed attention. His briefing ended.

"Any questions?" asked Deacon. There was silence until Ambrose spoke.

"So you and the corp ain't with us on this one then."

"No, we're on the kidnap raid. For tonight's sortie, you'll be under the command of Major Sawyer."

"Not the fucking turnips!" said Shaw. "Not the bloody Lincs."

"But you're still our officer, right?" said Kenny.

"Of course. It's only for tonight. Major Sawyer is a good soldier," said Deacon. "And he knows all the dodges, so don't let yourselves down. If you are better soldiers than the Lincs, then prove it tonight. But don't do anything stupid."

"Like what?" asked Lee.

Deacon gazed down at his men. Their tanned, gaunt faces drifted under cigarette smoke and stared blankly back at him.

"Like go and sign on for another four years," he said.

Deacon leaned against the shadowed arch of a derelict house and watched the troops about their business at the bottom of the hill. The sun was setting fast and the air began to gloom about him as he watched. The Al Malah was alive with troops and anxious Arabs with their hands on their heads were being led towards growling trucks. There were women and children bustling around them. But there was a quiet and compliant efficiency about it all. The lines of Arabs were being herded with hardly a protest. The operation seemed to be going well.

"Not exactly resisting, are they?" said Lockett. He too had been watching the activities. The rest of their small raiding party had retreated to the back room of the roofless house and were enjoying a pre-raid smoke.

"Would you?" said Deacon.

Lockett seemed to consider his answer.

"Yes, I think I would," he said. "And certainly more than they are. For God's sake, they are being turfed out their homes by a foreign invader! And they hardly protest at all. Odd that, don't you think?"

Major Villiers called for them to join the rest of the raiders in the back room. Deacon was surprised to see Sergeant Lamb in their party. Villiers was quick to explain.

"Lieutenant Peterson has gone down last minute with Yemen belly. Sergeant Lamb will take his place as translator."

The sergeant nodded a welcome. "Privates White, Ferris and Botley," continued Villiers. The three privates looked like a triplet of rodents, each a compact and eager rat. They grinned as one. Villiers cast an eye over his small troop. His face-blacking smeared like claws across his gaze. The pale blue eyes sparked. "We'll be going in soon," he said, " so we go in quiet like a snake, fierce like a tiger and determined like a... like a..." Major Villiers seemed unable to think of anything suitably determined.

"Like a donkey, sir?" said Lockett

Deacon kept an impassive face, and let the hidden smile ripple through him.

"A donkey, corporal?" said Villiers. "Are they known for their determination?"

"Oh yes, sir. And bravery and intelligence too," said Lockett.

Villiers looked at Lockett. He seemed to be trying to decide if he was being made a fool of. Corporal Lockett looked right back.

"Donkey is the symbol of the American Democratic party, sir," he said. "Them Yanks unlikely to get it wrong."

"True," said Villiers. "The Yanks know their business. Determined as a donkey then. That's how we'll take Alim Becha."

A sergeant from the Lincs appeared at the ruined archway, silhouetted in the dusk light. He was out of breath from running up the hill. He saluted as best he could.

"All cleared and trucked, sir," he wheezed. "Way is clear."

Villiers stretched to his full height and reefed his pistol belt. "Then let's do it."

The kidnap party moved out through the back of the derelict house and made their way up the cool, shadowed street. Night was falling heavy and fast and the Crater streets were already as forbidding as tunnels. Deacon's blood drummed loud within him, but the streets about him were silent. The small troop loped in single file up the hill and turned into an alleyway that led further up the side of the rise. No one stirred from the houses, the streets were empty and no lights shone from windows. Deacon felt the chill of the night begin to enwrap him.

They stopped and took rest at the edge of an open tract of ground as big as a town square but criss-crossed by the walls of bombed-out houses. The walls were low and rubbled and beyond them squat, lightless houses and the derelict shells of buildings loomed. Deacon checked on Lockett. He was sitting with his back braced against a wall nearby. They shared bravado grins they didn't feel. Villiers pointed towards a street that led up the hill into the Crater dark beyond the far side of the square.

"Just up that street, last house on the left," said Villiers. "Straight over the ground here. Spread formation. You lead the way, privates. Rest of us follow. Regroup at the bottom of the street on the far side. And we go as quiet as cats!"

The raiders set out across the rubbled square.

"Quite the zoo, aren't we?" whispered Lockett to Deacon as he took his place at his side.

The three privates fanned out and led the way with their Sterling machine guns primed and their eyes scanning ahead into the night. Sergeant Lamb followed just behind and Deacon fell to rear guard with Lockett and Villiers. A waxing gibbous moon hung low and lantern in the Crater skies and cast the ground and houses in an eerie half light, like a chalk picture on black paper.

They crept on, often stumbling over the loose rubble and pitted terrain until their way was made easier by an area of flat, open space.

The gunfire exploded from nowhere. Ahead of him Deacon saw flashes of violent muzzle lights and heard a fire-cracker world erupt over and around him. Someone cried out. He saw one of the privates stagger and fall. Sergeant Lamb was on his knees clutching his chest. Someone loomed up beside Deacon and then Lockett was on top of him, pushing him down behind a chest-high wall.

Villiers dived in after them. He was panting hard. The gunfire continued to crash and whine about them, puffs of rubble spat from the ground and the wall shook with the impact of machine-gun ferocity. The noise was mind-numbing. Deacon shook himself out of his daze and tried to take in the situation. Lockett and Villiers were crouched head-down against the protection of the wall. Ahead of him, out in the square, Deacon could see the gunfire dancing maniacally in sprays of dust and what looked like the shadows of two bodies lying still amongst it all. A further furtive scan revealed two other shapes, one was arched back over a low wall and was jerking spasmodically from the attention of concentrated fire.

"The others are down," said Deacon, "give me your glasses." He lifted the night vision binoculars from around Villiers's head. Villiers didn't seem to notice, his face was pale and his eyes stunned. Deacon crept a little way along the wall and studied the scene again with the aid of the glasses.

"What happened?" said Villiers. His body twitched and turned in the confusion about him. "They were waiting for us!"

Lockett knelt upright and sprayed a blind burst of fire over the wall towards the enemy. He leaned back to the wall and reloaded a fresh magazine into his rifle. He laughed.

"Seem to recall you are a betting man, major," he said. Villiers said nothing. He was scanning the terrain behind them, ducking the sounds of bullets as they pinged among the rocks.

"Well, I bet, major," said Lockett, "that Alim Bacha is not in that house up the street. Never was, never has been, never will be. Probably not even in the city. Care to risk your hat on that bet, sir?"

"Don't be ridiculous, corporal. He's there. They just caught wind of us, that's all. We've been betrayed."

More bullets cracked into the rubble about them and a yellow flare lit the sky behind them.

"No, major, we've been suckered," Lockett said. "You've walked us into an ambush. You've been played like a fish and you gobbled it line and sinker. You're a true fucking donkey. We need to get support up here fast. Who was assigned the radio?"

"Private Botley," said Villiers.

"And you put him on point?"

"War is chance, corporal."

"Well private Botley has certainly lost his," said Deacon. "Looks like they're all down. Caught head-on out in the open. Sergeant Lamb is down behind some rubble. Looks like he's wounded. I'm going to check."

The gunfire had eased off and now only sporadic shots could be heard.

"You can't go out there, sir!" said Lockett. "I'll go if anyone."

"No, you will not, corporal," said Deacon. "Stay here with the major and give me covering fire. That is an order. Right, major?"

Villiers seemed to drift back from somewhere.

"What? Yes. That's right. An order, corporal."

Deacon moved off before Lockett could protest. He crawled on his belly to the end of the wall and waited. He looked back to see Lockett squatting against the corner of the wall with his rifle primed. His face was pale and his watch of Deacon was intense. Deacon nodded and waited for Lockett's and Villiers's burst of covering fire to spray out into the night before he ran low and weaving his way to where Sergeant Lamb lay among the rubble. Deacon lay in the dirt beside him.

"Lieutenant Deacon here, Lamb. Where are you hit? Can you move?"

Deacon knew it was a stupid question. Sergeant Lamb was lying on his back, his breathing shallow. His eyes were open and wide and he was staring fixedly up into the Aden night sky with a passive, concentrated, calm. His large hands were cradled across his blood-soaked belly as if he was trying to stem the last leaking droplets of his life.

"Will you look at that beautiful sky!" he said. "Got a fag, sir?"

"Afraid not." A couple of bullets pinged nearby. Deacon realised that the Adoo rebels were now pretty much firing blind in the night. "I'll try to drag you to better cover." Lamb held up an imploring bloodied hand to decline the offer.

"Rather not do the dragging, sir, thanks all the same." He fell silent for a while. Deacon could see Lamb's guts bubbling through his shirt.

"I expect you'll be seeing Lieutenant Peterson when you get back, sir," said Lamb.

"Yes, I expect so."

"Then be so good to tell him he's a fucking bastard," said Lamb. His hand fell back to the dirt and life's last droplet ebbed from him on a sigh.

Deacon pressed himself to the dirt as more bullets came firing in. His anger was almost liquid. He cursed the world and everything in it. He cursed his stupidity and the waste and the whole fucking craziness of it all. What the hell was he doing in Aden, where the hell was his sham of a life?

The skies above him were suddenly lit by two blue phosphorous lights trailing grey-green smoke. The Adoo had launched a couple of night flares. Deacon could see the grounds and terrain about him begin to take visible shape as the flares floated down. Deacon was on his feet and running back to the cover of the wall before the guns could train on him. He sped over the rubble as the first shots sprayed at his feet. He could see Lockett giving diverting fire from behind the wall. Deacon ran towards him, leaping the low walls and rubble piles. As he stepped to take the last wall he stepped onto a trampoline. His foot sank as if into a patch of soft, deep mud and he was then propelled upwards into the air by an irresistible sprung force. He saw his boots and hands trace across the night stars and the ground become the sky and he was aware of tumbling in the air and a faint flash of light. A distant boom sounded and he crashed back to the ground. He lay on his back and felt ache sizzle through him. It felt ridiculous and unreal. He tried to laugh but was aware of a fear beginning to grow in his guts. He knew that this was a life's moment. A moment when his world shifted on its axis, when it would never after be the same again. Maybe even never to be at all. In his mind, he tried to feel his way through his body to seek out any injury. He couldn't discover one.

Deacon's shirt and collar were grabbed. It was Lockett. He looked anxious and frightened, his face night-blacking smeared in trickles of sweat. The gunfire started again.

"Its okay sir," said Lockett. "Don't try to move."

Deacon felt himself being drag-hauled over the rubble and back behind the safety of the wall. Villiers was there, firing blind into the night to cover their return. He looked at Deacon and then traced his gaze down to his boots. Deacon knew that he had stepped on a mine, but he couldn't bring himself to confirm it. Lockett was busy with checking Deacon over. When he spoke his voice was calm.

"You stepped on a mine, sir. A little one. Nothing too bad. Foot's a bit of a mess. No other injuries that I can see. Can you sit up? Who got assigned the medical kit, major?"

Villiers was studying the ground behind them, the way back down the path they had come. His eyes were wide, his movements erratic.

"What? Oh, we didn't allocate one. Not on the kidnap. Hardly seemed necessary for such a short trip."

Deacon saw Lockett gaze at Villiers. The gunfire continued to crack.

"Major," said Lockett, "you are one fucking idiot."

Villers turned on him, his face thunder. He then seemed to calm.

"I'll pretend I didn't hear that, corporal."

"I can say it louder if you like, sir," said Lockett.

"We can't stay here," said Villiers. "We have to get back down to Al Malah."

Deacon raised himself onto his elbows and steeled himself to look down at his foot. His boot was a shattered mess of blackened, smoking leather tongues and the flesh of his foot spewed from it like blooded offal. There was a glint of bone at his heel. He felt a wave of nausea surge through him and had to lie back down until it passed. The numbness of shock and adrenalin which dulled his pain began to fade and he gasped as a fire took hold and began burning up his leg.

Lockett took out his knife and split Deacon's trousers to the thigh. He cut a long strip of cloth and began to fashion a tourniquet above Deacon's knee.

"Must stay awake sir," said Lockett, his voice anxious. "Don't go drifting off. You hear me?"

Deacon could feel himself becoming light-headed, his body sagging under the weight of his terror. Lockett leaned forward, raised his hand and slapped Deacon hard across the face. The crack of the unexpected blow shocked Deacon awake. He raised himself on his elbows and shuffled himself to a sit against the wall. He rubbed his cheek.

"Army can shoot you for that, corporal," he said.

Lockett grinned.

"Army'll shoot you for anything, sir," he said.

Deacon saw shapes moving through the derelict buildings on the left flank edge of the square.

"They're on the move," he said.

Villiers and Lockett turned to follow his gaze.

"They're going to outflank us!" said Villiers, his voice rising to betray his fears. "Going to surround us. We have to move out now and quick."

"It's not us they're after, major," said Deacon. "They're heading down the hill to ambush any soldiers coming to rescue us."

"Then we must move now!" said Villiers. "We can't stay here. We'll have to make a break for it. Get to the cover of those bombed houses behind us and make out way back down the hill to Al Malah."

"The lieutenant can't make it unless we carry him," said Lockett.

Villiers said nothing. He was loading his pistol ready for the retreat.

"Speed is key to success," said Villiers. "The lieutenant understands that. The chance of war."

Deacon could feel his guts beginning to burn with pain. He struggled himself to an upright sit against the wall.

"He's right, corporal, and you know it too," he said. "You two can make it better alone than with me. Get going. That's an order corporal."

"It's a tough call, Harry," said Villiers, "but it's the only way. We'll be back with the cavalry before you know it."

"I'm not going," said Lockett. He fixed Villiers with a stare. "I'm staying with the lieutenant."

"I gave you an order, corporal," said Deacon.

"Then shoot me. One can bring back the troops just as well as two. I'm staying here."

Another flare rocketed into the skies above them. The gunfire began in earnest again. Bullets cracked off the stone walls above them.

"We don't have time to debate it." said Villiers, "It's now or never. You stay here if you must, corporal, but I'm going for help."

Deacon leaned forward and offered Villiers something from his hand. He dropped it into Villiers's palm. It was the silver golliwog badge. Villiers stared at it for a moment and then put it in his breast pocket and tapped it with a smile.

"I'll keep it safe for you until you get back Harry," he said. "Don't worry, I'll be back with rescue before you can spit."

Lockett laughed. He spat into the dirt at Villiers feet.

"Why don't you just take your tinplate golliwog and fuck off, sir," he said.

Villiers' face was pale with fury, but he said nothing. He turned, crouched low and headed towards the bombed-out buildings at their rear. He made it to the shelter of one and then turned to offer a hasty wave of encouragement before disappearing into the night.

Lockett returned to checking over Deacon's wound. He tightened the tournique and helped Deacon sip water from his canteen. Deacon gritted his teeth against the pain that now flooded through him. He could feel his body cooling and his mind fogging, he could sense himself drifting.

Lockett grabbed him by his shirt and shook him. Deacon looked up to see Lockett's tear stained, frantic, angry and beautiful face glaring over him. He continued to shake Deacon.

"Don't you die now, you bastard!" said Lockett. "I haven't waited for you all this time to lose you now. Don't you dare fucking die! D'you hear? I can't do this alone. Not now. It's too much. I need you to shoot me tomorrow."

Lockett began to sob, his shoulders heaving and tears dripping his cheeks.

Deacon lifted a hand and cradled it on the back of Lockett's head. His curled hair felt like warm moss. He gently pulled Lockett's head down onto his chest and allowed his fingers to stroke. He could feel Lockett's sobs judder through him.

"It's alright, David," said Deacon, "I don't feel like dying today."

He felt Lockett's lips brush his, as dry and hot as sand. He felt the burning touch of Lockett's tears on his cheek and the world exploding about him and in him. Deacon was aware of a sudden jolt and twist of the hemispheres locking as one. And in that moment, Deacon felt clean and renewed. A new energy swept through him.

"You must go now, David," he said, "Don't make me kill you like this. I couldn't bear it. Get out now while you can. Chi will need you. Save yourself. That is an order."

Lockett sat up and wiped his face on his sleeve. He grinned.

"Had me worried there for a while, sir. Good to see you back to ordering. You're good at it."

"But you never obey them."

Lockett thought about it.

"Sometimes on Tuesdays, sir."

Deacon laughed. And with the laugh came a cough and another wave of pain. He could feel himself drifting again, of his body numbing.

"I think I could do with a donkey," he said.

"Then you've got one," said Lockett.

Deacon felt Lockett's strong arms reach under him.

"Might be a bit of a rough ride," said Lockett, "they're going to throw everything they've got at us but I think we can make it. Are you ready to try?"

"I've never been more ready."

"Then let's go. Together."

Deacon was aware of a wave of joyful warmth surging through him. He felt himself being borne up towards the ocean heavens and saw the open arms of a thousand bright stars rushing forward to embrace him.

THE END

Also from Triskele Books

CLOSURE

Helen West is coming to terms with her husband's death and trying to cope with her six-year-old son's grief. Jake suffers from nightmares, and visions of what he calls his 'other life'. He talks about a boy called Jacob and a place known only as 'the island'.

Helen's journey to find the source of Jake's torment leads them to North Wales, where the university town of Bangor is in lockdown following a series of student abductions.

When Jake's nightmares start to mirror the abductions, Helen begins to believe her son might have second sight. But what could Jake's 'island' possibly have to do with these crimes? And how can they help without putting their own lives in danger?

It seems that decision will be Jake's alone.

Set along the beautiful North Wales coastline, Closure is a story of belief, revenge and repercussions of the past.

"Atmospheric, original and impossible to put down - this supernatural crime novel is a masterclass in good story-telling and will keep you hooked right to the unexpected ending."

- Sheila Bugler, Irish Crime Writer

Also from Triskele Books

RAW MATERIAL

Bank Holiday weekend. Beatrice Stubbs takes some holiday snaps on a secluded Welsh beach. Those innocent pictures reveal rather more than cliffs and seagulls, and someone wants them destroyed. But Beatrice has other things on her mind.

Assigned to the London Transport Police, she's pursuing the Finsbury Park Flasher, trying to pre-empt a serious sexual offence. Meanwhile, neighbour Adrian and companion Matthew decide to play Poirot, and investigate the mystery of the disappearing photographs. Amateur detectives and professional criminals are a dangerous mix.

From deserted Pembrokeshire beaches, through the shadowy underpasses of North London, to the remote Irish countryside, Beatrice discovers the darker side of human nature.

"The characters leap off the page, the prose is witty and intelligent, and the twist of plots keeps you hooked to the last. What more could you ask? –"

- Barbara Scott-Emmett,
author of European thriller, Don't Look Down

Lightning Source UK Ltd.
Milton Keynes UK
UKHW01f1938260618
324833UK00001B/177/P

9 780957 403109